THE REVELATION

THE REVELATION

JARED BEASLEY SHARPE

THE REVELATION

Copyright © 2021 Jared Beasley Sharpe

All rights reserved. This book or any portion thereof may not be reproduced or used in any manner whatsoever without the express written permission of the copyright owner except for the use of brief quotations in a book. Requests for permission should be addressed to the publisher.

The Revelation is a work of fiction. Names, organizations, places and incidents portrayed in this novel are either products of the author's imagination or are used fictitiously. Any resemblance to actual, events, locales, or persons is purely coincidental.

First Edition 2021
ISBN: 978-1-7353331-0-6

*For everyone I love,
especially my grandparents:*

*Darvin "Darwin" Beasley
Mabeth Jackson Beasley
John "Edwin" Sharpe Sr.
Frances Evans Sharpe*

PROLOGUE

Thirteen years ago

The contamination sirens wailed throughout every corner of Southern Guard's fortified cityscape. The concrete facades of the many homes lining the top of the Outer Wall only amplified the deep wailing alarms that pushed into my ears. Dad ran to the closest of our two living room windows and scanned the gray streets as people hastily scattered back to the safety of their homes.

"Cara!" Dad yelled, calling for Mom as he closed both of the blinds, shutting out what little light strained inside through the dark afternoon clouds.

Mom hurriedly rushed into the living room from the hallway. Dad turned on the lamp beside me, then picked up one of the toys I'd dropped on the floor and sat it in my lap.

"Where is Ruma?" Mom asked shakily.

"She hasn't made it back. Try calling her," he suggested, and Mom quickly returned to her bedroom to grab her holophone.

THE REVELATION

"It'll be okay," Dad said, trying to console me as he gently laid his hand on my head. "Why don't you keep playing?"

The toys I had received on my fifth birthday just a few days prior sat strewn over the couch around me. The relentless droning of the sirens kept me frozen in place.

"Erwyn, she's not answering," Mom said frantically, reentering the room.

"I'll go look for her," Dad said, throwing on his coat.

"They'll arrest you for not sheltering in place," Mom countered, grabbing his arm.

Without warning, my thirteen-year-old sister, Ruma, smeared with blood, burst through our front door.

"Please, help me!" she yelled as she threw the door shut and activated the security lock.

I pulled one of the couch pillows close to my stomach and clenched it with my fists. Ruma flung off her jacket and her trembling hands hung suspended in front of her body as if held by strings. Her gray undershirt, still wet from deep-red bloodstains, stuck to her skin.

"Ruma! What's wrong?" Mom cried.

Dad rushed quickly toward Ruma, asking, "What happened? What happened?"

"Stop! Don't touch me," Ruma commanded, backing hard against the front door.

Dad took another step closer, and Ruma shouted, "Don't touch me! I might be positive." Her hands shook by her side as she stood stiffly in place.

"What are you talking about?" Dad asked, his voice matching Ruma's panic.

As Ruma looked down at her stained clothes, her eyes seemed to freeze in place. For a moment, no one moved, except for Mom, who carefully reached from behind the couch, lifted me over the cushions, and set me down behind her.

Before that day, I'd only heard my parents mention perducorium a handful of times, usually when Ruma complained about not being able to travel beyond the Outer Wall. I struggled to pronounce the word, but I knew it was dangerous.

"Ruma, breathe. Just breathe," Mom said as soothingly as she could while squeezing my arm tightly.

"Listen to me," Dad said, trying to subdue his angst. "I need to know if you're hurt."

"No. I mean, I don't know. Salom rode in from the tracking line, and he was covered in blood. So I helped him. I had to."

"Why was he covered in blood?" Dad asked, his face heavily wrinkled with concern.

Ruma stood stiffly in place as her lips stumbled over incoherent words.

"It'll be okay," Mom reassured Ruma. Her grip was hurting my arm, but I was too afraid to say anything, peering from behind her shirt.

Ruma struggled to get the words out between shuddered breaths. "It was... He said it was a Stone."

Dad shook his head, and Mom kept saying "no, no, no" over and over again.

"I-I don't understand," Dad stammered. "How did you make it past the perducorium scanners? You can't—"

"We didn't," Ruma said. "Salom broke in through the emergency tunnels behind the stables, and we snuck in through the Outer Wall."

"Where is he?" Dad questioned.

"When we heard the sirens, he told me to leave him and

get home," she said as tears slid from her eyes. "They're going to take us away," she cried.

"You don't know that," Dad said hollowly.

"It's okay, baby," Mom whispered, softening her grip on me as she gently shushed Ruma. "Let's calm down."

"It's not okay!" Ruma fired back. "They'll take us all." Dad moved closer, and Ruma screamed, "Stay away!"

"Keep your voice down," Dad demanded.

All three were silent except for Ruma's heavy breathing.

"I have to get this off," she whispered softly, taking off her bloody jacket.

"We need to get you cleaned up," Dad said.

Mom carried me to the far side of the living room. I held her tightly so she wouldn't let me go. Ruma cautiously moved across the living room toward the hallway bathroom.

Before she turned the living room corner, a heavy blow struck the front door. I screamed, and we all stood paralyzed by the voice demanding we open the door.

"What do I do?" Ruma quietly pleaded for an answer neither Mom nor Dad could give.

Seconds later, the door was slung open as at least a dozen agents from the Perducorium Removal Agency invaded our home. The agents' defensive gear, concealing every inch of their bodies, made them appear more like robots. A few distinct red bands around their arms and legs lined the metallic-gray exterior of their protective gear.

Mom sobbed, reaching out one hand in protest as one of the agents aimed a gun at Ruma. He fired. Ruma shrieked as a small wire from the head of the gun embedded itself in her back.

"No!" Mom screamed as she clutched me close in her arms.

Ruma suddenly went stiff, like they turned her into a statue. As she fell to the floor, Ruma gashed her forehead open on the wooden end table my mom's father had made.

Her body thudded against the ground. Dad dove toward Ruma's side, and an agent flung him into the wall, shattering a few of our family pictures. Dad fought back, tackling that agent to the ground before he, too, went stiff from the wire gun. They braced his arms and dragged him out the front door, where I couldn't see him. Mom slumped to the floor as I cried in her lap. Two nearly identical agents lurched toward us and grabbed Mom's arms, prying me away from her. I saw my face reflected in the mirror of their helmets.

"Don't take my son! Please. He's my baby!" she screamed as they carried us outside to the eerily empty streets lining the top of the outer wall.

"It's okay, baby," a gentle voice said from behind the helmet. "We're here to help." I cried as she loosely carried me in her arms.

A moment later, another pair of hands pulled me from her and carried me along with my parents. No neighbors were outside, but curious and fearful faces filled the windows lining both sides of the streets. I couldn't see Ruma, but I heard one of the agents say, "Her reading is positive."

"Darvin!" Mom sobbed as they escorted her toward a strange van that might have been an ambulance. "Give me my son. Darvin!" Mom fought to free herself from the agents.

My body wouldn't move. In a moment, I watched PRA agents shove my parents and Ruma in the backs of the strange vehicles. They drove away in opposite directions. I was loaded into a smaller car with two other children; both wore oxygen masks and looked frozen like me. They sat encased in clear chambers like unopened collector's toys.

A young woman in a skin-tight white suit pointed at me. "What's the child's name?"

"Does it matter?" one of the agents responded.

"Yes. For now," she said flatly.

As another woman fastened me to the seat in my own strange container, my heavy breathing fogged her helmet's visor with a tiny cloud. After closing me inside the chamber, she shook her hands as if she'd just taken out a rotten bag of trash.

Someone with a droning voice said my parents' names and address, followed by words I couldn't understand. The woman in white grabbed my arm forcefully. Before I could resist, she stuck a thick needle in my arm with one gloved hand while she glared at a nearby medical monitor.

"Darvin Flint. Let's hope we're not three for three."

CHAPTER 1

I spent six months, including my sixth birthday, in a desert camp where heavy barbed wire choked the necks of every fence. They called these places purge camps, which I later found out were designed to help eradicate the perducorium outbreak that had wiped out an ungodly portion of our country's population.

I don't remember much about the purge camp. I'm not sure if that's because I was too young or if I instinctively blocked out as much as I could. I guess they held me in solitary confinement most of the time because I barely remember talking to or seeing anyone. Some days I would push my bed over to the window so I could look out and watch the desert sandstorms or lose myself in the stars at night.

When the nurses came, I remember the fear that gripped me when my veins caught the jabbing needles. Later, I found out they were pulling blood samples to test me for any possible flare-up of dormant perducoric cells.

THE REVELATION

My parents were taken to an entirely different camp somewhere up north. I asked my dad several times what his camp was like, and I never could get him to say anything more significant than "It was really cold" or "It was just a bad dream. But it's all in the past."

He has a few long, bright scars stretching across his back, like streaks of lightning against his dark skin. He pretends they aren't there, but Mom told me they came from a low point one time when he tried to escape. She didn't give me many details, but from what she did say, he got caught up in a barbwire fence.

Mom has a scar too, just below her stomach, and I've only seen it once. When I asked her about it, she said she'd always had it. I could tell she was lying, so I didn't push her further. Her skin is much lighter than Dad's, so hers is more of a pink scar, and because it's around her waistline, she can hide it well.

After about six months of showing no signs of infection, my parents and I were separately released from our purge camps and reunited back in Southern Guard. They drugged me for the trip back. No one told me I was returning home, so when I woke up on the floor of an empty metallic room, I assumed I was still at a purge camp facility.

My throbbing right wrist harshly welcomed me back from sedation. When I looked at it, I saw they'd tattooed three touching hexagons with small dashed symbols inside. Later, I found out the tattoo is called the *snare*, which is an encrypted symbol containing codes that store my purge camp records. The markings brand me as a purge camp survivor.

I'd never seen this myself in person, but from pictures, I knew some people in our capital, New Province Guard, had three touching hexagons tattooed on each wrist. My dad said the double-snare meant you tested positive but you had enough money to relocate to the capital to receive the treatments that kept you from undergoing the extreme physical transformation brought about by perducorium's complete takeover of every cell. From there, the medical branch of RedCloud Industry usually amputated the diseased area if necessary and supplied the spreader with a TASER, which is a Technologically Advanced Synthetic Extremity Replacement. Even the prosthetic replacements have the snare markings.

Any spreader who can't afford treatment is shipped to a purge camp to await being forcefully exiled to any number of nearly uninhabitable reservations. Fortunately, most of my family avoided that fate.

After I'd spent a few hours alone in the windowless holding room, a Southern Guard Protector led me out and into an unfamiliar customs line, where I joined a small group of people returning to Southern Guard. I saw my parents for the first time in months, spotting them before they saw me. My mother ran out of line even though the protectors were yelling at her to come back. I was too afraid to speak or move when she grabbed a hold of me. I remember shaking as she squeezed me so tight within her shrunken frame that I could feel her bones pressing against her skin as she cried. In some ways, that moment felt like my second birth into a different life without Ruma.

Dad grabbed a hold of me too just before the Protectors forced us apart again so we could individually enter the scanning systems, which granted us passage into the Outer Wall.

THE REVELATION

Upon returning home, we were told we had lost everything but the concrete skeleton of our home, but that also no longer belonged to us. The Southern Guard Quartering Department reassigned us new housing and gave my parents a small stipend to help get us back on our feet.

On our way to the new housing unit, my dad led us by our old home for one last look. I remember shaking as Mom held my hand. A part of me expected to see Ruma there again, but a new family had moved in, reclaiming the only home I'd known. Before we passed our old front door, a wiry redheaded little girl wearing a face mask ran up to me, blurting, "They melted your house."

I didn't know who she was or what she meant, and thinking back now, I'm sure she didn't either. Her dad, also wearing a mask that covered his nose and mouth, came running up behind her.

"Silver! Get away." He grabbed her hand, forcefully pulling her back while trying to avoid looking at us, as if we had no clothes on. "They don't want anybody bothering them."

"Why?" Silver asked, but he just turned away, pulling her back to their house.

Our new home came with no beds, so on the first night, we slept huddled together with a few pillows on the concrete floor. Mom quietly hummed the same song she used to sing to Ruma and me when we had bad dreams. I pretended to sleep while I watched tears slide down her cheeks, wondering if Ruma might actually never come home.

For a while, my parents worked tirelessly at undesirable jobs just for us to stay afloat, sometimes leaving me at home alone. Even though we had been cleared of any possible traces of infection, almost no one felt comfortable hiring someone who had been exposed to perducorium. Thankfully, my dad found work in the Southern Guard stables, taking care of the guardsmen's horses. His work ethic allowed him to move up the ranks pretty quickly, and now he's a guard captain.

It took a few years, but my parents managed to piece our home back together to create a new nest for us. It was a chance to start fresh, even though the ghostly absence of Ruma quietly haunted our hearts. I didn't know how to ask what had become of her.

My social life got a slow reboot too. During the first few months after moving into our new house within the Outer Wall, everyone's eyes dodged ours, and no one came near, as if instead of fighting near starvation in purge camps, we had spent the past six months rolling around in perducorium-infested shit piles. Eventually people began deeming us safe enough to stop dodging our shadows, and nearly a year later, I finally made a friend.

Despite her parents' warnings, the same young redheaded girl who greeted us our first day back, Silver, started following me one day when my mom took me to play in the commons courtyard. Silver's curiosity got the better of her, and she easily enticed me to play with her dinosaur toys.

It wasn't until Silver and I were nine years old that she told me about what she remembered happening to our home after my family was temporarily removed from Southern Guard. We were playing outside in the streets in front of her home when she said, "You want to know what happened to your old house? I'll tell you at the top of the wall." She took off running, and I chased after her.

We climbed through a few holes in a hidden section of a stone wall we used to sneak through so we could scale up to the top of the Outer Wall. From up high, we could look out over the farmlands below as the massive sprinkler systems spewed a watery mist that formed small rainbows over the crops. When we could manage, we liked to go to our secret spot so Silver could take off the mask her parents always made her wear and also so we could dangle our legs off the edge and have spitting competitions.

On that particular day, when we reached the top of the wall, Silver broke into her story about the "robot men" who sprayed green foam inside people's houses.

Silver made up weird stuff all the time, but she swore this story was real, so I asked her if that was what happened to my old house.

"Yeah," she said. "It was like a giant green bubble bath, but a bad one, 'cause it melted everything."

The foundations, walls, and roof of our old home were all made of reinforced concrete, and they were the only things that survived the chemicals. The PRA sealed the windows and filled our house with the acidic foam, which ate away everything we owned like a hungry disease.

All we have left of our past are our memories. Even those we've more or less tried to bury in our hearts so we could move toward a future not defined by the stains of our past.

Even so, there are nights I lie in bed filled with hopeful anxiety, wondering if Ruma is alive somewhere far away, thinking of me in the same moment, wondering if she, too, dreams of finding her way back to the family she lost thirteen years ago.

I try to leave the past in the past, because it's rarely a weight worth carrying. For my family, moving on was hard because even some of our worst memories are the only connections we have with Ruma. Her infection changed us forever, but thankfully we stuck together so we wouldn't lose the good we had left.

For the most part, I've figured out how to find happiness within the walls, but I can't shake the feeling of being trapped like a rabbit inside a burrow. Perducorium has made countless people seemingly disappear into the outer world beyond, and no one seems to know how to make things better, so we live comfortably but not freely. The best I can do is live in the present and take each moment as it comes.

CHAPTER 2

Asa rips up the ground with his hooves as we weave through rows of tall pine trees interrupted by a few sporadic oaks on our way home. Breaking past the hem of the forest, he gallops down a small hill just as my right foot slips out of the stirrup. I nearly barrel off his left side. He must feel my body shift because he slows down to help me regain my balance.

"Whoa, whoa, whoa! Take it easy," I say.

We come to a stop, and I readjust my body before leaning forward to pat his neck. His glossy brown coat shines even more brightly as it catches the light of the setting sun.

"Thanks, bud," I tell him while digging out a treat from one of the saddlebags. I toss half of an apple on the ground in front of him as I lift my feet out from the stirrups to dismount. The piece of apple tumbles out of Asa's reach. As he lunges forward, I nearly fall, trying to land both feet flat on the ground.

"Shit, Asa! You're gonna kill me."

THE REVELATION

A familiar ring sounds from my temporary tracking device, which has been locked around my arm by the Southern Guard Protectors Unit. The device tracks my location and allows me to send out a distress signal if I'm in danger, but I've never had to use it. Anyone traveling beyond the Outer Wall of Southern Guard has to wear one. It's a small price to pay for being able to wander within the tracking line, which is the protected perimeter that stretches one mile out around the entire circumference of Southern Guard's walls. I tap the receiver on my arm to signal everything is okay so the beeping will stop.

Boundaries don't sit too well with me, so I almost always ride beyond the tracking line and accept the consequences of having to endure the more extensive security procedures and full-body scans before I can go back through the Outer Wall. I make sure to always be on my guard in case I encounter a Stone.

One night, on a full moon several months back, a few of my Southern Guard Youth buddies and I took our horses and rode out a couple miles past the tracking line. The weight of night fell heavily across our shoulders as we rode underneath the bony winter arms of the trees above, but none of my friends wanted to be the one to cave and suggest turning around. I led the way through the dark shadows of the outlying forests until Asa suddenly slid to a stop, rearing on his hind legs.

Not twenty feet away, a male Stone rose up from his hands and knees like a wild beast. In the dim moonlight slicing through the branches of the overhead trees, I could see the dark gloss of fresh blood running down his face. The yellow shimmer of his eyes brightly contrasted with his diseased body, which was halfway covered by the hardened ash-gray skin unique to the Stones.

The glistening blood dripping from his mouth came from some type of animal carcass at his feet. Fortunately for us, he never came any closer, despite what I'd heard of the aggressive nature of Stones. He just looked us over for a second before casually putting a few items into some kind of backpack and clumsily stumbling away into the night. We all swore not to tell anyone what we saw in case our parents found out, but the encounter disturbed me enough to keep my wanderings closer to the Outer Wall.

Once Asa finishes his snack, I climb back in the saddle, and we continue forward. A soft hum rises and falls over me as we pass one of the hundreds of security beams that form the tracking line.

Each crisp white pillar stands twenty feet tall and has concave sides with circular energy receptors rising at two-foot intervals. On the rare occasion that the security beams are on, the receptors catch the streams of energy pulsing between any two parallel receptors. This forms a white-blue expanse of electric bars that protects our city from any outside threats, such as possible Stone invasions.

In school, we are taught about the Chemical World War, which nearly wiped out our entire country almost two hundred years ago. Foreign Naroke extremists strategically tore our country apart using bombs loaded with toxic gasses and chemicals, including perducorium, which causes severe physical mutations—if you're lucky enough to survive. The old society had to evolve into a new culture of isolationism in order to survive the outbreaks.

Nearly two centuries later, we've rebuilt the country of New Province by using what we call the Guard System. Each Guard embodies and upholds the same foundational principles of

THE REVELATION

the New Province Constitution. By forming separate, self-sustaining Guards, our country has split its heart into four distinct yet equal beating chambers, known as Southern Guard, Northern Guard, Western Guard, and Star Guard, which is between Western and Southern Guard. Our capital, New Province Guard, is more or less in a centralized location between the current four Guards. New Province Guard is the self-sustaining mother city, and the remaining four Guards are her children.

With a few tongue clicks and a quick tug on his reins, I ask Asa to slow to a canter. I'd like to get home soon because my stomach has been growling with hunger pains for the past thirty minutes, but I know Asa's tired. At this pace, I'll have a little more time to admire the sunset as the deep-orange waves of light spill between the tall building silhouettes towering above the nearing Outer Wall. I have to use one hand to shield my eyes, but I trust Asa to lead the way.

If I wasn't a member of the Southern Guard Youth, I'd have to sit through a few additional hours of detention, testing, and interrogation before being allowed to go home, but since I am, it only takes about fifteen minutes.

Over the past year, there have been several positive readings for perducorium, but they were effectively contained by the PRA, and none of the spreaders were allowed to enter Southern Guard. They were all detained at the first security checkpoint. Whenever this happens, our city has to undergo a week or so of living in an atmosphere super-saturated with paranoia and fear, but most people begin regaining a sense of peace and security once the lockdown protocols are lifted.

Asa and I reach East Gate, which rests in the long shadows of the late afternoon. After checking Asa back into the stables and making sure he's fed and watered, I head over to the East Gate entrance.

A few people are queuing through the exterior glass-wall security ports, but I head to the express line. I've probably been tested a few hundred times, but every time I enter the interior scanning chamber, one particular security worker treats me like I could be a full-blown Stone.

This particular woman in the Southern Guard Protector's Unit has always been convinced I'm a carrier of perducorium. Ever since someone told her about the incident with Ruma's infection years ago, she's been overtly suspicious of me. She frequently stares at the snare on my hand. It's visible proof I was declared clean after my period of detention, but it clearly means nothing to her.

This woman looks to be in her late fifties. She wears a scowl across her face like an ugly accessory, which matches the fake hair that swirls above her head like a dark tower.

"Single file," she grunts. "Have your ID ready or we'll send you to the back of the line. Step up."

From behind her glass cubicle, she waves her long fingernails at me as if I'm incapable of understanding her words.

"Hey. How's it going?" I ask, challenging myself to be cordial. She ignores my question, so I simply tap the holophone on my wrist to pull up my ID.

"You're lucky I don't send you to the back of the line," she says without making eye contact.

There are only six people in line behind me.

"I've had worse things happen," I assure her, pointing to the snare. She stares for a moment, snuffling loudly before continuing.

THE REVELATION

"Step forward. Wait for the light, then enter the scanner," she says, even though she knows I've been through the scanner enough times to do her job. I step forward as the ENTER light illuminates, and I move inside the glass chamber.

From the outside, people can see into the chamber, but from the inside, the rounded walls and ceiling are like mirrors. The ground beneath my feet moves me forward through a series of laser scans. The chamber maintains a dark-red glow, but several layers of colored lasers fall over me, scanning for any possible trace of perducorium.

When I was a kid, the first couple times I had to be scanned, I cried because I was terrified I would have to go back to purge camp, but after I got over that fear, I started to love the free light show. Once the scanning process is complete, the lights turn a whitish blue. The exit doors hiss open into a short concrete tunnel that leads into East Portal, which is one of the four main Southern Guard entryways.

As much as I love riding away from Southern Guard and into the deep breadth of woods, I still have a special place in my heart for the complex beauty of the city. At this time of day, there are very few people around East Portal. Purple trumpets and scarlet honeysuckle vines cover the massive bio-stanchions stretching all the way up to support the woven synthetic-glass ceilings, which occasionally release a light spray of mist for the plants below.

Several contouring benches rest on the edges of the transparent floor panels, which also serve as ceilings for the underground terrariums. Relaxing music from the cello of a young female street performer greets me as I make my way across East Portal to board the wall lift. The higher I rise up the spine of the Outer Wall, the more open the view of the melting sunset becomes.

From up here, it's easier to see the cityscape as it rolls out for miles. Freshly growing structures are always rising into view. Solar panels dress the structural faces of almost every building, making them shine like jewels. If I didn't have to head home to pack for Special Ops training tomorrow, I'd stay out late so I could watch the solar-harvesting roads glow like soft white rivers. They're not quite the same color, but the comforting glow reminds me of the bioluminescent canals we explored when I was sent to the nearby coastal grounds for Southern Guard Youth basic training. Ever since then, a place deep in me fires with euphoria and anxiety when I imagine traveling far beyond Southern Guard's walls.

Around this time, I usually see some of my friends out, riding the wall lift, but I'm not having any luck today. It doesn't really matter, though, because I have too much to do when I get home, so I don't really have time to stop and chat.

My holophone beeps, and Mom's picture pops up, suspended over my forearm. I tap my wrist to answer, and a sideways projection of our kitchen cabinets appears above my arm.

"Hey, Mom. Mom?" I say, but she's not there and can't hear me because she called accidentally. After I turn my outgoing volume on high, I pull my wrist to my face and yell, "Hey!" I hear her shriek, and her face finally appears above my wrist.

"Who is talking? Oh. Hello? Hello," she yells, still confused.

"Me," I say, rolling my eyes. "You called me."

"Oh. Good. I was just about to call you anyway."

I let out a long breath before saying, "I'm sure you were.

You have a talent for calling me about three minutes before I get home."

"Where are you?"

"Three minutes away. Well, now two minutes away." I hold my holophone out ahead of me. "See? There's the house. I'm right here."

"Okay, okay. Sorry. It's almost time to eat. See you in a minute."

"All right. Bye." I tap my holophone off and groan to myself to release a small dose of agitation. This week, Mom has called me at least three times as much as she usually does.

Like my old house, our current home is made almost entirely of reinforced concrete. My dad accented the frames of our front door and windows with natural stone. Thousands of nearly identical houses make up the upper portion of the Outer Wall, so it's a small way to distinguish our home from the rest. Mom doesn't like the location because it's farther away from the action of Southern Guard's central hub, the Court, but I don't mind because we have the best views of the city and the landscape beyond the wall.

I take out my scan-key, flash it across our door panel, and step inside. I can hear Mom and Dad talking in the kitchen, so I sneak to my bedroom and collapse on my bed for a few seconds of quiet.

Tomorrow, my best friend Merrin and I leave for training. Both of us are transitioning out of the Youth program and going straight to Southern Guard Special Ops. If we pass, we'll skip over the guardsman ranking and be directly promoted to the Southern Guard Operative status.

I first met Merrin when we joined the Southern Guard Youth regimen five years ago, after we turned thirteen. I joined a month before Merrin, so I always joke that he's playing catch-up to me. Back then, we enjoyed a confidence boost from thinking we looked good in our matching uniforms while completing obstacle courses more quickly than everyone else, but now things have gotten much more complicated.

Other than the intensity of our training being higher than ever, this year we will most likely share the responsibility of training the entry-level SGY. All the other Southern Guard citizens our age who chose to wait until they were eighteen to join—which is the mandated entry year—will begin their two years of service in the Southern Guard forces. We'll have to rely on our extra training experience to assert ourselves over the ones who bring their egos with them.

"Darvin, why haven't you started packing?" Mom asks, walking into my room and laying some freshly folded clothes on my bed.

"Because it will take me about ten minutes. Stop worrying."

"You'll be gone for four weeks. It'll take more than ten minutes," she scolds, picking up a pair of pants off the floor. "Are these clean?"

"Yes. They're clean. I got it," I grumble, sitting up to take the pants back from her. "Where's Merrin?"

"He went walking with Jaykin, and he's already packed."

Jaykin is my younger brother. He was born a year or so after we returned from purge camp. I cried when I found out he wasn't a girl because I wanted another sister after losing Ruma, but getting used to having a younger brother didn't take long. He's only ten years old, but our age gap has never kept us from being close.

Merrin has been as much of an older brother to Jaykin as I have. Before he moved in with us, our families used to

THE REVELATION

celebrate holidays together when we couldn't get our travel appropriations approved to visit my mom's parents in Northern Guard.

When Merrin's brother, Raythe, tested positive for perducorium, his parents had enough money to apply to RedCloud Prosthetics and the medical treatment branch for him to receive amputation and transfusion treatments, but for some reason, their request was denied. After that, they left everything behind, including Merrin, who was forced to move in with his aunt, and set out for the capitol of New Province Guard to appeal the decision with the insurance branch of RedCloud.

Shortly after, Merrin's aunt married into a new family of her own and didn't have room for him, so we agreed to take him in until his parents returned. New Province Guard is only a half day's travel away from Southern Guard by way of the shuttle drones, but his parents have been gone for four years, and we haven't heard from them since.

I hear the front door open, and Jaykin and Merrin come in. Jaykin's voice calls out, "Hey, we decided I'm going with them to training tomorrow."

"No, you're not," Mom yells down the hallway as she leaves my room.

"He'll be fine," Merrin argues jokingly. "Once he learns how to shoot and handle a little hand-to-hand combat—"

I enter the living room just in time to see Merrin grab Jaykin in a chokehold. I walk over to help Jaykin and try to smack Merrin between his legs, but he moves just in time.

Dad's voice calls to us from the kitchen. "You could also work on that hand-to-hand training by helping your mom fold your clothes."

"That's a terrible idea," I counter, but Jaykin sits down and picks up a pair of my pants to fold.

"Not as terrible as being lazy. Both of you come help me finish cooking," Dad says. Merrin and I choose the lesser of two evils and join Dad.

Tonight we're having a special meal. Stewed roast, squash casserole, fried cornbread, and twice-baked potatoes. We fix our plates and settle around our kitchen table. Dad prays for the food and for our protection during our training. I try to sneak a quick bite of potatoes.

"...and help Darvin to learn patience and self-control," Dad says, staring at me.

"Amen," Mom adds emphatically, and we all begin eating. She sips her sweet tea and barely makes it through one carefully chewed bite before saying, "I'm worried you both aren't going to have everything you need for tomorrow."

"I'm just hoping we make it home alive," I say.

"Don't even start. You think it's funny, and you're going to forget something important, and it's just going to be too bad for you. Who else needs a napkin?" she asks, getting up from the table.

"All right now, Negative Nancy," Jaykin jokes.

"I'm not being negative," Mom insists as she lays an extra napkin beside each of our plates. "I'm just trying to make sure they're prepared."

As Mom sits back down, Merrin puts his hand on her shoulder and tells her, "I'll take care of him. But you might want to pack him a picture of you just in case he gets scared."

"I already packed that," I say, winking at Mom.

"We really do want both of you to be careful," Dad tells us. "Neither one of you has been to New Province Guard, and

I know Ops training has probably changed since I've been there, but it's not easy. I can tell you that."

"I'm glad you told us. Thanks for the advice," I say, my voice flat.

"Don't be rude," Mom admonishes.

"I'm not. I'm just saying we knew that when we signed up for this."

The room settles for a few seconds before I feel the need to add, "We'll be safe."

Jaykin blurts out, "If you bring me back a flying suit, I'll be your servant for a year!"

Mom doesn't hesitate. "He's had a servant for years. Her name is Mom."

Jaykin jokingly throws his wadded-up napkin and hits Mom in the face. It startles her, and we can't help but laugh as she half-heartedly throws it back at him. I don't know how he does it, but Jaykin always makes things okay.

I catch his gaze while trying not to smile. "I'll see what I can do about that suit."

Eventually, to Mom's surprise, I finish packing, and the night pulls us all to our beds. That's when my nerves finally get to me. I can't sleep. If my mind were a library, it's like someone has pushed over every bookshelf, and now it's my job to put all my books back in order.

I stare at my ceiling to distract myself, imagining it's the black curtain preparing to open up to my dreams, if I can just calm my mind. I waste several minutes before I decide to just lie awake and let my thoughts run wild. I hope they'll eventually get tired like me, so for now I let my mind drag me through my cluttered memories of my SGY training, which I'll definitely need tomorrow.

A few months ago, the leaders of SGY assembled an elite squad consisting of the highest-performing protectors in their division. Of the several thousand protectors enlisted in SGY, High Commander Nebbuck himself, the head of the Southern Guard branch of services, selected just two dozen of us to participate in training in New Province Guard for advanced Stone-defense missions based on our aptitude and agility scores on a prerequisite training. Of the twenty-four chosen, I was told I earned the second-highest cumulative score, just behind someone named R. Shaer.

The officers tested us after school over the course of a few weeks by throwing us into various physically and mentally exhausting training exercises. If we didn't master every assigned task, they threatened to kick us out and send us back home to remedial training.

During special weapons training, a girl named Carrie from our team got two of her fingers nearly blown off in an accident. They had to force her to stop trying to complete the drill so the on-site medical team could properly stitch her fingers back to her hand. After only five days of recovery, she managed to pass the firing course using her other hand. Merrin didn't pass until day seven, so the rest of our squadron hounded him about it.

One day, they took us to a flight-simulation hangar that replicated flight patterns and maneuvers of the Southern Guard Falcon division. The first time I saw Falcon operatives was my second day of purge camp. A group of us were being transferred out of our camp to another location because of overcrowding issues. After several people tried to escape during the transition out, Falcon operatives materialized out of nowhere, subduing the deserters with force while herding the rest of us back in line.

Since then, I've periodically seen a group of Falcon operatives blast across the sky during infiltration drills. There has never been anything else I wanted to do more than fly. Even after experiencing the flight simulators, I felt like a new part of my spirit opened up, allowing me to breathe in a deeper sense of purpose from a place in me I didn't know existed before.

The more Jaykin found out about what Merrin and I were doing in training, the more he wouldn't stop asking questions about what guns we had fired and if we'd killed any Stones yet. The day we came home from flight-simulation training, I showed him a hologram of me flying in my mock Falcon gear. As he watched, the same light that compelled me join the Southern Guard Youth years ago came across his face.

That night after supper, the second Jaykin left the kitchen table, Mom clenched my forearm and said, "Don't encourage him about that stuff. Never again. Not about guns, not about killing."

There were tears in her eyes, but she got up from the table before any fell. Since then, I feel like I've taken on some of her worry for Jaykin's safety.

My dad used to tell stories of how he and his friends would rescue young children caught up in the Greylands skirmishes on the peripherals of Southern Guard. He told us that outside of the Guard cities, men and women would cut throats to secure resources or land. He risked his life for others, and I always wanted to find purpose in doing the same. Jaykin wasn't as interested as I was in my dad's stories, but I know he looks up to me. I worry he might follow in my footsteps.

The thought drops an uncomfortable weight in my stomach, so I roll onto my side and pull the covers off to feel the air from my fan. When I close my eyes, the disappointment on Mom's face hangs in my mind. I shake it away and force myself out of bed, then I quietly walk to the hallway bathroom to pee. A small stream of light leaks from under my parents' bedroom door. I hear soft mumblings, and it sounds like Mom might be crying. On the balls of my feet, I silently ease my way to their door.

"I've seen them," Mom says, her voice wavering. "The guardsmen are practicing defensive drills almost every day. Talia called me twice today to see if I had seen them training on the wall, out in the open. I'm not the only one. You can't tell me something isn't going on. You can't."

"I don't know," Dad whispers. "I've heard there's been some tension between RedCloud and the capital, but that's normal these days."

They say nothing for a moment.

"What is it?" Dad finally asks, frustrated. "Do you think I'm hiding something from you? I would tell you—"

"No. I'm not saying that. I'm saying I think you're not being honest with yourself."

He pauses for a moment, and I realize I'm holding my breath.

"We can't live in fear," he says. "We've done that before, and it doesn't work. Whatever it is, we'll be okay. They'll be okay. They will."

For a second, I think about going in to join them, but something holds me back, so I head for the bathroom before returning to my bed. Across the room, Merrin's lumpy shadow sleeps soundly in his bed. I hear the ebbing stream of breath

THE REVELATION

steadily leaving his nose. He always falls asleep before I do.

    I try to copy the slow rhythm of his breathing to help hit the brakes on my mind—in through my nose and out through my mouth. My eyelids begin feeling heavy, so I dip into my imagination once more with a different strategy. I place myself on the back of a sleeping hill under a gentle gathering of stars. Here in my mind, I whisper prayers for my family until I drift off into the night.

CHAPTER 3

The morning comes too quickly for me. My least-favorite part about having joined the Southern Guard Youth has always been waking up early. Merrin is already up and brushing his teeth. In this moment, it feels like one of the loudest noises I've ever heard, so I pull my pillow over my head. I hear a click, and light spills through the edges of my pillow.

"You up? Time to get up. I got breakfast when you're ready."

Dad talks obnoxiously loud in the mornings. I moan and stretch under my covers, and that's good enough for him.

When I make it to the kitchen, I see Jaykin is up too, but his face is still asleep. I ruffle his stiff hair, and he swats my hand away.

Mom hands me a glass of milk. "Did you sleep okay?"

"Yep. Good," I say, not wanting her to worry.

"I'm glad *you* did. I couldn't go to sleep, and your dad kept snoring like a bear."

Dad throws a half-hearted "sorry" over his shoulder while he fries a few more pieces of bacon. Merrin walks in to sit down with his coffee and begins spilling out the contents of his dream, assuming I want to hear it.

"I dreamed when we got to New Province Guard, all the people were wolves, so we startled crawling and howling so no one would notice us. But then this huge spotlight came out of nowhere, so everyone could see us. Then we ran up this weird tower thing that turned into a massive tree, and Silver was there, except it didn't look like her, and she gave us these weird swords. But somehow we got to the big spotlight and started hitting the shit out of it with our swords. And then the light turned this dark-red color because it was spewing blood, and then I woke up."

"That's demonic," Jaykin jokes.

"Way too intense for breakfast," I say, getting up to clean off my plate.

"Maybe you should start praying or reading before bed to clear your mind," Mom suggests.

"No, I normally don't dream stuff like that, but that one was just weird."

Getting our gear and bags together takes longer than we expected. Mom throws in an *I told you so* for her own enjoyment.

I slide my brace-comm over my forearm and power it on. "Merrin, our shuttle leaves in forty-five minutes."

He yells back from our room, saying he'll be ready soon, and Mom takes this time to tell me goodbye.

"I'm going to miss you being here." She hugs me, and I can tell she doesn't want to let go.

"I'll miss you too, but I'll be back soon."

"I know. Four weeks." She pulls back for a second to look at me. "I sure do love you."

"I love you too." I kiss her on the cheek before reaching over to swoop Jaykin up in an overdramatic hug.

"Stop! I have to poop," he says, laughing, and I know that's the best goodbye he can come up with.

"Save some love for me," I hear Merrin say as he walks up and gives Mom a good squeeze.

She laughs and tells him she loves him. Jaykin wraps himself up in his blanket on the couch, so Merrin falls on him to lovingly squash him. I pull him off because we don't have time to goof around. Dad offers to walk us to the shuttle, and I accept because we have a lot to carry.

We say our second round of goodbyes to Mom and Jaykin, and as we walk out the door Mom yells behind us, "Please be careful!" one last time. I call over my shoulder, assuring her we will, and moments later, Dad is leading Merrin and me along the Outer Wall passage that circles down to North Gate. We live in the Outer Wall Sector, Unit T67—twenty stories up, sixty-seven units east of North Gate, and around six miles out from the Court. Merrin used to live near the Court before his parents set out for New Province Guard. I spent the night with him once and felt like I was a prince in their mansion.

Our uniform gear catches the eyes of several people making their early morning starts, and I like it because it makes me feel superior. We keep walking until we intercept one of the exterior wall lifts, which we use to ride to the top of the Outer Wall concourse.

To my right, a bed of fog rests low over the land beyond the wall, as if the clouds are struggling to wake up. Most of the vendors to my left have opened their stores and are organizing their outside merchandise. Even though I've already eaten, the scent of fresh bread stirs my stomach. Some Saturdays, I bring Jaykin up here to browse around, and we usually end up bringing home a wrapped bouquet of flowers for my mom.

Someone calls to me from behind and grabs my arm right on my brace-comm. I instinctively pull away before I realize it's Silver. I haven't seen her for a couple of weeks, but that's normal these days.

"Sorry! Hey," Silver says. I must have startled her as much as she did me.

"Hey. It's okay. What's up?"

"Nothing. I just heard you're leaving today, and I wanted to say good luck and bye." She reaches out once more and gently places her hand around my brace-comm. She's never been an affectionate person, so I try not to let my face show my confusion.

"Yeah. Thanks. We're about to catch our shuttle drones now."

She waits a moment, as if waiting to see whether I have anything else to say, but I can't think of anything. Her cheeks have turned bright pink.

I catch Merrin's eyes over Silver's shoulder, and he's makes a dramatically awkward face.

Silver suddenly nods her head before hastily saying, "Okay. Be safe. See ya." She walks away without even acknowledging Merrin or Dad.

"That was gloriously awkward," Merrin says, thriving off my embarrassment.

Silver and I have mostly gone our separate ways in the past couple of years. Somehow, both of her parents became infected with perducorium. I tried to talk to her about it, but she shut me out, and ever since then, Silver has only gotten stranger. She moved in with a family friend, but she wouldn't tell me who it was or where she lived. I tried asking her how she managed to avoid going to purge camp, but she just shook her head and walked away. Ever since then, I've been trying to keep my distance while respecting hers as well.

Dad waits until she's out of earshot. "What was that about?"

"I don't know, but you should ask Merrin because he's the one who dreamed about her last night," I say.

Time moves too fast, and we are at the shuttle drone dock before I have mentally prepared to leave. I recognize most of the faces from our SGY group. Griff, Mage, and Carrie look like they've already said their goodbyes and are now waiting in line for the P-scan.

"All right, boys. This is it." Dad hands over our bags. Their weight in my arms makes me realize how glad I am he walked us down.

"We need to scan in," Merrin says.

"Yeah, okay," I say.

Dad reaches out, putting a hand on each of our shoulders. "It's going to be fun, but I want you to be smart. They'll teach you self-defense, but no one's going to teach you how to guard your heart and your mind. But that matters too, and it's probably the most important thing you can do."

He opens his mouth to say more, but he stops himself. I'm waiting for him to tell us whatever he was too afraid to tell Mom last night. Instead, he takes in a deep breath and abruptly lets it back out.

"We'll be good," I say to reassure him. "We have each other."

THE REVELATION

"When he starts crying, I'll hold his hand," Merrin jokes while grabbing my hand.

I yank my hand away and glare at him disdainfully to try and make him feel stupid, but it doesn't work. He hugs Dad and kisses him on the cheek to be funny. While Merrin picks up his bags, Dad turns to me and pulls a thin box out of his pocket.

"Open this later," he says, tucking the box into my hand as we hug. "I love you, boys. Have fun. Be safe for your mom," he adds, winking at us.

We tell him we love him too and head toward check-in. I turn to wave one more time, but the morning crowd seems to have swallowed him.

A tight-faced woman quickly grabs each of our wrists to access our brace-comms. She smudges her thumbprint against the screen before typing in some correspondence code she finds in the PRA database. I smile at her, but she is too busy waving me out of the way to notice. The guards herd about twenty of us into the clear P-scan tunnel, and the doors seal behind us. No one is talking, but a lot of eyes are busy reading faces.

I feel like a fish in a tank. I owned a fish when I was younger, but Merrin flushed him down the toilet after we got into a fight. I quietly remind him of this story, and he tries to look guilty before his laugh takes over.

The room compresses with air, and a wave of pale-blue light falls across our bodies, scanning for any possible trace of perducorium. I've never understood them scanning us as we leave. If one of us in here tested positive, we'd all be screwed.

"Whoa! That was cool," Merrin says as if he's never been scanned before, and no one responds. My face turns hot from embarrassment. A guard motions us ahead, and we're all clear from within the chamber. In front of us, a gate opens into the Outer Wall's interior.

We leave the natural light as the gate's metallic gears crunch shut behind us, sending echoing groans into the vaulting gray hollows. The flat-faced pillars stretching high above and the arching buttress bridges below offer us little more than a cold concrete welcome. We step into the next clear, dimly lit chamber underneath the dull infrastructure within the Outer Wall's frame.

Four PRA guards intercept us as we walk in. Some of the people in my group flash their digital tickets in front of a guard's scanner, and he directs them to step off to the side into another holding line. The biggest guard approaches Merrin and me, asking, "Are you two with the Southern Guard Youth?"

"Yeah," Merrin says. "We're doing the Special Ops—"

"Your shuttle is ready and waiting."

He points over toward a vehicle hovering on the other side of a huge drop-off. Soft blue light washes underneath our shuttle drone like a wave in the dark. Three narrow bridges reach over the pit ahead, which sinks into the dark workings of underground Southern Guard.

"Take the third bridge," the guard commands.

Merrin and I aren't particularly scared of heights, but once we step onto the last slender walkway stretching over the faint cavity below, I can suddenly feel my heart pulsing in my neck.

The thin railings lining the sides of the walkway give little comfort.

"Whoa," Merrin says, grabbing me while pretending to fall.

THE REVELATION

I string off a line of cuss words, both to release anxiety and to retaliate against Merrin.

He's laughing, and I feel stupid, because it did rattle me. A sudden rumbling shakes the bridge below us. I look through the grated steel below my feet and see another lighted craft of some kind hurtling up toward us. In the same instant, I feel and smell the mechanical musk of hot air violently swirling around us.

"Oh shit!" Merrin yells as we both scramble across to the other side of the pit.

Behind us, a shuttle rises up from the pit below the bridge and maneuvers into place directly behind our current loading drone before coming to a halt. I hear laughing, and when I turn around, I find it's coming from the four PRA guards who checked our group in.

"We could be off to a better start," I say to Merrin as he brushes past me to hide inside the shuttle drone.

CHAPTER 4

Sometimes I think about how strange it is that vastly different people from any two places can make the same decision that leads them to cross paths in the exact same moment. I see people and wonder if we're sharing an insignificant encounter in life only to be forgotten seconds later, or if I should be paying attention just in case someone I meet becomes a part of my life forever. I lean over to share this thought with Merrin, but he's already sleeping with his mouth open in his seat.

There's a beautiful dark-haired girl with bronze skin sitting a few rows up on the opposite side of us. She's the one who has me thinking about chance encounters. I've seen her a few times before, but I can't stop staring. I prepare my eyes to shift away if she turns around. I'm studying her sharp features when she turns her head to the side, and even from here, her eyes seem to catch and hold light. I'm kind of glad Merrin is asleep so he won't interrupt me.

THE REVELATION

She catches me off guard, and we lock eyes as soon as she turns around, so I quickly pretend to talk to Merrin, who is still asleep. Now all of a sudden I wish he was awake. I wait a few seconds and look back her way. She is laying her head against another guy's shoulder. As my stomach tightens, I grit my teeth and let my head fall against the seat in front of me. I look out the window to my right to find something to distract my thoughts. The heat from my breath spreads fog over the glass. I stare into the blurry landscape of skeletal buildings buried beneath wild overgrowth rapidly passing by and try to distract my thoughts away from the girl.

I was sixteen, and Merrin was fifteen, the first time we saw a Stone. We both got a little carried away with excitement because we were going on a rare SGY expedition beyond the walls outside of the tracking line. Our commanders wanted us to experience what it felt like to operate in the presence of danger. They said fear could alter or even take over our training instincts if we let it control us.

I don't know if the SGY commanders actually intended for us to come in contact with any Stones. Looking back, it probably would have been a huge liability to organize an intentional encounter, but either way, it happened. Eight commanders of various ranks had saddled up about thirty of us on horseback and led us to the edge of a dense forest. Broom sedge washed the ground gold all around us before giving way to the wildly overgrown tree line.

"We won't go too far in," Commander Fray shouted over his shoulder, gesturing toward the monstrously tall trees strangled by gnarly tendrils of vines.

"Now's the time to piss or put a little water back in your

tank. We're not stopping once we go in," another commander instructed.

We all took a few swigs from our water bottles, except for Merrin, who asked to borrow mine because he somehow forgot to bring his. Annoyed, I tossed him my canteen and walked off to pee behind a collection of nearby boulders jutting up from the grass like a giant skeleton.

I hopped onto a small rock face and instantly froze. I felt a presence around me before I saw anything. Soon after, I realized my movement had startled a Stone, who shot up from his haphazard bed of sedge between the rocks. He must have slept through our arrival, but his golden eyes immediately fixed on mine. His rigid, broken skin showed between the remnants of ripped clothes clinging to his gray complexion. I couldn't breathe as a surge of terror squeezed my chest tightly. We both waited to see who would make the first move.

As far as I could tell in the quick moment we stood before one another, the Stone was around my age. He was the first to move, darting around the other side of the rock formation. I scrambled in the opposite direction.

When my breath came back to me, I screamed, "Stone!"

Without hesitation, all eight of the commanders trained their weapons on the young Stone tearing out for the woods. The distance between him and the safety of the forest stretched too far. Within seconds, several high-impact lasers tore him apart, leaving behind little more than hot ashes and smoke. I tried to subdue my shaking as I watched the Stone's fingers still twitching on its detached arm.

Merrin's elbow hits my side and suddenly brings me out of my thoughts. I sit up and look at him.

"Oh my God. Look at that girl," he tries to whisper to me.

THE REVELATION

"Shhh. Don't you know how to whisper?" I say, modeling an appropriate hushed tone while I try to cover his mouth.

"I wanna go talk to her," he says quietly, swatting my hand away as if he needs my permission.

"No. I think she's with that guy."

I subtly nod my head toward the guy sitting beside her.

"I can fix that," he says, smiling as he gets up.

He stands up, and I whisper, "Don't." He ignores me, of course, and walks up the aisle. I roll my eyes as he pretends to bump into her seat. He uses his apology to segue into a conversation. I can't watch, so I look away.

My hand settles on my pocket, and I remember I haven't opened my dad's gift. I'll gladly use anything to distract myself from Merrin's intrusive conversation. Once I pull it from my pocket, I tear and slip off the coarse paper. I find a small picture of my mom taped to the top of a small box. My whole family probably planned this dumb joke together, but I still have to smile.

The lid opens easily, and I pull out a stainless-steel flint fire starter. Our last name is Flint, so I can't tell if this is an extension of a bad joke or if my dad really thought it would prove useful. Either way, I like it. While I'm turning it over in my hands, I notice the letter "R" has been engraved into the side. Just as I begin wondering if this used to belong to Ruma, I look up, and Merrin is gone. After a couple of minutes, he emerges from the bathroom and finds his way back to me.

"So how'd it go?" I ask while subtly tucking the fire starter and picture back in my pocket.

"At first, not too good," he says, plopping back into his seat. "That guy *is* her boyfriend, and she wasn't having it, so I just took a shit because I was already up."

"I'm glad you redeemed the situation," I say, glancing again in her direction.

"And there was a window in the bathroom, so it was totally worth it," Merrin says, and I'm sure he means it.

The countryside is indeed very beautiful. Most of what I've heard about the old highways made me imagine piles of overgrown ruins everywhere. I've seen some decaying collections of gray buildings connected by wild vines, but the farther northeast we travel, the more colorful everything seems to get. We pass alongside a wide river generously sharing its wealth with the neighboring fields, where clusters of yellow and blue flowers rise together. The terrain begins to roll up and down, gradually introducing us to the mountains ahead.

We're moving really fast, but the ride is so smooth I would have never known if I hadn't been watching everything fly past my window. I'm beginning to feel a little sick, so I lay my head back and close my eyes. The constant, gentle hum of the shuttle drone swiftly hovering along the highway makes me sleepy, so I let the sensation take me away.

Somewhere between sleeping and consciousness, I feel fingers pushing against my temple.

"Wake up, Sleeping Beauty. Get that drool off your chin."

The voice isn't Merrin's, or I would slap his hand away. It takes me a second before I recognize the sarcastically assertive voice. I open one eye and see my friend Griff sitting in Merrin's seat. He's leaning over, and his face is too close for comfort. He never has cared about anyone else's personal space.

"Griff, you're too ugly to wake anybody up that close," I say jokingly but also as a social cue for him to back up.

THE REVELATION

Griff is not really ugly. He's a ginger with a normal-looking face, but his body is ripped enough for him to maintain an unfortunately high ego. Keeping his head from exploding with confidence is almost a full-time job. We became friends several years ago when his family transferred in from Star Guard after his parents were recruited to implement new training tactics for SGY recruits.

"Are you flirting with me?" Griff asks before sliding his hand up my leg to make me uncomfortable.

"Stop. Stop!"

I grab his arm and push it away while he laughs. He knows he can annoy me more than I can annoy him.

"Where did Merrin go?" I ask.

"Dude, I think he's burning a hole in his pants," he says, wrinkling his nose in disgust. "My seat is by the bathroom, and I had to move before I died."

"Why'd you wake me up?" I ask.

"Look behind you, you big baby," he says, pointing out the shuttle drone's rear windows.

We're gliding along a narrow strip of bridge extending over a massive expanse of sunken, dead earth. Patches of unsettled fog fly by like ghosts above the dark-gray rocks below us, which stretch out for miles in either direction. The bridge angles slightly to the left, giving me my first view of New Province Guard.

"Well, shit," I say as we both stare out the window. The city details are hazy in the distance, but the instant reverence I feel just from the size of the city structures cues a deep shiver under my skin.

A voice calls over the speakers, announcing, "We are

approaching the city's Industrial Defense Quarter. Please prepare to exit."

God knows what kinds of weapons and military hangars are shrouded in the protective outer structures. My dad described the entire configuration of New Province Guard as looking like a bird's talons, with three outstretching claws and one larger claw at the back, where the heart of the city is located.

At this velocity, reaching the exterior walls of New Province Guard's Industrial Defense Quarter doesn't take long. As we decelerate, a concealed gate within the overlaid metallic walls opens like a giant mouth. Above the entryway, two massive New Province flags stretch out in the wind, showing off the vibrant eye of providence encapsulated within a triangle, poised between the majestic, outstretched wings of a phoenix.

All too suddenly, we are swallowed by darkness. The shuttle drone jolts as we reconnect with a grounded track. Some people let quick screams slip out before getting ahold of themselves. In the dark, a hand clenches around my arm.

"I don't like this," Griff shakily whispers in my ear after our lights switch off. "I don't do the dark."

Whoever is in charge of our drone must be having a little too much fun with the first-time visitors to New Province Guard.

"You okay, little buddy?" I ask sarcastically, without bothering to whisper.

"Stop. I don't do the dark," Griff quietly repeats.

"They're doing this on purpose. They're trying to scare us," I offer, trying to free my arm from his wrenching grip.

The interior lights streaking the tunneling roofs suddenly alleviate the darkness as we ride onward. We're all squinting

THE REVELATION

at each other in confusion, and Griff quickly lets go of me. His pupils are so dilated that his eyes look black in the passing light.

Merrin makes his way back to us. "The bathroom door wouldn't open, and I about had a panic attack in there."

A voice sounds over the speaker again. "Attention, SGYs. We are approaching our destination. Prepare for exit." While the lights remain on, the windows change color until they hold a completely black tint.

"I'll see you guys outside," Griff says as he returns to his own seat to collect his belongings.

I place my hand over the flint striker in my pocket, thankful to have something that connects me to my family. The rolling hum of the shuttle drone begins to lessen, and our compartment shakes a bit as we hit the ground. The side hatches lift open, and an officer covered with red armor enters from outside and immediately begins ordering everyone out onto the exterior platform.

"Let's go! Move! Move!"

As he yells, I can't help but stare at a massive scar streaking down the left side of his head, interrupting his hair and a part of his ear. Merrin and I exchange an anxious glance before quickly stepping outside to join the lines forming on the dark marble floors of the Industrial Defense Quarter's intake platforms.

I'd guess there are about fifty of us leaving the two shuttles. My neck tightens as rows of fully uniformed guards intercept us while others form a blockade between us and the structural pillars in front of us. I can't see their faces because they're all wearing dark, reflective masks. Every one of them matches identically in their bloodred gear, with the exception of a few who are dressed exactly like the PRA agents who took my sister. The memory triggers nausea in my stomach.

"Lights out," a voice calls, and I wait for the darkness again, but instead, several red guards step aside, changing formation as the agents move toward us with gassing guns.

Amongst the nervous shuffles and murmurs of our group, someone asks, "What's happening?"

Once the agents hit the triggers of their gassers, clouds of yellow fog engulf us all. We're all gasping and choking on strange fumes that burn my nostrils like hot sulfur.

I'm jostled from behind, and I realize it's Merrin dropping down to the marble floor. My vision turns black and white as Southern Guard Youth bodies fall on either side of me, their entangled limbs twitching in heaps as they struggle to breathe.

In the haze, I see only one other blurry figure remains standing above the fallen bodies, until every gas stream focuses on me. Finally succumbing to the citrine gasses, all my senses leave me as I hit the floor.

CHAPTER 5

When my eyes open to light, nothing looks familiar, so I quickly close them again. For a moment, I keep my eyes shut, because a small part of me hopes when I look again, I will find myself in my bedroom at home. My head feels like a bruised rock, and when I begin to move, I feel the pinch of needles moving in my arms and neck. I'm strapped to a bed, and I feel like throwing up. This isn't home.

My eyes open again to a white light flashing above a closed steel door. My mind struggles to make sense of my surroundings, and I start to panic. I try to get a hold of my breathing because I'm hyperventilating. The room is small but overflowing with medical equipment. A multifaced projector centered just beneath the ceiling is casting my vitals onto the silver walls. Before I can take in any more details, a woman quietly slips into the room.

Her skin is dark against her white uniform, which appears to be a one-piece outfit. After bobbing her head in and out of the door a few times, she cautiously closes it behind her. She's wearing red-tinted glasses but quickly takes them off as she approaches me.

"Don't fight me, and don't panic. I'm not that type of person. You got me?" She's locked in on my face and has her hand stuck out toward me like I'm a wild animal. "You hear me?"

"Who are you?" I ask, still feeling the putrid sting in my nostrils.

"My name's Ms. Diana. I don't have time to read you my bio. You just let me do my thing, and you'll be all right."

"I don't understand—"

"You like music?" she interrupts. "Let me put on some music. You got to get that panic out of your blood."

She runs her fingers across a smaller screen close by the door, and soft, ambient music settles in the room. I pull at a cord protruding from the crease of my elbow, and she firmly grabs my wrist.

"Now what did I just say? We can't have none of that now. Just trust Ms. Diana, and we'll get you on out of here."

I let her carefully remove the needles in my skin.

"What happened?" I ask weakly, realizing just how foggy my head is after trying to speak. My tongue feels like a wrung-out sponge, so I'm doing good to get out any coherent words.

"They don't pay me enough to keep secrets, so I'll tell you what I know." She continues untangling me from the medical equipment, and I try to distract myself by focusing on her words. Maybe that's why she's talking to me.

"One of y'all who came here wasn't invited, so they gassed the whole bunch and found a red-haired girl with no ID. That girl snuck up and thought no one would know the difference. They already locked her up down here somewhere."

"That's stupid," I mutter. "They could have gotten her without hurting everyone else."

"You don't have to convince me of that, baby."

Ms. Diana pats me on the back, signaling for me to move. As I slowly slide my feet off my bed and to the floor, I notice I'm only wearing a light gown that doesn't cover much, so I take care in how I stand up.

"Where's the rest of my group?" I ask, wondering if everyone else had to get hooked up to these machines.

"They're in their own rooms. You thirsty? You keep licking your lips," Ms. Diana says. She walks back to the front of the room, where she fills a small cup from a thin hose extending from the ceiling.

"Thank you," I say as she hands me a fresh cup of water. I hastily gulp it down. "Is this normal? I didn't expect it to start out like this."

"Stand right here," she says, pointing to a place on the floor beside her while slipping her other hand into one of her thigh pockets. "It's hard to use the word normal around here."

Ms. Diana's fingers fumble around in her pocket while her hand remains tucked away from sight. Suddenly, all of the power cuts out from the room. The dim white light above the door flickers back on and off sporadically as Ms. Diana quickly steps in front of my face.

"Look at me. You see me?" she frantically murmurs.

I can only see the dark pupils of her eyes between the small flashes of light as I ask, "Did you do that?"

"Listen to me," she whispers assertively while grabbing my shoulders.

THE REVELATION

"I am! I am," I affirm, suddenly feeling enveloped by her desperation.

"They want you for something," she says. "They shot chemicals in your veins before I got to you, and I don't know what they are. They did this to my son before they took him, and I never saw him again."

"What?" I whisper before moving back a step to put space between us.

She gets back in my face. "I don't have time to explain. Watch yourself. Don't trust them. That's all I'm saying, and it didn't come from me. You hear me?"

I look her in the eyes and nod my head.

"You hear me?" she asks more urgently.

"Yeah. Yes. I hear you."

She waits for a second, as if she's trying to catch a glimpse of dishonesty in me she might have missed before, but eventually she nods too. Her hand reaches back into her pocket, and the power instantly surges back into the room. Several machines hum deeply, as if trying to power up again, and the lights return as if they'd never left.

Ms. Diana taps her wrist a few times and begins speaking. "Yes. We just had a lapse of power in Room 1301-C. The room appears stable. Yes. Requesting approval for patient release. Okay."

The heavy wrinkles previously creased across her forehead and at the corners of her eyes seem to have abruptly vanished with the return of the lights. The same Ms. Diana I first saw enter the room looks at me differently now, smiling as if our conversation in the dark only existed in my mind.

"All right, then. Let's go, Mr. Flint."

I stare at her, looking for an additional cue to reconfirm

what we discussed in the dark, but she gives me nothing as she returns the reflective red glasses over her eyes.

"Follow me," she says, leading me out into a long empty corridor lined with bare silver walls.

"Where is everyone else?" I ask.

Ms. Diana pulls a card out of her pocket. "Some of them are here," she says, moving her card toward the left wall.

The card flies out and connects with the wall, and suddenly the previously barren walls give way to a clear stretch of window. I see other people behind the walls, none of whom I recognize, lying on elevated medical beds just like the one I was in a few minutes ago. As quickly as the room came into view, the transparent windows fade, and the people strung between the interwoven fingers of medical equipment disappear behind the wall.

"Did all of these people come in with me?"

When I ask this, she turns around, and a few wrinkles briefly streak above her thick eyebrows. "Let's just worry about you."

She continues forward in silence. Some of her facial features and her skin tone remind me of my dad, and for a second, I try to imagine what it would be like if she were my aunt.

We turn a corner and come upon an open circular room. I can already breathe a little easier with a little more space to move around. The ceiling stretches far above our heads, and symmetrical lines boldly divide the room like a giant pie. Numerous circular receiving platforms stand against the walls every few feet, but Ms. Diana takes me to a control panel in the center of the room.

From within her sleeve, she subtly pulls out an opaque

THE REVELATION

scroll, which quickly unrolls with a flick of her wrist. She places the sheet perfectly across the light panel, illuminated from underneath, and my picture and information instantly appear on the scroll. Ms. Diana begins tapping her fingers all over the place.

"Okay, baby, you are Tunnel 8. Head on over to the left, and it will light up."

"Okay, but what do I do?" I ask her.

"I think you can figure it out. Just step on the lighted circle and have a little faith. You'll get to where you're going."

"Do you mean training orientation?" I ask. I'm assuming a more organized version of our arrival would have included an immediate orientation if someone hadn't somehow managed to sneak onto our shuttle drone uninvited.

She silently shoos me away, and the tunnel marked with the number eight illuminates. I walk over and step to the center of the platform.

"Thanks for your help," I say to Ms. Diana.

She winks at me. "Baby, I just do what I'm told."

The words she spoke to me in the dark hang in the back of my mind, but the smile resting on her face now makes me second-guess our conversation entirely. A clear tube rises up around me from the floor, and I'm locked inside. Once I'm fully enveloped, the previously clear glass gives way to brightly colored advertisements. I'm caught off guard as High Commander Nebbuck appears on the screen in front of me. His ice-blue eyes shine bright, contrasting with his dark skin.

"Welcome to New Province Guard's Industrial Defense Quarter. You've made the long journey from home to begin a new chapter of your life as an elite member of our Special Operatives team."

I look upward, preparing to rise into the ceiling. Instead my stomach catches between my lungs as the platform quickly drops downward. I brace my hands against the walls and try not to throw up. Every second, a flash of white light falls over Commander Nebbuck's face, signifying each passing floor.

I've missed a line or two of the advertisement, but I focus in time to hear him say, "We rise for providence."

After fifteen or twenty seconds, the platform quickly comes to a stop, and all my insides fall back into place.

Without warning, an exterior wall outside the glass encasing of the tube drops down, revealing a massive military hangar in full-swing operation. My eyes run up the closest pillar, following it about fifty feet until it meets the ceiling. I'm startled by a hand knocking on the clear tubing as a young guy, probably a few years older than me, motions at me to look at him. He points some type of weapon at my face, so I flinch away. He hits the glass with his fist again and mouths things I can't lip-read, which is probably for the best.

He motions again for me to look ahead, so I do, because I seem to be locked inside with nowhere to go. What I originally thought was a weapon is actually some sort of scanning mechanism, which he once again lifts up toward my face. A few seconds later, he flashes his card across a security panel, and I'm no longer a fish in a tank.

Without introducing himself, the guy offers no other formalities before saying, "Follow me."

We step right into the bustling crowds, methodically shifting past one another while small swarms of drones fly swiftly above our heads. I'm not sure how far below the earth we are, but instead of windows, there are numerous screens, some of which mimic naturalistic scenery such as misty green forests and open-sky prairies drenched with colorful wildflowers, while others simply display interchanging messages. Most people appear to be dressed in various monochromatic tones of earthy greens, grays, and browns. While we walk hastily, I'm constantly engaged in a game of dodging humans.

"Where're we going?" I finally decide to ask.

"Where I'm taking you," he says.

"I figured that much. I'd like to get my clothes."

He turns around and inspects my gown before smugly commenting, "You seem like you'd be comfortable in a dress."

I'm not sure how to respond, so I coldly stare him down, then I dismissively say, "I don't care what you think."

We stay silent for a while. He takes me down an open lift, and we sink down a couple more floors before stepping out into a locker room. I count nine thick circular columns spliced with black lockers all the way around. We step onto grated rubber floor mats, and he leads me to the third column of lockers on the right.

After casually pointing to my locker, he sticks a key in my face and says, "Take this. Everything you need for now is inside." He gives two firm beats against my locker, and without acknowledging my confusion, he walks away and disappears back up the lift.

I look over the face of my locker and see no place for a key. Most of the overhead lights are either off or broken, which makes things even more difficult. I turn to my left and see a girl closing her locker. She's partially covered by shadows, but I can see she's looking in my direction.

"That guy is an ass," she says as she walks toward me.

"Yeah, I know."

It doesn't take me long to recognize her. She's the same girl who caught my attention on the shuttle drone. When she steps underneath the light, I can see her eyes are so hazel they look almost golden. Suddenly I am aware of every movement I'm making.

"You want me to show you what to do with this?" she asks as she politely takes the key from my hand.

I'm distracted because she touched my fingers, and I feel like my gown is increasingly becoming the most unfortunate outfit of my life.

She half-heartedly throws the key away from us where I can't see it. I stand there for a second, wondering if I should be insulted. "Why did you do that?"

"You don't need it," she says.

"What?"

"It's fake. That's why I said he's an ass."

"Are you serious?"

"Yeah. I was trying to figure it out for almost half an hour," she says, walking over to my locker.

"Here. I'll show you."

She taps the center plate of my locker, and a screen appears.

"Your brace-comm," she says, reaching toward me. I stick out my arm.

"Wait. Scan your eye real quick," she says.

I pull my brace-comm up to my face to unlock it. "That's new," I say, surprised.

"Exactly. Apparently they uploaded several things onto our brace-comms after they gassed us." She taps on a new icon, initiating a keypad projection, which she tells me to center on the locker plate. Most of the technology we used in our SGY training was outdated or discarded units handed down by the Southern Guard forces when they received updated gear.

"Now type in your SGY ID and password, and everything you need for now really is inside. *That* part was true."

"Okay, awesome," I say as it unlocks. "That wasn't too bad."

"Okay, good." She turns to walk away, and I realize our moment together is over before I noticed we were in one. Before she gets too far, I shout, "Hey! What's your name?"

She turns for a quick second and says, "Rhysk, like taking a risk. Just spelled different."

"I like it. I'm Darvin," I say, grinning, feeling a sudden twinge in my stomach as she moves farther away.

"And I like your dress, Darvin," she says before turning a corner.

I look down with a start, and I don't know whether I'm embarrassed or in love. I decide on embarrassed and strip off my gown to step into my new attire.

As Rhysk said, I find a few complete uniforms, extra bathroom amenities, and an in-depth training manual with an additional "Weapons and Devices" e-file to download on my brace-comm. Some of my personal belongings are already set out neatly on an inside shelf, like my fire starter and the picture of my mom. I hadn't even noticed they were gone, but I'm relieved to find them here.

"Don't mess with my stuff," I mumble, retroactively scolding whoever took my things without permission. I have a feeling I'm going to need to talk to myself every now and again just to keep my sanity. I open the manual and find the "Day One" checklist with very detailed instructions, everything from which uniform to wear at what time to how to find my assigned living quarters.

The uniform I'm wearing now has thick braces above each forearm and is reinforced with exterior joint shields, which thankfully are cushioned on the inside. There's also some kind of button above the crease in my elbow, so I press it. A thin strand of wire and prongs ejects from my arm and clasps around an I-beam in the ceiling.

"Shit!"

I hear the lift coming down again, so I frantically try to pry the wire free. It doesn't budge. Eventually I think to press the button again, and the wire recoils back into place with ease. Even though I'm no longer stuck, I decide to wait and see who is coming down in case Merrin happened to catch the next lift.

Four legs come into view, and then two faces, only one of which I recognize as the unfortunate guy who must be assigned to escorting all trainees to their belongings. The other guy is huge. They're laughing about something, and as they step over to a locker, the escort guy immediately shows the big guy how to open it. I didn't need another reason to hate the escort, but if I see Rhysk, at least we'll have something else to talk about.

After completing the first several small organizational checks on my list, my next set of instructions tells me to exit down the center hallway.

"To where?" I mumble to myself, hoping I'll finally get some clarity on where and how I'll officially begin training. I'm used to following specific orders from a commander, but this method of following instructions without supervision requires me to be more decisive and take initiative.

Rhysk never mentioned where she was headed, but of the three hallways to my right, she took the center hall. I head that way too. Arching white lights stretch over the tunnel in segments all the way down to the end, where I see Rhysk waiting. Just as I step under the first stretch of lights, a convex door revolves outward from within the wall's frame and quickly encloses her. I can no longer see her as I make my way to the end of the tunnel.

I reach out my hand and press against the semicircle barrier, wondering if Rhysk is still inside. The convex wall in front of me begins rotating around once more, revealing the now-empty concave entry point where Rhysk was standing only moments before.

To my right, I notice a keypad flashing with the words SIMULATION IN PROGRESS. I have no idea what I'm getting into, but I know I'm next. My stomach unhinges as I quickly scan my instructions again.

Enter access code #900658675 to retrieve virtual headwear. Failure to utilize headwear for the duration of this simulation may result in permanent loss of vision.

Muffled sounds thump against the padded doorway. My lungs begin drawing in all the air I have been forgetting to breathe. Without a formal warning, I prepare for my first Special Ops training session.

"Okay, okay, okay," I say, exhaling while I punch in the code. A compartment releases from the wall to my left and spits out some type of goggles attached to a headband. Before I even put on my virtual headwear, the keypad flashes a new message: PREPARE FOR ENTRY.

The front-facing wall of the entry tube previously before me spins around behind, closing me inside. Two illuminated footprints on the floor mark where my feet are supposed to go, so I step in place.

I quickly throw on my headband. Once I adjust the goggles, I see a new signal prompting me to select the red ENTER key. I would feel better if it were green. I hesitate for a moment until a numberless analog countdown projects onto the entry door in front of me. Below the receding countdown ring, I see the option to ENTER NOW.

"Who would press that?" I ask myself.

Unless it's a test. My fingers punch it before my head can object. The tubular door in front of me revolves, revealing a quiet moonlit forest, and it's as if I've been teleported to an entirely different place.

CHAPTER 6

Splotchy patches of grass and dirt stretch down the hill supporting the platform beneath my feet. My ears slowly perceive the distant trills of crickets hiding within the shadowed forest ahead. The short embankment rolls down from where I stand into a patch of thick grass that reaches into a wide stretch of trees. I pull one deep breath into my chest before stepping forward.

I move carefully at first, still trying to make sense of the starkly contrasting change of scenery. Once I reach the bottom of the embankment, the ground under my feet feels distinctly different than what I expected. Contrary to what my eyes anticipate, it's not soft folds of grass twisting under my boots. Instead it's the smooth flatness of a hard floor. I bend down, and my fingers pass through the grass projections, confirming my suspicions as I sweep them over the cool surface. I'm not sure how much, but portions of my surroundings are virtual.

Once I reach the nearest tree, my fingers reach out and

THE REVELATION

slide along the bark, wrapping around its trunk. The bark doesn't give way or chip, but my fingers still stutter over the hardened grooves—that's real enough.

I smell the air, hoping to pull in the sweet breath of tar and heart pine, which always reminds me of my rides with Asa, but the stiff, dry air reminds me more of the dark inner workings beneath Southern Guard's Outer Wall. A part of me wishes Asa would come trotting up through these strange woods, ready for a long ride home. As I raise my gaze to the simulated stars, I don't feel the sense of peace that usually accompanies me while I'm in nature. I doubt this training exhibition was designed with that in mind.

I look behind me toward the entry. The platform, swallowed again behind the rotating wall, is barely distinguishable against a structural replication of a rocky cave. The blending shades of darkness covering the walls would make any barrier nearly impossible to perceive had I not been aware upon entering the simulation.

Along the same back wall hosting my entry platform and about fifty yards to my right, a faint light catches my eye. Through the intermingled branches stemming from the surrounding trees, I can make out the shadow of another SGY trainee stepping from a chamber like my own at the top of a sloping hill.

A pale glow from my brace-comm catches my attention as it lights up. I look down and quickly read the lines:

Objective: Navigate to the extraction point before your opponent. Select the distress option on your brace-comm menu at any time to forfeit your mission.

I look up and can no longer see my opponent through the darkness between us.

What if I lose?

My competitive desire to win fights the anxiety churning in my stomach. Off in the distance, a red pillar of light streams from the ground, reaching far into the expanse of simulated sky. As identified by my brace-comm, the light, which is already fading, marks the designated location of my objective. I take a mental note of the cardinal direction and degree bearing of my destination just before the red indicator beam disappears completely. Thankfully, my goggles don't inhibit my span of vision.

Take inventory. Prepare means of defense. Determine route of travel.

I streamline my initial strategies to suppress my fear. The sound of snapping twigs interrupts my thoughts, and I quickly face the direction of the noise. My hands feel naked and vulnerable without a weapon. The crunching sounds move closer. Now there's more cracking from my left as well as from my right, accompanied by a low, guttural growl.

A limb falls from above and nearly strikes me on the head. When I look up, I can barely make out a dark figure perched about twenty feet up in the tree, and then I notice the glow of sickly yellow eyes. My heart is thudding quickly, like the heavy footsteps now pounding the ground from multiple directions around me. As I tear out in a full sprint toward the general direction of my objective, a consuming roar from behind makes every hair on my neck stand on end. Whatever creature has dropped down from the branches is now chasing me.

Judging from the volume of limbs cracking behind me, I know there are multiple creatures joining the pursuit. If I knew what was chasing me, I could develop my defensive strategy, but for now, running is the best plan I can come up with. I never was the strongest member of my SGY squad, but my feet always kept me ahead of the pack.

As I run, the texture of the ground suddenly changes again, and I feel the relief of padded floor beneath me. A glowing line streaks underneath my boots, which I realize is meant to be my path guide. Flashing symbols appear around me every so often. I've passed several of them by the time I realize these illuminating signs represent weapon and supply expos. From the sound of what's trailing me, I'm going to need something special.

As my eyes adjust to the night, I notice a wasp-link laser fastened to an expo stand about twenty yards ahead of me. As soon as I snatch the firearm off its stand, my hands feel strong again holding a familiar weapon. After disengaging the energy lock, I turn around and face the relentless mob wildly breaking through the undergrowth between us. With only seconds to spare, I spray a streak of silver laser into the darkness in front of me. The small amount of breath I hold catches in my chest as the streaming light reveals the nightmare before me.

In the momentary brightness, I see the sickening gray bodies of three terrifying Stones drop hard into the dirt.

They can't be real. The thought brings me little comfort because fear swallows me all the same. My original blast scattered those who managed to dodge my line of fire, so I release another silver blaze in front of me until the laser's energy cap is exhausted. Judging by the bellowing growls and the swell of rustling brush all around me, at least a half a dozen more have come to replace the ranks of the fallen three.

My heartbeat pulses in my ears as I sling the wasp-link under my arm and sprint ahead while waiting for the energy round to power up. This laser feels different than what I'm accustomed to. The recoil is nearly nonexistent, so I'm assuming the power threshold has been significantly lowered. I waste a small amount of energy hurdling over a patch of tall simulated grass and bound into a clear stretch of earth. Two separate trails flash before me, diverging in nearly opposite directions.

My brace-comm speaks to me: "Choose your path."

"What?" I yell, confused, hoping for additional information, which doesn't come.

I stutter-step for a moment before committing to the left. Once I do, the guiding lights disappear completely, and I'm stumbling my way through the night while a few synthetic branches slap across my face and body. I have no idea where I'm going. I just keep running while ignoring the sting of fresh cuts and the bitter dryness setting in my mouth.

About fifty feet away, a fiery blue electrical explosion ignites the surrounding foliage, and I catch a glimpse of a few other Stones taking a hit as my opponent dives into the brush. I'm relieved to see I'm not the only one struggling. As I refocus my attention ahead, a soft blue glow catches my eye, and I see a mag-scope sniper rifle fastened to a sycamore. I plan to leave it behind, but as I pass by, my hand reaches back at the last moment. I hastily rip the magnetic scope from the rifle's back and throw the gun itself to the ground.

Ahead, there's a clearing in the treetops, where a patch of moonlight is washing through the foliage. I stop here for a quick second to examine the scope and catch my breath. I'm used to having another set of eyes watching my back, so without the additional strength and security of having Merrin by my side, I have to adjust my tactical strategies and hope my ears will warn me of any possible threats.

THE REVELATION

I didn't have time to take inventory earlier, so I check the folds in my pockets, searching for additional gear. Other than my grappler wire on my forearm, the only useful item I find is a flat-tip knife. There's also a thin tube of ionized water and an energy gel packet, which I don't plan on using, considering I'm already feeling over stimulated.

I'm not sure if it will work, but I position the scope's lens in front of the wasp-link's muzzle, and I use the scope's magnetic fastening strips to secure it in place. It's not enough. My knife saws through the shoulder harness, and I cut it into strips that I can use to tie the scope to the laser's head.

I move to position myself at the top of a small embankment, which turns out to be the lip of a massive ravine that drops off into complete darkness. I'm trapped and can't go any farther. The group of Stones relentlessly pursuing me is now close enough for me to see their glistening yellow eyes. My legs feel numb as I shakily aim the laser at the snarling avalanche of Stones. There's nothing left for me to do but fire and hope for the best.

The scope refracts the solid laser beam into a widespread fan of energy. All in the same moment, the Stones crash over the ground like a broken wave. So much adrenaline is pumping through my body that my vision blurs, and I almost pass out. The sudden surge of brightness seems like it's swallowing me, so I shut my eyes. My knees hit the ground, and my hands brace in the dirt while I desperately hold on to my consciousness.

"Holy shit!" I exhale, realizing I need to focus on regulating my shuddering breaths. My fingers twist the dirt inside my palms. It feels real, unlike most of what I've experienced in the simulation. Slowly, my head begins to clear, and I start regaining my composure with each steady breath. I force myself back on my knees. Even though my breathing feels more normalized, exhaustion is seeping into my muscles as my adrenaline subsides.

My hand digs inside my pants pocket, where I find the energy gel packet. I rip it open without stopping to think and slurp it down. It tastes like bitter citrus jelly, so I wash it down with the small portion of water.

Pull it together. I reach over and grab my wasp-link. The scope broke and came undone, so I take it off. The fingers on my left hand are slick with blood from a cut on my middle finger. As I wipe my hand against a real strip of grass, a singular grunt startles me back to my feet.

Not more than fifteen feet away, one remaining Stone stands motionlessly before me. The dark crevices of her skin streak across her body like cracks in dry, gray earth. A web of black hair flutters from her head down across her bare chest, which heaves with each breath.

We have each other locked down with our eyes. My wasp-link won't recharge for at least another thirty seconds, but I might have five seconds at the most before she attacks. I haven't had enough time to rest to run at full speed again, so if I try to get away, there's a possibility she could intercept me and engage in hand-to-hand combat. She's bigger than I am. I think about aiming my weapon to intimidate her, but she would certainly charge if I did.

The standoff ends when she makes the first move, hurtling straight for me.

Her harrowing shriek sinks deep into my ears, freezing me in a near panic. My mind can think of no better solution than to prepare for impact. I manage to adjust my stance and ready my hands for a collision. A single resonating shot from somewhere behind me strikes the Stone in the torso, where a small patch of her skin lights up. She tumbles to the ground, nearly cutting me down at my knees. I jump over her as she passes underneath me and disappears down the throat of the dark ravine.

As I catch my breath, I realize now that the sudden chaos of the simulation has drawn me in so deeply that I've forgotten where I am. My heartbeat is throbbing in my ears.

This isn't real. This is a test. Stay focused.

Apart from the ensuing fall, the bullet didn't seem to cause any actual damage to the Stone's skin. The wasp-link's signature recoil was nearly nonexistent when I fired upon the other groups of Stones. I cling to these two details to calm my nerves.

You've got to pass. Focus. Where's your opponent?

I feel like I've done well so far, but I still haven't found the extraction point. I look over the pit to the other side, where an empty forest stands much like the one behind me. Whoever saved me from being tackled into the ravine remains hidden, tucked away in the darkness.

I waste no more time staying still and begin running along the drop-off, hoping to find a way to cross. A moving shadow about thirty yards ahead catches my eye—my opponent scampering up the trunk of a tall tree.

Something's chasing him. Even from a distance, I can see that despite his size, he's very agile, as he swiftly ascends the tree with ease. The undergrowth obstructs my vision near the base of his tree, but from the sounds ahead, I know what has him trapped. Between the ravine and another group of Stones below him, he has nowhere to go.

I can no longer hear anything coming from behind me, but I throw frequent glances over my shoulder for my own reassurance. The same red beam I saw at the beginning of the simulation illuminates the sky once more, signaling my target across the ravine. This time it's much closer. The energy gel feels like it's kicking in, but I'm still exhausted. My determination gives me the additional kick I need to keep myself steady.

As I cautiously near my opponent, I stop at a safe distance to observe the Stones attempting to scale their way up to him. He doesn't seem to have a weapon on him. My wasp-link is charged and ready, so I take aim. I count to five and prepare to take them all down while they're huddled together. My fingers feel for the trigger. Before I fire, I take a quick glance behind me to make sure I'm safe.

Another blue weapons display partially hidden by heavy foliage catches my eye less than twenty feet away. I lower my wasp-link and cautiously step closer. The symbol of an electric pulse baton glows on the side of a weapons expo. I'm not sure what good it will do me, but I'll need a secondary form of defense if my wasp-link loses its charge. The baton is retractable and fairly thin, so after I grab it, I easily stow it away in one of my leg pockets before continuing toward my opponent.

"Help me!" he yells.

I'm not sure if he has spotted me moving in his direction or if he's hoping someone else will come, but I keep quiet. Even so, one of the Stones finds my opponent's call for help curious enough to leave his group and move in my general direction. If I stay still, there's a chance I'll go unnoticed, but if he finds me, I'm not sure what will happen. I decide to take my chances by stealthily maneuvering away from his trajectory, crawling along the edge of the pit.

My eyes scan ahead. There's a giant fallen tree about forty yards away, stretching over the ravine to form a natural bridge. I've found my way across. For a moment, I debate making a run for it. I want to win, but my instincts tell me to be a team player. I continue crawling until I have a good vantage point of my opponent's tree. The Stones have him completely surrounded. I have no idea how he managed to get so high up the tree because there are essentially no low-hanging branches, but he certainly can't get down.

I figure now is my best chance for a clean shot while they're distracted. As soon as I engage the humming charge of my wasp-link, the Stones at the base of the tree all turn in my direction, just in time to meet the silver laser stream that throws their bodies into the dirt.

From my left, I catch sight of something careening through the brush. The Stone who previously wandered away from his group is now engaging me in a full-on assault. As I try to reposition my aim, my foot catches on a raised root protruding from the ground behind me, and I stumble backward, crashing into the dirt.

By the time I manage to scramble to my feet, the Stone is leaping through the air. As we collide, his momentum carries us into a backward roll. A sharp electric jolt pulsates over my skin as I thrust my boots into the Stone's chest as hard as I can. He sails over my head and disappears into the belly of the ravine, taking my wasp-link with him. Less than a foot away from tumbling over the ledge myself, I frantically get up and stumble toward my opponent's tree. I'm not sure if the Stone shocked me or if the pulse baton in my pocket was triggered by the impact, but I grip it—it's now my only form of defense.

As I reach the base of the tree, I cautiously step over the subdued bodies of the four Stones I struck down. Apart from the rise and fall of their chests, they remain motionless. Strung between a few gnarly branches, my opponent clings to the tree, watching me from above.

"What the hell are you doing?"

"Helping you. How'd you get up there?" I ask flatly, annoyed that his response to me helping him doesn't include gratitude.

"My grappler," he says, tapping his forearm on the same place where I discovered the wire I accidentally shot into the ceiling beam.

"You need help getting down?" I ask, noticing his pale skin seems rosily flushed with fatigue.

"I got it," he says curtly, firing his grappler once more into the tree's trunk. In seconds, he's scaling down to the ground. Behind me, the familiar growls of another group of Stones sound off in the distance. I sprint toward the fallen tree bridge, taking advantage of my slight lead. Even though his physique seems more built for strength, my opponent's previous displays of agility assure me he will be close behind.

Before I reach the base of the tree extending over the empty void, I drop to the ground and freeze. A large Stone, even bigger than my opponent, stands guard before the natural bridge preventing my way across. He's armed with his own pulse baton, so even if I wanted to approach him, I'm not sure he wouldn't take me down.

My opponent catches up to me and must not see the Stone because he barrels past where I'm crouching in the undergrowth. The Stone is already charging him before he finally notices his mistake. I jump to my feet and aim my right fist at the Stone as I fire my grappler. The prongs wrap around the Stone's arm, and his momentum jerks me a few feet through the brush.

My efforts have deterred the Stone from tackling my opponent, who continues onward with no concern for my safety. Once the Stone realizes I'm attached to the other end of the wire clenching his arm, he begins dragging me toward him through the dirt with ease. I grip my pulse baton tightly and stick it against my metal grappler wire. A bright white spark pops over the cable, signifying the sudden flux of electricity. After a few seconds of being surged with pulsing shocks, the Stone collapses to the ground. I retract my grappler wire into my arm and begin clambering toward the tree bridge behind my opponent, who's already hastily maneuvering over the trunk.

"Asshole," I mutter to myself, pushing up from the ground.

He's about halfway across before I jump onto the tree's spine. Our combined weight disturbs the trunk's balance, and I brace myself between two limbs to avoid falling into the mouth of the ravine.

The fallen tree shifts further down into the ravine before stabilizing itself once more with its clawlike branches. My opponent frantically tries to regain his footing as he tumbles between the hanging limbs.

Just before being swallowed by the darkness below, he slaps the button on his wrist, once again ejecting the compressed grappler wire toward the fallen tree. His body jerks as the wire connects with the trunk, and he swings just beyond the tips of the lower hanging branches.

"Help me! Please!" he pleads.

I can barely breathe enough to respond. "The third time is on you," I shout over my shoulder while carefully scaling the remaining expanse of the tree bridge. Without turning back, I step until my boots hit hard ground on the other side of the ravine. The now-familiar glow of the checkpoint light warmly greets me as I begin the last leg of my sprint toward the extraction point.

In the darkness ahead, I hear a thud followed by a high-pitched whistle. Something flies directly toward my face, and I shield my eyes with my forearms. Before I know what's happening, I'm constricted in a full-body net. I fall to the dirt as someone runs right by me to the ravine's edge.

"Bray!" she screams frantically.

Now I know my opponent's name. I hear a faint response ringing back from within the pit.

"Rhysk!" Bray yells.

I roll over just in time to see Rhysk fire a few quick bursts toward the other side of the ravine, where several fresh Stones fall one by one off the sides of the hanging tree bridge. The shots sound identical to the singular shot that took out the female Stone who nearly dragged me into the pit.

"Hey!" I angrily yell at Rhysk, but she's too busy shooting.

Once the remaining Stones drop out of play, Rhysk crawls out over the fallen trunk and manually releases her grappler wire into Bray's reach so he can safely secure himself. She's able to brace herself so she can hoist him up, and they both scramble their way across the tree to safety.

"How are you still in here?" Bray asks, pulling her into his arms.

I clench my teeth hard and inhale tight breaths through my nose while suffering the regret of saving him twice.

"The mock Stones took out my opponent pretty quickly, so I waited to see if you would come in next."

"I'm glad you did."

"Me too," she says as she gently wipes a streak of blood away from his forehead.

"You mean you're glad you cheated?" I ask, interrupting their conversation, still nearly unable to move.

Rhysk stops and looks at me. "I helped my teammate. I call that loyalty."

"Maybe you could teach your friend what that means," I spit back.

"You seem to have your own problems, don't you?" Bray responds condescendingly.

I have nothing to say as they walk away, leaving me to struggle alone in my netted prison.

While still in earshot, I hear her ask him, "Should we leave him?"

"He can press the distress button if he needs to," he says without hesitation.

The more I struggle against the ropes, the more I feel claustrophobia setting in. No matter how much I try, it appears there's no way to escape this netting.

Press the distress signal.

I struggle harder to ignore the thought. I suddenly remember my flat-tipped knife and pull it out so I can begin cutting myself free. About a hundred yards away, I see what must be the extraction point light up once more with the bright-red glow before it turns completely white.

Instantly, the lighting around me changes. Instead of stars, I see high industrial ceilings blanketed with optic panels. I manage to pull my goggles off my eyes, and now, instead of trees, I see a forest of wires and twisted beams dressed in strange hues of bright blue, green, and red. The whole facility is an enormous production studio. I've never experienced a more distinct break of awareness.

People begin emerging from doors and openings hidden in the floors and mechanical structures. They're all dressed head to toe in dark bodysuits that constantly shift in color, much like spilled oil reflecting waves of sunlight.

One particular group heads directly for the ravine, where they use special equipment to pull the fallen mock Stones back to the surface. The team hoists a tall dark-haired female up over the edge. As she removes her face mask, she smiles and laughs at a comment from one of the team members assisting her. Her countenance starkly contrasts with the hostile expressions I saw on the simulated Stone version of her face.

"We didn't really expect anyone to do that," a deep voice says, catching me off guard. I turn to see a uniformed man standing over me.

"Sir?" I ask, not entirely sure if he was talking to me.

"Your opponent. Most people who enter are more interested in deterring their opponents. You seemed to value what matters most—human lives."

I'm feeling particularly vulnerable within the confines of the net, but instead of looking away, I stare back at the man because his dark face seems very familiar. As he stoops down to cut me free, his clear blue eyes give away his identity. By the time I realize the man is High Commander Nebbuck, he's already pulling the netting off my body with one hand while extending the other to help me to my feet.

Other than the initial honor of receiving an acceptance letter signed by High Commander Nebbuck, the head of all of

Southern Guard's corps, my only previous interactions with him have been through advertisements and video messages disseminated for wide audiences.

All I can think to say as I shuck off the net is, "I guess it didn't pay off this time."

"No, it did. No need to worry about that," he says reassuringly. "I was very impressed with your performance."

I'm not sure if I really believe him, seeing as how he's just finished cutting me out of a trap, but he looks serious. His features are sharp and distinguished, so maybe everything he says seems serious. Either way, I appreciate the compliment.

"Thank you, sir."

He's looking at me with a question on his face, so I wait.

"I think you'll be surprised at what you can accomplish."

I smile and nod. "I'm just trying to make my family proud."

"Yes, there's nothing more important than family. Especially those we've lost," he says with a soft reverence.

His countenance shifts, and I can't decide which eye is less intimidating to look at, so I look away.

"Nice to meet you, Flint," he says, extending his hand. "We're sending a few of the others back home. Not everyone is cut out for this, but I think I can confidently say we're glad to have you with us."

"Thank you, sir," I say as he smiles and walks away. Two younger men quickly intercept me and escort me out of the simulation facility. High Commander Nebbuck's words resonate in my head.

Especially those we've lost.

Was this what Ms. Diana had been referring to when she told me not to trust anyone here? I'm suddenly unsure if High Commander Nebbuck's words were intended to intimidate me or empathize with me. After what happened with Rhysk, I suddenly realize if Merrin doesn't make it, I'm not so sure I'll have anyone here I can trust.

CHAPTER 7

My own voice startles me awake. Over the past two weeks, our training schedule hasn't left much time for rest, so my neglected thoughts have been finding me in my sleep.

I've been dreaming about Ruma. I don't know what she would look like now, so when I dream, my mind keeps changing her face as she talks to me. In some dreams she looks more like Mom, with her high cheekbones and bright eyes, and other times, like tonight, her thick brows and stretch of white teeth remind me of Dad. She was begging me to hide from someone. She said a name, but my mind lost it in between states of consciousness.

I click on my light and grab my journal from underneath my bunk. Lately I've been trying to write down my dreams. Sometimes I worry my light might bother the other eleven people assigned to my barracks, but if I dream something I feel is important deep in my gut, I make sure to write it down. My eyes struggle to focus on writing the words, but my mind is wide awake, so I use this as an opportunity to purge my thoughts.

Does God ever try to tell me things through my dreams? I'm a realist, so most likely my fears and uncertainties from encounters like the one I had with Mrs. Diana are simply manifesting in my sleep. Thankfully, Merrin ended up making the cut, so I have him to talk to in the rare moments we have downtime.

Only six of the original group that came from Southern Guard were sent back home. Rhysk and Bray both made the other squad, so I've been avoiding them when I can. My few interactions with Rhysk have consisted of little more than occasional eye contact and civilities when necessary, but I've developed a habit of keeping an eye out for her everywhere I go.

I thought I was the one who would need Merrin around for support, but he's been sitting on my bed every night before we go to sleep. He has no concept of a whisper, so this guy named Cain, who's pretty mellow and mostly keeps to himself, volunteered to switch his bed above mine with Merrin. Merrin just thought he was being nice, but I think Cain did it so he wouldn't have to listen to him talking all the time.

The whole mock Stone simulation determined who stayed and went home and also provided the information needed to split us up into two separate groups based on our performances. We've been spending a lot of training time with our new squad and our leader, Commander Locke. I haven't told anyone this, but his authoritative yet tranquil demeanor reminds me of my dad.

Our commanders let us name our squads. The other group is called the Hammer Squad, which came from some unclear inside joke about someone's made-up dance move, and we are the Pyrith Squad.

One night, we were talking about potential names, and we had almost given up when Merrin said, "We should be the Pyriths."

Everyone instantly agreed because most of us are in love with this character named Salia Pyrith from a show called *Coliseum*, which is about a slave-born woman with superhuman abilities who rises from the fighting pits to lead a rebellion against her conquerors. We've been watching it together almost every night when we have downtime.

Our instructors are jamming so much information into our heads that I can barely make space for remembering everyone's names. We even have a class called Stone Communication, where we learn how to negotiate and communicate effectively with Stones because perducorium affects different parts of their brain. I understand the initiative, but most of us feel like it's a waste of time. From what I've seen, sufficient weapons training and tactical defense skills seem to be the best tools to effectively "communicate" with Stones.

"Hey," someone whispers in the dark.

I look to my left and see one of my fellow Pyrith members, Jude, sitting up in his bed.

"I can't sleep with your light on."

"Yeah. Sorry," I tell him. I tuck my journal away and click off my light. My thought stream seems to be slowing to a trickle anyway. My head feels lighter without the weight of my thoughts, so I sink back into my pillow and focus on my breathing until sleep takes me back into the night.

THE REVELATION

When I wake, I throw myself into my morning routine without hesitation. I dress, knock out my stretches and hygiene regimen, and grab a gel supplement for breakfast. Curiosity and anticipation provide me with a good morning boost as I make my way to Professor Bolden's Cultural Ethics classroom.

Today she is leading an interactive study on Stone culture, which features really cool holographic displays of actual Stone settlements. After everyone finds their seat, she makes her way to the center of the classroom to activate the holo-dock. She's thrown half of her hair up into a messy bun, letting the rest fall where it may. With one hand, she pulls her tan cardigan more securely over her shoulders; the other firmly holds her coffee. Judging from a brown stain on her chest, she's already had one spill this morning.

"Is it working?" she asks as the light swells, creating translucent images that reflect off her glasses. "Yes," she says triumphantly. "Okay. Here we go."

Stepping to the edge of the holographic projection depicting a map of New Province, she begins.

"At the start of the Perducorium Pandemic, the initial rampant spread of the disease caused widespread chaos. Lack of understanding left room for fear, and with such an abnormally high contamination and death rate, everyone's initial reaction was, of course, panic."

Her fingers fiddle over the control pad, and the illuminated scene changes, now portraying a valiant-looking woman holding a flag while leading a mass of people.

"Wait. Wrong topic. Not Pérduca," she says, correcting her error. "Let's do this one."

With a single swipe, the projection switches to an ensemble of PRA agents shrouded in silver armor with red-accented bands, posing in front of a white background with a deep-red cloud in the center. The apparent comradery of the depicted agents triggers a quick flash of resentment in me that makes my neck twitch, so I look away. Even though I know those PRA agents are just doing their jobs, they wear the masks I associate with those responsible for Ruma's disappearance.

"Until RedCloud established the Perducorium Removal Agency, neither the normal nor diseased populations could exist in any sort of peace in a functioning society," Professor Bolden explains before quickly switching the hologram scene once again.

"Okay, I need everyone to move closer for this one. I'm talking to you, Griff," she says while eyeing him. His face is tucked into the crook of his elbow so only his red hair shows. He's in the very back row of seats, which might have gone unnoticed if there were more than twelve of us. For being afraid of the dark, he sure enjoys sleeping in it.

Jude throws a pen and hits Griff in the head, startling him awake. He stretches and groggily joins the rest of us up front.

Professor Bolden has us surround a projection of a male Stone as she explains the physical transformation of the disease. No one ever really talks about this process, so I'm eager to see it.

"Early signs of perducorium include dark marks taking shape, first on the person's hands and feet. These areas harden, and then the physical effects of the disease progress to the mouth, tongue, and throat, eventually completely covering the body."

Griff jumps at the opportunity to make an inappropriate comment, leaning up from behind me to whisper, "You'd have a hard-on twenty-four-seven."

THE REVELATION

I frown disapprovingly, turning halfway around to silence him with a sideways glance as Professor Bolden continues.

"Those with weaker immune systems generally die within two weeks of testing positive, but those strong enough to survive begin to undergo this painful physical change. The outer skin pigmentation turns varying hues gray. All parts of the body begin to harden significantly while maintaining dexterity at the joints. The disease actually recodes the individual's DNA to eliminate the production of fat, which results in most Stones having a significant increase in muscle mass."

The hologram flips through a few projected clips of Stones skirmishing with Southern Guard operatives. From within their armored transports, the guards open fire on a small group of a dozen charging Stones. After failing to see blood or penetrating wounds, I realize their bullets aren't piercing the Stones' skin. But from their physical responses and screams, I can tell it still hurts them. Even so, the Stones smash into the transports like boulders.

"We're not exactly sure how, but perducorium actually preserves the functioning organs of the Stone so that their life span dramatically *increases*. I can't personally confirm this, but I've heard stories of people who claim family members from numerous generations ago are still living as a Stone. You might consider that as a positive side effect, depending on how you view life, but as you can see from these projections"—Professor Bolden swipes through a few pictures of creatures who look like they've been snatched right out of a nightmare—"the ears, nose, lips, and hair gradually deteriorate over long periods of time."

Her fingers slide across the projections, and eventually

she selects a colorful image of a Stone's brain, which is now lighting up the center of the room. The various cerebral hemispheres illuminate as she discusses them.

"Over time, the hardening of the brain disables proper functioning of the prefrontal cortex, located, as you might've guessed—"

"In the front of the brain," Merrin says sarcastically, as if he's experiencing an epiphany.

"You got it," Professor Bolden says, playing along before continuing. "It's responsible for complex behaviors, prioritizing, personality development, etcetera."

"So that part of their brain must be nothing but a bunch of goop," Griff suggests.

"But look at all the synaptic activity," Mage says, pointing to the synaptic reading projected just above the highlighted hemisphere.

"Exactly," Professor Bolden says. "Although popular opinion might hold that Stones have very limited cerebral function, most of the scientific evidence I've seen suggests only limited and sporadic cognitive deterioration occurs."

I raise my hand and ask, "So how long does it take for them to lose their sense of humanity?"

"Well, that depends on how you define what it means to be human."

"If you don't have emotions, then to me, you're not really human," says Jude.

"I didn't say they didn't have emotions," Professor Bolden corrects, reaching for her rolling chair. She sits down and pulls at her cardigan that has somehow gotten caught over the armrest, then adds, "But do emotions truly make us human?"

"If they did, then that would disqualify a lot of the guys I

THE REVELATION

know," Carrie asserts, covering mouth as she yawns. Her pale face still looks sleepy, and she's not one to care enough to put on any makeup. Carrie is the only girl other than Rhysk in Special Ops training and possibly the toughest operative here. From what I've heard, most training groups are evenly split between guys and girls, so I was disappointed to only have two.

Jude brings the conversation back on track, again saying, "So then it is emotions that determine our humanity."

Professor Bolden adjusts her glasses. "My cat gets pissed at me when I forget to feed her. Anger is a very real emotion for her, but Peach isn't a human, despite how I treat her."

"I think it's language," Carrie offers matter-of-factly. "Our ability to communicate on a higher level makes us human."

"That's a good thought," Professor Bolden says just before Griff jumps in with his opinion.

"Do Stones even talk? I feel like they just grunt at each other like cave people."

Professor Bolden makes no effort to subdue her disapproval of his comment.

"I think it's the eyes. Anything with eyes can have feelings," Merrin says, seemingly unaware of Carrie's introduction of a new thought.

I can't tell if he's joking, so I ignore him and add, "You say the disease preserves life, but to me it feels like perducorium is more like a prolonged death sentence."

"Yeah," Griff says. "My family always talks about how much money the government wastes on the purge camps and reservations. If that money went somewhere else—"

"I think that's a pretty insensitive comment to make," Carrie says disdainfully.

I move my left hand over my right wrist as I settle both hands in my lap, covering my tattooed snare. I don't feel so much ashamed as I do protective of what my family has been through.

Everyone starts speaking over and interrupting one another with their own opinions until Professor Bolden quiets us. "What about a cure? What role could medicines play if they, theoretically, had the power to preserve our humanity?"

"Isn't there already kind of a cure?" Cain asks, entering the conversation for the first time.

"Yeah, a laser to the heart," Griff responds, aiming his invisible gun toward Cain before making an obnoxious zapping noise.

Most everyone laughs except for Professor Bolden and me. As she looks to me to commiserate, I'm glad I didn't laugh. She doesn't have a snare tattooed on her wrist, but I wonder if anyone she loves has been sent to purge camp or taken away like Ruma.

Professor Bolden stares at Griff disapprovingly. She's taking extra effort to tightly close her lips, as if holding back some weighted words. She breathes in once through her nose and swallows as if pushing down whatever comments she had for Griff before simply asserting, "That's enough."

Griff slightly rolls his eyes, but from the way he submissively folds his arms, he's gotten the message.

"As to your questions, Cain, there is no known cure, or at least not that I know of personally. None of you have been authorized to travel into the living districts of New Province Guard yet, but entire sectors, particularly within the capital, wouldn't have been able to exist without RedCloud discovering the medical success of amputation and genetic treatment procedures."

Merrin sits up in his seat and raises his hand, but before she can call on him, he asks, "How does that even work? I've never really understood how they do that."

"It's complicated, but I can give you my best answer," Professor Bolden says, taking a sip of her coffee. "Once they remove the established legions of perducorium on the skin, they administer the vaccine, which attacks the defective exomes responsible for duplicating perducoric cells. Unfortunately, it's not effective as a preemptive treatment, but once the antibodies prevent the reproductive spread of the disease, the recovering patients can live in remission as long as they have access to proper medication."

Jude snorts. "Yeah, but if you can't afford the treatments, the PRA will bag and drag you to a purge camp anyway, so to me it's just about survival of the fittest." His comment doesn't sit well with me.

"That's survival of the *richest*," Carrie says, before Professor Bolden continues.

"Survival of the fittest would mean evolutionary adaptation to the disease, if that's what you're suggesting, and there's not much research to support the idea of natural resilience. Recently, I did hear someone mention that there have been studies on something called *genetic reversal*. I don't know if it's real or just hypothesized, but supposedly there have been rare cases where people's bodies have fought back against the disease by genetically mutating DNA structures. I haven't heard or seen any actual evidence to support that theory myself, but it's certainly an interesting topic."

"What does genetic reversal have to do with preserving humanity?" Mage asks, bringing the focus back.

"Possibly everything," Professor Bolden says just as she receives a notification on her brace-comm. Her lips move silently as she reads. Her eyebrows knit together before she looks up. "I'm sorry, but we have to end early today, so let me leave you with this question. Actually, I have two. I wrote this down before class so I could ask you all."

She pulls out a small notebook from her overstuffed tote bag and reads, "One: Is our definition of humanity determined by one's ability to exist within a specific mental, physical, or emotional state? Two: Is the value we attribute to a life or a potential life subject to be taken away if that life doesn't meet our societal expectations of what it means to be human?"

"What do you mean by *potential life*?" I ask.

"That's the point. I'm asking *you* how you interpret it. I will send the questions out to all of your brace-comms so you can mull them over in your spare time. Come back to me prepared for discussion." She grabs her empty mug of coffee along with the rest of her belongings and slips out of the room.

We're all starving, so we head toward the cafeteria. Merrin and Jude race each other down the hall, which they frequently do. Every few steps they take, the motion-activated hall lights switch on, racing down the hallway with them. They have this stupid idea that the ultimate runner could run fast enough to beat the lights down the hall. Sometimes I play along, but today I need a moment to unwind from our classroom conversation.

Among my favorite moments are the times we get to slow down a second and eat together, like now. There are twelve Pyriths total, but today only half of us are sitting around the table. We had a late night in training, so some people decided to take their food to the barracks so they could catch a quick nap. The six of us remaining like to sit together and laugh and occasionally trash talk the Hammer Squad.

Mage is our go-to gossip. He somehow knows everything that goes on or what will happen next, so we all listen in when he sits down and says, "You guys hear about that guy Chrome?"

We all shake our heads, so he continues. "He got his arm blown off."

"No!" Cain gasps, dropping a spoon full of soup on his lap.

"How?" Jude asks, scrunching his face up tight in horror.

"Whatever gun they gave him backfired and tore his shoulder off."

"Oh shit," Merrin slowly whispers, leaving his mouth wide open.

"You're lying. You just made that up," I say, and Mage immediately starts laughing. He takes advantage of people assuming he knows everything, but over the last few days, I've been catching on.

"Seriously, though," Mage whispers, and we all lean our heads in close. "We're doing something big this week. I overheard Commander Locke talking about preparing for an operatives mission, and he's been going to several command meetings the past couple of days."

"That doesn't mean anything," says Jude. "We don't know what half these people are doing down here."

"Maybe it's a surprise princess birthday party for Carrie," jokes Merrin, gently elbowing Carrie. She returns the blow, nearly shoving him out of his seat. We laugh as she fixes her wavy blonde hair, pulling it back in a short and tight ponytail. Carrie's birthday is today, but you couldn't tell by her demeanor.

She stares Merrin down and then flatly asks, "Who's funny now?"

"What?" Merrin jokes, keeping his hands up as if expecting another hit. "You're turning thirty, so we're definitely doing something special."

Even though Carrie's only eighteen, she's the mom of the group. She's over six feet tall, but she usually keeps her shoulders slightly dropped as if trying to appear smaller. We all know she could probably beat up any one of us in a fight. I don't know her well enough to know why, but her face is stern. I always try to be nice to her to see if she'll loosen up.

Our brace-comms sound in unison, reminding us of our meeting at 1300 hours. We all finish eating, and I stuff an extra piece of bread in my mouth to chew while I turn in my empty tray. Our command meeting starts in about fifteen minutes, so we head toward the training facility to join the rest of our group.

I enjoy passing through the Britton Courtyard when I can, so I make everyone take a small detour to see the garden terrariums, even though it takes a little more time. The artificially replicated environments sustain beautiful plant life, which doesn't seem to be valued by many people underground. Normally I see Professor Bolden reading here after lunch, so when I don't this time, I assume she's still trapped in her meeting somewhere.

I run my fingers over the large bellies of a few snake plant leaves. They've just been watered, which is rare, so I wash my hands with the small droplets I've collected. Merrin opens the door for all of us as we enter the C-wing hallways that go past our barracks. We all decide to stop in for a short bathroom break.

THE REVELATION

Even with our unplanned stop, we reconvene and arrive five minutes early. Merrin has successfully managed to keep a smudge of honey mustard on his face since we finished lunch, so I tell him to wipe it off. We barely have time to greet the rest of our squad before a loud beeping noise echoes throughout the hangar. One of our training officers runs to the largest of the security doors as it sinks down into the floor.

"What's going on?" Mage asks.

"If you don't know, then you know none of us do," I tell him.

The security doors grind open, revealing a thick red cargo vehicle with suspended shocks between its four sets of wheels. The driver maneuvers the cargo bed sideways in front of our group before stopping. Commander Locke hops out of the driver's side, and we stand at attention until he signals for us to relax.

"I know most of you are too ugly to go on dates," Commander Locke says, "but what I'm about to give you might give you a little confidence boost. File around back."

He instructs us to form a semicircle around the side of the vehicle. After he initiates the unlock sequence, a few angry hydraulic hisses escape from underneath the vehicle as its entire structure begins shifting unexpectedly. We all take a few cautious steps back while watching the right side of the wheels fold down to catch the collapsing cargo wall. One side of the vehicle seems to be swallowing the other half as we watch the mechanical transformation unfold before us, revealing an embellished panoply of full-body armor.

"This is what we call Falcon gear," Commander Locke explains.

The structural design of the suits carries a uniform pattern of earthen tones with a glistening metallic finish. A lightweight reinforcing exoskeleton supports the arm and leg joints, and several boosting jets cleanly lay across the back armor, behind each calf, and beneath both forearms.

"Each of you has been preassigned a specific suit. The sizes vary, but they function the same. In the mission field, your suits will all be synced to reflect the camouflage of your surroundings, except for Flint's."

"Sir?" I ask, fearing disappointment and hoping for clarity.

"I'll explain in a second. Listen for your name. Captain Sheers will introduce you to your new best friend."

"Alderman," Sheers calls out, and Mage steps forward and follows Captain Sheers to his Falcon gear.

"Flint," Commander Locke calls, motioning for me to come closer.

"Yes, sir," I say, walking over to him as I prepare to be let down.

"I'm not sure how, but your armor went missing," he confesses.

"What happened?" I ask, wondering why someone stole *my* Falcon gear of all the possible choices.

"I don't know, but I'm sure they'll figure out what happened," he says.

"So what do I do?"

"We've got you covered," he says, slapping my shoulder. "The good news is, when we reordered your Falcon gear, you got the newest model."

"That does sounds good, sir." My initial worry quickly fades, and I can't help but smile, imagining all the jealous faces when I receive my replacement.

THE REVELATION

"For now, you'll have to use an older model we pulled from one of the storage hangars. It should do the trick."

He leads me over to a faded red suit marred by a plague of dents. A series of scratches infected with rust crawl over the exterior plating. Commander Locke spits in his hand and tries to wipe off a prominent smudge on the helmet, but it doesn't seem to respond to his attempt at cleaning.

"The best part is that she's worn in like a glove."

I'm not sure if that's a good or bad thing. Between the captain and Commander Locke, the twelve of us quickly learn how to deactivate the exterior locking devices at the joints so we can crawl into our new skins. As I manually unlock my Falcon gear at every joint and at the side of the neck guard, I realize everyone else is simply pressing three separate automatic buttons that conveniently shift all the necessary pieces out of the way for a clean entry.

The charcoal-gray interior smells like dust and oil. As I maneuver my way inside, I decide to put aside my initial disappointment and focus on the fact that I've been dreaming of using Falcon gear for years, and now it's actually happening. I imagine Jaykin's face and pretend he's watching me now. He'll want me to remember every detail from this moment, so I do my best to focus.

"You all right in there, Flint?" Commander Locke asks me while making one last attempt to wipe away the stain from my helmet. I realize I haven't done a good job of hiding my slight disgust, so I adjust my face accordingly.

"Yes, sir. I'm perfect," I respond convincingly enough.

He nods before calling everyone to attention.

"All right, everybody listen up. Falcon gear will be your mama, your daddy, and your best friend out in the wild if you're ever assigned to remote defense patrol. So pay attention unless you want to die or get a nice Stone makeover." Commander Locke raises his eyebrows and pokes Griff in the chest before continuing.

"When you're locked in, press your thumb and pointer finger together on each hand and say 'Power on.' Flint, you'll have to cross one wrist across the other and wait. Yours will eventually power up."

Everyone follows his instructions, and their suits hum to life. I cross one wrist over the other and hold them in place, but nothing happens. I switch up my wrists a few times before calling to Commander Locke for help.

"I don't think mine is turning on."

He walks over to me, scratching the back of his neck.

"Let me see here," he says as he beats his fist twice against my chest.

"Now try it."

I place my wrists together as I had before, and now my Falcon gear begins vibrating, shaking me as if I'm being electrocuted. Commander Locke gives one hard smack against my back, and the shaking subsides to a gentle hum. I feel as if everyone around me is a uniformed superhero while I'm wearing a Halloween costume. Thankfully, my squad members seem too enthralled with their own Falcon gear to be concerned with mine.

"That'll work," he says, walking away. "Now follow the instructional guide to make sure you know what the hell you're doing."

Once Commander Locke sees we're all moving around, he instructs us to follow him. As we walk, Griff tells us Mage thinks they're training us in these suits for a specific assignment.

"Something big," he says.

"I think I could figure that much out," Merrin tells him.

Commander Locke leads us through a few coded doors and into a part of the training facility that looks like an abandoned, out-of-place warehouse choked with electrical wires and metal piping. The Hammer Squad is already there, waiting in a collection of chairs thrown together in front of a holographic screen. For a second, I lock eyes with Rhysk and then quickly look away.

I have only seen her a few times since our last encounter in the initial simulation, and it's always from a distance when I can manage. I didn't even tell Merrin how she trapped me in a net to help Bray because I didn't want him asking me about her. I've mostly decided not to like her, and I've done my part to convey this by remaining visibly indifferent when she's around. Apart from my family, she still crosses my mind when I have downtime more than anything else.

The instructor hastily moves around the room with his shoulders hunched forward. I doubt he's that old, but his dark, unkempt hair and splotchy beard paired with his poor posture add several years to his appearance.

He absentmindedly instructs our squad to sit on the opposite side of the holographic screen, away from the others. He's more interested in scratching himself and clearing the phlegm in his throat than he is in adding any details of what to expect. Someone shuts off the lights, and a section of the floor directly under the screen is casting holographic images upward to create a virtual scene, where three unknown faces stand together, shrouded in Falcon gear.

Without bothering to share his name, the instructor launches into a full explanation of the design and functionality of our Falcon gear. He orchestrates his stuttered comments with one hand while clenching the other behind his back. He doesn't seem to be interested in making eye contact with anyone.

"Before... before every mission, all of the... the necessary camouflage design sequences will be programmed... *pre*programmed into your brace-comm database. Your commander will have complete control over all the... all functional controls to ensure squad unity. For example..." He trails off as he runs his fingers over his own brace-comm.

Immediately, all of our Falcon gear turns ice white. My camo flickers unstably, and the icy coloration only accentuates the distinct patches of rust that splotch my gear like giant freckles. After a few seconds, he waves his hand again, and every suit turns as black as night. He quickly takes us through a few more camo shades, like water, ground vegetation, and sky.

Cain leans over and whispers, "I guess this means we'll be doing a little flying and swimming in these things."

"Sounds fun until you think about why we'd need to stay hidden," I respond, wondering how dangerous our operatives missions will be.

Commander Locke takes over the instruction and leads us into the Falcon simulation room, where he explains how he'll be taking us through the air, water, and land training exercises so we can learn the ins and outs of our Falcon gear. We break up into groups of three within our squads. Carrie and another one of my squad mates, Wynn, end up being with me, and we take on the water exercise first. Wynn spends most of his downtime reading, so he's kind of a wild card to me. The

Hammer Squad sends over a trio to work beside us, but I don't know any of their names.

Our instructor is a slender young woman whose efficient movements and stoic expression suggest she's guided numerous groups through the same training activity. She directs our attention to a brief instructional video. A voiceover narration explains our objective as a faceless figure glides through a virtual representation of our assignment, making it look much easier than I'm assuming it will be.

"Your compressed oxygen tanks will enable you to remain underwater for several hours at a time if necessary," the narrator instructs us as the figure dives off a high ledge into a pool of water. An animation shows the exterior of the suit momentarily glowing blue beneath the water's surface before quickly transforming to a warm shade of orange. "And the thermodynamic engineering helps stabilize your body temperatures in extreme climates."

After the video completes a step-by-step portrayal of the course we'll be navigating, our instructor explains we'll be given ten minutes to complete the objective as a team. However, only one squad member is allowed to go at a time.

I tap the clear covering of Carrie's mask. "Do you want to go first?"

"I hate swimming," Carrie says, frowning down at the blue water. I shrug and step forward, but she quickly stops me. "But I'll go first. I'm still going to knock this shit out." She steps to the end of the ledge, where we have to plunge into a pool of water twenty-five feet below.

Her competitor toes the line beside her. Once the signal light shines green, he stares her down and asks, "Are you scared?"

She says nothing, just turns around, facing the rest of us. She flashes her middle finger toward him before flipping backward off the edge. He quickly follows her with much less style.

Wynn and I exchange a few comments while waiting, and another guy from the Hammer Squad interrupts us.

"I bet you're glad Rhysk isn't going against you this time," he says, waiting for my response.

Wynn looks confused, and I tightly clench my jaw. My inability to respond leaves me with a sensation not unlike that of having lost a good sneeze. My signal light cues me to jump, confirming our Pyrith trio is in the lead.

"Looks like Carrie just beat your friend's ass. I think I'll follow her lead," I say before copying Carrie's backflip, only mine is a double-bird combo.

Initially, the sharp chill of the ice-cold water snatches my breath away. My suit effectively adjusts and stabilizes to the new surrounding temperature quickly enough for me to regain my focus.

As instructed by the video, I swim down toward the hydrolyte laser lying flat on the bottom of the pool. As I retrieve the weapon, I aim and accurately strike my target with ease. Leaving the laser behind, I stroke my arms out in front of me while my legs steadily propel me forward into the mouth of a small, narrow underwater cave.

My headlight helps guide me through the dark, rocky passageway as I push away feelings of claustrophobia. The previously straight course suddenly begins obscurely twisting in unpredictable directions. My fingers grope along the slimy walls as I try to pull myself through the narrowing channel.

THE REVELATION

I think about my opponent's comment about Rhysk, and the thought fuels me to swim faster.

As I turn a sharp corner, the cave walls dead-end in front of me, but thankfully, as I look above my head, the surface of the water glistens with rippling light. While I hastily swim upward, I imagine Rhysk laughing with the Hammer Squad as she recounts how she trapped me with her net gun. Once I break the water's seal, my fingers struggle to find an adequate crevice so I can pull myself over the jagged stone ledge. My frustration drives me to finish the challenge, which only requires me to scale fifteen feet up a knotted rope to a final platform.

Carrie and I wait together at the end of the course until Wynn emerges from the water before his opponent.

"One down," he says, joining us on the platform before accidentally slipping, nearly losing his balance. I grab his arm to stabilize him, and we laugh as the three of us quickly dry off so we can move on to the next phase of training.

The flying exhibition requires a much higher level of focus, which is just what I need to get my mind off Rhysk. As a team, Carrie, Wynn, and I have to complete a land-to-air hybrid navigational course. Our new course, stretching over about a hundred yards, replicates a stretch of mountainous terrain where the crests and troughs form the shape of an M. We have to carefully navigate our Falcon thrusters from one rock ledge to the next, hitting each checkpoint along the way within eight minutes.

There's about a fifty-foot stretch where simulated rain falls, and one of Wynn's landings would have taken him over the side if Carrie and I hadn't caught him when he slipped. Fortunately, a cushioned external padding coats the replicated rocks around us in case we do over- or undershoot our trajectory.

We're given three trials of the flying exhibition, but none of the Hammer or Pyrith trios manage to break the eight-minute mark. Our trio has the second-fastest time overall of eight minutes and forty-three seconds, but we all leave determined to come back and accomplish our set goals—and to beat each other's records.

As a whole, the nautical and aerodynamic navigation systems take a while for us to master, so we essentially have to set up camp in the Falcon simulation room for several days while trying to master the controls. Even though completing each course proves to be strenuous, we manage to laugh and enjoy ourselves in the moments without direct supervision when we don't have to compete against the Hammer Squad. I'm pleased to see my rusted red suit is keeping up with the rest.

One night, Griff comes up with the idea that we should all sneak out to play extreme tag. Our training wears all of us down to the bone most days, but none of us can pass up an opportunity to grow together as a team. We decide to play Stone tag, where one of us starts out as the Stone with the task of tagging whoever they can catch first. Once they've tagged someone, that player becomes a Stone too, and that person is then also responsible for tagging others. The game continues until everyone is tagged out.

Mage volunteers to be the first Stone. He even shows us how to change our reflective camouflage to resemble smoldering ash once we've been tagged so we'll be able to distinguish who is and isn't "a Stone." He gives us one minute to split up, and

THE REVELATION

we begin disappearing underwater and behind fake mountain crevices until the game begins.

After thirty minutes of playing, only Merrin and I are left untagged. I nearly get tagged three times by Carrie and Wynn, who seem to be out to get me because I'm normally on their team, but I flip and maneuver myself across the mountain exhibition until I'm forced to give up when the whole group descends upon me at once.

There's something about the struggles we experience as a group that seem to pull us together. When we mess up, we all laugh with each other, but if someone masters a particular maneuver, we make sure to teach everyone else in our squad so we all move forward as a team.

The next day, after an uncharacteristically short training, Commander Locke gathers us together. "All right, we're done for the day. Plan for an early morning. Be geared up and ready to leave at 0600."

As soon as he walks away, we hit each other with questions, but no one has any answers. We're all exhausted, so we grab our dinners to go and head back to the barracks to try and get as much rest as possible.

I can't sleep, and I can tell I'm not the only one from the occasional sniff or squeak of metal as someone rolls over to try and get comfortable in their bed. I keep a few of my belongings in a small box attached to the side of my bed, and sometimes I'll pull them out to hold on to a small piece of home. It's only been two and a half weeks since I've been away, but tonight I feel the empty pang of missing my family. They won't let us contact home while we're here, but most nights I say the things I wish I could tell Jaykin, Mom, and Dad under my breath like a quiet prayer.

"You awake?" Merrin whispers, leaning over the side of his bunk.

"Yeah," I say, and he carefully hops off his bed and crawls into mine, forcing me to scoot over.

"You okay?" I ask.

"Yeah, I'm just thinking."

"About what?" I ask.

He pauses for a while to collect his thoughts.

"Do you ever wonder why you're here?" he asks.

"Like why am I alive?"

"No. Well, I mean, in a way, but I'm talking about why we spend so much of our lives doing all of this training."

"I don't know. I know we're doing it for our families."

"Yeah," he sighs, not seeming fully satisfied with my answer.

"Are you getting tired of it?" I ask, concerned, feeling a slight twinge of guilt for not checking in with Merrin more often.

"No, not like that. I like what we're doing, and I like our squad, but something feels off for me." He exhales and struggles to let his next words out. "I know when people ask me why I give so much of my time to SGY, I tell them I'm serving for Raythe and my parents, but I don't feel like this is getting me any closer to finding them. What if all of this is just a distraction?"

I let his words sink in for a moment, surprised I've never wondered the same thing myself.

"Maybe a part of it is," I tell him, processing as I speak. "But we're both trying to keep other people from having to go through what our families went through."

THE REVELATION

"Yeah. Yeah, that makes sense," he says, and we both lay in silence for a while as my eyes begin to hang heavy.

"We'll find them. One day," I tell him, but my words feel hollow as I let myself fade into sleep.

CHAPTER 8

Our barracks' morning alarm rings, startling me awake from a dreamless sleep. My whole body feels stiff, and my sore muscles are begging me to stay beneath my covers. After a quick stretch in bed, I'm up and moving before my mind has time to join the internal complaining. Even though most of us are going on just a few hours of sleep, we manage to dress and meet together at our lockers on schedule.

When I walk in, I see our Falcon gear individually stationed with the rest of our personal gear. Just the sight of them churns my stomach into an acid pool. Yesterday, our suits were more like an exorbitant accessory we used for having fun during training sessions. Today, they are protective armor meant to keep us alive. The quiet shine of the lights softly reflects between the tarnished spots of my armor. Merrin and I help one other suit up to make sure every lock and strap is fastened correctly.

"Those rust patches are going to screw up your camo sequencing," Merrin says, concerned.

"If we go stealth mode and you lose track of me, just look for floating brown spots," I joke, for my own comfort as much as his.

"I'm not losing sight of you. We're sticking together today," he assures me. Usually he's the one trying to lighten the mood, but I'm guessing that the residue of last's night conversation about his family is still clinging to his thoughts.

All twelve of our Pyrith team members meet in the commons area outside of our housing barracks, and just as Commander Locke ordered, we're geared up and ready to leave at 0600.

Two men from the kitchen units pass out gel packs for breakfast, and from the labeling, Mage points out our meal is specially packaged as a preflight meal. I convince myself it was served out of convenience instead of necessity. Commander Locke leads us through some exercise drills to get our blood pumping, and before long, I feel halfway decent.

He leads us to one of the many lifts that channel through the multilevel hangars, and we quickly rise several flights. From the posted signs, I figure we're heading toward the eastside exterior hangars.

When our lift comes to a stop, we step out into a small empty foyer. Before us are two massive metallic doors cut into one another to create a form-fitting lock. After Commander Locke scans his brace-comm in front of the security receiver, the doors release their grips from one another and open, revealing dozens of identical transport aerocrafts lined in neat rows, each large enough to carry at least three squads of twelve.

For a moment, my eyes pore over the incredible army of machinery. Several of the transports are coated with a reflective sealant, making it pretty difficult to distinguish where one starts and the other begins. Massive pillars stretch like teeth across the mouth of the eastside exterior hangar, strategically positioned to hold the rocky ceiling in place high above us.

What takes the breath from my lungs is the incredible panoramic view extending beyond the open hangar's edge. Morning light spills over the distant hills like bright-pink waves. The plant overgrowth has brought life back into the skeletons of dead buildings scattered across the land, which now look like watchful green giants. It's been several days since I've seen the outdoors, and I've barely had any time to take everything in before a strong female voice calls us to attention.

No one knows who she is, but by her clear and authoritative tone, we know to respect her. We immediately turn alongside Commander Locke, who joins us in our salute.

"As your commander elite, I'm here to make sure you don't do anything stupid. You won't impress me. Because I'm not here to be impressed."

Both sides of her head are shaved and covered with tattoos a deep shade of black, darker than her skin. She's pulled the hair on top of her head into tight braids that run down the middle of her back.

"You will call me Commander Elite, but you'll hear my commanding equals address me as Anger. Yes, I said Anger, like what you feel if you experience injustice."

Behind me, Merrin whispers, "Her parents really set her up to fail." I ignore him completely. My skin feels tight, and I try not to blink to ensure I'm staying focused.

"Today, our mission is to negotiate with a local Stone tribe that has been suspected of capturing traveling Provincians."

Griff turns to Jude and makes a comment, and Anger's striking black eyes cut directly to him. I'm not sure if she heard what he said, but her sharply clenched jaws almost seems ready to bite.

"You. Step forward," she commands while extending her finger toward Griff like a loaded weapon. Griff timidly points to himself before dropping his head in submission. He takes one small step forward.

"It seems you're undereducated in the subjects of respect for authority and procreation," she announces while slowly approaching him like a predator stalking its prey. "When I speak, your attention belongs to me. And I don't like people who take what's mine. Secondly, perducorium tends to disable the reproductive organs of most Stones, so there is not much sexual intercourse to be had, therefore your comment only served to accentuate your ignorance and immaturity. Would you like to learn more?"

Griff struggles to maintain eye contact with her. Apparently realizing she's actually waiting for an answer, he shakes his head.

"Use your words."

"No, sir. Ma'am. No, ma'am."

"A shame. I was enjoying our lesson. Fall in line," she says, exhaling her words over him. Griff stiffly sinks back into formation.

We all remain frozen in place while she and Commander Locke take turns explaining the details of the mission, including the location and population of the Stones we will be "herding," as Commander Locke calls it. Anger says something about the weather and how we'll be gone all day, but most of what she says slips through the cracks of my imagination as my mind envisions me being attacked by multiple Stones. My heart pushes hard against my chest while I soak in the reality of being in the midst of my first Special Ops mission.

Howling engines stir a warm storm of air around us, and Commander Locke leads us toward our aerocraft so we can begin to load up. Other than the twelve Pyriths, Anger, and Commander Locke, there are a dozen certified operatives and two of their commanding officers already strapped in within the aerocraft's hull.

I tighten my face and try to throw off any anxiety as I pull myself into a seat beside Merrin. Two rows of seats line both sides of the aerocraft's interior, so our group sits in front of the new faces that don't look like ours, mostly because they appear more relaxed. One guy directly across from me is cracking jokes with his friend. I notice two dark-haired female operatives with similar features sitting beside each other, and I wonder if they're sisters.

Mage asks one of the certified operatives what we're riding.

"This is a C6 Dueler," he says, "but the pilot calls it *Greedy 6*."

The engine power begins gently rattling our seats.

"Prepare for ascension," the pilot says, and I hear the air slamming into the ground as we thrust upward. My breakfast threatens to escape my mouth. In only a few seconds, we are flying high over the ground. There's a floor window between the seats in the middle of the cabin where we can watch everything below us grow smaller as we jet away from New Province Guard. My ears seal and crack, adjusting to the new pressure.

Merrin leans over, trying to whisper, "I should've stayed

in bed." His hands are clasped between his rapidly bouncing legs.

"I guess the fastest way home is to get this over with," I tell him, unsure of how loud I'm talking.

For most of the flight, we ride in silence. I imagine Jaykin excitedly watching a live feed of my mission from home, which helps me feel more comfortable as I imagine everything we're doing is for show.

Anger's voice comes over the cabin speakers and sends my heart racing. "Helmets on. Now."

A screen appears on the floor, replacing the window. I read the instructions on how to properly secure my Falcon helmet. No one needs help, including myself, but I follow the instructions for my own comfort. By the time I've latched my helmet, Anger finishes her string of instructions by saying, "We are over our mission drop. Prepare to jump."

I want to say something to Merrin, but I'm scared everyone will be able to hear me over the headset. My attention diverts to two aero-launch lines as they unfold and drop from within the ceiling. The certified operatives and guard captains waste no time latching up first.

"Split up into groups of three," Commander Locke yells above the droning buzz of the engines. "Focus on the exit strategy Anger outlined for you, and if for some reason you freeze up, follow the lead of the others in front of you."

I crave more instructions for security. The twelve of us quickly split up, locking in as four groups of three. Griff comes with Merrin and me. There's about a foot between the three of us, but we harness ourselves to our exit booster. I check three times to make sure I'm securely connected.

On the wall space above the seats in front of me, I watch

three small green figures jumping across a video screen over and over as they model the proper exit technique. The middle figure leads the way, jumping first, and the two others soon exit behind, splitting off to either side of the ramp in perfect formation.

The lights go dim, and the C6 Dueler's capsule begins filling with the deep hums and bright colors as our glowing Falcon suits power up. My heart unabatingly thuds in protest, as if begging me not to jump. I tightly squeeze my harness with both hands. Anger's voice occasionally disrupts the silence and keeps making me flinch.

"Remember, Pyrith Squad, you are backup. You're not here to be heroes, just to observe. Stay close to the ship for brace-comm reception. The mountains interfere with our receptors."

Anger makes her rounds to ensure the twelve of us have properly hooked our chutes to our Falcon gear without obstructing our exit boosters. She stops a moment and gives a hard tug on my back before moving on.

Is something wrong? I don't need another reason to amplify my apprehension, but I add the possibility of my secondhand Falcon gear malfunctioning mid-fall to the list. Once Anger is satisfied with what she sees, she steps toward the tail end of the aerocraft and opens the release hatch.

"Stay together. We are one."

The cold air whips in, and I wish I could say that's why I'm shivering. The guard captains command the operatives who are responsible for escorting our supply drop to exit first. After firing two package drones into the open sky, the certified operatives file out of *Greedy 6* so smoothly it's almost as if they're dancing.

THE REVELATION

I'm in the third of the four Pyrith waves preparing to go. I'd have hated to go first, but I'm not sure the anxiety of watching the others go before me is any better. From the looks of it, Anger and Commander Locke are waiting to see us all out before bringing up the rear.

"Your Falcon helmet will instruct you when to initiate your landing sequence," Commander Locke says.

"Time to fly," Anger yells, and she slaps the exit booster. For the first time, I notice a slight smile on her face.

The first batch of our group launches out like missiles. I hear faint screams in my helmet speakers, so I'm guessing if we have an emergency, we can scream for help. I look at Merrin, and he is laughing. Apparently he thinks it's funny that the first group screamed.

The second group of Pyriths ejects into the open air. The pull lines tighten, and we're forced toward the mouth of the exit. When I look down, I see Carrie, Mage, and Jude as they're swallowed by a dark-gray cloud below us.

I hear the words "Prepare to launch," and all the tension in my stomach suddenly transforms into a swell of euphoria that streams straight to my head.

I instantly lose my breath as I'm launched into free fall. Our SG training simulations were extremely helpful, but nothing could have prepared me for the sensory overload of being shot out into the open sky.

My instincts kick in, and thankfully, I'm effectively able to remember the training simulations for air evacuations. While free-falling with my stomach parallel to the ground, I soak in the sight of the earth below me, which looks like a bunch of color patches melted together.

A small electronic reading projects in the upper-right

corner of my helmet's face guard, showing my velocity and my current dive trajectory. I carefully try adjusting my angle of descent.

Something catches my eye below, and I watch as one of our Pyrith members spins off course, flailing wildly like a bird shot down from the sky. I can't see who it is, but I don't think there's any way they can regain their composure. Most likely they've passed out from the intensity of their rotations.

"Commander Elite, Alderman has lost control. Alderman from Pyrith group one is spinning out of control," Commander Locke reports.

Merrin, Griff, and I stay relatively close together. We're closing the distance on the second group, but we're too far away from Mage to attempt intercepting him before initiating our landing sequence.

From above, a bright trail of emerald smoke flies by us like a giant snake, headed straight toward Mage.

"Preparing for interception," Anger's voice calls out.

A mountainous cloud swallows them, and they both go out of view. My Falcon helmet notifies me it's time to pull my chute. I do so without hesitation. Nearly in perfect unison, Merrin and Griff do the same, and our chutes yank us upward into a steady glide.

"Where are they? Did she get him?" Merrin yells into our comms.

We all desperately look around us to see if we can get a visual on Anger and Mage.

Then our focus turns to navigating toward the others below us as our sensors remind us how quickly we're approaching the ground. Our landing sequences automatically initiate within our Falcon gear. Thankfully, my older model seems to be keeping up with the rest. Forceful bursts of air stream out from below our calves and forearms as well as from our backs to soften the impact of landing. The groups before us have already landed safely and are assembled to receive us.

"There they are," Griff yells, pointing several hundred yards off in the distance.

Seconds later, our feet are touching the ground while the operatives help us disengage our chutes. I notice three other operatives in Falcon gear thrust off the ground, flying in the direction where Anger and Mage should be landing soon. From where I stand, their bodies blend together into one shape that glides in for a smooth landing.

"We're grounded," Anger reports.

I'm not sure what condition Mage is in, but I'm sure he's considerably better than he would have been if Anger had not intercepted him. We all need a few minutes to let our adrenaline settle, so they let us take in our surroundings while the certified operatives help us pack up our landing gear to send back with the drones.

"We haven't even really gotten started," Merrin whispers, leaving his open-ended comment up for interpretation.

Anger returns with the three operatives supporting a stumbling Mage. Griff and Jude receive him, taking him under their care. Once he gives us a weak nod of affirmation, we all silently agree not to talk about what happened.

We trek toward an isolated collection of mostly barren mountains that, in the distance, looks like a colossal beast resting in the middle of the semiarid prairie lands. I'm not a fan of long distances, but the time on the ground gives me a moment to sort out my thoughts. I'm trying to feel confident that my training has prepared me for what's ahead. The mock

Stones in our initial simulation gave me a taste of how to strategically push my thoughts beyond the walls of fear, but the apprehension I feel now is stirring from an entirely new place. My gut knows this is real this time—my first *intentional* encounter with Stones.

We travel for nearly an hour at a pace that doesn't invite conversation before stopping a few miles from our target location.

"Why did we land this far away when we could have just flown in closer?" Merrin complains to us.

One of the female operatives asks, "Aw, do you need me to carry you?"

"You can carry me any day," he responds.

She turns around so quickly with her gun pointed in Merrin's face that he drops flat into the knee-high grass. A few of her friends see, and they all share a laugh.

As I help Merrin up, one of them tells us, "The Stones still buy and sell technological equipment and weapons from the Greylanders. They didn't want to risk them picking up our C6 Dueler on a radar."

Our electro-synthetic camo allows for covert daylight travel, but we're waiting for the sun to set behind the mountains to provide us with the good old-fashioned cover of darkness. It helps save battery life.

I walk over to check on Mage.

"So how you feeling?"

He takes in a breath and lets it out slowly as his words come. "I don't know. I don't know." He shrugs. "I'll be all right."

"You scared the shit out of us up there."

He smiles weakly. "Yeah, I was just putting on a show."

THE REVELATION

I wait without saying anything else in case he decides he wants to talk about it more, but he joins me in silence. Merrin comes up too.

"I don't know about this," he whispers. Pulled tight across his chest, his right arm trembles while holding fast to his left bicep.

"What do you mean? You okay?" I ask, caught off guard by his uneasiness.

"I don't know. I just feel weird, and it's kind of making me panic."

"I'm sure everyone's feeling a little of that," I say, putting my arm around his shoulder. "You'll be all right. Don't worry about it. You've just been in your head too much," I say, trying to believe my own words. "At least we didn't start our day off by flipping a thousand times in the sky," I joke, giving Mage a gentle punch in his shoulder. He offers a weak smile. I'm hoping that in trying to distract Merrin, I didn't make Mage feel worse.

Anger gets our attention, so we gather together. A few of the operatives distribute a prepackaged meal. I find several strips of dried jerky, dehydrated fruit, bread, peanut butter packets, and a portion of chocolate in a small plastic package. We also get a good ration of water, which helps me wash down what I don't enjoy chewing.

We barely have any time to finish our meals before Anger is back to work.

"Prepare to move. Tonight our objective is to negotiate the relocation of a local Stone tribe. Our operatives are prepared to guide the group to a reservation where they can be properly monitored. We're demanding cooperation, but we do not expect it."

I've never seen a Stone reservation, but I'd assume it'd look something like purge camp. I guess forcing them to live in a central location helps control any further threats of contamination.

"Pyrith Squad," Anger calls out, addressing us. "This is no simulation. Keep your distance, and stay on guard."

Her gaze lingers on me for a second before she looks over the rest of our group, as if she's scanning for any signs of fear or doubt we are trying to hide. Does she suspect I'm afraid? I do my best to loosen my face from the fear I'm holding.

"Let's go," she commands.

The last strands of light cutting over the mountain's back throw a dull glow against the dark clouds forming behind us. As we move forward, drops of rain begin pinging against our Falcon gear.

"Engaging camo," Commander Locke says, and everyone turns nearly invisible amongst the rocks. Our helmet screens outline team members in silver so we can track each other's movements.

We hit the base of the mountain and climb until it's not practical for us to move without scaling ropes and grappler wires. Blasting our Falcon gear boosters would certainly compromise our attempts to move stealthily. A few of the certified operatives control anchoring drones flying high above us. After testing the security of the ropes, they attach the power ascenders, and within seconds, they are pulling themselves over a ledge about thirty feet up. Once the operative team signals an all-clear from above, the rest of us latch up to meet them.

"Approaching target site. One hundred meters," one of the guard captains says over comms. My eyes keep catching glimpses of dark faces in the shadowed rocks that take my breath until I realize I'm just imagining them.

We've reached a rugged but defined pathway leading up the mountainside. The certified operatives lead the way, and we follow close behind. The rain has picked up a little, which helps muffle our movements. Still, we move cautiously. Ahead, the operatives are huddled together on a ledge jutting away from a corner turn. A moment later, they cautiously disperse in various directions and are soon out of sight.

Once we catch up to them and make the turn ourselves, we see our pathway leads straight into the black hollow of a cave, looming high above our heads like a midnight cathedral. For a second, I imagine if I was one of the operatives up front, preparing myself to be among the first to intercept whatever is in that cave, and I thank God now is not my time.

"Prepare for contact." The guard captain's voice is unwavering.

As we close in on the mouth of the cave in two formational waves, I can see faintly glowing embers of a dying fire farther back in the belly of darkness.

"Fire lumen flares," Anger commands, and after a few barely distinguishable thuds from the flare guns, the cave is illuminated with a deep-red haze.

Bodies are visible everywhere. They quickly begin to stir, releasing strange groans that echo together out from the cave's throat. I've had very few interactions with Stones, and certainly never with this many. Dozens of them watch us with the reflective red glimmer of the flares hanging in their eyes. The atmosphere feels thick, as if the mountains themselves are pushing against my chest. I realize Anger has been talking for a while now, but I haven't processed anything she's said, so I try to focus.

"Listen to me," she's saying to them, her firm voice ringing within the mountainous hollow. She's standing out in front of our group just beyond the overhanging rocks forming the cave's roof. "I need to speak to your leader so this encounter can be civil. Who carries your voice?"

Within the darkness, the sound of a small child crying rises and quickly stops altogether.

There's a child? I feel a shift in my gut as my forced, cold aggression begins to give way to uncertainty. I begin to wonder who these Stones were before they became infected—if at one time they had a life and a family somewhere like Ruma.

Anger stands ahead of the rest of us. She might as well be our queen. Two silhouettes cautiously walk forward into the light of the full moon and stand before Anger. One is male, and I assume the other is female from the sparse, wiry hair dangling down from her head. They both are loosely dressed in little more than rags that leave most of their rigid gray skin exposed. I can't stop staring at their cold faces.

The male Stone speaks first, his eyes fixed on Anger. "What voice do you think we have?"

Anger stares at them, unmoved.

The female adds, "Civility didn't follow us into this cave, and I doubt you've brought any with you."

I swallow down my initial shock. I've never heard a Stone talk before. Until now, I never really imagined them being able to speak, much less to express themselves intelligently. The deep, guttural hums of each word almost seem to vibrate my skin as I stand perplexed.

"I've got orders for your relocation," Anger addresses

the Stones coldly while shifting her laser between her hands. "Your presence has been deemed a threat to our New Province supply transports. I'm sure you understand."

Both of the Stones silently stare at Anger while a few unsettling grumbles resound from behind them.

"If not, I have other ways of explaining," Anger says, boldly interrupting the silence. She drops one of her hands by her side, and with two fingers, she signals to one of the guard captains, who whispers over our comms for his operatives to keep their weapons ready. A few yards in front of me, the lines of certified operatives shift their weapons into their hands.

From the corner of my eye, someone moving forward catches my attention. I turn my head to see Merrin stepping from our ranks out into the open. My heart instantly begins pumping so hard, it's as if it's attempting to climb up my throat. He has already taken off his helmet before the certified operatives intercept him.

What is he doing?

The male and female Stone turn to him, alarmed.

"Merrin? Merrin. That's Merrin," the female Stone says loudly, suddenly shaking as she moves in his direction. The male Stone grabs her.

"They're my parents!" Merrin yells. Someone grabs his arm. "Let me go! I need to see them!"

My mind struggles to comprehend what he's saying. My chest aches, and panic surges quickly throughout my body.

"Stay back!" Anger raises her laser, screaming at Merrin's mother, Mrs. Palice.

"That's our son," Mr. Palice shouts, struggling to keep his composure while holding his wife within his arms. They're both within the reticle sights of several operative lasers trained on their thick, ashen forms.

Two operatives restrain Merrin and begin dragging him to the back of our squad. He desperately fights against them, screaming for his parents. Mrs. Palice breaks away from her husband's grasp and continues toward her son.

"You're hurting him!" she yells as the operatives pin Merrin against the mountain rock. The deepening lines in Mrs. Palice's face make her appear even more desperate. Between his broken groans, Merrin calls out for his mom. As she steps fearlessly toward the rows of lasers between her and Merrin, a single red beam of light strikes her chest. She drops down to the mountain rock at her feet.

Commander Locke turns his aim away from where he struck down Mrs. Palice and steadies his focus on Merrin's father, who wails deeply as he stumbles toward his wife's body. As he kneels down by her side, the cave erupts with furious growls as hordes of Stones begin swarming out from within the darkness like angry hornets.

Several lasers fire into the Stones, separating their bodies in a steamy vapor. I rush to help Merrin off the ground, but I'm intercepted by a Stone jumping toward me from a high ledge above my head. Before I can lift my weapon, the Stone hits the ground in two separate halves on either side of me. A single glowing beam fired from behind me split him in two across his torso.

I've barely realized what's happened before a heavy force smashes me into the ground. I violently scramble around on my back and realize Commander Locke is yanking me up. Then we're both scrambling down the mountain, enveloped by chaotic screams and red pulsating lasers.

THE REVELATION

"Go, go, go!" he roars into my ear, dragging me away from Merrin. I don't know why he's focused on helping me out of all the people in danger.

I quickly realize we're heading toward the belly of the C6 Dueler, which has materialized into view about fifty meters ahead on a large flat bed of rock. Most of us seem to be opting out of using our Falcon gear to maneuver. The sharp, wet rock formations would make a clean landing from a high thrust nearly impossible.

As scrambling operatives pile into the hull of *Greedy 6*, Commander Locke leads us both across the rocks in the dark toward a secondary aerocraft that's much smaller than our C6 Dueler.

"Where are we going?" I yell, confused, still trying not to lose my footing over the slippery rocks below my feet. Instead of an answer, Commander Locke screams in pain as a bright red laser surges past me only a few inches away. His previously wrenching grip on my arm releases as his body crashes to the ground. When I turn to see what has happened to him, a quick glance tells me he's not going to survive his wounds.

Whoever misfired their laser has burned Commander Locke's arm completely through his shoulder, leaving most of his left side exposed. The smell of his seared flesh overtakes my lungs like poison. His blood pours into the puddling rain beneath him while his body convulses. As I kneel by his side, his life quickly gives way to death.

I feel overstimulated to the point of numbness. When I stagger away from Commander Locke's body, I see Merrin being dragged off. For a moment, I wonder if he's the one responsible for Commander Locke's death, but with his arms locked behind him, he'd have been incapable of doing so. I tear out in a mad scramble across the broken rocks to get to him. Commander Elite Anger screams my name from somewhere close by, but I ignore her. I'm leaping over jagged boulders, and for the first time outside of training, I risk engaging my Falcon gear.

A force inside me ignites my blood. I have to get Merrin away from the operatives. He's jeopardized the lives of our squad by disobeying orders, and he's probably bordering on hysteria after seeing his parents as Stones and watching his mother die all in the same night.

I position myself at a higher vantage point and see two operatives dragging Merrin closer toward the C6 Dueler. From above, I have the advantage. I'm not thinking. I'm acting.

I make a nearly blind twenty-foot jump, only slightly easing my fall with my leg jets. I use the remainder of my momentum to slam my feet into both of Merrin's captors, and we all crumble to the ground.

I quickly grab Merrin from behind and brace my arms tightly around his chest before blasting us away as far as I can. We clumsily land about a hundred feet away from the nearest operative or Stone on a semi-flat ledge somewhere higher up and out of sight. As soon as we land, he starts cursing and fighting me.

"Get off me!" he yells.

I struggle to restrain him while trying to recover my breath, which has been partially knocked from within me.

"It's me! Stop! Stop! It's Darvin," I tell him.

He struggles a moment more before dropping to all fours. The rain pours down over us and lightning splits the sky open with its purple claws. Merrin releases an agonizing, guttural yell. For a moment, I panic, because I think he's hurt, but I quickly realize physical pain isn't what's gutting him.

"Shh! They'll hear us!" I tell him because I don't know what else to say. "Merrin, they'll hear us. It's okay. I got you." I grab him and pull him close, gripping him with a mixture of sorrow and fear. "I'm sorry. I'm sorry," I keep saying. He relaxes in my arms, so I say, "We have to keep moving. We can't stop here."

I begin to move, and he refuses. Uncomfortably close by, I hear the familiar sound of the C6 Dueler's engines flaring up in preparation to take off. The backlit shadows within the hull of *Greedy 6* secure themselves in their seats as another stream of lightning flashes in the distance.

An aggressive wind from the engines kicks the rain hard against us as our squad members quickly rise from below us. The belly of *Greedy 6* rolls away from the mountain's face and flies off to safety, disappearing into the dark apathy of the night storm. The smaller aerocraft stalls for a few moments before it too ascends out of sight, leaving us in a sea of darkness.

I stand there panting, wondering how many have been left behind at this new mountain grave. I choose to hope everyone on our Pyrith Squad, with the exception of Commander Locke, made it out alive, although my better judgment tells me that might not be the case.

I'm exhausted, and Merrin is bigger than I am, so if he's not going to move, we're not going anywhere. I lay down on the rocks, cold and soaked, with nothing more to do than watch the night storm rage on.

CHAPTER 9

Between the cold rain and immovable rocks, I can barely sleep. I spend most of the night between a state of extreme exhaustion and lucid dreaming, unable to escape the horrific images relentlessly replaying in my mind during possibly the most restless night of my life.

After seemingly endless hours of reimagining the agony on Merrin's face upon seeing his parents as Stones, Mrs. Palice's sudden murder, the chaotic eruption of Stones that ensued, and Commander Locke's death, the merciful appearance of morning light brings just enough soft colors and warmth for me to find a couple hours of rest.

I lift my hands to my face, and then my fingers crawl their way up through the matted kinks of my damp hair. The deep ache pushed into my bones from the mountain rock compels me to get up. With my hands still tingling from lack of proper blood circulation, I shakily force myself up. I quickly notice that Merrin isn't with me. My eyes race over every nearby rock. Thick wisps of fog floating all around me like giant ghosts limit my view.

I'm too fatigued to panic, but a sudden weight of anxiety and sorrow sets in my stomach as I continue searching. I don't want to call for him because I still don't know if there are any Stones around who'd likely smash us into the rocks. Of the two of us, Merrin might have a better chance of surviving if the Stones knew he was the son of their leaders. I imagine Professor Bolden would certainly believe this possible. After seeing his parents, the Stones might be exactly who Merrin is looking for now.

I begin struggling my way up the mountainside. Every new movement reminds me of the pain and soreness that has seemingly burrowed in every muscle. As my aching fingers pull me up onto a small ledge, my eyes meet a pair of dead gray eyes. I cry out and almost fall backward as I lose my footing, but I manage to regain my grasp of the ledge.

My heart feels like it's taken over my body, pounding so hard I can barely breathe. The air tastes like hot decay, so I can't help but gag. The last thing I want to do is look again, but I have to in order to pull myself to a secure position.

I take caution to move around the body, one of the male certified operatives, and I pull myself up on the ledge. One of his arms is tucked underneath his torso, and his legs are pulled in tight as if he was struck in the abdomen just before dying. I recognize him. He sat across from me on the C6 Dueler. I don't even know his name, but the weight of loss turns my skin cold. I quickly move past his body while trying not to step on the pools of dried blood. Somehow it feels disrespectful.

I try to engage my mind in each step I take as a distraction. I begin counting my steps in my head, and occasionally I say a number out loud. When I lose count, I just make up a number and keep going.

For a while, I just keep moving, because that's all I know to do, but when my eyes catch a glimpse of Merrin, I feel myself slipping back into full awareness of what he's suffered through. He's kneeling beside his mother's body just inside the mouth of the Stones' cave, which appears more like a tomb as I move closer.

He has his helmet on, so at least some part of him still cares about being cautious. I slowly walk toward him, avoiding several rigid Stone bodies spilling across the ground like sacrifices left on a giant altar.

When I reach him, he doesn't turn to see who's standing over him. I don't think he cares, but I put my hand on his shoulder with no words to offer.

He sits for a second in silence. I stare at Mrs. Palice's face, and I'm frightened by her familiarity. I never thought I could recognize a Stone after they had undergone the complete transformation, but somehow, even with the extreme physical alteration, she has maintained her gentle countenance.

"He killed her. We killed them. *We* did this," Merrin says, his voice breaking. His body shakes as another swell of fresh pain crawls over him, so I try to distract him from it.

"You didn't do anything," I tell him.

"Yes I did!" he screams into the cave. Really, it's more like a roar because whatever he was feeling inside just came out.

"Stop! Listen to me. You can't do this here. They could still be in there," I plead, trembling.

He cuts me off, yelling again, but this time I'm not the only one who hears. A Stone stumbles from within the cave and

THE REVELATION

comes into view. I turn to Merrin, and we both freeze. Our eyes never leave him as he staggeringly approaches.

My instincts come alive, and I scan my surroundings for a weapon. I find one of the lasers left behind from last night nearby, so I snatch it up. I view the Stone's movements through the sight of my weapon, my eyes darting back and forth between the Stone and Merrin. Merrin's eyes look different. They're holding heavy emotion, but there's no fear in them.

"Stay back!" I yell, trying to intimidate the Stone, but my words seem to float past him and slide over his shoulders. Shuffling into the bleak sunlight, he shields his blinking eyes as he steps toward where Merrin is kneeling.

"Who are you?" Merrin questions, his voice deadpan.

"No one. A memory, maybe," the Stone responds, stopping to look at Merrin for a moment before continuing toward him.

"Get away," I yell, sending clamoring echoes into the mountain caverns.

"I know who you are," the Stone says, ignoring my demand. I watch his dark, rigid mouth move as he continues. "Merrin Palice. They told me about you."

His eyes match the darkness inside his mouth, but the rest of his body is ash white, like a charcoal skeleton inside of a breathless fire. The thick crevices of his skin divide his body's complexion into jagged pieces, like an unsolvable puzzle.

"Where is he?" Merrin asks stoically. "Where is my dad?"

"I don't know. Gone. Maybe dead if he's lucky." The Stone weakly gestures his dry, charcoal-like hand toward Mrs. Palice's lifeless body. "There never was life for her here." As if falling into a hazy trance, he emptily stares over the broken collection of bodies strewn over the mountain rock like fallen statues. "We all died two hundred years ago."

"What do you mean?" Merrin asks, seemingly as confused as I am.

The Stone suddenly winces, stuttering through a few breaths as his hand moves to his side. The pain appears to bring some level of awareness back to his previously desolate countenance. Before, I hadn't noticed the open wound wrapping around to his lower back. He closes his eyes as he stabilizes himself, inhaling slowly a few times through his nose.

"The Chemical War didn't end when the last bombs dropped. Two centuries later, look at where we are," the Stone painstakingly utters. "You may not have perducorium, but we both know what it's like to live in a world where our skin separates us from the people we love."

The Stone breathes heavily, as if his own words drained his life. He takes a weak step in Merrin's direction.

"Stay back! Please," I implore him, demanding with my aim as much as my words.

Merrin stands up from his mother's side, his face keenly afflicted by the Stone's words. The Stone continues dragging his feet forward.

"Stop!" I scream, engaging the charge of my weapon, but the Stone is unmoved. I don't know why I'm hesitating to pull the trigger.

He stops an arm's length from Merrin, who cautiously steps back to widen the gap between them. The Stone turns his face toward me, his dark eyes dropping tears. "Do you think I have anything left to lose that I haven't already lost?"

As I look into the Stone's black eyes, I think of Ruma. This Stone could have been her, given another circumstance. Taken away from his family with no motivation for life, emptied of everything he valued. The smallest form of empathy, or maybe pity, holds me back from pulling the trigger.

"You already killed me when you feared me," the Stone mutters, now locking Merrin in a brief stare.

He silently trudges away, carefully walking between the maimed bodies of his fallen companions until he reaches a nearby ledge stretching out into the morning sky.

"Don't," Merrin says.

The Stone takes his last step, disappearing over the mountain's edge.

CHAPTER 10

Hear my voice, I'll lead you on,
Find my face among the stars,
Embrace the warmth that comes with dawn,
Like morning light, I'm never far.

Each word flows across my ears as my mother's voice flutters away like a bird in the wind. I feel myself slowly slipping back into self-awareness, which quickly translates to pain.

My head feels like it's being pressed between two boards. I open my eyes and see the stars above. I lift my head after hearing an unsettling howl not too far away, but after traveling all day back down the arduous mountains and across a stretch of grassland, my deep desire to rest outweighs any present worry.

I lay back against the ground. I can't escape my pain. I can't escape the possibility that we still aren't far enough away to escape other Stones who could be anywhere around us. All I can do is close my eyes to find a second layer of darkness. I breathe in through my nose and exhale slowly through my mouth.

I hear Merrin get up, and he comes to settle down beside me. He doesn't have to tell me he's afraid. I already know it. I'm scared too. Between the two of us, we've barely said a word since we left the cave after the Stone jumped to his death.

I keep my eyes shut and try my best to imagine we're both anywhere but here. I think of my parents and Jaykin, and then of my squad mates and Rhysk, wondering if anyone has reported our failed mission to them, or even worse—if we have been declared missing or dead.

It's strange that no one has come to check on us to see if we're alive, but I don't have the energy to take this thought too seriously because my body feels so heavy I could sink into the ground.

The constant sound of chirping birds hiding beneath the thick grass occupies my mind. The longer I listen, the more I realize how incessantly annoying morning birds can be. Even though I intentionally spent time doing several painful stretches this morning, I almost feel more sore than I did the day before.

After spending a few hours walking, my blood seems to finally begin carrying some of the pain and swelling out of my system. With both of our Falcon gears low on power, we've decided to turn them off to save what little energy reserve they have left. Walking seems to have given Merrin something to occupy his mind, so I make sure we keep moving south.

I've spent most of my time turning over possible scenarios

of what would happen if we head home to Southern Guard versus trying to communicate with New Province Guard. I assume they're already searching for us, but after Merrin compromised our mission that arguably led to the death of Commander Locke and an unknown number of operatives, he may not want to be found.

After suggesting we need to find some kind of sustenance, Merrin begins helping me search for food and water. We discuss maneuvering farther out into the open prairies. We'd risk being seen, which could be a good or bad thing, depending on who finds us, but we also would have a better chance of picking up a signal on our brace-comms to try and contact my parents, or anyone, for that matter.

We travel in silence for a good while. Silence is good. I'm pretty sure we both have shut everything out of our minds, other than the desire to eat and drink.

For a few hours, we pass over empty grasslands, with the exception of a few bushes growing here and there, embracing their lives of vast solitude. Whatever water we had in us is quickly passing back out through our sweat, and my mouth feels like I've been chewing cotton balls.

The land begins steadily sloping downward, and ahead I notice a few trees standing out from the grasslands.

"Hey, you see that?" Merrin licks his lips as he points ahead.

My eyes have been watching my feet push into the yellow grass for a while, so it takes me a second to make out what looks like a stream of water glistening in the distance, where the stretches of grass shift from pale shades of tan to deep green.

The potential to rest and rid our mouths of their dry, bitter

THE REVELATION

taste puts just enough wind back in our sails to help us reach the small stream.

Merrin kneels down beside the gently flowing water weaving around the sporadic collections of mossy stones.

"You think it's safe to drink?" he asks, cupping the water in his hands.

"It's clear and it's moving, so I don't care," I tell him as I lie down to stick my face in the water. We both drink indulgently, only stopping between gulps to breathe.

We strip down to wash all the sweat and dirt off our Falcon gear, which has formed a disgusting paste on our skin. It feels good to be clean.

Merrin sits on his knees with his eyes closed, silently feeling the water as it whispers between his fingers. I imagine he has more to wash off of him than what's sticking to his skin.

As I dry myself off, I wonder if he needs to talk anything out. I can't bring myself to ask him any questions, so I decide to give him space. He grabs his clothes off of a nearby branch. Our soggy attire is uncomfortable at best, but we're clean.

"I should've asked him about Raythe," Merrin says suddenly.

"What do you mean?"

"The Stone. He might have known Raythe, or at least he might've heard what happened to him."

"He knew your parents, so if Raythe was around, I'm sure he'd have mentioned him too," I suggest.

Merrin sits there, thinking this over. He seems to agree, but the doubt on his face is quickly turning into something worse.

"I was afraid of them. That was my first feeling when I saw them."

"I know," I say. "It's too much for anybody to take in."

"I keep seeing their faces over and over again. I almost wish I hadn't seen them. I thought knowing would be better, but I wish…" He doesn't bother to finish his sentence.

I watch him cry, and I know he needs it. A part of me wants to cry too, but now is his time. I'm not ready to face what he is facing. I try to imagine how Merrin is feeling in this moment, seeing his parents trapped inside the shells of a disease that never let them go, seeing his mom die in front of him. I've always hoped that Ruma was still alive somewhere. I still can't let her go, but now I'm scared to let myself think about what it would be like to find her.

I'm not sure what to say, so I walk over to Merrin and reach out my hand. I pull him up to his feet and wrap my arms around him. He hugs back tightly until I feel his breathing soften again. I step back, still holding his shoulders with my hands. Merrin wipes his face as he looks across the land.

"You look like your mom. I could still see it," I tell him, offering what comfort I have left to give.

"I'm not sure what to think about that," he says, halfway smiling, and I do the same.

I know he has more to say, but now isn't the time. We start walking, letting the stream guide us on its winding journey south. The entire time we walk, my mind flashes with images from the previous nights—the broken Stones and dead faces. I haven't been able to reconcile the thought of Commander Locke trying to save me out of all the operatives. Why? Why was he leading me to a separate aerocraft away from the others? I choose not to share these thoughts with Merrin because he already has too much to process as it is.

A familiar beeping escapes our brace-comms and breaks

me away from my thoughts. I notice a tiny red light flashing at the bottom corner of the display screen.

"The battery is too dead to even turn back on," I say, getting no response from the brace-comms as I repeatedly tap the screen. "You think there's some kind of reserve energy in here? Do you think it's sending a signal?"

He shrugs. "If it is, we don't know who would be picking up our signal." There's a subtle uneasiness to his voice.

The brace-comm's beeps are most likely an automated distress signal, but I'm not so sure we want to be found, especially given what Merrin did.

In line with my thoughts, Merrin says, "Maybe we should get rid of these."

We look at each other for a second, and that's all it takes for a silent conversation to pass between us. I take a few strong steps and hurl the brace-comm as far as I can upstream. Merrin does the same, and both units sink into the water. I know eventually we want to be found, but not knowing who will find us first isn't a risk I feel comfortable taking. With only reserve power, they are essentially useless anyway.

"I'd feel better if we find cover," Merrin says, moving toward a patch of thick bushes to his right.

We barely have time bring our legs into a sprint before the sound of pulsing turbine engines rising from the distant sky hits our ears. We dive into the brush to hide. Within seconds, the deep-red belly of a RedCloud Legionnaire's ship flies overhead like a phoenix and lands precisely where I hurled my brace-comm.

"Why is a Legionnaire ship searching for us?" Merrin asks breathlessly in disbelief.

"Maybe they just picked up our signals," I say, trying to

rationalize to myself as much as to Merrin why a RedCloud ship would have any interest in searching for SG operatives in training under the jurisdiction of New Province Guard.

Even from a distance, the ship's hot air sweeps around us, and at least a dozen Legionnaires stride out into view. Their polished silver uniforms seem to absorb the colors of their surroundings as they move. They are less than fifty meters away, so we can see a commander signaling orders to the Legionnaires, who split into pairs. The synchronization and calculation of their movements as they file out in various directions unsettles me. One pair in particular heads directly for us, like they've been given an azimuth toward our exact location.

"We've got to move. Now," Merrin says, grabbing my shoulder. Whether it's a mistake or not, we're running again. I don't look back, but they had to have seen us. I'm still too stiff to move with much agility, but the swell of adrenaline from having Legionnaires gunning for my heels helps me overcome the pain. We break directly for a thicket of trees. Merrin and I both pant heavily, fighting to keep our breath. The limbs begin clawing us with their fingers as we run deeper into the trees.

An incredibly strange whistle penetrates the forest, followed by a heart-pounding thud. Merrin and I drop to the ground, shielding our heads as a surge of energy blasts the skin off the nearby trees. Ahead, another burst explodes out into a bright sphere of light that hurls everything in its vicinity crashing to the ground.

"Run!" Merrin screams, pulling me to my feet. I try to run but feel myself slowing, as if the air I'm heaving in is weighing me down. We reach a clear stretch of land dressed with golden broom sedge, settled between us and another thick patch of forest ahead. Merrin strides out in front of me.

Another whistle slices by my ear, cueing a blast that flings Merrin to the ground. I reach him in seconds. He's sprawled out on his back, dazed with panicked eyes. His mouth moves as he tries to heave in air, but he can't because the wind has been taken out of him. Eventually, he pulls in a desperate gasp of air. On my hands and knees, I position myself over him to protect him. Between the clustering shafts of broom sedge concealing us from view, movement catches my eye ahead. I look up to see someone in a uniform black as death soaring straight toward us like a missile. I am petrified, closing my eyes while bracing for capture.

From behind me, fresh weapon fire crackles across the air like water on hot grease. After realizing the dark assailant wasn't coming for us, I look over my shoulder just in time to see the black shadow careen down on top of two men nearby. Not appearing to possess any weapon, the dark figure then streaks into the oncoming assault of Legionnaires, stretching out both hands toward the remaining attackers.

A high-pitched sound fills my ears, and I reflexively cover them. My skin vibrates and stiffens against my bones while every one of the Legionnaires convulses in unison, writhing within their reflective gear against the strange force that raises them several feet in the air before eventually slamming them all down. Their bodies disappear into the sea of thick, golden grass. My head begins to spin with a combination of extreme fatigue and irreconcilable bewilderment. A sudden rush of vomit rises from my stomach, and I heave out a mixture of bile and water.

Still seemingly disoriented, Merrin sits up beside me. He

cradles his head between his hands. My stomach continues to quiver while I hunch over the ground. The ringing inside my ears slowly dissipates. Whoever just destroyed the RedCloud Legionnaires wastes no time in approaching us. Neither of us moves. There's no use in trying to crawl away. We sit in silence, stumbling over the impossibility of what we just saw. I have never experienced anything supernatural, so I'm struggling to sort it out in my mind. Another bout of throw-up splatters from my mouth across the grassy dirt.

Merrin's hand grabs my arm from behind, and when I look up, the black suit standing before me glistens like the shiny back of a king snake. If we even attempt to run, which we physically couldn't manage, I'm confident we'll be struck down instantly. As terrible as I feel now, that doesn't seem like the worst possibility.

"Who are you?" Merrin manages to ask. I'm surprised he's brave enough to speak.

The figure reaches its hand up and places two fingers behind its ear, initiating the helmet's release. The other hand lifts the dark mask free. For a moment, against the fading sunlight, she steps closer while extending her hands down to us. As she nears, sharp features edged against her dark complexion reveal a familiar face.

I reach my hand up to meet Anger's as she pulls both of us off the ground and to our feet.

CHAPTER 11

We travel for about six hours straight, struggling through thick clusters of woods stretching over the backlands of New Province Guard. Thankfully, Anger allowed us a quick rest and provided us with some desperately needed prepackaged food and water before we set out after the Legionnaire attack.

"Where are you taking us?" I venture asking for at least the fifth time since our trek began.

"Home. The long way," Anger answers dryly.

Although we're heading northwest and home is southeast, it's the clearest answer I've gotten so far. Maybe she has lost interest in sarcastically avoiding my questions like she's done for most of the day.

During our trek, Merrin has remained mostly silent, but I've tried to ask Anger several questions. Like "Why did you attack the Legionnaires?" and "How did you take so many down at once?" She's dodged my questions with creative insults or by insisting I mind my own business, as if where she's leading

THE REVELATION

us has nothing to do with me. Apart from fearing to refuse her demand that we follow her, navigating our way home without Anger's help would've proven extremely difficult at best. For now, it seems more practical if we stick with her for safety.

Anger has forbidden us from flying to make sure we maintain a low profile. I told her we lost our brace-comms and have barely any reserve power, but our Falcon gear continues to provide significant joint support for the long hours of traveling.

We stop to set up camp amongst the darkness of the overhead forest canopy. After tossing Merrin and me another serving of prepackaged food and water, Anger quickly gets a suitable fire burning. She's carefully cut and cross-laid several thick logs to keep the flames alive and breathing. The firelight reflects within her dark eyes. She looks all around us like we're being followed. Even so, she seems too casual to be worried. When she stares into the darkness, her face carries the slightest hint of a smile, as if she's hoping to find someone out there willing to challenge her.

After we finish devouring our rations of jerky, rice, and greens without waiting to heat it, Merrin and I help each other out of our Falcon gear. Once free, we spread ourselves out over a soft patch of grass to rest. Anger settles on the ground beside her pack and pulls out two dead quail she killed around sunset. Utilizing the same perplexing telekinetic method she used on the Legionnaires, Anger had knocked the birds down from flight as they retreated from the wild brush into the open sky.

On several occasions, I've carefully inspected her black form-fitting armor, searching for any possible signs of hidden weaponry. Even now, as she skillfully begins dismembering the quail and removing the gray and brown plumage from the birds with her fingers and a small pair of shears, I see no evidence of any technology on her arms or body that would be capable of producing the power she exhibited today.

Anger's legs shake as she removes the birds' innards and tosses them into the fire. Merrin has already fallen asleep on the ground. I roll over and face the fire. The eccentric flickering entertains my mind, pulling me away from other thoughts, and I allow myself to get lost in the flames. Anger's voice startles me back to awareness.

"You should sleep."

"I will," I tell her plainly.

She pulls a small metallic plate from her pack and carefully arranges several pieces of meat on it. She extends an attached handle and sets the plate on top of the low-lying orange flames that curl around the plate's edge. We sit quietly, waiting for our dinner to roast as the stars slowly shift behind the woven branch canopy above our heads.

"How is he?" she asks, nodding toward Merrin.

I stare at her for a moment. Her face is dark and yet glowing. Merrin and I are both trying to function while in this weird state of existential confusion. Our lives were more or less predictable before we left for Special Ops training. Even with people talking about rising tensions between Stones and the various Guard outposts, I never felt the need to invest in worry or fear about my life.

And yet within a few days, Merrin's mom was killed by Commander Locke, his dad is also potentially dead or missing, and he's nowhere closer to knowing what happened to his only brother, Raythe. For all I know, my family has been told Merrin and I are both dead. We've also witnessed

THE REVELATION

Anger displaying supernatural abilities, unless she possesses some undetectable and otherworldly form of technology. Whatever the case, the way I viewed my life a few days ago is irreconcilable with how it is now. I doubt she'll care for my honest answer, so I shake my head and shrug my shoulders to avoid answering.

"He'll have to answer for his actions if they find him," she says decisively.

"What do you mean *if*?" I ask, immediately defensive.

Her lips move slightly and close again, just enough for me to know she's decided against voicing another thought. Instead, she turns aside to her pack and digs around for a moment before pulling out a few things.

She's holding some kind of pipe in her right hand, and with her left hand, she squirts a small amount of liquid from a syringe into the pipe's mouth. She also drops in a tiny pill, which causes a chemical reaction. A smoky vapor swirls from the pipe head, which she quickly inhales through her nose. Both disturbed and triggered, I have to look away.

My mom went through a time where she got pretty deep into drugs after we returned to Southern Guard after purge camp. Between trying to cope with Ruma's abduction and whatever happened to her and my dad at purge camp, she turned to some pretty intense drugs that nearly killed her. One day, I found her passed out on the kitchen floor, and I thought she was dead.

When the medics came and took her away, she was gone for six weeks and came home the day before my eighth birthday. Ever since then, she made up her mind to stay clean. I don't know what Anger has been through, but she did rescue us today, so I decide to suspend my judgment and offer her gratitude.

    I sit up, facing Anger. "Thank you. For saving us today." It's as much sincerity as I can muster up.

    My appreciation seems to confuse her. As she skeptically looks me over, she takes another puff from the pipe's mouth and presses her thumb over the small opening.

    "Can't sleep?" she finally asks before holding out her pipe toward me. "Take this."

    "No. No thanks. I'm good."

    Anger exhales, raising her eyebrows while flicking her outstretched wrist at me.

    "What is it?" I ask, trying to buy myself time to think.

    "Chenoo."

    "What does it do?"

    "See for yourself," she says while I hesitate and avoid eye contact. She's not wavering.

    "I don't want to," I finally bring myself to say.

    She shrugs and inhales another puff. "Then go to sleep," she huffs.

    We sit in silence for a moment, listening to the crickets and crackling fire talk. Anger carefully pulls the plate of smoking meat away from the fire. She takes a quick bite, chewing with her mouth open so she can blow out the heat. After handing me my portion for the night, she wraps the rest of the cooked meat in cloths and tucks it away in a pouch for tomorrow. I nearly inhale most of my food before slowing down to savor the last few bites.

    Although Anger suggested I should sleep, my mind isn't ready for it. The chenoo seems to be calming her down, and I wonder if she'd be more likely to talk when she's relaxed.

THE REVELATION

"How about this? I'll smoke if I can ask questions," I say before fully realizing what I've just said.

"Fair enough," she says, gesturing for me to come get the pipe.

Without thinking further, I sit up and walk toward her. Unbothered, she shows me how to hold it. Maybe the smoky vapor looks worse than it really is. It might actually help settle my mind so I can finally get some good rest.

"Like this?" I ask, trying to repeat what she did before. She nods, and I start to take a quick sniff before I stop myself. She looks up and her eyebrows turn down while she stares at me.

Fearing further hesitation could make me seem afraid, I lift the polished wood close and briefly inhale through my nose. The fumes sting my nostrils, leaving me with the sensation of needing to sneeze. I sniff again with more force and cough the fumes out with less suaveness than I had hoped. Whatever the side effects are, I'll be finding out shortly, so I make sure to ask my question quickly.

"I smoked first, so I go first," I say, my voice raspy.

"That's not true, but okay," she agrees, signaling for me to pass the pipe back to her.

"How did you take out those Legionnaires like that?" I ask, pinching the bridge of my nose.

"You should be asking *why*," Anger suggests.

She says nothing else, so I ask again, "How did you—"

"Magic," she says, widening her eyes while snapping her fingers at me to pass the pipe.

"My turn," she says.

"What? You didn't—" I start before I'm interrupted.

"Would you die for your friend there?" she asks, pointing

at Merrin. She takes the chenoo from my hand and inhales once again before passing it back my way.

"Yes. I would," I say without hesitating.

"Would he do the same for you?" she asks quickly, as if continuing the same question.

"Yes," I answer confidently before adding, "You asked two in a row."

"You answered," she responds smugly.

I inhale. "What do you mean when you say you took them out with *magic*?" I ask, specifically trying to enunciate my words as they begin to feel like they're struggling to make it off my tongue.

She points to her left middle finger, touching a ring I hadn't noticed until now. She gently removes it from her hand and extends it to me without hesitation.

"Here. Place this on your hand. Any finger will do."

My fingers tremble as I cautiously take the ring from her. I pull it close to my eye, framing Anger's body within the center of the metal band. The golden firelight catches in the grooves of a few symbols engraved on the ring's interior. After examining it more closely, I read the initials "E.C.M." She catches where my eyes have landed.

"E, C, M," I read aloud, feeling like my words are becoming increasingly sticky.

"Yes," she says.

"What does that mean?"

"*Éohleen cazshées dí la magicae*. E, C, M. It's a Barottossen translation meaning 'hidden wind of magic.' Place it on your finger."

"You're full of shit," I mumble, eyeing Anger closely for any signs of dishonesty. I have to close my eyes for a moment

THE REVELATION

as a sudden wave of dizziness rolls over me. Still without any other logical explanation for what I've seen her do, my curiosity compels me to slip the ring on my right hand. It's a tight fit, but I force it over my knuckle.

"What does this have to do with my question?" I ask.

"You asked me a question, and I'm answering it. Another. A big one," she says, pointing at the pipe.

I take the tube and breathe in the biting fumes. I nearly stumble over trying to pass the pipe back to her. My movements have slowed significantly. My head feels like it's floating over my body, which feels terrible and amazing all at once.

"Okay. Here," she says while walking over to the trunk of a pine tree. "You're going to take this tree down," she tells me, slapping the bark with her hand to mark my target.

"What? How?"

"I'll tell you. Get a good look," she commands. "Now, close your eyes and stick out your ring hand and clear your mind. Think of nothing. Not me. Not you. Only see the tree in your mind. Imagine it standing before you as if it is the only thing that ever existed."

"Okay," I say, feeling swept into a sudden state of tranquility while shifting my stance to steady myself. I unintentionally sway from side to side in silence for a moment, doing my best to clear my mind, which seems to be swirling with bright colors like melting fireworks.

"Focus. Focus," she says, directing me. "If you open your eyes too early, it won't work." She lowers her voice to a whisper. "When you hear the whistle, open your eyes and force whatever strength is inside of you out through your fingertips."

"Just push it out?" I ask, still unsure of what she means.

This makes me laugh for some reason, but I'm still determined to keep my eyes shut tight.

"Quiet! Let everything else go. Listen for the whistle, and release."

The whistle sounds, and I clench my teeth while stretching my fingers outward. My arm shakes, but nothing happens.

"Did I do it wrong?" I ask, trying not to fall because the ground is moving like ocean water.

"Just close your eyes and try again," she demands. "Clear your head. Let it go, and release." She lets her last whispered words slide out, barely audible, like a cold breeze.

I set my feet and wobble against the shaky ground. My head feels as if it's floating gently to the surface in a dark pool of water. I relax, and my focus tightens on the bright purple-and-neon-green pine tree I'm imagining that's slowly spinning in my mind. I wait patiently until it turns upright in my mind before I stretch out my hand.

The high-pitched whistle sounds in the dark, and I imagine forcing all the energy I have left in my mind outward. I open my eyes just in time to see the trunk of the pine tree explode, shattering into hundreds of splinters. The blast wakes up Merrin, who now looks just as perplexed as I do, but for a different reason.

"What the hell are you doing?" he asks.

Anger's laughing at me, and I realize my right hand it still outstretched. The last vapors of chenoo are floating out of the tube in my left hand. I try to explain what happened, but all I can do is mumble pieces of words that are barely making it from my brain to my tongue. I stumble backward and fall. When my body hits the ground, it's as if I fall through the forest floor into the earth.

THE REVELATION

Merrin's hands grab my face. I hear him speaking, but I can't open my eyes. My body is limp, like I'm floating down a soft river.

"Darvin, what's wrong? What's wrong with him?"

"Don't worry about him," Anger explains. "He just needed a little magic to help him sleep."

A stab of pain in the crease of my arm sends a sensation firing throughout my body like my insides are being burned. I hear myself yelling, but my voice sounds far away.

When I come to, the sunlight is burning my eyes. I cover my face with my hands, and my skin feels warm and baked. A strange but soothing hum runs smoothly over my ears, and while squinting through my fingers, I see the silver backs of two seats of a moving vehicle. I groan while painfully trying to stretch out the kinks in my neck and shoulders. Merrin turns around from his seat and sees my eyes open.

"You awake? Oh, you look like shit."

I struggle to push myself up and find Anger's eyes in the rearview mirror. My blood feels as if it's sludging through my veins like syrup, and my skin feels tingly all over.

"Give him water and this," Anger tells Merrin, who obeys.

"Take this," he instructs, holding up a pill.

I grumble in protest, shaking my head as I snatch the water from his hand. I drink vigorously. He offers the pill again, but I still refuse.

"It's either that or take another shot," Anger says over her shoulder. "You screamed way too loud last time."

I take the pill and wash it down with the last swallow of water I have left. My stomach rumbles, and I remember the quail Anger stowed away from last night. I'm not sure where she's stored the bird meat, but I could use something substantial to eat. My head falls against the window as I piece together what I can remember of my hazy memories from last night.

Did Anger tell me she had a magic ring? Somehow it made more sense in my state of delusion, but with my hazy recollection of what happened last night, I'm not exactly sure of anything now.

The rolling hills heighten my sense of nausea. In the distance, I spot the seam of a small city peeking just above the horizon. Anger switches on some high-energy music I might like on any other day. I pull my face off the window when I hear her singing along because I'm trying to confirm that I'm not imagining it. In the rearview mirror, her lips flow along with every word. Her singing voice is much smoother and more pleasant than when she speaks. As soon as she catches me looking, she stops singing, as if I took all the breath out of her.

Disregarding her personality, Anger is actually beautiful in her own way. She's a little darker than my dad and has no wrinkles in her complexion. The strong contour of her jaw angles down toward her lips, which further accents her smile on the rare occasion that she does. I'm guessing she is in her late thirties, but her appearance almost transcends age. Really, she could be anywhere from twenty to fifty.

We are hovering over the ground, which is nice considering the dry, broken terrain below us would make for a hell of a ride on wheels. I don't know how long we've been moving or where Anger found this vehicle, so I wonder if Merrin has tried to ask any questions. I've spent a fair amount of the time we've

THE REVELATION

been with her trying to imagine any possible reason she would care to help Merrin and me. I can't think of anything. In the mirror, I lock eyes with Anger again.

"Take it easy back there. You'll need to be rested up for where we're going."

I look away, trying to push down the urge to throw up.

"Where are we going?" Merrin asks.

I expect Anger to jump at the chance to play mind games with Merrin. Instead, she looks him in the eye and says, "The Black Valley."

CHAPTER 12

After a full day's drive, we park our hover vehicle inside a hollow underneath a large collection of boulders and continue walking on foot. The stagnant pools of water littering the surrounding wetlands catch the moonlight breaking between the crumbling clouds. Anger points ahead toward a murky orange glow rising from the darkness like a grave fire. Not having traveled far outside of Southern Guard, neither Merrin nor I have ever heard of the Black Valley.

"This is a rebel settlement, so never mention where you're from," Anger cautions. "They don't like anything that looks or smells like government surveillance."

"God. Then why would you bring us here?" Merrin asks brazenly.

"I have a few things to take care of," Anger says without turning around. "Be on your guard. Fighting is a way of life in the Black Valley. They have no real fluid currency, no governing body. And for that matter, no real moral code."

"You must fit in well here," Merrin quips.

"We'll need to find you both a change of clothes unless you want your Falcon gear to be beaten and stripped off your body," Anger continues, as if oblivious to his comment. We both exchange an uncomfortable glance, not wanting to part with our Falcon gear.

"For now, engage your Falcon gear camo. I'll link your camo to mine."

"We barely have any charge left," I remind her.

"Then let's hope what's left is enough to get us where we're going. We'll take the high route over the rooftops just to be safe."

From within our suits, our helmets move up and around from the back of our necks to cover our heads. Our night vision improves significantly. Now the distant lights swell whitish-green, like a brewing witch's cauldron. From her own brace-comm device, Anger engages and synchronizes our reflective camouflage to cover our movements. Before, walking behind Anger was like following a dark cloud of smoke. Now her body outline is clear, and I notice other small outlines forming in the distance.

"You see that?" Merrin's voice trembles as he whispers into his headset.

"Are those people? How do they defend themselves against the Stones?" I ask.

"There's no need," Anger claims.

"*No need?*" I repeat.

"How do they keep from getting perducorium?" Merrin asks.

"When you're not considered a threat or valuable to the

right people, you'd be surprised what you can accomplish," Anger says.

I wait for her to say more because I don't understand. When I try to speak, she sternly motions for us to keep quiet.

Our helmets are built to enhance sound decibels from far away, so we're beginning to pick up on strange noises and voices. Anger moves quickly and fluidly, like a snake on water. Merrin and I stay close behind her, uninterested in being left behind to fend for ourselves on the wild edges of a foreign settlement.

A quarter moon hangs above us. Little by little, the dark shadows begin materializing into view as a junkyard of chaotic structures welcomes us to the Black Valley. Strange metallic creaking and industrial groaning sounds echo in the night. As we sneak past the poorly built structures, they sound as if they're grumbling to one another about the inhabitants moving around inside. I hear children crying and dogs barking for a moment, and then silence.

No one appears to be outside the muddy streets until a window above us bursts open. We duck for cover just in time to miss a rain of vomit that splatters onto the ground at our feet.

Even in my Falcon gear, the rank city air seeping into my nose smells like the swollen carcass of a dead animal. A stumbling figure turns the corner of a tall wooden structure right in front of Anger. She maneuvers herself behind him and pinches his neck in the crook of her arm. The smell of alcohol leaks from his clothes and mouth as he struggles. I hear him choking under her grasp. He quickly falls limp. After Anger releases him to the mud, he gurgles and sputters like a washed-out engine.

"Let's go," she orders.

"Where are we going?" Merrin whispers frantically.

Anger gets a running start and leaps up to grab a plank jutting out from a rooftop. She quickly swings herself up, looking back our way while signaling us with her hand. She expects us to do the same. Merrin mumbles a few words about Anger under his breath. An automated beeping announces my sudden loss of power. My Falcon gear's camo sequence flickers momentarily before I'm exposed with only the thin cover of darkness to hide me from plain sight.

"Keep moving," Merrin says, shoving me from behind. "Can't stop here."

I chase after Anger and make the jump first, and then Merrin follows. We climb our way up after her over three stories above the ground and maneuver with about half the grace as she does. Anger's hands and feet carefully find every possible ledge along the sides of several houses that have been smashed, one on top of the other, in a bramble of wood and scrap metal.

We manage to scale our way up to the tops of the broken rooftop spines, forming a rickety sky bridge. From here, we can see the stretch of cluttered slums littering the townscape like skeletons in a boneyard. In the distance, a fiery glow rises from what appears to be a massive hole in the ground.

"What the hell is that?" Merrin asks, uneasily staring at the glowing light.

"I don't want to know. Keep going."

I grab Merrin's arm and pull him forward, and a familiar beeping signals the loss of power that coincides with his camouflage covering disappearing. The muted tones of his exterior armor still provide a more favorable covering than my rusted red gear.

Bounding out ahead of us, without bothering to look back, Anger doesn't appear to care if she loses us anymore. Stepping cautiously on creaking boards and crumbling shingles, we chase Anger's dark silhouette. I hear a whipping sound that's followed by Merrin yelling. Electrified by adrenaline, I turn around in time to see him sliding down the roof side.

"Help me!" he yells, frantically trying to keep himself from sliding farther down. Many of the thick ceramic slates crumble beneath his grasp while he struggles to maintain a hold.

"Something's got my leg!"

"What is it?" I cry, clamoring to reach his side. When I grab hold of his hand, I see his leg is caught in a noosed trap.

"I've got you," I grunt, trying to reassure him. While I hoist him up toward me, Merrin tugs at the rope tied around his ankle.

"Snatch him down!" a gruff woman's voice yells from below.

Someone at the other end of the rope is pulling hard. Merrin slides backward across the rooftop, so I start pulling on him in the opposite direction.

"Get it off!" Merrin yells. "They're going to pull me down."

"Stay quiet," I tell him firmly. Against the wooden planks of a dimly lit wall below, I see the shadow of someone savagely yanking at the other end of the rope.

Then a second gangly figure hops onto the rooftop. Whoever it is begins scrambling straight toward us across the broken structures. He's growling like an animal. I panic and forcefully pull Merrin backward, desperately trying to break him free. The ragged man grabs a loose brick from the rooftop and hurls it right past my head.

Now only a few meters away, his eyes wildly shine between the splits of stringy hair hanging over his face. His mouth is wide open, snarling as if he's ready to bite. My fingers tense like claws ready to strike him down. An explosive blast bursts through the ceiling directly below the man's feet, and he falls headlong off the roof. Through the newly blown hole, I catch a glimpse of a young girl, no older than ten, angrily pointing her double-barreled gun in the air.

"Got 'em, Mama!" she yells.

The sight of the spindly man crashing down from above must have frightened the person tugging on the other end of the rope enough to let go because Merrin finally frees his leg from the noose.

"Merrin!" I shout, eyeing the little girl below, once more aiming down the barrel of her shotgun directly at him. He swiftly jumps away from the fragmented holes blistering the ceiling as another blast shreds a portion of the roof to pieces. Luckily, her second shot doesn't find its mark, and we both noisily continue scrambling over the tops of several conjoining homes.

Nearly too late, Anger has finally returned to find us. She hastily leads us to a secure cable that's fastened on one end to a tall steel pipe jutting up from the roof. The other end of the wire appears to be secured a few stories down to a lower, adjacent scaffolded dock about fifty feet away. I'm guessing she left us behind to secure our way across, which makes me feel a little better.

"Is it safe?" Merrin asks doubtfully.

Anger risks a moment to stare at Merrin crossly. "I made sure it was secure. Both ends."

"But how?" Merrin asks, both of us wondering how she had time to accomplish this in a minute's time. Either she's lying, or she's again displaying seemingly impossible abilities.

Anger shakes her head and hands me and Merrin a double-headed safety harness so we can connect our Falcon gear to the makeshift zip line.

"Just don't fall, or the swamp dogs will eat you."

"Swamp dogs?" Merrin echoes, stretching his neck to scan over the dark, boggy waters beneath the running line.

Anger grabs the crossing wire with one hand and attaches her harness to her waist before flinging herself forward. I wait a second to make sure the line is secure before connecting myself. Anger makes it safely to the other side in just a few seconds.

"See you on the other side," I tell Merrin, who's taking several deep breaths. I push off the roof, zipping out above the muddy bog. My eyes dart around, catching the movement of several massive alligators in the swampy water below. I've seen enough, so I focus on the end of the line. Anger waits with her arms prepared to receive me on the balcony of a double-stacked row of shabby homes.

The line tightens as Merrin hooks himself on to slide across. Anger cushions my landing as I reach the other side. I release myself, turning to focus on Merrin.

A few seconds after Merrin leaves the rooftop, I see someone standing where he just was. If he cuts the line now, Merrin will be a fresh meal for the swamp dogs. We helplessly watch the man, but instead of cutting the wire, he begins climbing out on the rope across the bog. Just as Merrin

THE REVELATION

reaches us, the man loses his grip only about ten feet out and plummets to the ground, screaming the whole way.

We hear his body smack into the mud like a broken dinner bell. Three or four of the swamp dogs quickly slither in his direction. We don't hang around to watch. Anger leads us quietly past several disheveled huts and down a tattered ramp, which ends at the base of a small dirt path winding up a hill. We follow her around a few curves and then off the trail to the base of a huge tree, which supports a small house in the arms of its branches.

Anger's hands fumble around the ground as she digs at the base of the tree until she pulls up some kind of bell, which she rings three times before hastily scampering up the tree trunk. She climbs onto a small porch, barely large enough to be deserving of the word, and kicks off a rickety rope ladder. I follow her lead and reach the top just as she slips something under the front door.

Seconds later, the wooden door creaks open on its hinges, and Anger disappears inside, shutting the door behind her.

"Why is she bringing us here?" Merrin whispers, trying to catch his breath as he leans against the thick base of the tree.

Between heaves of air, I tell him, "Best way to find out..." Then I pull myself the rest of the way up the ladder.

Merrin follows. We both struggle to fit on the stoop. Pressing my ear against the thick wooden door, I hear unintelligible voices carrying on a quiet conversation. Merrin gently knocks before I swat his hand. The door cracks open, showing only a portion of Anger's face. She shoves something toward my hand, saying, "Put these over your heads. Both of you. Cover your whole head."

She's handed us two thin, towel-like cloths not much bigger than a pillowcase.

"What about our Falcon gear?" Merrin asks.

"Don't worry about that here. That's a problem for tomorrow," she answers.

"Why? I don't—"

Anger shuts the door in my face. Merrin and I sit, looking between one another and the fern-and-leaf patterned cloths in our hands.

"What is this about?" I ask, hesitant to accept Anger's demand.

"I don't know," Merrin says, scrunching up his eyebrows, "but I hope there's a bathroom in there."

I laugh soundlessly. I'd rather be just about anywhere else but in this place, but at least I have Merrin to help me stay grounded.

Merrin shrugs his shoulders, and we both throw the cloths around our heads. The fabric smells smoky and sweet, which is pleasantly contradictory to what we've seen of the Black Valley so far. I give a light knock on the door. When it opens, hands grab me and pull me inside. I'm guided a few steps before I'm pushed down. Thankfully, a chair catches my fall. There's a similar shuffle beside me, so I assume the same is happening to Merrin.

"What's this about?" Merrin mumbles skeptically.

"That's enough from you, ma'am," Anger responds curtly to Merrin. A few other small voices whisper around her, so I know there are children here.

"What's wrong with them?" a child whispers frailly.

Another whimpers, this one on the verge of being upset, as a third high-pitched voice uneasily says, "That one's big."

THE REVELATION

A woman's whisper responds, but unlike Anger, this voice sounds gentle and motherly as she drawls her words.

"These young ladies came from a long way away, and since they've traveled all day, their hair looks awful, so they're covering up with these drapes until they can have a good washing."

I'm guessing the child who asked about us is satisfied with the answer because she starts giggling.

"Lou, take my dish towel off your head," the lady says, softly laughing. The children laugh too before she shushes them.

"Now let's get y'all to bed so these poor ladies can wash their hair and let the crickets sing them to sleep," the woman says playfully.

Some feet shuffle into another room. I hear a few more muffled laughs, and as soon as a door clicks shut across the room, a hand snatches the fabric off my head. I catch Anger yanking Merrin's covering too before my eyes find the woman belonging to the new voice. Her tangled brown hair hangs down over her chest. She's standing cross-armed, leaning against a thick trunk rising through the center of her cluttered home.

"Welcome," she offers plainly. We nod to avoid speaking.

I can feel her using all of her senses, raking us over for any negative signs that might reinforce her suspicions of us. A long pink scar runs across the right side of her sharp jaw, from her ear down to the crease of her sharp lips. In the candlelight, her caramel skin warmly glows like her honey-colored eyes. She appears weary, unkempt, and yet very beautiful. I couldn't imagine the struggle of raising three kids in such a terrible place.

Without bothering to introduce herself, she walks across the room and casually grabs my face in her hands. I pull back slightly. She addresses my discomfort by loosening her grip, though without letting go. I feel like further protesting her proximity might be perceived as aggression.

"Don't worry, I'm just checking your eyes for secrets. We do this here, or at least I do, because, well, hell, I barely trust my own right arm. So who are you? Which one of your parents is the dark one?"

Anger sighs impatiently and rolls her eyes. I don't react because the woman is too close to my face for any expression I make to go unnoticed.

"Here. I'll let go of your jaw so you can speak," she says, gently patting my cheek. "Now, them hazel eyes are too pretty to come from a man, am I right?" She looks to Anger for confirmation but gets none.

"My mom has blue eyes. My dad's are brown," I tell her, watching Anger as she turns to go through one of the kitchen cabinets.

"Yep. Yep. My grandma had blue eyes. I mean, they were cold blue. Colder than a witch's titty. But see, my husband had these dark eyes that could swallow you whole, but the devil's dice if not one of my kids got his eyes. He's gone now."

"I'm sorry to hear that," Merrin says awkwardly, trying to help carry the burden of this strange conversation.

"Yeah. Yeah. Here. Sit down now. Both of ya. Let's drink," she says with an excited clap. She realizes her clap is too loud, so she tries again more quietly to remind herself and us that her kids are trying to sleep.

Anger approaches Merrin and me with several sticks of

THE REVELATION

dried jerky in her hands. Before she reaches us, she briefly stops to lift the jerky up for the woman to see.

"Of course," she confirms, flicking her hand toward Anger approvingly.

Merrin and I gratefully receive the much-needed snack and devour three sticks apiece. The bold spices burn my mouth, but not enough for me to regret eating them.

The woman picks up a wooden rocker and carries it across the room to help herself reach a high cabinet. There's not much room to move around in her home. With the lack of space, she seems to have adopted an eclectic but organized lifestyle. Tons of clear jars filled with all kinds of things like spices, nails, and colored feathers line the many shelves clinging to the walls.

I notice an assortment of stacked boxes builds an extra layer of wall halfway up past one of her windows. There's not much space to sit, so we gather around her weathered wooden table, which rests under the warmth of a light made from a hanging jar.

She unsteadily rocks back and forth while standing in the rocking chair, nearly falling before finding what she's looking for and returning to us with two aged decanters in hand.

"Y'all want whiskey or shine?"

"Neither," Anger answers for us. "Too young."

"Don't drag those laws into my house like shit under your boot. These boys can pick their poison here," the woman says while she continues rummaging through another cabinet by her kitchen sink.

We both look at Anger, who sternly shakes her head. She gets up from the table, settles down into a suede cushioned chair, and busily fiddles with her ring between her fingers.

"If you don't mind, I just need to use the bathroom. But I

might like a water," Merrin says, standing up from the table.

"Water sounds good," I add.

"Right through that door," the woman tells Merrin, pointing to a thin slab of wood with no handle hung over a small closet. Merrin thanks her and closes himself in the tiny bathroom, which is not much wider than his shoulders. While he's away, she quickly collects three glass mugs off a hanging shelf. After filling them with water, she sets two of the glass mugs in front of me.

"Thank you," I say for myself and Merrin, sliding his mug over as he returns to the table.

She stares back and forth between us as we sit in silence.

"So why'd you drag these pearls into the pig pen? You risking their lives just to get a fix? What would Jael think of that?" she asks, mockingly raising her eyebrows as she hands Anger a glass of water.

Anger slaps the glass out of her hand, and it shatters across the planked floors.

"Cut the shit, Adalene," Anger growls through her gritted teeth.

"I swear to God, if you scare my kids..." Adalene says calmly, her tone distinctly contrasting with her wide eyes and huffing chest.

"Trying to guilt me when you need it more than I do," Anger mutters condescendingly.

One of the children begins crying from behind the bedroom door.

"See? You scared them," Adalene says, jabbing her finger toward Anger. She hurries to the door and disappears into the room.

Anger tightly grips the arms of her chair. Her left leg

THE REVELATION

bounces restlessly while she stares at the floor. I'm afraid to speak, but there may not be a better time to figure out what's going on.

"I'm sorry, but I don't understand why we're here."

"Yeah," Merrin adds quietly. "I feel like it would help us to know when we're going home."

Anger ignores us as she stoops to pick up the pieces of broken glass on the floor. Standing up from the table, I grab the drapes we used to cover our heads to help her sweep up the scattered shards. Anger swats away my hand before snatching the rag from me. I shrug, then Merrin and I move across the room to sit on the only couch in Adalene's home. Anger inspects a cut on her hand that's leaked dark splotches of blood on the decorative fabric. She wraps her hand carefully and quietly continues working to collect the scattered shards from beneath the chair legs and tattered edges of a stained rug. She suddenly stops cleaning, closes her eyes, and slowly inhales a few times.

"Her kids are scared of men," Anger says, nodding toward the closed door. "Every now and then a bastard will try to break in here. Adalene tells me she fights them off, but I don't know." She pauses a moment before shaking the thought from her mind. "So I covered your heads. The kids wouldn't have been able to sleep if they saw you."

We sit in silence while Anger continues cleaning. After a while, I risk upsetting her to ask again, "Why are we here?"

Anger gets to her feet again and throws the glass shards she's been able to gather up into a wicker basket.

"I have things to take care of that are bigger than you. And you," she says cuttingly, looking directly at Merrin. "You directly disobeyed orders that compromised a mission, resulting in multiple deaths." Anger shifts her focus back to me, continuing, "And you aided him in his escape. Without me, there is no way home for either of you. For now, I suggest you keep your eyes open and let the world beyond your small walls speak to you. Maybe then you can find your own answers."

Merrin and I sit stiffly frozen as if under a spell of deep oppression. Heat rises in my forehead, and my teeth clench so hard I could bite through an iron rod. Not only has she stifled my hope of returning home soon, but she's also informed me and Merrin that we are essentially prisoners of our circumstances and at her mercy. With a few new wrinkles across her forehead, Adalene slips back into the living space and returns to the now-empty table.

"We need meat," she tells Anger. "Venison is best. You get me that, and I can afford to give you what you need. And salt. If not, I can't spare much. My stash is already small. The kids aren't much thicker than their clothes. I can't afford to lose profit."

"Done. We'll go tomorrow," Anger confirms, even though we have yet to hear why or where we will be going.

Adalene reaches into her pocket and flings something at Anger, which she quickly catches before tucking it away.

"What time is he coming?" Adalene asks dryly.

"Don't know. He knows I'm here," Anger responds impatiently, moving toward the heart of the tree stretching through the center of Adalene's home. Her feet step up onto a few pegs spiraling diagonally up the tree's spine until she has reached the roof.

"When he comes, y'all keep it quiet up there," Adalene adds.

Anger's hands push through a small opening in the ceiling.

She pulls herself out into the night and carelessly flings the hatch closed.

"Don't worry about her," Adalene says dismissively, taking over Anger's vacant chair as she joins us in her cramped living room. "If she didn't let me hate her, I couldn't love her."

I barely hear her. I'm so mad it's as if fumes are rising from my smoldering shoulders. How could Anger possibly benefit from preying on our circumstances of unintentionally compromising an operatives mission? My mouth feels dry from all the anger I've swallowed, so I take a sip of my water. Surprisingly, it tastes clean, and I appreciate the small sense of relief.

"I have a hammock between some branches up there where she likes to go smoke or shoot up," Adalene tells us. "Hate to say it, but it is what it is. If I didn't have kids, I wouldn't let her have it."

"What do you mean?" I ask, my stomach churning as I remember my last encounter with chenoo.

"She helps me get what I need for the kids. See what happens when I try my luck out there?" she says, pointing to the bright scar running beneath her jawline. "We don't have laws here, and we don't have money. You trade or you fight. That's about it, unless you give your body. You might try fighting when that's the only thing left to trade."

She gets up and pours herself a drink, but this time she doesn't offer us any. Her clothes are tattered. I can see where she's stitched a medley of fabrics together to make what she has on now. Most of it is brown and gray, but there are patches of floral patterns here and there. She turns the glass up and empties it in a few quick gulps.

"I hope y'all don't mind. It's hard being a mother, especially when you feel like you're not good at it."

She walks over near the back wall and pulls on a curtain I previously thought served as a cover for a poorly constructed wall. Instead, she reveals a tiny room not much bigger than the bed resting inside.

"You'll have to sleep here. Both of you. It's all I got. If you don't like it, blame Anger for bringing you here. I'm sure you'll be doing that tomorrow anyway."

"It'll work fine," Merrin says politely.

"Yeah, thank you, Adalene."

She quickly corrects me. "It's Widow. Don't call me anything else."

"But I thought—"

"I know, I know. She called me Adalene. And that was my name a long time ago."

"How'd you meet Anger?" I ask.

"It's been years ago, now. That was back when my husband was still around. He found that poor bitch out in the rain late one night. He heard her screaming in the woods and ran up on her as she was pinned down by three cockheads with rusty knives. Course, she'd have held her own if those suppressive meds hadn't still been in her system, but it didn't matter cause my husband beat them inside out before they could hurt her too bad. So he brought her here all pitiful and angry. I mean, she was spitfire, so we calmed her down and figured out a bit of her story."

Widow sits down and pulls out a picture from her pocket.

"See this here? That's Nyle, my husband. I let Anger keep this picture with her, so when she slides it under my door, I know not to grab my gun and blast her into swamp-dog bait."

THE REVELATION

She stares at it for a moment before passing it to Merrin, and when he's done, he hands it to me. The picture is weathered from handling, but I can see a decently clear picture of Nyle. He's good looking, which doesn't surprise me because even now, as tough as Widow lives underneath her grit, she's beautiful. I pass the photo back to her, and she stares at it again.

"He was different, that's for damn sure. And I miss him. I do. I do," Widow says, more to the picture than to us. For a short while, she doesn't look up. I can tell her mind is taking her somewhere deep, so we wait for her to come back.

"Either of you two heard of the Revelation Territory?"

"No, ma'am, we haven't," I answer for us. I lean forward, resting my elbows on my knees, eager to make some sense of why Anger intercepted us.

Widow's eyes lock with mine. She's always reading us and never stops. "She really hasn't told y'all anything, has she?"

"No. Nothing," Merrin says, sitting up, as if expecting an answer.

"She tried to tell me something last night about magic, a-and her ring," I stutter, trying to piece together the hazy fragments of my drug-impaired memories. "We both saw her take out about a dozen Legionnaires at the same time, but I never saw her with a weapon. That's when she found us, but I doubt she would've mentioned anything if we hadn't seen that."

"You said magic? That's a weird way to put it. So you know she's got..." Widow says slowly, as if she's trying to avoid spilling vaulted secrets.

"Yeah, she told me about her ring."

Widow looks particularly confused before saying, "I'm

sorry, but what in hell's fire are you talking about? A ring?" she asks, her face scrunching up tight.

Nothing I'm saying seems to resonate with her, so I continue. "She showed me her ring. Her power, or whatever you want to call it. She said that's where it comes from."

I barely have time to finish before Widow bursts out laughing. She quickly covers her mouth and tries to speak, but she's still laughing.

I scratch the back of my head, and my face starts to feel flushed.

"Is that what she told you?" Merrin asks, like he's joining Widow's team to make me feel even stupider. Without having a moment alone since last night, Merrin and I haven't had a chance to discuss what happened.

"That bitch told you she had a *magic ring*?" Widow asks, wheezing out a few more laughs. She finally catches her breath to say, "She was shitting you worse than spicy food. Maybe she's actually learning how to be funny."

The unsettling stab of humiliation makes me feel defensive. "It's not funny to me. She's dragging us around out here when my family thinks I'm dead—"

"Keep your voice down," Widow demands sternly. The whole atmosphere shifts in a second.

"Why did she bring us here?" I fire back.

"I don't know," she answers, her eyes narrowing on mine. "You're asking the wrong person."

I look down and bring my hands to my forehead.

"I think we've said enough for one sitting. It's time for bed, anyways. Goodnight," Widow offers, getting up from her chair.

THE REVELATION

Just before she reaches her bedroom door, Merrin asks, "Why'd your husband leave?"

I know he's only asking to try and keep her from leaving our conversation. She stops immediately, her back still turned. Her fist is clenched by her side. She turns around and slowly steps toward us.

"I don't know you, boy, and you sure as shit don't know me." Her words are dark and cutting. Her amber eyes flicker in the candlelight. "My husband is none of your damn business."

They stare each other down. I can smell the sweet scent of smoke from whatever Anger is smoking as it leaks in through unseen cracks of Widow's home.

"My family is dead," he says, taking no offense at Widow's aggressive response.

Widow silently stares at Merrin, reading him for signs of dishonesty.

"They were missing for years," he says, his eyes cold, "and on my first Ops mission three days ago, I found them. They were Stones. When my mom tried to come to me, they shot her down."

My skin prickles with chills as he pauses, struggling under the weight of his emotions.

"I don't know you," he continues shakily, "but if you could please help us figure out why Anger brought us here..." Merrin sighs as if giving up on the rest of his sentence.

Widow looks away, rubbing the crease of her elbow as she takes a moment to think.

"Anger comes to get a good fix. It's what she's up there doing now. I'd like to say she missed my kids, but she don't feel that way. I don't know what she wants with you. I don't. But I know she's got one stone and two birds to kill coming here, the other bird being some high and mighty she's meeting on my roof tonight. Falyn Dire, if ya heard the name before."

"No. Who is he?" Merrin asks. I let him do the talking because he seems to be getting somewhere.

Widow scratches the back of her neck, and her hand settles there. "The freeworlders here call 'im *the Revanchist*. Don't know why or what it means, but he and his Saints got a big following, even with some of the Stones."

"What? That doesn't make sense," Merrin says, as confused as I am.

"Confusion is the way of the world, baby," she says, bending over to pick up her husband's photo.

"I guess you're right," Merrin says softly.

Widow stares down at her shaking hand, losing herself in the photo before speaking again.

"I don't know where my husband is," she whispers without breaking her eyes away from the picture. "Don't know if he's dead or if his heart just dried up. He'd stay gone for weeks, then come home for a few days like nothing was wrong. It was like that for months, and one day he just never came back."

Widow tucks the picture away in a fold of one of her pockets and steps over to a nearby drawer. She pulls out a syringe from inside and begins rubbing her forearm and slapping it with her hand.

"The night I met her, Anger was covered in blood, and I... I couldn't tell if it was hers or someone else's, so I cleaned her up as best I could. When Nyle came back that night, he wasn't the same. I don't know what happened."

After tying a strip of cloth tightly around her arm, she finds a vein and carefully injects herself with whatever substance was in the syringe.

THE REVELATION

"Look what you made me do," Widow mumbles to herself, as if she's blaming someone in her mind rather than us.

We don't say a word, and she continues.

"We were broken together, me and Anger, and we healed together too. We gave each other new names. She didn't like Anger at first because she said it sounded like a word men use to insult powerful women, but I said that's why I liked it. We figured if you claim a name, you control its meaning. Tried to forget everything else, but you can't do that. At least I can't. So we just started over."

Widow carefully replaces the empty syringe in the drawer before saying, "I need to get to a bed before this shit kicks in."

We watch her stagger toward the only real bedroom in her home, where her children are sleeping. Before she goes in, she whispers, "You know, Falyn Dire is famous. It's not every day a famous person meets your friend on your roof."

She slips behind the door, and we sit in silence for a moment before deciding to climb into the rickety bed, which is barely big enough to fit us both. I close the curtain around our cramped space, and it at least provides a small comfort of separation. I lay my head against a lumpy pillow and pull the woven blanket up to my chin.

Merrin speaks softly, without prompting. "Anger said we'd be surprised with what the people of the Black Valley can get away with since they don't mean anything to important people."

"What about it?" I ask, knowing he has even more on his mind than I do.

"She's meeting with that famous guy tonight. Seems like they're important, so if she wants us with her, we must be something they value."

Merrin's revelation connects my thoughts back to Commander Locke. I roll on my side and whisper, "Before I got to you on the mountain when we all were escaping, Commander Locke was trying to protect me. He was leading me to a separate aerocraft away from everyone else before he got shot."

On the wall, there's a small window covered by a cloth so thin it lets the moonlight leak in. Merrin pulls back the drape, and I find a few stars between the tree branches. They just might be the only beautiful things in the Black Valley.

"Do you think they knew my parents would be there?" Merrin asks as he stares into the night.

"I don't know," I whisper. The idea of our disastrous encounter being intentionally planned sits so heavily on my chest I can barely breathe.

"Maybe it's you they want," Merrin says faintly, watching the puffs of smoke from Anger's pipe float past our window, like small clouds chasing after the stars, as she waits for Falyn Dire to arrive. I can't help but be curious to see him, but lying tucked away in this worn bed behind a curtain makes me feel hidden and small.

Merrin's hand drops the curtain back in place, cutting away the night sky, and we both lie in silence. I can't see his eyes, but I know he won't be going to sleep anytime soon. Neither will I. I wonder if Mom and Dad are lying awake at home wondering where I am, fearing the grief of losing their second child. I imagine Jaykin living his life, pushing against the ghost of me while feeling responsible for filling the emptiness plaguing his parents' hearts.

Ruma may or may not be alive, but I still am. If I can't find her, the next best thing I could do would be to spare my family the grief of losing not one but two children.

"Merrin," I quietly say.

"Yeah," he responds, lying still.

"Tomorrow, we'll find the right moment to run. Let's go home."

CHAPTER 13

My vision is hazy until I see her. The faceless girl standing before me transforms into Rhysk. My mind perfectly remembers her attractive face—the sharp angles of her smooth jaw line, the definitive contour of her cheekbones, and her bronzed hazel eyes. She accuses me of killing Commander Locke, and I begin to chase her.

Suddenly we're running beyond the Southern Guard walls toward the edge of the one-mile tracking line. She's running faster than I am. I can only move in slow motion. She runs over a hill and out of sight. I yell her name, and even though I can't see them, I know a group of Stones is on the other side waiting to ambush her. She's running directly toward them.

I can't see her, but I hear loud screams and terrible noises. I yell for her again, and a hand grabs my shoulder. I look behind me, and my eyes meet with a PRA agent coming to take me to purge camp. He's in my face, grabbing me, shaking my shoulder, and I wake up from the nightmare.

THE REVELATION

Anger's face is the first thing I see when my eyes open, which puts me on edge more than waking up from a nightmare.

"Get up. Time to eat," she says, releasing her grip from my shoulder.

I rub my hands over my face and stretch my spine for a moment in an attempt to unkink some tension I gained from sleeping on a worn-out mattress. I smell some kind of meat cooking, which is the only thing motivating me to get out of bed.

"Get dressed," Anger says, tossing unfamiliar clothes in my face. She herself is dressed in what appears to be jeans and an undershirt. Her light black body armor suit hangs from a sturdy curtain rod above one of the windows.

I examine the coarse shirt and find a hood of a different material sewn onto the neck. The dark pants unfold into some type of overalls, which fit a little loosely when I put them on. Merrin is already up and dressed. His attire looks similar to mine, except his fits him more appropriately.

"Do you think they were Widow's husband's?" Merrin asks me.

"Probably."

Merrin and I don't have to mention our conversation from last night for me to know we'll both be planning our potential escape from Anger once we've figured out what her plans are for us today.

I sleepily slip into to the same spindle-back chair I sat in last night in front of a small assortment of breakfast foods. I want to ask what the meat is, but I decide it might be easier to eat if I don't know. It looks like sausage, so I tell myself that's what it is. Everything tastes good, considering a lot of what we've been eating the past several days has been packaged preservatives for light traveling.

"You'll need to fit in with the Soots," Anger quietly explains.

"The who?" Merrin asks.

She gestures around us. "The people here. They're dirty inside and out. Soots."

"These aren't dirty," Merrin says, observing his clothes.

"They're Nyle's. He wasn't a Soot, but they'll work. We'll leave your Falcon gear here for now. People here would rob their own mother's grave."

"Yep. I've seen it myself," Widow says, emerging from her room. Her hair crawls in every direction, and her discolored face appears as if her blood stopped flowing altogether. She's staring at us wearing her husband's old clothes. I can't imagine myself feeling any more uncomfortable than I do now, even if I were naked.

"You could ask next time before you take his clothes," Widow says groggily.

"You were asleep. I'll wake you next time," Anger says, more politely than I expected.

Widow accepts her comment with a nod and pops a piece of meat in her mouth. Anger holds up one additional jacket to Widow for approval, and she looks it over before nodding. Anger pulls her arms through the oversized jacket and wraps a gray headband around her forehead before covering her hair with Nyle's hood.

"The kids are still asleep, but they won't be for long if they smell the food," Widow tells us, slumping into a chair beside Merrin.

Surprisingly, Anger gives us a rundown of where we are going before we ask.

THE REVELATION

"We'll travel to Beggar's Grave first. It's an organized fighting pit where the people of the Black Valley fight to win scarce valuables."

"Like food," Widow chimes in.

"Widow gave me the things I need, so I want to pay her back if I can."

"So you're planning to fight?" I ask her.

"No, I'm not. Not this time."

"That's surprising," Merrin says.

"How did it go with Falyn?" Widow asks.

"We're on the same page now."

"None of us knows what page that is, but as long as you feel good about it," Widow says, winking and shaking her piece of sausage at her.

Anger looks at Widow, and her eyes linger disapprovingly before she continues. "We'll be back before night with your rations, so get ready to store it."

Widow gives a delayed nod of approval, and Anger files us out the door. Widow's hoarse voice follows us out. "Bring them back."

At first I thought she was talking about Merrin and me, but now I feel like she could just as easily have been talking about her husband's clothes. Either way, I plan to bring myself back fully clothed. Once we leave, Anger also gives us each a black bandanna to cover our noses and mouths. Although she has assured us we don't need to worry about contracting perducorium in the Black Valley, I feel more comfortable knowing I'll have at least a small layer of protection against any possible airborne pathogens.

We scale down using a retractable rope secured to the

porch's side. When we hit the ground, it shoots back up on its own. Anger leads us on toward the Black Valley.

"So what's the plan?" Merrin asks, cautiously trying to find his footing on the less-saturated portions of the sludgy trail.

"Stay with me. And don't use my name. Not around here," Anger says, only stopping long enough to finish her sentence.

"Why? Who are you hiding from?" Merrin asks.

Anger pauses again, looking straight into his eyes as if she's searching for any sign of Merrin having a brain. He stares back at her, eyes wide. Then she continues ahead.

"Okay. I think I have a couple good names I can call you," Merrin adds, still staying close behind her.

Our morning journey takes us downhill into the thick fog hanging over the Black Valley structures. When we hit the streets, I realize I'm barely breathing. I'm particularly thankful for the bandanna because the smell of sewage is so overwhelming it's as if I can taste it. Most of the Soots' faces are dirty or covered by matted hair. Their tattered clothes leave more skin exposed than covered, and instead of shoes, half of the people only wear the black mud sticking to their bare feet.

I scoop some sludge off the ground and smear a little on my face. I show Merrin and suggest he do the same when no one is looking. He objects at first but quickly catches on.

I notice several people with maimed limbs and gruesome scars. Others have tattoos etched across their sunken faces. I feel their bony shoulders brush against my arms as we pass through the thick masses of Soots. The further we walk into the shambles of the Black Valley, the dirtier the people become.

I see one man on his knees, smashing flies against a wall and then eating them. Along the paths we are taking, there's

THE REVELATION

little more than mud and scrap homes infested by garbage. We reach a small circular patch of ground sludge where, in the center, several people are chained to posts like dogs. A dingy, rusted sign hangs above them reading "Theeves Lot," which no one has bothered to correct.

Anger reads the sign. "That's new. I guess they're testing out criminal justice for a change."

A little girl catches my eye as she's being dragged by someone who I assume is her mother toward a nearby food stand. Her features remind me so much of Ruma that I can't help but stare. While her mother engages the stand owner, the little girl looks around to see if anyone is looking before she reaches her hand into a barrel of peanuts. With her hand tucked away, she runs up to the chained thieves and throws a handful of nuts at no one in particular. The emaciated thieves rattle their chains against their bleeding skin just to get a small bite of food. The sight makes me want to throw up.

Looking back over my shoulder, I follow the young girl with my eyes as she runs back toward her angry mother, who slaps her down into the mud. Several slouching bodies obstruct my view of the girl, so I mumble a prayer for her and continue shoving my way forward. My soul feels tainted, and just breathing in the thick air makes my insides feel coated with slime. Even so, with Anger throwing glances over her shoulder every few steps, I resolve with myself that now isn't the time to run.

We dodge through the crowded markets between several thrown-together vendor stalls displaying pitiful selections of starving chickens, worn-out boots, and other items I would deem a step above trash.

The Soots scream, trying to get the attention of the various vendors by shouting what items they have clenched within their dirty hands for trade. Hundreds of desperate faces nearly crawl over one another, intertwining their arms and legs until the crowd looks more like a writhing millipede. I stare at the back of Anger's hooded jacket to avoid focusing on the terrible living conditions around me.

Ahead, poorly organized lines of people are filing down a sloping path between two stone embankments. Somewhere close by, the rise and fall of cheering crowds echoes from down in the pits. We approach the mouth of the exterior entrance to the fighting pits where the queuing Soots are shoving one another forward. A large, weather-beaten sign sways from horizontal chains strung between two of the only brick and mortar buildings in sight. The darkly engraved letters hammered across the rustic, metal sheet reads, "Beggar's Grave."

I slap my hand against Merrin and signal for him to look at the sign.

"I know," he says, even though neither one of us knows what we're getting into. The dehumanizing culture of the Black Valley feels suffocating. I can almost feel the burdensome curse of extreme emotional and financial poverty hanging in the air.

Massive bodies of stone form a substantial circular battlement around the walls of the fighting pits. My guess is the founders of Beggar's Grave created the pits using extremely powerful explosives to blast craters into existing rock structures. The Soots can barely build four standing walls, so more than likely the history of this place was swallowed by the shadows of the Black Valley settlement.

My feet are beginning to hurt, but I'm not about to

THE REVELATION

slow down in case I lose Anger. As we continue around the outer walls of Beggar's Grave, the crowd thins noticeably. A cobblestone pathway leads us down to the iron doors of a guarded gatehouse.

Anger confidently steps toward the guard at the entrance. He's almost seven feet tall. His skin is deeply tanned and weathered, and between his coarse beard and charcoal-black half-helmet, I can't see his face.

His hand moves to his side, where his gun hangs. Anger quickly pulls back her sleeve, exposing the inside of her left wrist. What I thought was a gun is his scanner. He shines the purple light over her wrist, revealing a previously invisible tattoo. I can't make out what it is, but the guard seems satisfied.

"You're late," he says, relaxing his stance. "Bout didn't recognize you."

"I'm not fighting today," she tells him, making me wonder how many times Anger has fought here before.

We follow Anger ahead, and a powerful hand grips my shoulder. I freeze, as if my subtlest move could cause him to rip my arm off.

"Not you," he says to Merrin and me. His voice falls over us like an avalanche. Against his size, I have no real choice but to be submissive while trying to contain my uneasiness.

Anger turns, firmly grabs his arm, and lets her hand slide down his wrist. She's gentle with him and almost seductive with her smile.

"I would've left them behind if I didn't intend for them to enter," Anger tells him.

He hesitates as if he's lost in her eyes. Her sultry voice seemingly melts his hold on me, and I cautiously slip away.

Even though his hand is gone, the ghostly presence of his grip lingers on my shoulder.

"I'll leave them in the inner ward. They'll go no further," she says smoothly to polish over any of his reservations about allowing us to pass.

Merrin offers an unwanted thank-you as we continue toward the next gate. The guard aims his gun at a panel beside the gate, and it begins lifting. The rustic iron bars grind in unison with the metal cogs. I clench my teeth and press my fingernails into my palms in rebellion against the deep sounds of crunching metal.

In school, we learned how the model for Southern Guard's walls and its inner workings evolved from nearly extinct structural ideas used several centuries ago. Beggar's Grave seems like one of the old-world strongholds stricken with twenty lifetimes' worth of dust and decay.

"What's holding this place together?" I whisper to Merrin.

"Dark magic," he says sarcastically, but between the strangely anachronistic architecture and the mystery surrounding the origin of Anger's unnatural abilities, I wouldn't entirely discount that possibility.

Just beyond the gate, we stop. Above us, sharp beams of light cut through two brightly colored stained-glass windows set high into the stone walls. One depicts a beautiful woman kneeling beside a sleeping man. In one hand, she holds a metal peg against the man's temple, and with the other, she's rearing back with a hammer.

The right window shines with an image of a warrior burying a sword deep into the stomach of a king. An angel stands close by, blowing a golden trumpet. I stare at the windows as Anger commands us to sit on a nearby bench painted by the colored light falling through the windows. She walks a short distance away, which gives Merrin and me a second to exchange thoughts.

"Why would a Commander Elite come somewhere like this?" I ask.

"It doesn't make sense, and we sure as shit didn't sign up for it." He swipes the gray cobwebs away from the bench so we can sit.

"We might've done better to let the RedCloud Legionnaires take us," he says.

His statement stops me for a moment.

"There's no way Anger just happened to be close by when they intercepted our brace-comms' signals," I say. "To get there that quick, she had to be tracking us too. In her own aerocraft."

"I know," he whispers. "With the Legionnaire ship being so close by, we'd never have made it out if she tried to fly away. Could've been why we've been walking so much. But why would either of them want us?"

I shake my head as we both watch Anger pacing quietly. Her eyes keep casually peeking around corners and following strangers who pass. I sense Merrin looking at me and turn to see what he's thinking.

"Do you think this has anything to do with Ruma?"

"I don't know," I say, dismissing his comment before the overwhelming realization strikes me that it could be true. My mind goes into overdrive as it tries to form a cohesive narrative to explain how my current circumstances could possibly connect to Ruma. Instead of answers, I find the sudden and heavy onset of enervating anxiety and mental fatigue.

As we sit in silence waiting for Anger's next move, I calm

my mind by studying the stucco patterns of interwoven circles that climb across the arching ceilings. Time has washed the elaborate designs with dark coats of dust, and I wonder how a quaint old-world cathedral built with such intricate beauty ever came to feel more like the mausoleum of Beggar's Grave.

"Who do you think they are?" I ask Merrin as I look up at the figures depicted in the stained-glass windows.

"They look like they don't belong here," he says.

Anger's focus is lost deep in some communication device she's holding in her hands. Her back is turned to us, so I lean closer to Merrin.

"Do you still think we could make a run for it?" I whisper.

In the light of the stained glass, Merrin's eyes are bright like clear water. He sits upright as the thought settles over him. "Yeah, but we've got to have a plan," he says, brushing the palms of his hands against his pants.

"I know. I don't mean now, but when the time is right. I'd feel better if we had our Falcon gear when we do."

Someone passes behind Merrin and brushes up against him. She draws both our eyes and leaves a wake of bittersweet incense behind. She walks straight up to Anger, who doesn't seem surprised to see her. I assume she's been waiting for this woman all along. All of her features are swallowed underneath her dirty cloak.

Their exchange is brief as they pass a few quiet words, none of which I can make out. The lady pulls something from within her cloak. They make a subtle trade between hands as they kiss each other's cheeks. The mystery woman disappears down the right of the three open corridors situated along the back wall of the cathedral, and Anger quickly rejoins us.

"Let's go."

THE REVELATION

We begin walking through the inner ward, heading for the left passageway.

"So much for staying in the inner ward," Merrin whispers. "I'm not about to fight that giant at the gate."

Anger hears him. "I'll apologize for lying when we leave."

The tall ceilings abruptly end, dropping down to an archway no more than eight feet high. The walls narrow significantly, putting us uncomfortably close to the blazing torches illuminating the winding hallway. Spasms of light flicker against the emerald mold, which crawls along like the spiders nesting across the damp stone walls. The stiff air smells like a collection of dying breaths that haunt the pale corridors.

"What are those?" I ask, pointing to the faded symbols painted above two passageways that extend to either side.

"Sigils. Family crests of the old champions of this arena," Anger tells us as she slaps a sign, which looks like an upside-down arrowhead. Disturbing growls echo up from the connecting passageways.

"What's that?" Merrin asks.

"It's either sex or torture, or maybe both," Anger says, unmoved.

Faint chanting and shouts stiffen the hairs on my forearms. As we continue deeper into the corridor, the sounds strengthen. We turn left into the face of a door made of wood and iron. Anger gives a couple hard slams against the door before a small eye-level window opens, revealing a solid purple square of light. A tiny circular plate also extends from the bottom of the opening.

Anger reaches into the same pocket where she stowed away whatever item the cloaked woman passed along. Her fingers reveal what looks like an intricately designed queen from a chess set.

She positions the figurine above the center of the miniature platform and lets it go. The queen statuette floats in place, suspended by some sort of magnetic field. The silver plate carefully rotates the figurine full circle as the purple light scans every detail of this unusual key. Accompanied by a satisfactory clearance sound from within the panel, the door moans open.

The space is not much bigger than a bedroom, with three velvet lounging chairs and a bar table. Directly ahead, instead of a wall, there is a full display screen.

"What is that?" Merrin asks.

"It's a video feed."

Anger squints her eyes and walks up to the video wall. She's watching the people on screen engage in hand-to-hand combat. I don't see any weapons as I walk up, but there are about eight people standing, with several others sprawled out on the ground around them. As the combatants fight, the cheers from outside the walls coincide with each major blow.

"Wait, is this live?" Merrin asks, on the same wavelength with my thoughts.

"Right there. That's K-Balt," she answers while pointing at one particular fighter with thick wild hair that's mostly braided behind her head. Anger's finger traces the female combatant's movements across the screen as she takes down three people in less than ten seconds.

Anger laughs out loud, which is about as strange as seeing an animal talk.

"Yes!" Anger yells, lost in the action. For a moment, her

countenance carries a playful energy that makes her almost appear friendly.

An overhead camera shot follows K-Balt as she leaps across a few closely laid boulders rising around the edge of the arena, which is filled with orange dust.

For a few moments, the screen's perspective shifts to K-Balt's view as she grabs someone's arm, rolling over her combatant's body and forcing them into the dirt.

"Are they killing each other?" Merrin asks, horrified.

"No. Watch," Anger says irritably.

The woman pinned beneath K-Balt's body taps out, slapping her hand into the dirt. The crowd gets to their feet, cheering, as K-Balt is the last woman standing. Several uniformly dressed attendants enter the arena and begin dragging the fallen fighters toward the outer wall.

K-Balt sprints toward a rock platform standing near the center of the arena, where the copper statue of a kneeling warrior rests. The weathered metal figure, rising three times its height above K-Balt's head, depicts an armored woman supporting her weight by gripping the hilt of her standing sword.

K-Balt bows respectfully toward the statue. As she returns upright, she rips off her shirt, exposing her chest. The crowd cheers approvingly. She beats her fists against her breasts, and I can't help but stare at the muscles flexing all over her. Her abs are finely cut and tanned. I don't have time to take in much more before the screen pans across the audience chanting K-Balt's name.

From a higher perspective, a camera follows her as she jumps down from the rock and heads toward a door on the pit wall, which opens simultaneously as the side door to *our* room opens, revealing the fighting pit and K-Balt jogging our way.

As soon as she sees Anger, she yells and sprints the last few steps, almost tackling Anger to the ground.

Merrin and I back into the corner of the room, desperately trying to figure out how to act normal in front of a half-naked woman. We don't have to think too hard because she extends her hand toward us with a comfortable smile across her face.

"I'm Kalee. These your kids?" she asks, turning to Anger while making an exaggerated long face.

Anger replies with her usual deadpan before cracking into a smile.

K-Balt shakes Merrin's hand first, and then mine, while I try to focus on keeping eye contact.

"Sorry about parading my girls around," K-Balt says, undoing her braids to fluff out her hair. "You just get caught up in the hype. It seemed like a good idea in the moment."

"That's okay," Merrin answers for both of us before turning back to me with tightly pursed lips and wide eyes.

The door we entered opens, and a young girl around my age stands holding medical supplies.

"Nope. I'm good, but thanks," K-Balt says, waving the girl away.

For being the last woman standing after a prize fight, she appears surprisingly uninjured. I assume that to be a further testament of her skill.

She turns her back to us, pulling her thick brown hair back and collecting it with a band at the crown of her head. My eyes trace the scars dug across her back and sides.

"Why didn't you join me? Those bitches were weak," she says, looking over her shoulder.

"You just answered your own question," Anger responds, settling into one of the decorative velvet chairs.

K-Balt makes a face and looks her up and down. "What the hell are you wearing?"

"Don't worry about my clothes. You're the one with your tits hanging out."

K-Balt gives a little dancing shake before laughing at Anger's comment. She walks to a drawer and pulls out a blue body wrap. She quickly wraps a few strips over her torso and around her arms and then finds a simple shirt to throw over herself.

"What's the blue stuff for?" Merrin asks inquisitively. I feel like he's just fishing for something to say so he can talk to K-Balt.

"Healing," she says. "I know I talk shit, but some of those women can crack a rib."

"I need a favor," Anger says, interrupting.

K-Balt wipes the blood off the corner of her lip and shakes her head as she grins.

"I was waiting for that. Go ahead and cash it in."

"I need a part of the voucher you just won for Widow's kids. And I need you to keep an eye on these two."

"Okay, but why? And who are they? No offense," she adds, looking at us to offer a polite nod as if to cushion her blunt manner of asking.

"I would have told you if it was important," Anger says plainly.

"That's rude. It sounds like you're saying they're not important, and you wouldn't have come here to ask me if they weren't. I can't do your 'everything's a secret' shit. Just tell me."

Her bluntness brings me relief. I say nothing to derail the conversation, hoping we'll learn more about Anger's intentions if K-Balt continues to force her hand.

"You should trust my judgment, but I'll say it. Mallins came back. I know where he is. We'll need to move soon for me to take care of him."

Her words fall heavily over K-Balt, who draws her arms right across her chest. "How do you know?" she asks, her face overlaid with concern.

"I've been communicating with Falyn Dire and a few of his Saints. We met last night. They made sure he got here, and it's my end of the deal to take him out."

K-Balt remains silent until Anger says, "I need a yes or a no. Tell me now."

"Yes to what?"

"Will you protect them while I take care of him?" Anger says, her voice rising. I don't know what we could possibly need protection from, but the thought doesn't settle well.

"What do you mean *take care of him*?"

"You know what I mean."

K-Balt's eyes nearly glaze over as she sinks into her mind.

"Falyn Dire and his Saints will have their targets, but I asked him to leave Mallins for me. But it's your choice."

K-Balt continues staring silently.

"It's yes or no!" Anger demands.

"Okay! Yes. Yes. Of course I'll do it. When are you—"

"Now," Anger says. "He's betting high on his combatant, who's expected to win. He's already locked in to compete. I'm ready if you are."

K-Balt nods, her face flushed. "Why did you bring them for this?"

THE REVELATION

My stomach and lungs are firmly knotted up, and as much as I don't want to be a part of what seems to be Anger's assassination mission, I'm certain Merrin and I couldn't find our way out of this place alone.

"Because they're my responsibility, and I need someone I can trust to look after them," Anger explains with an uncharacteristically empathic tone. I guess Widow wasn't the one she'd trust for that job.

"Ready?" Anger asks, grabbing K-Balt's arm before exiting the viewing room. As she goes, K-Balt follows, and left without a better option, Merrin and I do the same. Anger leads us back through the torch-lit corridors, and we turn too many times to ever be able to find our way out without help. Now, more than ever, I feel like Anger's possession. The thought makes my entire body tense and seethe with heat. The only comfort I can find is knowing I'm waiting for the right moment to escape.

The mouth of the tunnel ahead opens up underneath a high stone archway and leads us into an uncharacteristically elegant great hall. Ornate chandeliers dangle like earrings from the vaulted ceilings, which are supported by the marble hands of nine titan statues. The chiseled expressions on their faces capture agony and distress so perfectly that I almost fear the stone giants will drop the ceiling on our heads.

"How is *this* here?" Merrin asks. His mouth stays open as we walk underneath the massive statues.

"If you bury your gold under a pile of shit, you don't need to worry about someone sniffing out your wealth," K-Balt says.

"Where is everybody?" I ask as our footsteps echo throughout the hall.

"They're waiting for me. They just don't know it," Anger says.

At the end of the great hall, a glowing pool shimmers like a portal to heaven at the foot of three rising staircases. Above the pool, a circular opening allows white light to pour into the water, where reflective pebbles busily refract brilliant hues of blue.

K-Balt whispers to us, "That's called the Eye of God. Before you attempt a Trial of Talos, you look into the water to cleanse your spirit in case you die."

"What's Talos?" Merrin softly asks.

"It's the name of a mythical beast that was said to have feasted on the dead bodies left on the battlefields thousands of years ago. That's supposedly where the architect got the name and inspiration for designing his sadistic obstacle course."

"What obstacle course?" Merrin questions.

"It's on the other side," she tells us, pointing beyond the pool to the three separate staircases, which lead up to identical stone archways. Instead of doors, swirling light, like soft white flames, engulfs each of the entrances. Angel statues stand guard above the three entryways, and the trains of their white-marble robes flow down either side of the illuminated doorways. Despite the artistic elegance of the hall, I feel a haunting presence, like the décor is a sheepskin hiding a wolf.

Anger stops, taking a moment to stare into the Eye of God. She dips her hands into the cool water and washes her face. We stand ten feet behind to give her space. I hear her whispering inaudible words, then she spits into the water. She quickly walks back toward us and whispers, "Follow me."

We return to where we came in, passing the towering pillars until we reach our original entry point to the majestic hallways preceding the Trial of Talos. To the right of the archway, Anger reaches out and pushes against one of the many large tile panels making up the exterior walls. The tile shifts back into the wall, and I realize it's a door. Anger swings it forward to reveal a hidden stairway rising into the darkness.

Once we all clear the doorway, Anger slides the wall panel back into place. The darkness swallows us.

"Hold on," Anger says.

A subdued purple glow from a light Anger holds in her hand provides just enough visibility for us to see the outlines of our bodies and the stairs below our feet. Anger moves around us to lead the way. There seems to be no specific directional flow as we wind our way higher. Our footsteps echo even as we try treading carefully. Merrin gasps as the dark outline of a rat scampers between our feet.

The faint presence of light softens the darkness ahead. Anger conceals her own light as she turns a corner at the top of the stairs. We slip into the shadow of a small spectating balcony. Two small rows of chairs divided by a center aisle separate us from the balcony's edge, which obstructs our view of what's below.

"It's down there," Anger whispers as she points.

"What is?" I ask, almost afraid to look.

"Talos," she says.

We all silently crouch forward to get a better view.

Talos looks like an enormously complex machine that abstractly resembles a nightmarish monster chained in the center of an expansive arena. A series of bridges, ropes, stairs, and beams weave throughout the deadly obstacle course forming the treacherous pathways coursing over the beastly structure. The only significant light source in the arena falls from the various staging lights hanging from the ceiling. Talos itself appears to be suspended in a frozen sea of darkness.

"Wait here," Anger commands before vanishing into the black.

"Where is she going?" Merrin asks K-Balt.

"She's taking care of something," she tells us. "Just keep quiet."

Merrin pulls me close and whispers, "We should've run a long time ago."

His words don't have time to settle in as a groaning horn echoes from the belly of the room. A shudder climbs up my spine like a family of spiders. My stomach feels heavy, as if I swallowed the sound. The machine parts begin cranking, groaning like a dragon disturbed from its sleep. Radiating silver blades rhythmically slice over and around one another like swiping claws while other spinning cogs awaken larger ironclad parts that begin to crunch and pound into one another like monstrous teeth.

From within Talos, occasional bursts of fire lash out from hidden pores, scorching the stagnant air. K-Balt points to the front wall, where three contenders stand separated by three bridges connected at the mouth of Talos.

"Holy shit. Are they all going to do this?" Merrin asks shakily.

"What if they die?" I add.

"There's no way out but to go through Talos," she tells us. "The fire behind them keeps them from going back. The dark pit below them makes them go forward."

"What happens if they get to the other side?" Merrin asks.

"They'll win a shit ton of vouchers and rewards. So will the people betting on them. Do you see the faces?" she whispers, pointing out beyond the balcony.

At first, I have no idea what she's talking about, but my

THE REVELATION

eyes are beginning to adjust to the darkness. Pale shadows begin to appear around the perimeters of the arena like the dim faces of stars after nightfall.

"So this is the real fighting pit," I say, more as an outward revelation than a question.

K-Balt nods.

"Who are those people?" I ask her, pointing to the barely visible suits and elegant dresses hugging the edges of the surrounding viewing balconies.

"I don't know who most of them are, but I know what they do."

"What do you mean?" I ask.

Her face is shadowed when she speaks. The few small rays of light reaching her face are caught for a moment by the moisture gathering in her eyes.

"Most of them are old- and new-money millionaires, but there are a few politicians from New Province Guard. Trafficking lords too."

"Which of those is Mallins?" Merrin asks, and I'm glad he does because I wouldn't have.

She's silent for a moment while her eyes stay trained on the distant shadowed faces.

"Trafficker," she finally says stiffly. "Did you see my scars? The scars on my sides and back?"

I want to pretend I didn't because acknowledging I did feels intrusive.

"Yes," Merrin responds honestly.

"Most of them didn't come from my pit fights. They came from him."

"Then I hope Anger takes him out," he says, resolute.

She pauses. I can tell she doesn't want to continue, so I don't push the matter.

"Do either of you know who she is?" she asks, leaning back from the balcony's edge.

I know very little about Anger. I know her name, which Widow told us isn't real. I know she somehow has supernatural abilities, which I still haven't been able to reconcile. I know she saved my life, but I don't trust her. Something in me feels cold when I'm around her. I decide to keep all of this information to myself and simply say, "No. Not really."

"She's the matron benefactress of Beggar's Grave. Almost no one knows that because she doesn't talk to people. She gives purpose to women like me who'd be abused or dead without her. She pays for defensive training and housing for dozens of us. All we have to do is put on a good show a couple times a week in the pits. Sometimes it's tough, but at least in there we are in control."

"You were pretty incredible out there today," Merrin says. "I know I wouldn't want to face you."

K-Balt gently laughs through her nose as she peeks back over the ledge.

"Why do you think she brought us here?" Merrin asks, leaning up beside her.

"I don't know, but I don't think this is about either of you. Whatever happens, just stay calm and stay with me," she says reassuringly.

In the center of the arena, above Talos, several giant video screens suddenly appear, casting additional light on the room as they provide close-ups of the competitors dressed in light armor—two young males and one woman with a shaved head.

THE REVELATION

A loud voice, smooth as water, announces the start of the Trial of Talos.

"Competitors, prepare to enter." Something is also said in a foreign language I don't recognize. All three of them mouth the words in unison, so I'm guessing it's some kind of ritualistic creed. After the last words leave their mouths, they all reach their hands out, as if grabbing something out of the air, and they each place a hand over their hearts.

The room is rigidly quiet. A resonating thud interrupts the silence like a thick heartbeat as the video screens count down the seconds until the competitors play with death. A sanguine shade of red light pulses up each of the three runways toward the contenders. The dark, creeping lights swiftly transition into a pale white glow as they simultaneously reach the base of the three platforms. With a single, hollow blast from a horn, the contenders' shadowy figures sprint toward Talos like hungry wolves in the moonlight.

My fingers clench the edge of the balcony as I follow the combatants as they leap and climb their way past whirling blades and spurts of fire. The woman with a shaved head swings from a platform she's scaled, and in midair, the rope snaps. She screams as she smashes against a curved wall forming a portion of Talos's hind leg, but she manages to grab hold of a large spinning wheel, which she desperately clings to while she catches her breath.

One of the male combatants has disappeared from sight within the inner workings of the colossal obstacle course, but the other skillfully balances atop the plated scales forming the rear of Talos. Unpredictable blasts of fire erupt on all sides as his feet dance around the searing flames.

Some distant screams mingle with sounds of crunching

wood and pitching metal slicing across the air. My hand reaches out and finds Merrin's shirt, and I grip it tight. I hear K-Balt breathing in and out as if she's trying to calm herself. One of her hands finds me and squeezes my arm.

"Stay together. She'll come back for us," she whispers gruffly.

Too afraid to risk peeking back over the balcony, we stay huddled together, awaiting Anger's return, assuming she hasn't been killed. We take turns jolting as the resounding booms and skin-tingling clangs of metal striking metal echo from within the arena. K-Balt lets out a small shriek as another body pushes into us. We all jolt away until we hear Anger confirm, "It's okay. It's me. We're leaving. Hold together."

"Did you do it?" K-Balt asks.

"Yes. It's done."

"Oh my God," K-Balt utters, her voice trembling.

"We're leaving. Now," Anger says, dragging us through the thick coat of darkness filling the stairwell we came in through. Even though I'm sure K-Balt's abuser was a horrendous person, the thought of closely following Anger just after she murdered someone turns my stomach.

We round a corner, and I smack into a wall, knocking myself off balance. I fall and take Merrin down with me. We're quickly pulled back up to our feet and continue shuffling forward. Any second, I expect something to smash into my face. After a few minutes of chaotic scrambling, I hear a loud crash ahead. Warm light breaks over us once again, forcing our eyes to squint. We emerge back in one of the torch-lit hallways underneath Beggar's Grave with no time to stop.

"How could she see where we were going?" Merrin asks me.

"Quiet!" Anger scolds without slowing down.

Now I'm wondering what other secrets she might have that she's kept hidden from us.

Anger stretches her hand toward an iron-bar door coated with rust and cobwebs. After hearing the increasingly familiar sharp whistle that accompanies Anger's telekinetic abilities, the metal hinges crack like bones as the door falls flat on the ground. The light of the setting sun breaks against our faces as we emerge into a fenced-in pen choked by green overgrowth. My lungs gasp in air as if I've just emerged from underwater.

"They'll notice you out here," K-Balt says, grabbing Anger's arm. I hadn't realized until now that Anger's jacket and headband are gone, possibly because they were stained with Mallins's blood.

"After your fight today, they'll want your attention too. So just keep moving," Anger tells her. For a culture that highly esteems fighting, Anger and K-Ball very well could be famous here, which might've been why Anger didn't want us to use her name.

A few large hogs squeal threats from their mud hole nearby as Anger unlatches the pen's gate. She hastily snaps away several vines entangling our exit so we can escape into the crowd of people coming and going between prizefights. We've emerged on a different side of Beggar's Grave, but I have a pretty good idea of where we are now in respect to where we first entered the underground levels.

The foul air soured by unkempt livestock pens and barbaric human hygiene heightens my disgust of the numerous dirty faces sliding past us. A hand slides into my right pocket. I try to turn around, but someone kicks my legs and throws me to the ground. I can't tell who it was, as they disappear behind all the legs passing by me.

As Merrin pushes his way back to me, he accidentally knocks an elderly woman to the ground, who doesn't seem to mind, as if she falls a hundred times a day. Merrin helps both the woman and me back to our feet. Between the hard wrinkles on her face and her croaking protest to let her go, she seems more annoyed that Merrin helped her up.

"What happened?" he asks, ignoring the seething insults from the old woman as she shuffles away.

"Someone tried to rob me," I tell him.

Whomever it was thankfully didn't steal my flint fire starter, but as I take inventory of my pockets, I feel a smooth slip of unfamiliar paper between my fingers. I pull it out and unfold a picture of my family.

"What is it?" Merrin asks after seeing the confusion on my face. I frantically look around as my chest stings with anxiety. I show him the picture.

"Someone *put* this in my pocket," I tell him as he stares fixedly at the photograph.

"What if it's a threat?" I ask, feeling an increasingly constricting sense of panic rush beneath my skin. "What if we get blamed for what Anger's doing, and they go after my family?"

I look ahead. Anger and K-Balt are shoving their way through the crowd of fans that appears to be forming around them.

"This is our time," I tell him. "We can get away. We've got to go home."

He pauses, confused, as if trying to confirm whether I'm being serious.

"This crowd is the best natural camouflage we'll have. We need to go. Now," I demand, feeling my heart strongly pumping in my neck.

He glances back toward Anger and K-Balt, who are now completely out of sight.

"We could try to get our Falcon gear back from Widow before we go," Merrin suggests.

"Why?" I ask. "They don't have power."

"I know, but if we can find a way to charge them, they might make getting home a lot faster," he explains.

"What if they're heading to Widow's house too?" I ask as I begin taking myself through a few quick self-calming strategies to relax my anxiety.

"When they see they've lost us, they'll have to come back for us. They won't expect us to go there if they assume we're running away."

I'm not sure if he's right, but having the reinforced joint support of our Falcon gear would make escaping Anger and the Black Valley significantly easier.

"Let's go," I say, taking a deep breath before I begin dodging around the many Soots loitering around the perimeter of the fighting pits.

"Okay. Go. Go," Merrin says, pushing behind me.

We quickly break away from Anger and K-Balt's trail, unapologetically shoving past anyone obstructing our way through the mud-covered streets. The shadowy threat of night falls heavily over my mind as we race the setting sun, which descends over the Black Valley as if sinking into the grave. My blood streams with adrenaline as I feel in control for the first time since Anger took out the Legionnaires. As much as it terrified me that someone placed a picture of my family in my pocket, I cling to the photo tightly for reassurance as Merrin and I hastily trace our steps back to Widow's home.

CHAPTER 14

For a while, we don't even really know where we're going. The swarm of people has significantly thinned, so we cut into a bramble of trees and overgrowth to keep a lower profile. Up ahead of us, a small girl is eating something her little brother just pulled from a pile of trash. Her skin sinks against her bones, and her black hair has fallen out in patches. Our eyes meet for a split second, and a part of my heart shatters. We keep moving. Wild green vines slither amongst the clustered piles of junk thrown out behind every building. I focus my attention away from everything but maneuvering my way through the overgrowth.

"Look! Up there," Merrin says, pointing to a sign that's barely readable.

Theeves Lot.

Now that we're secure in our orientation, we quickly retrace our steps to Widow's tree house. The night pulls the last strands of sunlight over the edge of the horizon. There is a possibility Anger will assume we'll return to retrieve our things, but I'm hoping against it. Hopefully we've made good enough time to grab our things and escape while she and K-Balt search for us elsewhere.

We reach the base of Widow's tree, our limbs sore from exertion. Merrin bends over, catching his breath.

"Don't stop. Not yet," I tell him. "Almost there."

I interlace my fingers to make a step for Merrin and, gritting my teeth, I boost him up to the lowest branch. We use the last of our energy to scale the tree trunk up to the outside porch. I try not to think about how much farther we have to go to be safe. One step at a time will do for now.

Merrin slaps the door with the side of his fist as he calls out Widow's name.

"It's Merrin and Darvin," he adds. I'm glad he thought to say our names so she'll be less likely to blast our brains out if she opens the door. I reach into my pocket and pull out the picture of my family so I can slide it under the door. Once I do, I hear the latches clicking, and she quickly pulls the door open just wide enough to show her face. I realize we haven't come up with a reason why we are returning without Anger.

"What are you doing?" she asks, holding out the picture in her hand. I take the photo and carefully return it to my pocket.

"Sorry, I really have to pee," Merrin says, offering a quick excuse for getting inside.

He tries to push in, but she stops him.

"Wait. Where is Anger?"

I try my luck with lying.

"She's lagging behind with your meat. She said to go on ahead because she had business to finish."

"I'm guessing y'all are too fragile to help her carry that,

huh?" she asks. I can't tell if she's doubting our story or sarcastically insulting us.

"She's not the type to accept help," Merrin responds.

She shrugs agreeably.

"Can we come in, or should we wait out here?" I risk asking, hoping my offering will diminish any suspicions she might have of us arriving before Anger.

Widow's eyes flash back and forth between ours. I can tell she's holding something back, and it's unsettling.

"What's wrong?" Merrin asks directly.

She peeks her head back behind the door, and I listen for who's inside. If Anger is in there, I might just jump off the balcony to try and get away. I don't hear adults, just the soft whispers of children.

Widow bites her lip, then speaks. "The kids. They ain't seen a man, at least not a good one, in a long time. They're afraid of them," she explains, confirming what Anger told us before.

"But I can't hide them forever," she says, more to herself than to us. She steps back hesitantly, half-heartedly giving us permission to enter. "Please be good to them. And stay away if they're scared."

In the flicker of candlelight, I see the thin faces and body frames of two girls and a boy, who is the smallest. They remind me of a batch of stray kittens, with their wildly patched clothes and wide eyes full of fear and weakness. They can't be eating more than one meal a day, if they're lucky. I feel an urge to pick all of them up in my arms, but I know I need to keep my distance.

"Babies, these nice fellas are from a long ways away.

THE REVELATION

They're special boys, just like your daddy. They're nice to people. And they got a gift for y'all."

Widow nudges me. "What special prize did you bring? See, they're like the Winter Fairy, but they just come one time. I think," Widow says clumsily.

The only things I have in my pocket are my flint fire starter, the picture of my mom, and the new photo of my parents, Jaykin, and me. The pictures won't work, but I don't want to part with my fire starter. It's one of the only pieces of home I have with me. My hand sinks aimlessly into my pocket. I signal Merrin with my eyes, hoping he'll have better luck, and he clumsily begins fumbling his fingers around his jacket pockets. His face lights in surprise, and I'm relieved to see him pull out something that resembles a smooth, polished pendant. For some reason, he hands it to me.

When I open my palm, I see it's a decorative charm. It's simple, but exceptionally well-crafted. I pull the black-gold charm closer to inspect it and trace my fingers over a downward-facing triangle enclosing a triquetra in the center. Above the triangle is a two-headed cross. The larger top bar connects to a tiny ring to support a chain.

I extend the charm in my hand toward the children, who simply push closer together. Widow reaches out and snatches the trinket from my hand. Her eyes remain fixated on it.

"Where did you get this?" she asks Merrin.

"I didn't get it. It was just in my pocket," he explains.

"That's not your pocket. It's my husband's."

"I know that. I'm just saying that's where I found it," he says defensively.

"What is it?" I ask her.

"It's Anger's," she says coldly. "You'll have to ask that bitch what it is." Her eyes narrow at us. I can only assume what story Widow has put together in her mind, but she's clearly infuriated with Anger. Her small son begins to cry, and his oldest sister, who's barely twice his size, picks him up in her frail arms.

"Why isn't she back yet? Where'd you say she is?"

I'm not sure if this is the right decision, but I feel like honesty might get us further with Widow in this moment.

"We don't know," I confess, releasing the tension I've been holding in my chest. "We ran away and left her behind. I don't know what she wants with us or why, but I need to get back to my family. If you can just let us grab our gear, we'll leave these clothes behind and get out of your way."

Widow's eyes are still fixated on the charm. She seems lost in a storm of thoughts and emotions until her youngest daughter, no older than six or seven years old, walks up to her mother's side and clutches her tightly. I can tell she's watching us as much as her eyes will let her. She looks almost exactly like her mom, except for her coiling dark hair.

She whispers something as close to her mom's ear as she can reach.

"Yeah, baby," Widow says, giving her daughter a soft kiss on the cheek. "Just give me one minute. I'm going to tuck them in. Just one." She holds up a finger while leading her children into their room.

"Is it okay if we change out here?" Merrin asks just before Widow closes the door.

"You can keep the clothes. I don't need them," she says, shutting the door behind her.

We begin shedding Nyle's clothes and throwing on our operative base wear so we can lock back into our Falcon gear.

THE REVELATION

Even though she suggested we keep her husband's clothes, we fold them neatly and place them at the foot of our bed before throwing back on our dirty clothes. Merrin helps secure me inside my Falcon gear before I return the favor. Out of habit, I check my battery. I'm momentarily confused because my diagnostic reading displays a full charge.

"Merrin, look. Check your battery. Mine's saying it's full."

He checks his quickly, and his gear signals full power as well.

"How did this happen?" I question, unaware Widow even had access to electricity.

Widow silently slips from within the bedroom and startles us when she says, "Anger had me charging them while y'all were gone."

"Thank you," I offer, and Widow nods in acceptance.

"All right, let's go," I tell Merrin. "We need to move fast."

Widow suddenly reaches out her hand, and it finds mine. She transfers the charm Merrin found in her husband's pocket back to me.

"It's yours now. Sell it. Keep it. Hell, you can eat it for all I care. Now, get," she says with just a touch of kindness.

The front door crashes inward. The kids scream in the bedroom as I'm tackled to the floor from behind.

"Turn them off! Turn them off, you fucking idiots!" Anger shouts.

"They're coming," K-Balt yells from outside.

I'm getting used to all my moments of fear and anxiety being associated with Anger's presence, so I let out my frustration as I struggle to free myself from her grip. I slam her back against the floor planks, momentarily pinning her down. She scissors her legs around me and somehow flips me over until she's on my back, pushing the side of my head into the floor with her hand.

"Stop fighting," K-Balt screams.

While Anger fights to keep me pinned, Merrin throws her off of me, and she crashes into the kitchen table. She quickly rolls over onto all fours, and she drops Merrin to the floor by kicking out his legs from under him.

From behind, K-Balt's hands twist my right arm into an unnatural position against my back. I cry out in pain, but she's unbothered and maintains her hold.

Widow screams angrily, cursing all of us.

"I reconnected a tracking signal to your Falcon gear. Turn them off now!" Anger screams, exasperated.

"Why did you do that?" Merrin growls back, hopping up from the floor. We both power down our suits and wait for an explanation. I'd hoped escaping would be easy. I shouldn't be surprised. Nothing about the past several days has been.

"In case you tried to run!" Anger shouts in Merrin's face as her words grind between her clenched teeth.

"What the devil is going on?" Widow yells, grabbing Anger by her shoulders.

"Are my kids safe? You tell me now if I need to move them," she says, growling the words from the back of her throat.

"No. No, don't leave. You'll be caught, and that will tie you directly to me," Anger tells her.

"*Who* is coming?" I demand.

"The Legionnaires," K-Balt barks at me. "They're already here searching for Falyn Dire. Any outgoing signal will pull up on their radars."

Anger begins frantically slapping down shelves and knocking pictures off the walls.

THE REVELATION

"Have you lost your fucking mind?" Widow yells. Her daughter cracks the door enough to where I can see one wide hazel eye.

"You were attacked," Anger says. "I attacked you, and you fought me to protect your kids. That's what you'll say."

"What?" Widow asks, raking both hands through her hair while Anger continues.

"That's what you'll say when they come for you."

"Why are the Legionnaires coming to my house?"

"They're coming for them!" Anger yells, pointing at Merrin and me.

My mind reels at the idea of intentionally getting caught by the Legionnaires. If what Anger said about Merrin and me being wanted for compromising the operatives mission is true, then it's possible that New Province contracted out to the Legionnaires so they could take us into custody. If I risk those odds to get away from Anger, Merrin could be the one who'll suffer the most.

"Listen to me," Anger says to Widow, whose stern eyes begin to fill with tears. "You don't know me. I tried to break into your house. That's it!"

Widow turns to her oldest daughter, who is still peeking through the crevice of the door. "Baby, shut that door. I need you to trust me. Keep them quiet in there, okay?"

Her daughter nods quietly and immediately obeys.

"Hit me," Widow says to Anger. "I can't spin that chickenshit lie with no bruises."

Anger stalls, her face rigid.

"Do it, bitch!" Widow taunts.

Anger slaps her across the face. Widow still wasn't prepared for it and lets out a little yelp. She bares her teeth and punches her fist into her hand before turning back toward Anger.

"Again. At least two more."

Anger obliges. She also squeezes her wrists and cuts Widow's skin with her fingernails. Fresh blood falls from Widow's nose and down her sharp chin. When she wipes her face, the blood from her nose smears into the slits scratched into her arm.

It's not until Widow asks me to grab a rope from underneath her kitchen sink that I realize I've been frozen in horror, helplessly spectating for the last minute or so.

"Tie me up nice and tight. Do it!" she instructs me, seemingly resolute.

Merrin helps me fasten the hemp rope tight enough to be convincing.

"We need to leave," Anger demands, throwing a small pack of supplies over her shoulders as we gently lay Widow on the floor.

Outside, from high above us, a faint searchlight drags over the house. For a second, I'm startled by a black figure swiftly bolting out the front door.

"No! Kalee!"

Anger's voice chases after K-Balt, who disappears into the night.

"She has your suit. She's trying to distract them," Widow says, confirming what Anger already knows. She seems torn between chasing after K-Balt and staying with us. For a brief second, Anger's lips tremble, and she stares at Widow. "I'm so sorry," she offers sincerely before looking to Merrin and me. "If you want any chance of seeing your family again, follow me." Then she leaps out through the front door.

THE REVELATION

Merrin and I look to Widow. Succumbing to the bleakness of the current situation, she doesn't bother fighting her tears. She uses our last moment together to say, "Follow her. She's your best chance. She knows what she's doing."

We're out of time. Merrin and I look at one another, and he nods. His eyebrows hang low below the creases in his forehead. We have no better option as we jump blindly into the night.

K-Balt is gone, but Anger's shadow is close enough for us to follow. Anger leads us in the opposite direction of the spotlight above us, which is aggressively chasing K-Balt. Aerocraft engines growl above our heads. A faint chorus of collective screams rises over the Black Valley.

Thankfully, the canopy provides a natural shield over us. Several streaks of green light flash down through the trees right behind Anger, striking the ground like night owls after mice. Merrin curses with each blast.

Anger darts back in our direction. She rapidly closes the distance between us. "Turn your Falcon gear on!" she yells.

"But you said they'll track us," Merrin yells back as we briefly stop, sheltered by the dense undergrowth of the woods.

"They've already found us. They're trying to hit us with a nexus grenade," Anger says, drawing in rapid breaths.

"If the Falcon gear is on, it'll fry the circuits," I tell her, confused at having to remind her.

"No. The energy core in your Falcon gear is surrounded by an electromagnetic shield, but your trackers are not."

"So the EMPs will disable the trackers but not the suits," Merrin says.

Anger grabs my arms, forcing my wrists together until my

armor powers on. Merrin simultaneously powers on his own Falcon gear.

"Now what?" I ask, reluctantly considering Widow's advice to follow Anger.

As if in answer, a burst of ice-blue light explodes only a few meters away. Anger dives out of the way as Merrin tackles me to the ground.

A barrage of electric currents rains down over Merrin and me like a lightning storm. Anger manages to avoid the pulsating cracks and sizzling hums striking all around us. A searing sting ripples over my tingling skin, and my muscles convulse spastically for a moment. I barely have time to recover before Anger snatches me off the ground.

We all manage to get up and shake ourselves back into a run. My leg feels numb, but my pulsing adrenaline is delaying the pain.

"Engage your helmets," Anger commands. "We've got to lose them."

She stops us in our tracks. We're only yards away from where the woods break off into the fringes of the Black Valley swamps. I look over my shoulder up to the distant hill where Widow's house stands. A hollow ache sinks low into my stomach. Lights brighter than anything Widow owns illuminate her home. There's no telling what the Legionnaires are doing to her, but I say a prayer that whatever story she comes up with keeps her and her kids safe.

"Disable your rear booster. I need to climb on your back," she tells Merrin.

"Why?" he protests.

"You'll have to fly both of us. K-Balt has my gear, and you won't make it far without my help."

THE REVELATION

We've never had a better opportunity to leave Anger behind. I watch Merrin to see if the same thought has formed in his mind. Widow's last words hang within my mind. *Follow her. She's your best chance.* When I look back at Anger, her eyes pierce into mine as if she's reading my thoughts.

"I know you want to leave, but those Legionnaires are after both of you. I'm only telling you what you need to know for your protection. Either trust me or I'll have to rip a suit off of one of your bodies and leave you both behind."

"No, you won't. You brought us this far for a reason, so you need us too," Merrin says boldly.

I'm not convinced she wouldn't do exactly what she just said, so I stay quiet. Merrin and Anger stare each other down, waiting for someone to make a move. Merrin decides first. He extends his hand toward her. "Climb on."

She hesitates, as if deciding how to exert her dominance over him, but she steps forward and grabs Merrin's arm. His helmet slides over his head as she climbs on his back. From behind, she reaches under his arms and fastens her hands over his shoulders.

"You ready?" Merrin asks me.

I engage my own helmet and nod.

"Stay low to the ground," Anger says.

We engage our thrusting power, and Merrin and I instinctively recall our training to select the reflective-terrain camo output so we can avoid easy detection. We blast off through the trees along the hem of the night sky. I would much rather be leaving the Black Valley without Anger, but she needs Merrin and me for a reason that I need to know. I don't trust her, but sometimes curiosity is much more dangerous and entangling than trust.

While we fly away leaving behind the barrage of Legionnaire EMP explosions, the rushing winds fill my nose with the stagnant stench rising from the putrid mire below. After a few miles flying against the wind, we're relieved by a vast stretch of thick forest. The dark shadows of the treetops sway beneath us like a swell of waves in an ocean storm. We're in the air for a solid thirty minutes before Anger and Merrin begin descending. I follow them.

Our thrusters fire forcefully as our feet prepare to connect with the ground. My momentum carries me forward a few steps, and then the forest floor is crunching beneath my feet. We've landed by a small running stream. Merrin drops to his knees, sticking his face down into the water to drink.

"Wait," Anger says, snatching him backward.

"It's running water," Merrin snaps, licking the water from his lips.

She unclips a pack from her shoulders and pulls out a water purifier. Anger draws the water into the clear tube and pushes against the compressor until the water filters into the drinking chamber. She takes a quick swallow and passes the rest to Merrin and me. While we drink, she hastily scrambles around, collecting small sticks and tinder. Once she has assembled it in a pile, she digs around in her pack. I can tell she's lost something.

"I need your fire starter," she says, reaching her hand toward me.

When I reach into my pocket, I feel Widow's charm tumble over my fingers as I pull out my fire starter. I extend my hand toward Anger but then pull it back.

"How did you know I had a fire starter?" I ask.

"Hand it over," Anger demands impatiently, her arm still outstretched.

"So you've been through my stuff."

"Obviously," Anger confirms.

Realizing the confrontation isn't worth my time, I reluctantly toss it to her, and she catches it. She strikes the flint into the tinder and blows the sparks so they stir up a small puff of smoke, which quickly turns into a blaze. Returning to her pack, she removes some metallic poles connected by several thin tinted squares. With Merrin's help, she unfolds the pieces and hastily assembles them to form a geometric dome, which she carefully places over the fire. I don't want to help her, so I stand by and watch.

"The heat can escape, but the light stays shielded," she explains to Merrin, mumbling as she works.

She sits down close by to warm her hands. I watch her pull three small packets of food out from her bag, and she positions them over the fire cover to heat up what's inside.

After warming his hands by the covered fire, Merrin walks away to join me around thirty feet away, where I sit plucking up tall pieces of grass and rolling them between my fingers. I've already detached from my Falcon gear, and he does the same.

After a few minutes of silently listening to the night whisper around us, Anger bluntly says, "Time to eat."

Neither of us responds. As hungry as I am, I'd rather not give her the satisfaction of coming when she calls.

"All right," she grunts, pushing herself off the ground. "You want to talk? Let's talk."

"What do you mean?" I ask tonelessly.

"I mean exactly what I said. Let's talk. Sit."

She motions for us to join her by the concealed fire. Merrin and I move slowly and cautiously. Still skeptical of what she's trying to do, neither of us cares to sit close to her, so we settle down together on the opposite side of the fire. She throws the warmed prepackaged food our way, keeping one for herself. We're too hungry to really care what's inside. I open it up and squeeze the mashed-potato-like paste into my mouth. It tastes like a blend of vegetables with salt, but it's not bad to swallow. She takes a swig of her water and wipes her mouth before tossing it to me.

"Words aren't my weapon of choice," Anger begins. "I've had better luck with actions. That's one of the reasons I brought you with me today. Some things just sink in more if you see them for yourself, so I am showing them to you."

"Why?" I ask, already taken aback by her offering a few sentences of conversation in a row.

"So you can form your own opinions. Right now, neither of you live in the same world as I do," she says, forcing the last bits of food clinging to the inside of her package into her mouth.

"What do you mean?" I ask.

"You live in a story written by RedCloud loyalists," she explains, rubbing her hands clean against the grass. "So does everyone else hiding behind the walls of the Guard system. Did you hear anyone mention Stones in the Black Valley? Did anyone there seem worried about getting perducorium?"

"You said something about how they weren't a threat to important people," Merrin says, seemingly unsure of his recollection of what Anger previously said.

"I said the Black Valley and its people aren't a threat to the ones in power, so no one cares about controlling them with fear or a disease," Anger says, looking between us as if to see if we're following her.

"So they don't worry about the Stones taking them over?" I ask, trying to make sense of the first significant conversation Anger has offered us.

"What would the Soots have that the Stones would want?" she questions, sitting up to shove a few pieces of wood into the fire.

"I don't know what Stones want, but I know they have violent instincts," I say, immediately feeling unsure of what I've just said. I remember the grief-stricken faces of Merrin's parents and the Stone who ended his life by stepping over the mountain's edge. In that disastrous encounter, the operatives had initiated the violence. Merrin has suddenly gone quiet. Without having to ask, I know his mind has taken him back to that night.

"You don't know that for yourself," Anger says, leaning down to blow the coals beneath the covered fire. "You're just repeating the story RedCloud wrote and convinced you to believe."

I'm struggling to follow what Anger is trying to say. I feel myself growing tense because even though she has finally agreed to talk, she seems more interested in discussing conspiracy theories than helping me understand why I am here with her.

"Okay, then tell me. What story would you have me believe? Why am I here?" I ask, struggling to hold on to what little patience I have left. Merrin puffs out a chest full of air and lies down on his back. He buries his face in the crook of his arm.

"You are here because I'm helping you," she says matter-of-factly, sitting back to stick the heels of her black boots near the edge of the fire.

I lift my hands to my face and rub my eyes, very aware of my rising urge to yell at Anger. Between my fingers, my eyes follow the thin sheets of smoke escaping the fire's cover as they dissipate into the empty darkness above.

"Okay, then. Why are *you* here?" I ask impatiently, getting to my feet.

"To help people like you rewrite the stores that were taken from you," she answers intently, holding her gaze on my eyes until I look away.

"How do you know what was taken from me?" I ask, my frustration washing over me until it shifts unexpectedly into a deep, sweeping wave of disappointment. I close my eyes and breathe in and out, as long as it takes for my words to come. "I wake up and go to bed every day thinking about how much I miss my family," I say, looking into Anger's dark eyes. "Merrin already lost his family, but my family still considers him one of us. But for all we know, they think we're dead. I don't know what story you want me to believe, but I don't need it. We have a family to go back to, but now we can't because you showed up."

She stares at me, and I stare back, determined not to let my eyes break away, even though I'm uncomfortable.

"Let me tell you a story about a family," Anger says calmly, getting to her feet. "There once was this young girl who got caught up in some terrible things much bigger than she could imagine. But it wasn't her fault." She slowly closes the gap between us. "One day, her friend was ambushed by a wandering horde of Stones, and while trying to save her bleeding friend, she was exposed to perducorium."

THE REVELATION

My heart races uncontrollably, and my back prickles with chills as she continues.

"She ran home as fast as she could, thinking maybe if she could just get back to her family and wash the dark-red stains from her clothes, everything would somehow be okay, but it was too late. The PRA knew, and they were already coming for her."

I've never told Anger about Ruma, but her story feels as if she's pulling the words straight from my past. I continue staring, completely vexed by her words, almost afraid for her to continue.

"She was tied up, and her family was pulled apart. For many years, she lived with questions that were only answered with lies that made her more confused, until she no longer knew what was real. Her own story was sacrificed—and so was she. There was no one there to stop her captors from turning her into someone else. Into something else entirely."

Anger's obscure eyes almost seem to be leaking with enticement.

"So that's what happened to you?" Merrin asks curiously, sitting up.

"No," she says. "That's what happened to Ruma. And I know where she is."

CHAPTER 15

When I hear Anger say Ruma's name, I can't reconcile her knowing my sister, much less knowing a part of her story I've never known. Somehow I feel as if she has violated my privacy by knowing a part of my history I didn't want her to know.

But how does she know?

"Who told you that story?" Merrin asks, as if reading my mind.

"Does it matter?" Anger asks, still waiting for my reaction, which is suppressed within the fog of my sudden emotional and cognitive processing.

"Of course it does," Merrin insists. "Whoever told you about Ruma knows us too." Merrin's eyebrows dig deep into his forehead. "Whoever that person is, they want us alive and need us for something."

"I think you've both had enough information for the night," she says dismissively.

THE REVELATION

"Where is Ruma?" I ask, forcing myself out of shock and into the conversation.

"I can't tell you that now," Anger says firmly.

"How can you expect me to be okay with not knowing more? I've been wondering what happened to her for almost my whole life, and you know but can't tell me?"

"Probably because she's lying and really doesn't know shit," Merrin scoffs, walking away from us.

Anger stalks after Merrin. Once she reaches him, she grabs his shoulder and pulls his body around to face her. Clenching a fistful of his undershirt, Anger stands nearly nose to nose with Merrin.

"Don't mistake your boldness for authority," she snarls, her voice thick with warning. "This has never been about you. Know your place."

Merrin glares fixedly back at Anger, and neither of them moves. His face remains strained as they stare each other down. Anger shoves him away, releasing his shirt. He stumbles briefly but stands his ground. As if satisfied with making her point, Anger returns to tend the fire while Merrin furiously walks away, stepping into the darkness. Anger's eyes follow him for a moment before she looks back at me.

"Come take this," she says, pulling something from within her pocket while squatting back down close to the concealed fire.

"What?" I ask sharply, not bothering to hide my agitation from my face.

"It's for sleep. You'll need rest for tomorrow," she explains, extending an open palm cupping a barely visible pill.

"You're not going to shut me up by giving me drugs again," I say disdainfully.

"It's not like that," she says, shaking her head. "It's a sedative."

Between my instincts and the firing triggers formed from my past experience with Anger offering me the chenoo, I silently refuse her offer. Knowing her well enough to not expect further conversation, I decide to look for Merrin instead.

As I walk away, Anger stops me, saying, "I know you don't understand what I do. I don't expect you to. But prematurely sharing information before necessary action only creates liability."

I repeat her words in my mind until they make sense to me. This does little to alleviate my anxiety.

"You don't have to take it, but if you do, it will calm your mind," she says.

I turn around to see her once again offering me the tiny pill.

After a brief hesitation, I begrudgingly walk to where she sits, just close enough to take the pill from her hand, along with some purified water she's offering. I pretend to take the pill, but when she's not looking, I spit it back into my hand and slip it into my pocket. I don't trust Anger, but making her think that I do might encourage her to be less cautious and methodical in her potential strategies of deception. Anger stretches out over the grass and pulls out her pipe. Disgusted in more ways than one by the sight of her pipe, I walk into the darkness once again to try and find Merrin.

The little bit of information Anger gave me is enough to have my mind swirling as I high step my way through the tall, rustling grass. Thoughts fire across my head like shooting stars, bright for a moment and vanishing the next without clear resolve.

THE REVELATION

What's so strange is that I don't even know Ruma anymore. To a large extent, my parents shaped the ideas I have of her now. They wanted me to remember her so she'd always be with me. But I haven't seen her in thirteen years, so who I imagine her to be now isn't much more than a preservation of who she was as my thirteen-year-old sister. Ruma's disappearance became a source of motivation for me. I've tried to honor her memory by being strong and unrelenting with my training and everything else I do, but it's made Ruma more like an ethereal force of inspiration than my living, breathing, twenty-six-year-old sister existing somewhere out there in the world. I don't know if I ever really believed I would see her again, but now I'm closer to finding her than ever before.

With each trudging step up the overgrown hillside, my mind and body more persistently demand rest, but I don't feel good about the way things left off with Merrin. It doesn't take long to spot his shadow against the starlit sky. He's standing on a naturally formed ledge ahead of me that overlooks the surrounding stretch of grasslands bordering the forest. As I approach, he turns his ear in my direction, but he doesn't bother to look back.

"You okay?" I ask, allowing him some space.

"Does it matter?" he mumbles stiffly, his arms crossing tightly below his chest.

"Yes. That's why I'm asking."

"Then no."

I pause for a second, trying to figure out what's going on with him and what I can say to help.

"What's going on?"

"Just forget it," he says, irritated.

"No. I came to talk."

"I don't want to."

I'm not used to seeing Merrin so defensive and closed off. His blunt responses test my patience.

"What's your problem?" I ask.

"You!" he yells, finally facing me.

I pause for a moment, confused. "What do you mean?" I ask, my frustration rising.

"All of this. It's all about you and your sister. Anger needs you to get to her."

"What are you talking about?" I ask. Merrin and I have had plenty of disagreements in the past, but he's never looked at me with the contempt I'm seeing now on his hardened face.

"Don't you ever wonder why she's protecting us? Do you think she cares about you finding your sister again? She didn't give a shit about me watching my family die, but Ruma, she's worth it all, *right*?"

He stops to take a deep breath and wipes the corner of his eye.

"I don't know what to say," I tell him finally, taking a step back. I'm torn between recognizing his hurt and my own offense at his words. My eyes wander out over the tree-speckled grasslands and the hanging stars until my words find me.

"I should've asked you about your parents," I say, trying to swallow the tightness in my throat. "It's been on my mind a lot too, but I've been scared to bring it up." It's both a confession and a realization. "I know there's nothing I can do to make it better, but I feel your grief too. But I should've asked you. I'm really sorry."

We both soak in the weight of the night. I don't know how to continue or what else to say, but I commit to waiting here

THE REVELATION

until he decides what he needs next. He turns around again toward the open stretch of moon-washed prairie. With his back to me, I assume he might just need time to process. I don't want to leave him alone, but maybe that's what he needs.

"I've been trying to remember them," Merrin says just as I begin walking away. I stop to listen. "One time in school I wrote a poem about them. I really wanted to win this poetry contest because the first-place prize was a dinner for four at Stacks, and I wanted to take my family there for my mom's birthday. When I wrote it, I knew I was going to win.

"But when they announced the winners at school, they didn't call my name. I cried and pretended like I was sick so I could go home, but my teacher knew why I was upset. Dad came with Mom to pick me up, which he never did because he had work, and I remember we walked home a different route than usual until we ended up right in front of Stacks. They had Raythe meet us there, and we all ate as a family as if I had won. That was probably the best meal I ever had with them." Tears are falling down his face.

We've both lost a sibling, but his story has taken a completely different turn from mine. All he had was a sickening flicker of hope to see his family again, and that was lost when he watched his mother die and his father disappear again.

"They loved you so much," I say, hoping he truly knows it.

"I shouldn't have said that," he says, wiping his eyes.

"Said what?"

"It hasn't been all about you," he says, looking at me again.

"That's okay. I know."

"I just wish I had something to help keep me going."

"You have your brother," I say.

Doubt flashes over his face. "No. He could've died years ago. I'll probably never know."

"You can't think like that," I tell him. "I thought the same thing about Ruma. Sometimes I just made myself pretend she was alive."

"I don't want to pretend," he says wearily. "That doesn't work for me."

"Then hope. That's stronger anyway."

Merrin hesitates, as if he's cautiously choosing his next words. "What if Ruma's not who you've imagined? What if she's not what you've been hoping for all these years?"

"I don't know," I say quietly, and we both stand in silence.

I'm sure Merrin is just trying to protect me from the same hurt he felt upon seeing his parents. My mind is tired from digging up thoughts I've worked hard to bury. The wind sneaks up around us, and a herd of gray clouds ride overhead like wild horses in the moonlight.

"You know what's crazy?" Merrin asks me as he half-heartedly reaches out his fingers as if trying to catch the wind.

"What?"

"That we've seen more of the country in the past few weeks than we've seen in our whole lives, and we haven't really stopped to say anything about it. This place is gorgeous."

"I haven't really thought about that," I say, taking a second to breathe in the night air.

"That looks like it's going to get pretty nasty," Merrin says, pointing at the clouds overhead. "We should get back to Anger."

"Maybe she'll get struck by lightning tonight and we can run home," I say, trying not to smile.

"It wouldn't be the worst thing," he says, unable to hide his own grin.

We haven't talked about what's next since our failed attempt to run home, but something in me has shifted since hearing Anger say she knows where Ruma is. Even though we'd both be happy to get away from Anger, I'm not sure where my stirred curiosity will leave me once I've had time to rest and process.

We return to find the fire has tapered out, just like Anger. I need sleep, but I'm not sure if my thoughts are going to allow that, regardless of my exhaustion. My fingers find the pill Anger gave me in my pocket, and I swallow the tablet along with a quick gulp of water.

Within minutes of laying my head down, my heartbeat slows drastically. I focus on my breathing as the gentle darkness settles over my mind like a thick blanket.

Asa's hooves rip the earth like loose flesh as we race across the land beyond the Southern Guard wall. Once we cross a shallow run of water, I hop off and let Asa turn back to drink.

After I secure his reins to a nearby tree, the sky suddenly darkens. I grab a few nearby exposed roots that run down the back of an eroded embankment and pull myself up to see a blood moon melting in the sky. The dark, crimson liquid pours down and spills like liquid fire over the horizon and sets the earth ablaze.

I try to find Asa to return home, but as my eyes pass over the starlit blackness, I realize I'm alone. I see the tracking-line markers blinking in the distance, and then they disappear entirely. I begin running through the low, dead branches of gnarled trees, which hang down like skeletal fingers waiting to claw me.

I come upon a shallow grave dug into the center of a small cove within the trees, and in the dim starlight, I peer into the dark hole. A body pushes from beneath a layer of soil. Blood runs down the dirty face of the decaying figure. As it rises up from its grave, I recognize the mangled body of Commander Locke.

"You left me," he groans, and I'm paralyzed, unable to move or scream. As Commander Locke reaches for me, a sudden agony grips his face and he abruptly dissolves into gray smoke. My intense urge to escape what I'm seeing jerks me into the early morning light.

As I awaken, my head feels swimmy and slightly throbs with pulsating beats of pain. My neck and shoulders lay stiff against the dirt. The wind forces me upright as it kicks up some of the smoky ash from last night's coals into my face. I don't think I moved all night long. I begrudgingly make myself stand up. Squinting my eyes, I look around for Anger or Merrin.

Merrin is walking about twenty feet away from me. From the way he's moving, he's clearly been up for a while. I'm not sure what time it is, but the low rising sun has yet to dry the residual dew coating the rolling waves of grass.

I drag myself following behind him as he makes his way down to a nearby stream to wash up. I do the same. The smoke dried out my eyes, and rubbing them just makes it worse, so the cool water brings much appreciated relief. The stream unwinds from the skirt of our small mountain and disappears into its rocky folds below.

"You sleep okay?" I ask Merrin.

THE REVELATION

"Not really," he offers. "Did you?"

I shake my head and decide not to mention taking the sedative.

After Merrin washes up, he leaves with his water filter filled. I take extra time to wash the night away, massaging the kinks out of my neck as best as I can. After I drink a few gulps of water, my stomach wakes up and is ready for food.

When I return to our camp, the fire's coals glow with life as Anger cooks the breakfast she caught for us.

We all fill our stomachs with enough meat to keep up our energy for the day. No one cares to talk, so I find myself listening to each of them smacking. We don't sit long before we get moving toward another collection of mountains in the distance. Resuming our same method of flying from last night, we follow the stream against its flow for a while. The way the sunlight swims in the water mesmerizes me.

Just as we reach the foot of the mountain range, Merrin and Anger land together, and I plant my feet down beside them.

"It won't be safe for us to boulder-hop while I'm hanging on your back. We'll need to climb on foot for a while," she says.

We hike over endless rock faces, climbing higher by the minute. I say a few comments to Merrin, but he answers me flatly, so I fall back into silence. We continue like this the entire day, rarely stopping for breaks. I'm not even sure where we're going. I hope we're on our way to Ruma, but I know better than to ask while we're traveling. I plan to wait until our next stop to revisit last night's conversation.

The high back of the mountain shields us from the sun a few hours before nightfall, so we don't make it very far before we have to stop. This time we have no stream, so we are forced to rely solely on the water we collected at the previous stop.

Anger carries out the same fire ritual from the night before, and she tosses us another condensed meal.

"I thought we ran out?" I say.

"Why would you think that?" Anger asks.

"Because you had to hunt this morning. I figured we had already eaten what we had."

"Just eat," she says without looking up from her own food.

"Where are we going?" I ask.

"I'm eating," she mumbles through a mouthful of warm paste.

"Do you ever have a normal conversation?" I ask her impatiently. "I mean with anyone? Ever?"

She keeps eating, as if she's unaware I exist, so I decide to push some of her buttons.

"Did your parents not teach you basic social skills, or did you just decide they weren't important?"

Anger stops eating long enough to burrow her dark eyes into mine for a moment, and then she resumes her dinner.

"People don't hide unless they have something to lose," I say accusingly, unbothered by her glare.

"Yeah," Merrin joins in. "You definitely need us for something."

"Yeah. You need us to help you. What is it—"

Anger shoves her hand toward me, cutting me off, and I can't breathe. My bones quiver like I'm experiencing an internal earthquake, and it's like my blood is pushing against my skin. The constricting vibrations squeeze so tightly I feel myself fading from consciousness. After a few seconds, she releases me from whatever force she held me with, and I fall onto my back.

THE REVELATION

I lie shaking and struggling to catch my breath while Anger walks toward me. She stands over me, looking down.

"Be careful what you ask. You might not like my answer."

Whatever motivation I had to ask questions evaporates.

"Now get up," she commands.

Trying to recover my breath, I ignore her. Still in shock, my body isn't ready to move, but in my internal rage, I hope she thinks I'm just being rebellious.

Merrin yells a string of curse words at Anger. She quickly subjects his body to the same pressure she put me under, her hand shaking as she stretches it toward Merrin. He chokes as his body hangs stiffly in the air. I grab a nearby rock and fling it toward Anger's head. She ducks out of the way, releasing Merrin from her grasp.

A sudden streak of electricity momentarily blinds us as a thunderous crack rumbles the ground. Anger drops flat. She's sprawled out on her stomach over the rocks so that I can't see her face.

Merrin catches his breath and shouts, "Holy shit! Was that lightning?"

I'm not sure what happened, but I move quickly to Anger's motionless body.

"I don't think that came from the sky," I tell Merrin, my blood going cold. I feel a strange instinctive caution swelling in my stomach, as if someone is watching us. I glance over my shoulder and catch movement in the corner of my eye that ignites my adrenaline.

Not fifty yards away, two wild men rapidly close in on us as they leap down the rock faces like mountain lions descending upon their prey.

CHAPTER 16

My first instinct is to raise my hands in surrender. It's my best chance at survival considering my current physical state. Merrin hasn't noticed the rugged aggressors bounding toward us because he is too busy trying to shake Anger awake now that he sees she's breathing.

"Merrin! Stop!" I say, and he freezes.

"What?" he asks and then quickly answers his own question as he spots the two men bouncing from rock to rock with incredible agility. We'd certainly have a better chance surrendering than we would running.

One of the men isn't wearing a shirt, and from the looks of his tanned skin, I'm guessing he doesn't make a habit of wearing one. His long hair matches the length of his beard, both of which are rugged and dark brown like soil.

"You both okay?" he asks kindly, as if he expects us to trust him after what we've just seen. The closer the men get, the more I can see they look very similar. They might even be twins. Neither is holding a weapon, so I'm not sure how Anger was struck. Regardless, their size and build still heightens my anxiety. The other man wears a worn shirt and shorts that are so stained that I can't tell what the original color of either would've been. He hangs back several feet from his brother and slightly waves at us, adding a respectful nod.

"I hope you guys weren't friends with her," the shirtless man says.

Merrin and I both stand dumbfounded.

"We've been watching her for a while, and when she went after you, we figured you guys might need some help," the other says as he scratches his ribs beneath his tattered, dirty shirt.

"How did you do that?" Merrin asks, finally able to speak.

"You mean shocking her?" the shirtless man asks.

"*You* shocked her?" I ask, my mouth dropping open.

"Yeah. We did," he confirms. "We both did. Together."

"We're twins," the shirted brother chimes in again as he approaches us.

"I know it's probably confusing enough already. My name's Edwin," the shirtless, longhaired twin continues, "and my brother is Brooks."

As Brooks comes closer, I notice that while the facial similarities between he and his brother are striking, his frame is slightly thinner. He stoops down over Anger's body and pokes her shoulder a few times. I'm relieved to see her move. Regardless of my growing dislike of Anger, she's my only potential link to Ruma. Her limbs move stiffly as if she's just woken up from a long cryogenic sleep.

"Ah, she'll be fine," Brooks says, looking up at us. His clear blue eyes seem friendly enough. "The battery of that device she's wearing on her arm will probably be messed up, but other than that, she'll be all right."

"That might not be good news to you based on how she was treating you," Edwin says, smirking.

It's too soon to trust them, but I feel safe enough to introduce myself.

"My name is Darvin," I say, extending my hand to Brooks.

He hesitates to do the same but sticks his hand out eventually. "Well, this will feel a little weird, but it's just electricity."

I pull my hand back a moment. "What do you mean?"

"When people shake our hands, they feel a strange tingle. It's more awkward if you don't say anything. Here, just watch."

He grabs my hand for a brief shake, and my whole arm feels like it's fallen asleep.

"Whoa! Whoa. That was weird," I say, trying to shake off the numbing sensation.

"I told you."

Merrin's face strains. "Are you—"

"Twins?" Brooks interrupts.

"No. I heard you say that. I mean...how?" Merrin asks, stumbling over his words.

"Are you like her?" I ask, looking down at Anger. She still hasn't come around enough to try and stand. Even after seeing Anger's strange abilities and hearing the men say they shocked her, I still feel ridiculous asking.

"We have a genetic-reversal ability too, but ours is different," Brooks says. I look to Merrin to see if he understands, but his eyebrows are furrowed.

"Do you think she escaped?" Edwin asks Brooks, pointing

at Anger. "We thought we were the only ones to have ever done that."

"I don't know," Brooks says. "That could be disappointing. Do either of you know where she's from?"

"What's her name?" Edwin asks, adding to Brooks's question.

"We don't know her real name. She says it's Anger," Merrin explains.

"What do you mean by *did she escape?*" I ask, wondering if they could be referring to wherever Anger came from before she was rescued by Widow's husband, Nyle.

"Maybe she was there before us," Brooks says to Edwin. Then he turns back to us. "So you really don't know her?"

"She was our commander elite in Special Ops training," Merrin explains, "but we got lost, and then she saved us from some Legionnaires. We didn't really know why they were coming after us, so we've been stuck with her ever since."

"We're both from Southern Guard," I tell them.

Brooks nods.

"So why did she save you?" Edwin asks.

"We were hoping to figure that out soon," Merrin says, answering for both of us.

"Do you know the effects of her genetic reversal?" Brooks breaks in.

"What does that mean?" Merrin asks.

"It looked like telekinesis," Edwin says to Brooks before turning back to us. "I assumed you both knew, but maybe I'm wrong. Now I'm confused." His voice trails off.

"Yeah. Let's start over," Brooks says, rubbing his forehead. "So you knew she could telekinetically move things before today. Right?"

"Yes. But we don't know exactly what it is or where it comes from," I say.

"She told Darvin her power came from a magic ring, and he believed her at first, but..." Merrin says, letting his sentence abruptly end after noticing my immediate vexation.

They both give a little chuckle. I'm sure Merrin feels the affirmation of their laughter was worth unintentionally embarrassing me.

"It wasn't like that," I quickly throw out.

"So she's never mentioned the Revelation Territory?"

"No." My growing awareness of how little I seem to know about New Province is making me uneasy.

"Wait. Yes. We've heard that name," Merrin says. "That's what Widow was telling us about."

I'd forgotten. "Right. No. Yes. We've heard of that."

"She had to have come from there," Brooks says.

"How do you know?" I ask, feeling enlivened by the openness of our conversation.

"We can feel the energy of her genetic reversal coming off of her," Brooks tells us. "It's very strong. Every person gives off energy waves. You may be able to feel them too sometimes if you pay attention, but we just have a particularly heightened ability to manipulate energy."

"We work together to control electrical impulses," Edwin explains. It's a lot simpler than you'd think."

"I doubt it," Merrin says, unconvinced.

"Where is the Revelation Territory?" I ask.

"I could just about spit on that slave hole from here. It's right behind us," Edwin says, looking back over his shoulder where a rising plateau stretches out like a rocky shoulder leaning into the fading sky.

THE REVELATION

"Do you think that's where she was taking us?" Merrin asks me.

"You don't *go* to the Revelation Territory unless you're captured and taken there," Edwin tells us.

"If they're diamonds, she could be a jeweler," Brooks suggests to Edwin, who quickly reads the confusion on my face.

"Jewelers abduct and sell people who have potential genetic-reversal abilities. If that's you, then you're a *diamond amongst Stones.*"

"What's the purpose of the Revelation Territory?" Merrin asks.

"That's a loaded question, but it's a medical and scientific research facility privately funded by RedCloud Industries. Well, Empire. Now they're saying RedCloud Empire."

"So that could be why RedCloud Legionnaires were trying to capture us when Anger saved us," I say, making the connection out loud.

"She doesn't look like a savior to me," Edwin says plainly, as if he's surprised we haven't figured this out before now. "She's attacking you and won't tell you where you're going—that sounds more like you're being held prisoner."

"Why do you care?" Merrin asks aggressively, catching us all off guard.

"No need to be offended," Edwin says.

Anger's croaking groan startles us all. She weakly pushes herself up off the rocky dirt and begins inspecting her cuts and bruises.

Edwin and Brooks focus intently on Anger.

"We can feel what you're trying to do. It won't work against us, so stop now," Edwin says without the slightest hint of fear.

Brooks takes his own jab. "We'll just reverse the channel of your energy back onto you." He extends his hands toward her. "Can you feel that?"

Anger's entire body stiffens.

"Give it up," Edwin tells Anger.

She seems to realize she's fighting a losing battle. The pressure releases from her body, and she lies back on the mountain bed for a moment, breathing heavily before sitting up again. Suddenly Merrin's body shoots up thirty feet above where we stand.

"Stop! Stop! Bring me down!" Merrin yells.

I demand the same as I step toward Anger's outstretched arm. She's already stated that her intentions for intercepting us have never been about him. Merrin seems to believe her too, so if he's right, then I'm terrified of what she might do to him to leverage her control over me.

"Put him down," Brooks demands calmly.

"We've seen worse things than strangers dying," Edwin confesses, unmoved.

Rain droplets begin falling in a spastic rhythm as we stare at one another.

"So you haven't told them where you're taking them?" Brooks asks. His face darkens, and his eyes glisten with light even in the falling darkness.

"Some knowledge is dangerous. You should know that," Anger snaps.

"So is deception and manipulation," Edwin snaps back.

Anger suddenly drops Merrin, and he screams as he falls. Edwin, Brooks, and I jump forward to try and catch him, but we're too far away. She stops Merrin's body less than a foot away from crashing into the rocks. Our temporary fear seems to satisfy Anger.

"And no. You're not the only ones to have escaped the Revelation Territory," she says, getting to her feet. She releases her hold on Merrin, and he drops to his hands and knees, breathing heavily. I rush to his side and hold him down as if to protect him from being lifted again.

The sky breaks free and releases a steady downpour. In the distance, my eyes catch a sideways vein of lightning streaking out across the sky, quickly followed by a raw crack of thunder. Several thoughts hit my mind at the same time, forming a sudden feeling of epiphany, which grows as I lace my thoughts together. With Anger close by, I'll have to wait for the right moment to process my thoughts with Merrin.

"How did you escape?" Brooks asks Anger.

"I don't know why you're surprised when you've apparently done the same."

"No. It wasn't the same," Brooks says, standing alert as if trying to anticipate Anger's next move.

She isn't showing any signs of interest on her face, but she lingers in silence as if waiting for more.

"We need to find cover," Anger suggests.

The twins exchange a short glance as thunder rumbles over the dark storm clouds. Brooks subtly nods at Edwin.

"Follow us," Edwin commands.

Whether out of curiosity or having no better choice, Anger lets the twins lead us deeper into the mountains.

"You all right?" I whisper to Merrin.

"No," Merrin says flatly, so I leave him alone. I'm not used to seeing him carry so much pain and frustration. I know he needs space, but it's beginning to feel disconcerting and isolating.

The sun is taking its last breath over the horizon, so I can't see much of anything in the distance. A couple of times I slip and have to catch myself from falling off the various stones as we leap across the wet mountainside. Brooks and Edwin easily scale our path, leading us up to a rocky plateau, but the rest of us struggle to keep our footing as we trail behind. I reach my hand over my brace-comm and almost power it on to finish the ascent, but my pride decides against it. By the time Anger, Merrin, and I reach the brothers, we're bent over our knees and panting heavily.

"You see those lights out there, and way over there?" Edwin asks, stretching his arm out into the night. The rain mixes with the moonlight and makes his skin look like wax. We've all been too busy watching where our feet have been hitting the rocks to notice the ghostly collections of lights flickering across the darkness on two separate mountain peaks.

Edwin continues. "Those lights closest to us there, that's the Patmos Monastery and a school for young boys. We were raised there. And those lights way over there are from the sister convent, St. Mary's Haven for girls."

"What do they do there?" Merrin asks.

"They're both live-in schools for the children produced by the Revelation Territory," Brooks says.

"Wait," Merrin says, "what do you mean by *produced*?"

"It's honestly hard to explain," Brooks says evasively as he continues leading us, "and you have your own problems to deal with now, so I wouldn't worry about it. We'll be able to see them both better in the morning."

My stomach is agitated by my unnerving interpretation of

what he meant by the word *produced*, as if they create children on some kind of scientific assembly line. As disturbed as I felt walking through the impoverished slums of the Black Valley, this thought makes me feel even more estranged from the world I thought I knew.

We continue moving as the thunder chases the lightning into the night. We slip down a natural stairway into the mouth of a dark cave. I hesitate to enter, but the relentless pelting of the rain makes my decision a little easier. Pulsing wind echoes within the cave, as if it's trying to catch its breath like we are. A quick strike of electricity flashes our silhouettes against the hollowed walls. One of the twins sparks a fire from his fingertips into a pile of dry wood. The firelight gently fills our temporary shelter.

"So you like to show off," Anger says.

Brooks pays her no attention, but Edwin scrunches up his face.

"Convenience, actually," Edwin says.

"Merrin," I say, drawing more attention to myself than I intend. Anger watches me as I walk toward him. "Come with me," I whisper.

We settle down at the far edge of our rock shelter, just out of reach of the water pouring down in broken sheets. The moonlight filters through the rainfall, adding a smooth white shimmer to the puddles forming on the cave floor. I take extra caution to quiet my voice so the echoes don't carry to the wrong ears.

"They said they were in the Revelation Territory because of their genetic-reversal abilities, right?"

"The twins? Yeah," Merrin says. "And Anger was there at some point too and escaped."

"Right. Professor Bolden told us about rare cases where some people were exposed to perducorium and their DNA shifted to help their immune systems combat the disease. Remember? She wouldn't really answer other questions when we asked her about it."

"So if Anger and the twins were exposed to perducorium, then we're screwed," Merrin says, his face stiffening.

"No," I say, pausing to take a breath. "Not if their bodies did the whole genetic-reversal thing. If that's where they take people who are resilient to the disease..."

I see my thoughts click across Merrin's face.

"What if that happened to Ruma?" he asks, forgetting to whisper.

"Who's Ruma?" Edwin asks. We both turn back to them in alarm. "Everything echoes in a cave," Edwin says, shrugging.

Merrin looks at me, waiting to see if I'll respond.

"That's not your business," Anger cuts in.

"She's my sister," I say, answering the question more to annoy Anger.

"What happened to her?" Edwin asks, seemingly concerned as he sits up from where he was lying by the fire.

"Is that where she is?" I ask, walking toward Anger. "Is she in the Revelation Territory?"

After a moment of sitting in silence, Brooks addresses Anger. "If you made up this story about his sister being in the Revelation Territory just so you could sell them off, then we'll personally make sure you burn in hell as soon as possible."

Anger tilts her head slightly, as if she's amused. Her fingers glide over her brace-comm, which, contrary to what Brooks suggested, seems to have been unaffected by the twins' previous electrical shock. Within seconds, a holographic image of someone's face appears above her arm.

"Everything okay?" asks a hooded man with a richly compelling voice.

Edwin and Brooks's faces seem frozen in awe as they silently stare at the projected image of the man wearing an elaborately embossed golden headband. Whoever he is, they clearly recognize him.

"Just making sure you're close by," Anger says.

"Of course."

Anger touches her pointer finger and her thumb on either side of her eyebrows and gently slides them down her face, as if removing an invisible mask. The cloaked man does the same before Anger dismisses the holographic image.

"You have no idea the host I could have at your throat within minutes if I made the call," Anger says coldly.

"Who was that?" I ask without reverence for her attempt to humble the twins.

I wait for a response that doesn't come from Anger.

Edwin breaks the silence with his answer. "That was Falyn Dire."

"Where have I heard that name?" Merrin asks.

"He's the leader of the Saints. They're the only public anti-RedCloud coalition I know," Edwin explains reverently.

"You met with him above Widow's house, didn't you?" I say.

Anger appears to lose interest in the conversation and steps toward the fire to warm her hands.

Seemingly intrigued, Edwin approaches Anger until he's close enough to touch her. "You're not trying to get people into the Revelation Territory, are you? You're going to help them break out."

"It must be lonely searching for purpose in other people's business," Anger says contemptuously. "Stay out of my way." She leans in even closer to Edwin without breaking eye contact.

"We can help you," Brooks says kindly, I assume to help break the tension between his brother and Anger.

"No. We don't need you," Anger says, rudely. "You'd be chasing a snake's tail when you can't see its head."

"You don't know what we know," Edwin says. "We can pretend you followed us here because of the rain, but you want to know how we got out."

"Then what of it?" Anger barks. "Let's hear your little story."

"What's your problem? Do you even care about them?" Brooks asks, flashing a glance at us.

"She obviously isn't helping out of charity," Edwin jabs.

"And what about you?" Anger asks, nearly spitting her words. "Do you make a habit of risking your life for strangers?"

Neither Edwin nor Anger are backing down.

"I don't know what your deal is," Edwin says, "but it looks to me like *you're* the snake, and I see your head just fine."

As soon as Edwin finishes his sentence, every hair on my body stands on end. The current of an electric charge tingles across my skin.

"Don't!" Brooks yells, extending his hand toward Anger and Edwin. "You're wasting your time."

Flickers of electricity pop between Edwin's fingers as if they're carrying a storm. My skin feels like a thousand tiny ants are marching over my body.

"Stop! That's enough," Brooks shouts again.

THE REVELATION

Anger and Edwin stare one another down as if waiting to see who will strike first. Edwin's pupils glisten as they reflect the electric currents hopping across his fingertips.

Merrin darts from within the cave out into the black downpour. I chase after him, leaving the twins and Anger to handle their own problems. With the two of us gone, Anger won't be able to use us as pawns in her power struggle against the twins.

"Merrin!" I shout out into the night, trying not to slip as I'm pelted by cold rain.

Merrin's shadow is sporadically relieved by the strobing flashes of lightning. I yell his name again, and this time he stops, standing soaked and breathing heavily. Thunder shudders faintly around me as if the distant sky is complaining to the surrounding mountains.

As soon as I reach Merrin, he says, "I can't do it. I can't be in there anymore."

"Me either," I agree, still catching my breath.

Merrin sits down on a smooth slab of rock. The insides of his elbows cradle his knees, and he clasps his hands together. I join him by his side and duck my head down to keep the rain from my eyes. We both submit ourselves to the downpour until we're so drenched that the persistent rain becomes nothing more than a tranquil sensation on our skin. I feel a welcomed sense of peace within the storm that's neither asking nor expecting anything from me.

"Is it okay if I join you?" The nearby voice startles us. Brooks calmly walks to meet us.

Left with no real choice, we both nod, and he sits down on my left side.

"Are they going to be okay back there?" Merrin asks,

concerned. I'm also surprised Brooks left his brother with Anger, considering the tangible tension between them.

"They're working things out now," he says, unconcerned.

I can only imagine how to interpret what he means, but I'm just thankful I'm not a part of it.

"I promise you, we can help you," Brooks continues, nudging me with his elbow. After spending time with Anger, I'm leery of trusting anyone who offers unsolicited help.

"Why do you want to help us?" I ask, for the both of us.

"Because we know what it's like to lose a sister," Brooks says sincerely, as if he's reluctantly pushing the words from his mouth. He puffs out, blowing the rain dripping from his beard.

We wait in silence, anticipating more, but Brooks says nothing else until Merrin asks, "What happened to her?"

Brooks leans in front of me to look at Merrin.

"She's alive, but we haven't seen her since before we escaped. She's lives at St. Mary's Haven—it's basically a feeder school. They raise the girls who'll eventually become citizens of the Revelation Territory."

"So if you know where she is, then why do you say you lost her?" Merrin asks.

"We can't get into St. Mary's Haven. Even if we did, there's no guarantee we'd find her, and we'd risk getting sent back to the Revelation Territory."

Brooks slicks back some wet hair that sticks against his forehead and wipes the water from his thick eyebrows.

"Honestly, we're hoping Anger will find our undiscovered way out of the Revelation Territory useful enough to make a bargain with us. She seems to have the right connections through Falyn Dire that might could help us get our sister out.

But if not, we can at least feel good about giving someone else the chance to see his sister again."

My gut tells me Brooks is being genuine, so I choose to believe him because I get it. I'm not sure what Anger has planned, but if there's the slightest chance she can help me find Ruma, I'm willing to sacrifice suffering through the uncertainty of not knowing the big picture.

"So Ruma is in the Revelation Territory?" I ask, squeezing out my words.

"More than likely," Brooks confirms.

"Why would she be there?" Merrin asks.

"I think you know why," Brooks answers softly, as if to cushion the shock.

"Holy shit," Merrin mumbles under his breath. "So she *is* one of you guys."

The thought instantly overloads my brain. Suddenly I'm remembering the moment Ruma was taken away, playing it over and over again in my mind. Did the PRA agents know then? Did the vehicle she left in have different markings? Maybe? I always assumed she was taken to purge camp and shipped off to a distant Stone reservation once she was confirmed as testing positive.

I shake my head for a moment and ask Brooks, "How can we get to her? I want to know exactly where the Revelation Territory is. I know it's close."

"Come with me," he says, pushing himself up. He helps Merrin and me up, and we carefully follow him across the sloping ledges, trying not to step into the small puddles of water forming in the rock indentations. The wet surface of the mountains catches just enough moonlight for me to see where I'm going.

Brooks stretches out his hand. "See that mountain crest over there? The tallest one?" He points toward a dark shadow not two miles away.

"Yes."

"Edwin showed you where the Patmos Monastery lights were, right? Okay. See the sister peak to the left over there? St. Mary's Haven. Now follow your eyes straight down the center of those two mountains into the valley down there."

"I don't see anything. It's just trees."

"Wait for it. Keep your eyes open and wait for lightning to strike," Brooks instructs.

We wait for a while, but nothing happens.

"What are we looking for?" Merrin asks, sneaking up behind us. Immediately after he asks, a slit of lightning splits the sky below us. Only for a few seconds, we see a massive portion of the tree canopy disappear, revealing an expansive sea of hazily illuminated panels that flicker like a malfunctioning screen stretching over the entire breadth of the valley. Thunder drums across the mountains as the shield stretching over the Revelation Territory shifts once again to a simulated tree canopy resting between the two mountains.

"What is that?" I ask, mesmerized.

"Lightning disrupts the energy output of the electronic shield covering the Revelation Territory, so it makes the camo panels flicker," Brooks explains.

"So she's really down there?" Merrin asks, pulling at the hair on the back of his head.

"She's trapped in one of the world's best- and worst-kept secrets," Brooks tells us.

"How does no one back home know about this?" I ask, dumbfounded by the apparent ease at which such secrets can

THE REVELATION

so easily hide beyond the protective walls of isolation and ignorance I've lived behind for eighteen years.

"People know, but not many. When almost everyone else lives inside walls their whole lives, you don't have to worry too much about being found. Even if someone finds them, no one could stop what they're doing in there."

Lightning strikes uncomfortably close once more over the mountains. This time, the shield remains unaffected. The rainfall gains strength as it rides a surge of fresh wind.

"We should get back. I probably shouldn't have left those two alone for this long," Brooks tells us, returning to the cave to rejoin Edwin and Anger. Merrin and I remain outside, staring into the blackness, waiting for lightning to stab the shield one more time. After several minutes of nothing, Merrin pulls at my shoulder.

"We need to get out of the rain."

I hesitate, half expecting lightning to strike the second I turn my shoulder, but I give up the ghost and join the others around the fire. Edwin and Anger are whispering to one another, having a strangely civil conversation from what I can see. Brooks joins them after tossing Merrin and me pillows they've stored farther back in the cave.

As soon as my clothes dry and my blood flows warm again, I move away from the fire and the secretive conversations to try and sleep. My imagination is overrun with thoughts about Ruma and the Revelation Territory. I try to silence the chaos by meditating on simpler, more grounding thoughts. I think of Rhysk. I try to recollect the details of her face, like how one of her cheek dimples pulls in when she smiles. Does she ever wonder what happened to me?

I think about Jaykin at home. He's probably facing the

same emotional struggle I faced, not knowing whether I'd see Ruma again, except he's older and more capable of feeling. My parents don't know where I am, and I'm sure they're reliving the fear of losing a child all over again. The heavy thoughts keep breaking through my best efforts to drive them away, so I sit and watch the fire as a distraction until it slowly burns away all my exhaustive worries.

Merrin settles down beside me, and with the help of our two borrowed pillows, I'm hoping we can get a few hours of sleep. I'm thankful we've set ourselves where we're hopefully out of earshot from the others. Between the rain washing me clean and the comforting warmth of the fire, my body is ready to embrace rest. I tuck my thick, smoky-smelling pillow behind my head and try to convince myself it's more comfortable than it really is.

Merrin rolls over and nudges my arm. "I have an idea."

I don't feel like talking, but I suspend my selfishness and roll over to face Merrin. "What?"

"It's nighttime, and we're at home," Merrin says. "Jaykin is playing video games on your bed, and you have to make him give you the controller."

I close my eyes and try to imagine seeing him.

"Your mom is watching TV while your dad reads one of his books. And tomorrow they're going to cook us a big lunch, but we get to sleep in."

He goes on for a couple minutes, making up all kinds of things. I try to mumble occasionally to let Merrin know I'm still awake, but eventually I slip into sleep.

When I wake again, I have no idea how long I've been asleep. It could have been ten minutes or several hours, but Merrin seems to have fallen asleep. I hear whispers, just barely audible enough for me to understand. Anger is quietly conversing with Edwin and Brooks. To still be in conversation, I'm assuming Anger has taken an interest in whatever information the twins are offering.

My body is trying to force me back to sleep, but my mind is locked in on trying to pick out their words.

"I can't get her out now," Anger whispers. "I can't risk that, and I haven't planned for that."

One of the twins says something. I can tell he's frustrated from the rise and fall of his vocal inflections, but I can only distinguish the pieces of his sentence that he enunciates.

"...no way we're...selfish..." It's barely enough to piece together their side of the conversation.

"I already have the resources to plan and execute this. You don't," Anger says, whispering as though her teeth are gritted. "Falyn Dire always keeps his word."

"We don't know that. Why would we risk leading you out for nothing? All we have is *your* word, which..." The rest fizzles out before it gets to me.

Anger mutters something, which I decipher after piecing her broken words together. She says she will do it with or without their help, and then the conversation ends. I accept that the rest of the night will be spent ruminating over endless anxieties and uncertainties.

I will find Ruma, I tell myself, realizing that getting her back could be more difficult than I ever imagined.

CHAPTER 17

A faint choir of voices finds my ears as my eyes open. For a moment, I wonder if the echoing song came from a dream, but when I sit up, I can still make out the singing. Anger and the twins are nowhere in sight, and even though their absence leaves me feeling a little skeptical and uneasy, I also feel relieved to be given a moment of solitude.

Merrin isn't up yet, so I nudge him awake.

"Merrin. We need to get up."

He ignores me and rolls over onto his stomach. My body is sore, my mind scrambled and disoriented. We've lacked adequate food, water, sleep, and even alone time over the past several days. Right now pain is my most pressing feeling, so I make myself stand up and stretch my limbs while trying to rub out the soreness. A place in the crease of my elbow stings, and I notice my skin there is agitated and oddly discolored. There's no raised bump, but it feels like a spider bite.

I step out of the cave, careful not to slip. The sky hangs

THE REVELATION

heavy and low. There's moisture in the air as the breeze slides across my skin. The dew polishes every rock with a clear, glistening coat. I walk toward the lookout where Brooks showed us the Revelation Territory last night in the rain. As I walk, I keep an eye out for Anger and the twins, who still are nowhere to be seen.

The air is too thick to see the convent or monastery, but every once in a while, the wind carries a few faint notes of music that catch in my ears. For a short time, I sit staring out into the mist, wondering about the lives of the captive children. Refusing to engage in additional worry, I close my eyes and tell myself my only purpose in this moment is to breathe, taking in air and giving some back.

Before long, I feel myself disconnecting from my thoughts and connecting to a physical sense of self-awareness. No one is around me. My feet plant firmly into the ground. I gently flutter my fingers by my side, trying to feel the thick fog. For the first time in weeks, I soak in the presence of being alone.

Peace settles over me, and I feel ready to head back to check on Merrin. I scan the area around the cave's perimeter and still see no sign of the others. I didn't notice before, but when I return to the cave, I notice they've cleared out all of their belongings. Against my efforts, a growing anxiety churns my empty stomach as I consider that they might have left us. Merrin is finally sitting upright and rubbing his arm while inspecting it.

"What's wrong?" I ask.

"I don't know. I guess something bit me."

"Yeah, something got me too," I say, showing him my own mark that's coincidentally around the same location as his.

"That's weird. Why did it turn that color?" he asks, rubbing the splotchy purple-and-green circle in the crook of his arm. "That pillow did nothing for me last night," Merrin says, stretching. "Where'd they go?"

"I don't know," I tell him as I scan the perimeter of the cave once again. "They were gone before I got up. I looked around outside for a second, but I didn't see anything."

"Please, God, let them be bringing back food. Right now I'd kill for a plate of bacon," Merrin says.

"I wouldn't count on it," I say dismissively.

The thought of us being left alone makes me feel increasingly uneasy. The fire has died out, so I reach into my pocket to find my fire starter, but it's not there. The pictures of my mom and my family are gone too.

"My things are gone."

"What things?" Merrin asks, finally sounding concerned.

"My fire starter and my two pictures. I had them in my pocket, but I can't find them."

"Maybe they fell out when you were sleeping. I'll help you look for them," he says. "Where's our Falcon gear?" he asks me, as if I'd know.

Our search for our belongings is cut short when Anger calls our names from somewhere outside the cave.

"Come help me carry this," she commands.

Merrin and I look to one another, unsure of what to do.

"Where are the twins?" I whisper uneasily.

He shrugs his shoulders, and we both leave the cave out of curiosity rather than obligation.

"Where are you?" Merrin calls out, still wiping the morning light out of his eyes.

"Over here," she yells with no further instruction.

"Where is *here*?" Merrin calls.

THE REVELATION

As best as we can, we follow her voice back up the rocky stairs that we descended last night.

"Hey. Look," Merrin tells me while nudging me from behind. The mist has begun to clear, and the two blurry mountain strongholds Edwin and Brooks pointed out to us last night are becoming more visible across the valley.

The monastery and convent stand like beacons nestled against the necks of the sister mountain peaks. The valley between them still hides the Revelation Territory underneath perfectly simulated tree cover. As I reach for Merrin to remind him Anger is waiting, I jolt upon hearing an unfamiliar, deep voice commanding us to place our hands behind our heads.

"Get on the ground!" another yells.

Several identically uniformed bodies ambush us from multiple directions, leaving me no time to think or attempt escaping. Apart from the slightly distinguishable dimensionality of their full-body protective gear, their reflective camouflage makes them nearly invisible, even up close. The silvery tinge of their mirroring uniforms instantly reminds me of the Legionnaires who nearly captured me and Merrin before Anger intercepted us.

Anger steps into view nearby, and I watch her to determine my next move. I expect her to unleash her wrath on these strange assailants, but instead she simply watches as the five identically uniformed men, who are pointing weapons at our heads, aggressively approach us. The exterior of their protective gear uniformly phases into a reflective shade of bronze. I can more clearly distinguish their armor, which appears more minimalistic and form fitting than our Falcon gear.

"Get on the ground," the guy with the deep voice spits out again as if he's choking on testosterone.

"What are you doing?" Merrin yells at Anger, who stands by idly while the men force us on the ground, folding our arms against our own backs before securely locking them in place.

Why would she allow the Legionnaires to capture us after all this time?

"She lied to us," Merrin says accusingly. "You piece of shit!" he yells at Anger. His voice is muffled from his face being pressed against the ground.

In the chaos, I hadn't noticed her before, but a young girl standing in a white pleated dress smeared with stains catches my attention. Her eyes are like cold lightning, striking a chill down my back. Some of her silky blonde hair is matted against her forehead, stuck in a paste of dried blood and dirt. She can't be much older than eight years old, but for some reason, the Legionnaires have her restrained by shackles connecting from her neck down to both of her wrists.

A hard knee presses into my ribs, which deflates my lungs. Callused fingers fumble around my neck as a cold, metallic ring is locked around me like an animal collar. I don't know the purpose this contraption serves, but the click of its lock makes me shudder with fear. Two of the men pull me to my feet, now that I've been securely restrained.

Merrin decides to go down swinging, so while I'm swimming in a pool of utter confusion, he's wildly resisting entrapment. Even after several days of extensive travel and malnourishment, Merrin reels back against the men, holding his arms together, and pushes off their bodies. He rears a boot high and smacks the guy with the deep voice in the head. The

THE REVELATION

kick knocks his helmet off, revealing the man's shaved head and pale face that's creased with deep wrinkles.

Merrin's rebellion is short-lived. Even after taking a blow to his head, the man quickly retaliates by sticking Merrin with some kind of pronged baton, which seems to both shock and sedate him.

"Don't! Stop!" I yell in protest, unsuccessfully struggling to break free from the unrelenting grasps on both my arms. I call Merrin's name, but he doesn't respond. My inflamed breathing seethes in and out between my gritted teeth. From where he lies unconscious on the rigidly compacted dirt, I'm relieved to see Merrin's chest still moving. Considering his weight and muscle mass, I'm sure the Legionnaires will regret having to carry him. Previously distracted by the conflict, I realize Anger is now standing beside me.

"Where are the twins?" I yell at her.

"The more you know, the less you tell," she remarks, unfazed, her black eyes and sharply flat countenance holding an air of smugness.

I spit in her face. She backhands me in return. I spit at her again, and she kicks me in my stomach, completely taking the breath out of me. I manage to keep my footing and count it as a small victory.

"Get him up," says the bald-headed man who knocked Merrin out. He then stomps his way over until he's in my face, close enough where I can smell the stomach acid on his breath.

"I could stick you too, you know," he threatens, tapping the double-headed black tip of the electric baton against my chest.

I try holding my breath, but the stench continues to crawl

in my nose. Right as he turns to walk away, I can't control myself.

"You're a piece of shit, too," I say.

As soon as I finish speaking, he turns around and jabs his baton into my stomach, and I fall to the ground. The relentless pulsing of electricity firing inside of me I feels like every tendon in my body is being yanked out by the baton's head. When the surge finally stops, my muscles continue convulsing as I gasp for air.

"Call them now," his voice commands, and one of the other men speaks into a device similar to a brace-comm.

"Berringer, RT6 requesting an evac."

I stay on the ground for a moment, trying to catch my breath. The longer I'm down, the more desperate I am to stand up and show him he can't keep me down. At least, that's what I'm telling myself. My limbs are frustratingly weak, but my determination and stubbornness make up for what I lack in strength.

With my arms still fastened tight behind me, I pull my knees underneath myself so I can attempt standing. I roll my shoulder off a nearby rock, and thankfully my feet are sturdy enough that I can stand upright.

My mind channels all the pain I'm feeling into anger. I deeply heave in each breath and exhale quickly to make room for more air. My nose drips blood, so I try to wipe it on my shoulder. I don't know where Edwin and Brooks have gone, but if they were planning to intervene, they've already missed the better moment. For all I know, Anger could've gotten rid of them in the night.

I look to Merrin, who is still unconscious, and then to the small bright-eyed little girl watching me intently. Smudges of dirt and dried blood stain the white ruffled fringes of her dress's collar. I wonder what she did to get the roughly bandaged gash on the side of her forehead. As we look at one another, she pulls her lips into a smile that quickly gives way to misery once again. Off in the distance, I hear the sound of aerocraft engines. The Legionnaire team, which I'm assuming Anger is now an honorary member of, prepares for evacuation.

In a quick scramble, the little girl runs to my side. I'm not sure what to expect, so I freeze.

"Where did you come from?" she whispers gently, her voice eager.

I stare into her eyes, which now look like a fresh pool of water, and I feel like we're on each other's team. Before I can answer, she is quickly snatched away by a pair of camouflaged arms. The deep hum of throttling engines is quickly approaching, but I see no sign of any aerocraft. The evacuation ship almost lands on top of our heads before its invisible exoskeleton reveals the characteristically deep-red underbelly of a Legionnaire ship. The boarding ramp extends from underneath the aerocraft, exposing the silver hull within.

"Hey!" one of the Legionnaires suddenly shouts.

I turn just in time to see the little girl bolting away from our group. One of the men tries to grab her, but she disappears, leaving a hazy cloud behind where she once stood that swirls like an airy ghost over the mountain plateau until she suddenly reappears nearly a hundred yards away.

"There she is," one of the men yells as he points his finger across the rocky plateau.

The young girl's bright blonde hair swishes behind her in the wind as she desperately tries to hop over the rock face to get away.

"How're we supposed to catch her?" one of the men says helplessly as their commander steps forward, unsheathing a weapon from his side.

"Move," he growls, right before hastily aiming a single, ear-piercing shot. He seems to have hit his mark, as the little girl tumbles to the ground, out of sight. Whatever fight I have left in me subsides to an aching sense of grief and a numbingly cold hatred toward the Legionnaires.

Everyone is frozen in place, as if time has stopped, except for the bald-headed man, who unapologetically curses us all for not loading up quickly enough.

"She's tagged, so go get her. Call an evac and take her back to St. Mary's in case she survives," he says to one of his men, who quickly runs off in the direction where the blonde girl fell.

Is that where she's from?

I don't know who these people are or why they've been wanting to capture Merrin and me since our operative mission fell apart. Ms. Diana warned me the first day I arrived in New Province that *they* wanted something from me. She mentioned something about her son being taken, but how could that have anything to do with Legionnaires, or for that matter, Commander Locke? Him trying to rescue me over the rest of the operatives before he died still doesn't make any sense.

All this time, I've been following Anger out of nothing more than fear and curiosity, as if I was helpless, and now I have no idea whether anything she said about Ruma is true. A part of me still hopes that Anger is lying and that Edwin and Brooks will save us any second. I tell myself *hold it together* over and over again. It's all I can do to keep myself from running to the

THE REVELATION

little girl so she doesn't have to be alone, whether she's alive or dead.

I close my eyes to escape in my mind as they drag me onto the aerocraft, and suddenly a surge of vomit runs up my throat. I throw up on one of the guys carrying me, and he shoves me away.

He curses at me and is immediately ordered to continue moving me. He doesn't have time to clean himself. Instead, he and his partner toss me into one of the seats, strapping me in like a child. I feel no need whatsoever to cooperate. In this moment, going limp seems to be the only bit of control I have in my current situation. Three men dump Merrin into a seat beside me and secure him as well. His eyes remain closed.

There are seven other passengers, eight including Anger, hastily taking their seats around the circular loading deck. We're all facing the center, where a cylindrical holographic projection portrays a live feed of all of our faces with our corresponding medical statistics. My body temperature is 101 degrees. My heart rate is 118 beats per minute. Several of the other measurements registering in front of me don't make sense, but the ones I do understand don't look good.

The pitch of the aerocraft engines steadily increases, and my stomach suddenly drops as we take off. I close my eyes, hoping that when I open them again, I will be somewhere completely different. Instead, when my eyes open, the screen in front of me projects our coordinate reading.

The man I threw up on finally has time to clean my orange-red bile off his silver-sheened uniform. The name "Cabben" is engraved in a dark-gold symbol on his sleeve, just below his shoulder. The emblem's distinct pattern instantly triggers my memory back to Widow's home and the unusual charm in her husband's jacket pocket. I trace the design pattern with my eyes, scanning over the two trapezium wings that form the double-barred cross that holds the upside-down triangle encapsulating the three interwoven circles below.

In my state of disorientation, I still try to remain aware, to learn as much information as I can about who has captured us. Even so, no secrets are revealed on our short flight. From the central holographic projections in front of me, I assume we're landing around the outskirts of the Revelation Territory, opposite from Brooks and Edwin's cave.

Anger has been avoiding eye contact with me, despite my attempts to murder her with a glance. From her slouching posture to her unassuming, empty stare, she seems as if she's taken on a completely different persona. Her hand slips into her pocket, and she pulls out my flint fire starter, fidgeting with it between her fingers. I start to react, but she fluidly slips it back into her pocket as if it were never there. I can't decide if she's trying to intimidate me or sending me a subtle message. Maybe she means nothing at all, but her eyes never look my way for any sort of confirmation.

Once the bottom hatch opens, our captors force us out into a relatively small and mostly empty aerocraft hangar with reflective honeycomb-like walls. Apart from paling in size, these unfamiliar structural designs are exorbitantly more impressive than the hangars of New Province Guard. We're quickly escorted into one of several geometrically dynamic armored vehicles. The exterior skin of the vehicles appears to be constantly shifting, like a living organism. The perplexing optical illusion makes my head hurt and yet captivates me all the same.

The Legionnaires throw me and Merrin onto the metal

vehicle bed as soon as the back hatch is opened. The impact jolts Merrin awake. He slowly stares with his parched lips agape, looking extremely confused, which I probably would find entertaining under different circumstances.

Anger follows the bald captain to the back of our caravan and disappears into her own vehicle. The vomit-stained man forcefully shuts the door, leaving Merrin and me lying on the cold metallic floor. As the vehicle moves, we bounce around at the mercy of the natural terrain.

I try kicking my feet against the back door. I don't expect it to open, but an anxious swell of frustration in my gut is in need of a physical outlet. The hatch is unmovable, absorbing each muffled blow without the slightest hint of damage. I kick until my will breaks, and I start crying. If there is a time to appear weak, now is better than ever, with only a half-aware Merrin to witness my emotional breakdown.

My breathing stutters irregularly for a while. Merrin mumbles something, which I can't hear.

"What?" I ask, even though I don't care.

"I can't do this," he barely gets out, letting his head fall against the vehicle bed.

Drowning in my own fresh apathy, I have no response for him. He's right. Maybe he can't psychologically take this. Maybe I can't either, and at some point, one or both of us will snap.

"What is she doing to us?" I ask Merrin.

"Who?" he asks foggily.

"Anger," I say, remembering he's not in a clear headspace.

"I don't know," he mumbles weakly. "Where are we?"

"I don't know. Maybe the Revelation Territory," I offer, with no better guess.

"Then we'll be that much closer to Ruma," he says as reassuringly as he can manage.

After a few more minutes of bouncing around with our arms still strapped firmly against our backs, we come to a stop. My neck has kinked up pretty good, and my shoulders are throbbing from confinement.

"What do you think they'll do to us?" Merrin asks, almost void of emotion.

"Guess we'll find out soon," I say. "Right now it's just you and me without Anger. That's good enough for me."

A fist bangs twice on the side of the vehicle, and we begin moving again. The inside lights dim to a dull florescent glow. While we've traveled, my eyes have tried to find details to study in the back of our mobile prison cell, but other than a few air vents, inactive screens, and bolt covers, the plain metal walls give away nothing.

Like a tire quickly losing air, a hiss sounds from above us, followed by thin red smoke, which billows down over us from the air vents. Instead of choking on the fumes, the strangely sweet-smelling gas makes my body feel weightless and numb, as if I'm suspended in the air. Within seconds, Merrin's eyes roll closed, and his body goes limp. As I close my eyes, embracing the inevitable blackness, I hear my mother's distant voice singing, *Keep me close, I'm never far.*

CHAPTER 18

Unfamiliar beeping and humming sounds from an assortment of machines speak to me from all around. My eyelids struggle to open under the heavy weight of sedation. A mask covers my mouth and nose as fresh pulses of air chill my teeth. I'm strapped down in a slightly elevated medical bed. My blood flow feels lazy, as if my organs are functioning in slow motion.

Apart from the crisp copper floors, clean white metal dresses most of the room. The textured design of a burgundy metallic door directly ahead of me reflects the ceiling lights. My arms are turned outward and strapped down against the shiny steel bed frame. Several thin strips of tubing connect to thick needles nestling in my veins, which appear deep green on the surface of my skin. My usually light-brown skin appears much paler, more closely resembling my mother's complexion.

There are very few wires, buttons, and keys on the plain

faces of the machines. I assume most of the cleanly designed mechanisms serve some medical purpose unknown to me. To my left, there's a video monitor depicting a row of people positioned in a similar fashion as I am now. I count eight faces before the display changes, focusing on a singular person. It takes me a few seconds to realize the face belongs to me. My eyes look too empty and soulless in the display to really seem like mine.

The screen's display shifts back to the original picture of the eight faces I saw before. After scanning over the same set of faces three cycles in a row, I don't recognize any of them, which is worrying. For the first time in weeks, Merrin isn't with me. I observe the placid faces of different ages, sexes, and colors, wondering how we all managed to be lured into the same trap.

Another peculiar hum, like a mechanical complaint, coincides with a sudden tugging in my veins. I look down at my arms, and the translucent tubes turn dark red as the machines pull blood from my body. I follow the streaming blood spiraling down until I have to close my eyes to keep from passing out. I almost feel like my spirit is being drained from me.

A female's voice from behind my head startles me, so I'm wide-eyed and alert. I must have passed out, because somewhere within the incoherent darkness, I've been transported into a long hallway, still very similar in design to the white steel walls and copper floors of my previous holding room.

A firm hand presses tightly over my mouth. My nose is already clogged, so I'm having trouble breathing. I try jolting away and realize my wrists and ankles are still tied to the edges of my bed railing. A voice shushes me from behind my head.

"You were screaming. Keep quiet," a voice whispers, sounding uncomfortably similar to Anger's.

As the soft hand lifts from my face, I glimpse a pale arm slipping back out of view. At least I know the woman isn't Anger. My neck strains as I try looking behind my bed to find the face that goes with the voice, but I quickly give up and lay my head back against the firm cushion. Trying to sound fierce, I attempt to fire a few sharp curse words over my shoulder, but instead, my voice sounds like a deflating balloon.

The hand again returns to my lips, accompanied by a quiet scolding. "Stop it! Please. Just stay quiet for a little while longer."

Still struggling to breathe, I twist my neck away and snap at whoever's fingers are trying to silence me. The hand jerks away to avoid being bitten, which thankfully allows me to breathe through my mouth again. I can see a clear reflection of myself against the glossy white ceiling panels above. My outfit is clean and white, trimmed by deep-red rings—one at my neck and a few on my arms and legs. Looking in the reflection, I'm able to see that the woman behind me looks nothing like Anger. Her blonde hair and pallid skin blend together so that it's hard to distinguish one from the other.

A lady worriedly peeps her head out from the only open door I've noticed so far in the hallway. She's dressed in a tight-fitting crimson bodysuit.

"Oh. I didn't expect to see you here," she says submissively. Her perfect teeth shine like polished jewels, and her smile stretches over her face without causing a single wrinkle.

"Did they miscalculate his dosage of anesthesia?" she asks

my attendant while adjusting a crimson headband that neatly collects all of her platinum hair behind her head.

"Unfortunately. He's still adjusting to the dremaline," my attendant says sympathetically. Whatever drugs they've got me on have left me at the edge of delirium, making any efforts to focus or think feel burdensome.

"I can take him if you have other places to be," the young woman responds, leaning halfway into the hallway. After being beaten and drugged to get here, wherever I am, their cordialness is jarring.

"No, thanks. I got him. Don't worry about it," my attendant insists as my medical transporting bed continues gliding along.

"Take care," the young woman says, timidly touching my bed railing as I pass by. From up close, I notice the strange interwoven symbol of three interlaced circles with the double-barred cross embroidered over her heart. The silver shade of it matches the pair of horizontal stripes across each of her sleeves. My eyes lock on the symbol until we pass her as my attendant pushes me around a corner.

"Who are yo—"

"Lay your head back. You need to rest," she commands, pulling my forehead back down to my bed cushion.

"Where am I?" I ask, still completely confused.

My attendant stops pushing and steps around the transport bed to face me. Her eyes are not dark like Anger's. They're a rich green, like pine needles.

"Listen to me," she says sternly just before leaning close by my ear to whisper, "Don't tell anyone your name. No one can know who you are."

"Why?" I ask, swallowing hard as she adjusts the thin

pillow that's slid down my back so it's propped back up behind my head.

"For the protection of you and everyone you care about," she utters so close to my ear I can feel the warm fog from her breath. "Tell no one. Do you understand?"

My head swims hazily as I experience a moment of déjà vu, remembering my previous experience with Ms. Diana in New Province Guard when she warned me that I shouldn't trust anyone there because I was wanted for some unknown reason. Even though I'm still confused, I don't have the energy for her to keep lecturing me.

"I need to know you understand," she whispers emphatically.

"I understand," I say, licking my parched lips, hoping she'll leave me alone.

"Good," the pale woman says before briefly pinching the inside of my nostrils with a pungent ointment.

I try to wipe my nose against my shoulder to shield myself from the stinging fumes. Her hand gently pushes my forehead back against my pillow as I weakly resist.

"Rest," she tells me, steering my bed once again from behind.

It's all I can do to keep my eyes open. My head drops to the side as we pass by a collection of windows lining the long hallway. Inside the rooms, rows of clear vertical holding tanks host the bodies of developing babies suspended in fluids. My attention moves to an attendant who seems to be cleaning out one of the emptied tanks. She has a small baby not much bigger than her hands, and she's holding it by its feet. Then she discards it in a bin, along with her cleaning wipes.

I lock eyes with the attendant, and she watches me as the

pale woman continues pushing me onward. She smiles and gently nods before my eyes give way to darkness.

My eyelids peel open at the same time I become aware of a burning pain surging in the back of my neck. There's a young man leaning over my face, and his mask only allows me to see the features above his nose. His hazel eyes squint to focus on the screen he's poking at behind me. The white of his skin almost shines, distinctly contrasting with his black hair.

"Sorry about that," he says gently before removing the needle from my neck. He carefully rubs the point of entry with a soft swab. "I just do what I'm told. You can blame my boss for that one." He smiles so genuinely that I don't fault him.

"What's your name? I know your friend's name over there, but you only came with an encrypted medical file," he says, flashing me a glance at the information on his tablet. "I have some of your information, but they replaced your name with a code sequence."

My memory of the pale woman asking me to keep my identity hidden feels more like a dream than a memory. I don't know who she is, and I have no reason to trust her, but I decide my silence gives me more control, so I ignore his question. I look over to see if Merrin is okay. I wouldn't have noticed him in the room if the man hadn't pointed him out.

"He's all right. Don't worry," he says, reading my face. There's a good fifteen feet of open space between Merrin's bed and my own.

"Your blood work actually came back with more extreme results than his. He should be worrying about you," he explains, playfully raising his eyebrows.

I stare at him, deciding whether to ask questions or to stay silent.

"I'm about to wake him up. Maybe he'll tell me your name," he says before prepping another needle to inject into Merrin.

I decide to play my hand at leveraging the conversation where he answers my questions first.

"Who are you?"

"I'm definitely one of the least interesting people here, but my name is Jerrico. I stay busy trying to keep people healthy, like you and your friend here."

"What did they do to us?"

"That's a better question," he says. "You both registered positive readings on your blood chemistry samples that show signs of genetic-reversal capabilities. From what I can tell, your exome screening looks like you have genetic immunity to perducorium. I've only personally met a few people who do. So right now, more important people are deciphering those results and deciding what to do with them while I keep you comfortable—except for when I'm having to stick you with needles," he adds while sliding the needle into the back of Merrin's neck.

"There you go, my friend," he says.

"I don't understand," I tell him, confused. "Genetic immunity to perducorium? That can't be real."

Within seconds, Merrin's eyes start to flutter, and his breathing strengthens. As soon as he opens his eyes, he begins wildly scanning the room. He sees me almost immediately and sits up before clumsily stumbling to his feet.

"Are you okay?" he asks, coming to my side, ignoring Jerrico's suggestion to take it easy.

"Yeah. I'm fine. Take it easy," I tell him. I barely sit up in my bed before Merrin awkwardly wraps his arm around the back of my head and leans his head down beside mine.

"What did they tell you?" he anxiously whispers in my ear.

"Nothing. I don't know anything," I quietly confirm as he releases me. I read the uncertainty imprinted on his eyes as a sign that he knows more than I do. As my friend, he's always taken on the role of being my protector, even when I didn't need him to be. I'm sure he feels no different now, wherever we are.

"You have to lie down. Now," Jerrico commands Merrin.

"What did they do to you?" I ask Merrin, hoping he can help me make sense of what's going on.

"I don't know," he says with a hint of suspicion as his eyes cut toward Jerrico.

"So what's your friend's name?" Jerrico asks Merrin, interrupting our conversation as he pulls Merrin back toward his bed.

I look at Merrin, preparing to subtly clue him in that I'm not supposed to share my name, but he quickly says, "Eden Evans." His eyes linger just long enough on mine to see if we're on the same page.

Eden Evans is my cousin's name. I don't know why he's saying this, but at least now I know we have both been told to keep my identity a secret for some reason. I risk a subdued nod to let him know that I'm not completely lost.

"You could've asked him yourself," Merrin adds.

"I actually did, but he didn't seem too interested in telling me," Jerrico tells him.

"Why do you care?" I ask Jerrico flatly.

"I told you," he says calmly. "Parts of your file are encrypted, and I was just curious. But now I know."

"Did you read the part about how we were taken against our will?" Merrin asks cuttingly.

"You're right where you need to be," another voice breaks into the room.

Shifting my gaze, I recognize the same blonde woman who told me to hide my identity stepping in through the open doorway. Her tone makes her seem as if she's had a few too many cups of coffee. The fluorescent lights only accentuate her ivory skin and white-gold hair. Her gray work suit fits tightly to her narrow body. Several sharp fabric edges jut out like fake armor around her neck and sleeves.

"I'll take it from here, Jerrico," she says, dismissing him by flicking her wrist a few times in his direction. With a submissive nod, he obliges, disappearing behind the automated doors.

She quickly addresses my visible suspicions of her as she says, "Good to see you again, and welcome to the Revelation Territory."

My chest instantly tightens along with seemingly every other part of me. Even though she's confirming what I already assumed but was too afraid to believe, her words are no less distressing. Ruma's name whirls around in my mind like a wild bird trying to escape a cage. We remain silently stunned, waiting for a continued explanation of why we've been captured and brought here.

"I do realize you might feel uncomfortable considering your current situation, but we have your best interests in mind here, I can assure you," she says with forced cordialness. Her demeanor is starkly different from the last time I saw her.

"And what exactly is my best interest?" I ask, still trying to reconcile the memory of her whispering in my ear to not let anyone know who I am. I want to confront her, but what if we're being watched? Maybe that's why she's acting different.

"Anything concerning your physiological well-being," she tells us. "You both have been recently exposed to perducorium."

I look to Merrin, whose eyes instantly drop to the floor.

She continues. "And yet your bodies seem to not only be fighting the disease, but traces of your DNA have triggered positive responses for genetic reversal, and in your case," she adds, nodding at me, "genetic resilience. Do you know what this means?"

I remember the twins, Edwin and Brooks, briefly explaining this occurrence shortly after we met them. I decide pretending I know less than I do could play to my advantage.

"No," I say. There's enough doubt in my voice for her to continue without missing a beat.

"Perducorium not only hardens the exterior regions of the body, but it also ossifies internal organs, including certain regions of the brain," she explains, as if reading from a cue card. "In most cases, the central region of the brain responsible for emotional regulation, known as the deep limbic system, is compromised."

"We already know all of that," Merrin interrupts. "What is genetic resilience?"

As she stares at Merrin, her tight, creaseless face appears as if she's hoping he'll vanish from sight. "As I was saying," she says, regaining her composure, "we've collected a positive reading from the molecular structure of your DNA, which tells us you both are genetically predisposed to resist the effects of perducorium. Just in different ways from one another."

I stare at her blankly.

"That's good news," she reassures us. "But we're currently unsure to what extent that is. Your friend Eden seems to be immune to the effects of perducorium altogether, which is uncommonly rare, with nearly one-in-a-million odds. You should feel special." She clasps her hands together. "We'll be running various tests to produce a more detailed analysis of your condition."

"What if I don't want to be tested?" I ask disdainfully. "Am I wrong in assuming I still have rights?"

"Your right is to live in a country where the government fights to protect you, and as I've said before, we do have your best interests in mind."

"From what you've just told me, I don't need protection," I say as my neck begins to feel hot with anger.

Her flat expression shows no amount of sympathy for my frustration.

"I've oversimplified my explanation of your condition so you could understand, but I can assure you, you're where you need to be," she tells us.

"And why should we trust you? Because to me, anyone who captures another person against his will doesn't come across as reliable."

"I'm sorry, but you're mistaken. We have official records, signed by each of you, with your authorization to participate in our treatment program."

She strides over to the wall and enters a key code into a panel beside the door. After positioning herself in front of a screen rotating out from within the wall, she slides her fingers fluidly across an interface full of icons and pulls up our personal information. Her movements are so formal it almost feels as if she's performing for an invisible audience.

Her fingers tap a handheld screen she has pulled away from the wall, and I see an alphabetical list of individuals by

THE REVELATION

last name. I can't decide if she's trying to taunt me or if she's sending me a secret message. My eyes slip over names until I read FLINT, RUMANOR B. She's only one of two Flints in the database, and the other name is one I don't recognize. She scrolls away quickly, saying, "Evans. Yes."

"Go back," I tell her before I can stop myself. She pays me no attention.

"One moment... And here...we...are," she says as she pulls up my photo identification. It looks like a slightly altered version of the picture that was used for my Southern Guard brace-comm. Below my picture, I see the name EDEN L. EVANS with a conglomeration of organized statistics, which actually seems to reflect most of my real personal information.

She scrolls down to a document that appears to contain my signature.

"Here is yours, Mr. Evans. And would you like to see yours, Mr. Horner?" she asks without looking up.

She selects the name Wyatt Horner, and there's Merrin's face above the name.

"No," Merrin says quickly as his short but intentional stare keeps me from asking, *Who is Mr. Horner?* Whatever he knows, he won't be able to tell me here.

She flings the information off the screen, and a few keystrokes later, the display disappears as if we'd never seen a thing. I'm not sure why I've been asked to hide behind my cousin's name, but the thought of my real identity becoming lost makes me think again of Ms. Diana losing her son after he was subjected to a series of blood tests. I know he vanished from New Province Guard, but for all I know, I could be facing a similar experience here in the Revelation Territory.

"You're both set to be received at your orientation

appointments. So let's get moving. You'll need to be checked into your temporary barracks as well as assigned to your occupation and field of work."

"I don't understand," I object, feeling trapped.

"You will get used to the daily routines after a few days," she says.

"What are you talking about?" I ask. She ignores me, but I persist. "Why are we here?" I yell, struggling to keep my composure.

"Don't question me," she retaliates sharply. Her eyes grab hold of mine, and she shakes her head with the subtlest movement. "I need you to keep it together. I'm sure you and Mr. Horner will have more time to discuss any further questions you might have."

She cuts her eyes toward Merrin, who comes to my side. "We'll be all right. We just need some time to adjust."

His forced reassurance is unsettling, but his hand lightly squeezes my shoulder and lingers for a moment, just long enough to let me know he's leaving some things unsaid. He restores a weak smile to his face, and I can't help but shake my head. My breaths feel short, so I spend a few moments trying to stabilize my anxiety.

I remember the last words my dad spoke to Merrin and me before we left Southern Guard. *No one's going to teach you how to guard your heart and your mind.* I've overcome too much in the past several days to give in when I'm possibly closer to finding Ruma than I've ever been before. Even though I feel like I could lose control at any moment, I meditate on those words as the woman begins disconnecting any remaining medical cords we failed to pull out ourselves.

THE REVELATION

She's wearing an ID badge, but instead of a name, it reads *Dean of Biochemical Research.*

"What's your name?" I ask her, realizing I don't have a name to which I can attach my frustration.

"Rose," she says casually. "Please stand up."

I haven't noticed until now, but Merrin and I are both dressed in unflattering white medical gowns. Neither of us have any other clothing in sight, so when Rose pulls open a storage drawer and empties out two fresh bags of clothing, I appreciate it. She turns away to provide us with privacy but remains close by, as if she expects us to bolt away.

These suits seem to be almost identical in style to the one I was wearing when I first awoke to find Rose pushing me in my medical transport bed down what I assumed to be a laboratory hallway. The only difference is, the color scheme is reversed, so most of the body is crimson while a few white stripes ring my neck, arms, and legs.

"Your boots fasten the same way as the back of your suits do," Rose explains. "The hyper-magnetic strips in the fabric will lock your clothes in place. You'll have to fold back the shielding alloy strips to redirect the magnetic fields when you want to take them off. Let me show you."

Rose shows us how to fasten and unfasten our suits and shoes properly, which makes me feel all of four years old.

"We are actually on schedule if you both wouldn't mind following me, please."

"On schedule for what?" I ask, flattening out the wrinkles of my uniform.

"Orientation, remember? You'll need a proper introduction to our expectations in the Revelation Territory."

She quickly spins on her sharp heels and makes her way

toward the solid metal doors, which slide back into the wall with a faint flick of Rose's wrist. She tucks her exit card away in her breast pocket and swings her hips, turning an ordinary trip down a hallway into a runway exhibition.

Merrin chooses this last moment before we exit to whisper, "We're here for a reason."

"What do you know?" I whisper back.

"That we trust each other," he says.

We stand in silence a moment, each waiting for the other to take the first step toward the door.

"So you're Wyatt," I whisper after leaning in close enough to his ear to avoid being heard in case we're being monitored.

"Of course. Wyatt Horner. And you're Eden Evans," he mutters even more softly.

Rose peeks her head back in the room. "I don't mind holding your hands if you're afraid." She winks before strutting away once more.

"She's annoying," Merrin whispers, and we cautiously follow Rose as if she is our guide through a minefield, which she just might be.

CHAPTER 19

The cylindrical elevator thrums a singular note as we ascend, without which there wouldn't be much evidence we are moving. Sometime after we left our medical release room, Rose dressed her smooth, almost buttery face with a pair of scarlet-tinted eyeglasses.

I don't remember any noticeable markings on the hallway walls we traveled before. Even the elevator, apart from the empty ice-blue display screen, shows no numerical or coding identification of any sort, which would make maneuvering this place incredibly difficult if Rose didn't have her glasses. From the way she keeps looking around and adjusting them on her nose, I derive they must reveal all the hidden informative symbols we can't see.

The door makes no sound to cue its opening. I'm startled when the concave door revolves back into the wall and opens up to another room, which also keeps with the circular theme in its design. I'd guess the diameter of this room is a little more than fifty feet, and the ceiling is about the same—almost like a planetarium.

The dark walls glow faintly enough to where I can see four slightly elevated shadows standing in the center of the room. Rose quickly leads us as she strides down an aisle outlined by softly pulsating white lines guiding us toward the other strangers. The walls turn bright white, and I realize the room's exterior is a panoramic video screen. Rose waves us toward her just before engaging the small group now surrounding her. Their passive postures seem so cold and disconnected that I assume they've also been abducted against their will.

Rose doesn't appear to be introducing herself to anyone, so they must already know her. Merrin's curiosity is stronger than my apprehension, so I follow him as he moves to join the others.

Again, the familiar deep-red symbol I keep seeing flashes on the screen. The design repeats about every five feet around the circumference of the room.

"That's gotta be the Revelation Territory's emblem," I tell Merrin. "I've seen it everywhere."

"Makes sense to me," he says, surveying the numerous icons.

As we reach the four figures, I see other relatively young faces—two guys and two girls. They could be from another guard post for all I know. Two have dark hair and skin and look similar enough to be brother and sister, and the other two have their arms around one another. As we join them in the center of the platform, Rose begins her introductions.

"I would like you all to meet Wyatt, and that's Eden behind him," she says, as if I'm an uninvited guest at a party.

They share their names with us and shake our hands. I'm

too distracted to remember what anyone says. Rose explains how we all have one commonality: being new to the Revelation Territory. She rambles for a few minutes about understanding how we all must feel and how we shouldn't worry because we will soon feel at home, as if my parents and Jaykin are little more than disposable memories to be replaced by new faces. My stomach burns and tightens, and I squeeze my fingers into my palms to let out my surging aggression.

"Fortunately, everyone here has a friend, or in your case"—she nods toward the dark-haired pair—"a sibling to make settling in here all the more comfortable," Rose says, in a weak attempt at empathy.

I can't imagine being here without Merrin. Other than the idea of possibly finding Ruma, he's the only force that keeps me grounded when I think about being separated from my family.

Rose quickly punches a sequence into a keypad attached to the railing encircling the platform we're standing on. My eyes follow a humming sound to the ceiling above, where a 360-degree projector lens descends.

"You will need to wear these protective lenses. Without them, the projection's intensity might cause permanent retina damage," she says casually.

"Is this really worth the risk?" Merrin asks, holding his glasses on either side of his ears as if afraid they might jump off.

"There is no risk involved if you follow instructions," she states flatly without looking up from the glowing keypad.

Once our eyes are properly shielded, she begins the video, which initially stretches across a portion of the screen. A pleasant musical score circulates in our ears as an aerial shot of greenback mountains flies in front of us. Slowly, the image expands, first to the left and then to the right. I couldn't dream of a clearer blue for the skyline, which begins expanding above us like a dome. Our feet tremble beneath us as the floor shifts, making way for the projection to expand below us as well. Our platform rises off the ground until we're perched halfway between the ground and the ceiling. Within thirty seconds, we are fully encapsulated in a holographic projection of nature.

Rose points to steer our attention in the right direction. I notice two small structures quickly rising on two adjacent mountain peaks. As our perspective brings us closer, I realize we're watching a simulated rapid construction of the monastery and convent crowning the sister peaks outside the Revelation Territory. A deep, soothing voice begins narrating the history of the two massive structures.

"Before the first stone was set to rise on either peak of the Revelation Mountains, there was born a man named Isaac Kane, Father of the Patmos Monastery and benefactor of St. Mary's Haven."

We're only a couple of lines in, and I'm so immersed in the creation story of the Revelation Territory that it feels like I'm there during its birthing moments. The platform beneath us simulates movement in all directions, so we shift according to the movements of the projected story.

Dozens of muscular men painted with sweat-smeared dirt haul blocks of stones, stacking them into high-formed arches and pillars towering into the sky. Others chop tirelessly at the foot of trees to harvest lumber from the fallen trunks. Time-lapse reanimation shows us the progressive stages of construction as the Patmos Monastery grows before us like a living creature.

Distracted by the alluring three-dimensional projections, I only catch a few details of history provided by the narration.

"Bishop Isaac Kane, along with his establishing partner, Rebekkah Casborn, the First Mother of St. Mary's Haven, birthed the vision of establishing a sister convent to the monastery. The simultaneous construction of St. Mary's Haven began in the thirty-third year of Patmos's construction on a twin peak towering over the opposite side of the Gateway Valley, which is home to the present-day Revelation Territory."

A brief narration explains the past century's transformation of the monastery and convent into educational facilities for the Revelation Territory's young children. After watching a similar rapid construction of St. Mary's Haven, our perspective carries us high up into the simulated sky, where we get a full view of both establishments standing like sentinels over the valley between.

"It is here, at the foot of the mountains in the Gateway Valley, where RedCloud began their research and rehabilitation program for those experiencing the biological effects of genetic reversal in response to becoming infected by the perducorium virus."

Merrin pulls my focus out of the simulation by saying, "So it's basically a glorified purge camp that you never leave."

After a brief introduction to the founding of the Revelation Territory's medical research institution, we're guided through a quick virtual tour of the different facilities we're expected to visit that will help us get acclimated with our new environment. Through the voiceover, we're given details about the designated assignments each of us will carry out in exchange for food, shelter, and other essential needs.

THE REVELATION

An assigned task lasts for one month, unless someone shows expertise in a particular area and is given special authorization to continue that specified task.

From the musical inflections and the narrator's tone, I can tell he's begun his closing remarks. My eyes and mind have swallowed enough stimulation to feel heavy with new information.

"In a world full of sickness, peril, and uncertainty, we vow to be your haven of wellness, security, and prosperity. Welcome to the Revelation Territory," the narrator announces reverently as his last words blend into a triumphant musical hum gently vibrating the room.

A large Revelation Territory emblem appears before us, only this time the familiar symbol glistens gold with three words written around the perimeter of an additional circle enclosing the logo.

"Sacrifice, serve, and preserve," the narrator reads aloud in a way that clearly assumes we'll be chanting with him.

Rose mumbles the words to herself with less enthusiasm than I would've expected. The screen fades to black, taking all the light from the room. The moment of darkness is refreshing for my overstimulated eyes. No one says a word. I feel as if I've traveled to an entirely different planet, a world far away from my family and the familiar culture of Southern Guard. *You're observing, not embracing.* I internally repeat this mantra, which helps me feel I still belong to myself rather than to the Revelation Territory.

The hydraulic pistons below our platform sigh and occasionally squeal off-key notes as we descend toward the ground. I steady myself against the handrails, trying to return a sense of equilibrium to my stomach.

A ring of dimmer lights around the top of the wall's circumference gradually makes our faces visible again. I catch the girl with the darker complexion quickly swiping a tear away from her face. Her eyes glisten, contrasting with her dry, leaden expression.

"Now for your pendants," Rose says slowly, drawing her words out as her hand searches for a hidden compartment attached to the backside of the platform. "Here they are," she says, pulling out a handful of fabricated wristbands, each pinned with the shiny Revelation Territory emblem.

"You each get one. Please place them around your left arms to signify your induction into the Revelation Territory so that others will know to assist you when needed. And it's not a pleasant experience to get caught in the wrong place with no excuse," she says, smiling as if to soften the severity of her advice.

I quickly secure my armband, hoping it will provide at least a temporary excuse to sneakily explore restrictive areas without getting punished. The others do as well, and Rose leads us through the exit opposite of where we entered.

The brother whispers to his sister, "There will be people here like us. We'll figure it out."

I really want to connect with them so they don't feel alone or confused, but my desire for self-preservation pulls at me to be silent and do nothing. That feels wrong too, so I raise my hand and tap the brother on his shoulder.

"Hey. Are you two okay?" I ask.

He looks at me for a second before nodding his head.

"We don't trust this place either," I whisper, trying to reassure them. "I'm sure there'll be other people like us here."

THE REVELATION

"Thanks. What's your name?" he asks, his previously austere face softening to appear more courteous.

I catch myself just before I say *Darvin*, and stutter a moment before saying, "Most people call me Eden. And this is my friend Wyatt." I feel guilty for having to lie, but I'm not willing to risk disclosing my identity just yet, even if I don't understand why I've been told to keep it a secret.

Rose interrupts our conversation as the door before us, which previously seemed to be made of thick iron, dissipates into scattered light, revealing an energy shield that gradually vanishes.

"This way. We have to keep to our schedule. They'll be waiting to assign you to your transitional quarters up ahead."

"My name is Endon, so it'll be easy to remember yours," the brother says, reaching out to shake my hand. "And my sister is Hara."

"Nice to meet you, Endon. Good luck in here to both of you."

"The same to you," he says before continuing ahead.

Hara gives me a slight smile as well, which makes me feel better.

"What was that about?" Merrin asks after uncharacteristically keeping his distance from my brief encounter with Endon and Hara.

"I just wanted to make them feel a little more comfortable. We might need as many friends here as we can get."

"Let's just lay low," he says quietly.

"We need to make a plan," I tell him.

"That's not our job," he responds, interrupting me when I try to ask him something. "I know. We just need to figure out one thing at a time."

I grip my fingers tight, balling up my fists. Merrin is clearly trying to keep me from talking, and I can't go much longer without knowing why. I'm sure he's waiting for us to be alone, but there's no guarantee that is going to happen.

The domed hallway is unnecessarily long, as if the only purpose of its length is to inspire anxiety before we reach the reception desk at the end. The lighting around us emanates a smooth blue glow, like the kind of light that attracts unsuspecting bugs before zapping them dead. The arching metallic walls mirror our reflections. I empathize with my own apprehensive expression—first in the walls and then again in the reflective black marble floors. It's like I'm watching myself from another dimension. How did I ever end up so far from home?

I count seven workers standing alert and prepared to receive us as if they're expecting an influx of new residents any minute. We divide ourselves amongst the different workers.

Merrin pulls on my arm.

"Look. Look at her," he says, pointing to a beautiful, golden-haired young woman standing in the third line from the left.

"That's the last thing on my mind here," I say, somewhat annoyed.

"No. I don't mean that. She's not moving," he says, staring skeptically.

I pause for a few seconds, watching her as she stares ahead, motionless, with a smile strung wide across her face. Just as a white light shines down from above her head, her eyes find mine, and she says, "Please step forward."

Her crisp, clean voice is as smooth and rich as her ivory skin.

THE REVELATION

"I mean, is she... She's not even blinking," he says.

"Is she real, you mean?" I ask.

I scan the other workers helping the people in front of us, but they all seem normal enough. There's nothing immediately suspicious about them, but upon closer examination, their movements seem too fluidly precise to be real.

I take a few steps toward the woman, and once I get within ten feet of her, her head shifts, and she quickly finds my eyes.

"How may I help you?" she asks pleasantly.

I hesitate to move.

"Is something wrong?" Rose asks me, concerned.

"What is she?" I ask, confoundedly staring at the astoundingly realistic human replica. "Is she—"

"Able to help you?" Rose interrupts. "Yes. But you and Wyatt should follow me."

"No. I mean, she's not human," I mumble quietly, still worried I might offend the anthropomorphic robot.

"She's as good as one to most," Rose responds, unamused. She motions for Merrin and I to join her.

"Please step forward when you are ready for me to assist you," the mechanical woman instructs smoothly.

Merrin steps around me. "Hello. How are you today?" Even in these circumstances, he's finding opportunities to amuse himself.

She moves with realistic precision and fluidity once engaged.

"I'm very well today," she says cheerfully. "Thank you for asking. Please place your chin in front of the facial recognition scanner."

"Wyatt, that's enough. You and Eden, come with me," she says, pulling her phone out of one of her pockets.

I follow her as she approaches who I assume to be the only real human behind the registration counter. Unlike several of the inhabitants of the Revelation Territory, he has lines creasing his face. His shirt is slightly wrinkled and untucked at his sides.

"How can I help you?" he asks Rose. His expressions are much less animated than his android co-workers.

"I have a pre-authorized clearance from my department for patient code 82-171V." She extends her phone toward the man, who squints his eyes as he scans the screen.

He mumbles while reading over his own computer screen and seems confused for a moment before realization crosses his face.

"Okay. Okay. Yes. I see it here," he says, clearing his throat. "If you'll just take this sleeve and place it on your left arm."

I slip the metallic sleeve with a cushioned interior on as he watches to make sure I'm doing it correctly. From inside one of his reception drawers, he pulls out a transparent green sticker in the shape of a common battery and places it on the platinum surface of my new sleeve, which reminds me of a brace-comm device.

"As long as this remains green, you will know sufficient energy is being channeled from your body to power your T13 unit. Give it one second," he says, firmly pressing the patch against my new sleeve device.

Within a couple seconds, the sleeve activates a 360-degree wraparound screen over my forearm.

"You have your basic information, like time, date, and temperature here, and these preloaded apps will provide all the other information you need. For example, click on the compass here, and you'll have your map with your current

THE REVELATION

location as well as a tracking communication system, which can guide you to wherever you need to be. Sound good?"

"As far as I know," I say plainly.

"Great. You're assigned to Beasley Pass," he says, seemingly avoiding eye contact with us both.

"What's that?" I ask, trying to follow his explanations.

"It's your housing pass, where you'll be assigned a living space. So if you click here and follow the instructions, you'll be guided through the necessary steps for resident intake."

Hara and Endon finish their intake before I do. They step behind their service counters and into two of the seven clear cylindrical chambers built into the back wall. Once they're inside, the chamber walls spin, revealing the silver backside of the tube. They're out of view for only a second, but when the clear side of the chamber spins back around, they're both gone.

My attention returns to the man behind the counter. "If you have any additional questions, Dean McLoud should be available to assist you."

I don't know who he's talking about, but I nod anyway.

"For now," he continues, "I just need you to step onto the platform behind me and keep your arms by your side. Once the chamber closes, it will open up to the other side, where you'll meet your group."

I quickly read his nametag. "Thanks for your help, Journey."

For someone with his name, I can't help but feel disappointed that he's stuck behind a desk. I step into my chamber at the same time as Merrin. I place my feet onto the designated shoe prints on the floor and hold my hands tight against my side. The wall in front of me quickly rotates open to a waiting area. The dull silver walls funnel ahead, converging at a double-door exit. The white floors glow under our feet as Rose gathers all of us at the center of the room.

"Everyone needs to look at their T13 units and find the personal identification, or PID, icon," Rose instructs. "It's the red Revelation Territory symbol on your home screen. All the necessary information you will need to pass through each security checkpoint will automatically load once you tap it. Go ahead and tap. We're about to clear security now."

We all do as she says. Instead of listed information, I see my fake name, my picture, and a bar code, which hides my personal data, as if I don't have security clearance for my own medical information.

Rose uses her authorization card to get us past the exiting doors, and we're intercepted in a dark room by heavily armed security guards. All at once, our upper armbands illuminate red, and the same faint color appears on the ground in lines, signaling our path ahead. Apart from the dull red glow, I can barely see anything, so I'm assuming the guards are using some form of night-vision equipment.

"Stop at the red line cutting off the path," an unfamiliar voice instructs. Guided by Rose, we do as commanded, stopping just before the red-outlined entryway.

"This is Sect Guard 161 requesting entry for six recruits escorted by Dean McLoud," the original guard says.

"Who is Dean McLoud?" Merrin whispers to me.

"Maybe it's Rose," I suggest, remembering the title on her ID badge.

"She doesn't look like a dean," he whispers.

"Permission granted," a voice responds from some speaker hidden in the darkness. "Step forward, please."

THE REVELATION

We enter a small elevator, and as soon as the door shuts, the lights come back on, revealing everyone's faces again. Our eyes squint, readjusting to the brightness.

"See? That wasn't so bad now, was it?" Rose asks, looking at no one in particular.

"What are you the dean of?" Endon asks Rose.

"I'm an interdepartmental dean of biochemical research. See?" she says, pointing to the title badge I noticed earlier. "I don't normally work intake, but I decided to tag along today." She stops. "And here we are."

The elevator doors open, revealing a vibrant marketplace hosting a bustling crowd of people just beyond a set of glass doors. Almost everyone is wearing uniforms, stylistically identical but varying in color scheme. I immediately begin scanning the many faces, looking for anyone who could resemble Ruma. I know the odds of finding her this soon are against me, but I can't help but try.

Just as we step past the entry doors, Rose announces, "This is Center Hub. Once you've earned buying privileges, you'll be able to find everything you need to live modestly around here." She waves her hands toward various kiosks as if she's conducting an invisible symphony.

Around us, vendors sell fresh produce and a diverse assortment of pasteries and sweets. Further in, we stop in the middle of a large indoor marketplace. My stomach is tight with hunger, and I'm already entertaining thoughts of buying food, even though I don't even know what currency they use. The bright environment on this side of the security doors seems peaceful and happy enough to make me wonder if people actually enjoy living here.

On the opposite side of Center Hub, there's a fifty-foot glass wall revealing a refreshingly picturesque view of the outside cityscape of the Revelation Territory, which contrasts greatly with what I'd expect of such a restrictive and authoritarian organization. I feel a sense of natural harmony reflecting off the eco-fashioned structures symbiotically rising amongst the rich green trees and flowering vines. Gray stone mountains glimmer like a majestic rampart surrounding the perimeter of the Gateway Valley, which hosts the Revelation Territory. People busily move around, investing themselves in a variety of tasks like landscaping, gardening, or selling goods.

"This place is like its own planet," Merrin says in wonder, sticking close by my side.

"It looks a lot happier than I would have guessed," I tell him, feeling a twinge of revulsion at offering this place any form of compliment.

"I guess insanity is much more enticing when it's attractive and organized," he mutters, incredulously surveying our new surroundings as we continue walking with our small group. I don't notice any form of ground transportation among the people walking on foot, but a few single-passenger aerocrafts hover higher up in the distance.

All of our T13 units vibrate in unison. Several strangers around us look at their units as well.

"That's just a life update," Rose explains, "which you all will receive periodically." She looks down. "Let's see. What does it say? Tomorrow night's meeting, yes. When you receive these, just follow the details provided. Meetings are mandatory, so do not miss them."

Rose maintains our attention long enough to inform us of our first task, which is to use our T13 units to find our way to our housing pass.

THE REVELATION

"You'll need to check in within the hour. You'll find your assigned living pass under the *Base* tab," Rose instructs.

"What pass? I don't have a pass," Merrin says nervously.

"Yes, you do. It's your assigned living passageway," Rose asserts, tapping her T13 unit, seeming flustered. "Just ask your friends. I'm sure they'll help you. Best of luck," she says distractedly before quickly walking away, leaving our small group unattended for the first time.

"So that's it?" Merrin asks. The six of us look between one another for a moment before realizing we all are equally uncertain.

The couple walks away together without bothering to say goodbye. I nudge Endon's arm and tell him and his sister, "Maybe we'll see you around."

"Yeah," he says, nodding politely, and we go our separate ways, moving out into the exterior courtyard of Center Hub.

"Look at the sky," Merrin says in awe. The transparent ceiling stretches the entire breadth between the encompassing mountains.

High above us, clear square panels cross-laced by thin muntins reach across the expansive sky, revealing a host of white clouds. From inside, no one would ever know that from above, as Edwin showed us in the storm, the panels project a simulated tree canopy that completely conceals the Revelation Territory.

"This place is a giant, beautiful cage," Merrin says faintly, shaking his head.

"Don't say that. It makes me want to panic."

"Panic won't do you any good. It'll be best if we just go with the flow until we figure out what's going on."

"What's happening to us?" I ask, clenching my jaws as acid

in my stomach threatens to climb. "How long are we going to be here?"

"We'll be all right. Let's just keep walking," he suggests, pulling my arm along.

I focus on breathing as Merrin leads us away from the high-traffic areas until only a few people are around us in a tranquilly shaded rest area. We step off the paved walkway just under the shade of a low-hanging tree.

Merrin suddenly hugs me, and I'm thrown off guard.

Before I can ask what he's doing, he presses close against my ear and hastily whispers, "Listen to me. We won't be here long. Ruma is here. Don't ask questions. They could be watching or listening to us."

My heart races, and my skin runs cold with chills. He pulls away, and I hold on to his shoulders. I don't know what to say. So many questions flash across my mind that I know can't be answered here.

"So how do I find my pass?" he asks, breaking away from me. I need a few seconds to mentally and emotionally change gears.

"Uh..." I mumble uncertainly, trying to come up with an answer. "Look. Right here," I say, tapping his Base tab.

How much does he know? How does he know Ruma is here? I want to ask him, but if our conversations are being monitored, I'm afraid to risk being heard. Hugging him again to whisper might seem suspicious if someone might be watching us as he says.

"Oh. Got it. So let's find Hansen Pass," Merrin says, blowing out a tight puff of air.

"Mine says Beasley Pass. Why is mine different?" I ask, worried we might be assigned separate living quarters. I'm not sure how I'll psychologically hold up here on my own.

"What?" he questions, grabbing my T13 unit to see for himself. "Well, shit. I guess we'll have to separate for a little while. How many passes are there?"

I scroll through. "Looks like four. Our two, and then there's a Shalland and a Rae Pass."

"Okay. Well, I guess we should go check in and try to meet up after," he suggests, nodding reassuringly as he tightly squeezes my arm. "It's going to be okay."

The sensitive discolored splotch in the crease of my elbow stings as Merrin releases his grip.

"The bites," I say as a thought hits me.

"What?" he asks, concerned.

"It's not a bite. Anger injected us," I say, inspecting my arm.

"Don't worry about it," he urges, pushing my hand away as if to divert my attention from the suspicious bruise. "Let's just do one thing at a time."

I stare at him, confused, but I quickly realize he's trying to evade my previous comment, so I don't force it. Our T13 units sound again, reminding us of our intake schedule.

"Thirty minutes until check-in," Merrin reads aloud tranquilly.

My T13 unit vibrates again on my arm. I tap the screen to view the message, *Follow your navigation system to Regents Core.*

"You didn't get this?" I ask, showing him my message.

"No. Not yet. We'll give it a second."

I stare at his arm. We wait, but nothing happens.

"I guess it's just for me," I say, still watching Merrin's T13 unit. Unable to process openly with Merrin for fear of being heard, I can't help but wonder if the continual instances of being singled out—from Ms. Diana, to Commander Locke, and now with being summoned separately from Merrin—all have to do with being Ruma's brother.

"Do you want me to go with you?" Merrin offers worriedly, reading my unconcealed angst.

I can tell he's trying hard to act normal when I know we're both feeling anything but that. My mind keeps trying to reconcile why Anger turned us over to be captured and how she might have made some deal with the twins, but nothing is making sense. If Merrin is right about Ruma actually being here with us, then for now, finding Ruma is the priority.

"You hear me? I can go with you," he repeats.

"Yeah," I decide, trying to focus.

"Okay, good. Let's do one thing at a time," Merrin says coolly. "Take a few good breaths. Breathe."

I do as he says and feel my short breaths begin to stretch out into full inhales.

"Keep doing that. Now tell me what it says on your screen."

I look back at my screen to see a timer counting down the seconds from my allotted travel time.

"It says I have eight minutes. Why is there a timer?" I ask while clicking on the navigation icon.

"At least it doesn't look too far," Merrin says, following the projected trail.

"So we have to follow the line to the destination."

"Sounds easy enough. Let's go, then," he says.

Our directions have us retrace our steps back to Center Hub. This time, we enter the vaulted glass doors and turn to the right, dodging more expressionless faces and shoulders busily filling their uniform satchels with fresh vegetables and goods.

An aroma of freshly baked bread turns my head. Three elderly women stand side by side, kneading bread in nearly perfect unison behind a silver counter. Across from the women, at another exhibition stand, a circular platform rises from beneath the ground, releasing a cool puff of frosted air. Two identically dressed men disperse packs of neatly sealed meats to their co-workers before disappearing once more underground.

We walk until the navigation marker on my T13 unit leads us past the crowds and vendor stations to the back corner of Center Hub. Here, the sharply geometric walls and bright ceiling beams of the marketplace appear to melt down in design, forming a more rugged, naturalistic stone passageway. The cavernous tunnel, full of colorful nestling plants, feels more like a portal to another dimension than an exit leading away from Center Hub. Softly glowing bioluminescent flowers fill a curved walkway designed like a wind-weathered mountain pass.

"I don't know if this is right, but my navigation route is telling me to go that way," I say, pointing to the tunnel.

"I guess we'll find out soon," Merrin says, following me as we walk toward the funneling passageway.

My attention focuses on the suspended plants hanging among the assembled stone fixtures. Once Merrin and I enter the cave, we reach out to touch the numerous glowing flowers blossoming, giving off small patches of light against the dark walls. Others walk past us, uninterested in stopping to appreciate the beauty.

The opposite mouth of the tunnel opens up into another

security checkpoint, which seems more like we've stumbled upon a hidden entrance to heaven.

"Oh my God," I say, slowly dropping the words from my mouth as I marvel at the incomparably lavish architecture.

Merrin doesn't respond. His mouth is slightly open, and his eyes strain as if they're struggling to take in all the detail. Two giant golden statues stand with open arms, greeting everyone who walks before them. Rising behind the two figures, a high white-marble wall embellished with golden floral designs serves as the backdrop of a decorative iron fence partitioning the entryway. Golden letters inlaid on the bright metal archway display the word REVELATIONS.

Beyond the gateway, the massive white-marble wall stretches at least eighty feet high, serving as the front edifice of one of the Revelation Territory's interior facilities. Amongst the golden flowers, the wall hosts a legion of flawlessly carved marble angels trimmed with golden accents, each poised with purpose and splendor. Several of the angels hold overflowing bowls of water that spill from the top of the wall and pass water into the other bowls below until the water reaches a bottom pool, which runs the full length of the white wall.

As we move closer, the bright diamond eyes of the angels sparkle with increasing radiance. A glowing assembly of warm lights overhead breathes down on the angels like the last sacred whispers of light spoken by the sun before it sinks below the horizon.

Our final destination is an inferiorly designed white elevator a short walk away from the decorative archway. The timer on my T13 unit beeps, reminding me I have less than three minutes remaining, so I decide to use my last moments to soak in the unexpected beauty.

THE REVELATION

"Look at the names on the plaques," Merrin says, pointing them out as we approach the two golden monumental statues.

"Bishop Isaac Kane and Mother Rebekkah Casborn," I read aloud.

"They're the founders of the monastery and convent that were in our introduction video," Merrin says. He looks at me. "Are you going to keep going?"

I pause for a second. "I didn't even think about it being an option *not* to go."

"Do you think I can go with you?"

"I don't know," I respond, but I think he won't be coming with me.

"Your time is almost done," Merrin says, pointing at my T13 unit with some concern.

The seconds count down in the teens on my timer.

"Yeah, I know, but sooner or later I'm going to buck this place, so I might as well start now just to see what happens."

I watch the timer hit zero, and Merrin and I stare at the screen, awaiting any further instructions. Suddenly I feel a stinging pinch in my arm underneath my T13 unit.

"Shit!" I say, shaking my left arm.

"What's wrong?"

"This thing poked into my arm," I tell him, squeezing my arm.

"What do you mean?" he asks uneasily.

"I mean it poked me. It stuck something in my arm," I tell him quickly. "I think it injected me with something. My arm is tingling."

"Are you sure?" he asks, examining his own T13 unit as if trying to understand what could've happened to mine.

I repeatedly bend my fingers at their joints, trying to gauge my sense of dexterity. I notice a commotion in the crowd to my left.

"That's Endon and Hara," I tell Merrin as I point in their direction.

Hara is holding her wrist as she panics. Did the same thing happen to her? My head starts swimming, and the daylight becomes increasingly bright. A sharp whistle begins filling my ears with a steady crescendo.

"Hey. Hey! You okay?" Merrin asks, grabbing my arm.

Over his shoulder, I notice two men in matching uniforms approaching Endon and Hara, weapons pointed in their direction. They fire, one after the other.

"No!" Endon screams, throwing himself in front of his sister, even though he's too late.

The Revelation Territory inhabitants cautiously scatter away but don't protest.

The first shot strikes Hara with a strand of wires, which appear to latch on to her skin. The second blast fires a powerful energy wave that throws Endon's body across the ground before he limply slides to a halt. Once he's out of the way, the first marksman fires pulsing electrical waves through the wires connected to Hara. In a moment, she is engulfed by a small black cloud burst, and then she's gone.

Merrin and I stand paralyzed. What's almost more disturbing than seeing Hara vanish from right in front of me is that no one around us seems to be bothered by what's just happened.

Several needlelike prongs pierce my back, and I scream in pain. Merrin grabs me, and I feel him tugging at the cords latched on to my back for a moment before hot wind rushes over both of us. Other than feeling that stabbing pinch from

THE REVELATION

the cords tugging at my skin, I'm unaffected by the blast of energy. I watch in terror as Merrin's body tumbles across the white-marble floor.

I close my eyes, unable to focus on anything but my escalating sensory overload. All I feel is an incessant tingling throughout my entire body, as if a million tiny, panicking ants are crawling over me.

My consciousness passes into what feels like an entirely different realm, like I'm floating amongst the chaos between worlds. I hear sounds, but I can't distinguish between my senses and my thoughts. My body feels loose, as if I were melting into vibrating waves, almost like my mind has split into pieces.

White light fills my vision, and the tingling sensation in my skin quickly begins to subside along with the harsh trilling sound in my head, which now gives way to the deep, rhythmic thumping of my heartbeat. I heave in stuttered breaths. A few more colors break into my vision as abstract shapes slowly resolve into a fuzzy outlines of figures moving around a thickly furnished room.

I'm in an entirely different place from where I left Merrin, and I'm not alone. Is Merrin here somewhere? Several stripped bodies stand fastened into strange medical holding devices, which are still too blurry to make out. Other bodies busily move around the room as blotches of color.

Harsh noises soften into words, and someone calls, "Eden. Eden, I need you to relax. Can you hear me?"

A fresh sting burns in my forearm, and I'm almost relieved because the pain is one of the few things grounding me to reality. A pair of white-gloved hands carefully maneuvers a needle into one of the more prominent veins in my left arm.

Someone straps both of my arms out, perpendicular to my body.

As my vision clears, I notice my T13 unit is gone and so are my clothes, with the exception of an undergarment covering me from my waist to midway down my thigh.

The lights hanging above shine too bright for me to see the ceiling. The holding mechanism fastened around my body raises me to an upright, standing position. I now clearly see the other faces, trapped in my same condition, positioned around the room in a semicircle formation.

A deep swirl of sound whips into the room. My eyes flash over to a dark billowing cloud that disappears as quickly as it came, leaving behind a naked body curled up in the fetal position. *They've teleported us here.* My head throbs incessantly as I'm unable to reconcile what I've just seen. Two attendants quickly intercept a girl around my age, covering her and lifting her into the arms of a medical holding device, where they strap her down.

I look away and pinch my eyes closed. I continue opening and closing them over and over, trying to wake up from what I fear isn't a hallucinogenic dream.

When I look back to where the attendants have positioned the girl, they've sparsely covered her groin. Her head slumps over her left shoulder, and dark hair covers her face and chest. As she is brought to an upright position, her head swings forward and then backward, so her neck is stretched tight. She lets out a loud groan, and the attendants quickly sedate her. My heart swells in my chest and my throat tightens. Her head falls forward again as she scans the room, bewildered.

Her eyes meet mine. Neither of us can look away. Whether by impossible coincidence or disturbing intentionality, I realize the Revelation Territory has stolen Rhysk Shaer away from her Special Ops trainings in New Province Guard. Now the two of us stand strapped and nearly bare within the cold confines of the same medical observation lab, miles away from where we first met.

CHAPTER 20

Why did they bring us both here? Hysterical shrieking breaks my attention away from Rhysk. Hara is screaming out of her mind. In my initial scan of the room, I'd missed seeing her. I should have expected her to be here after watching her get zapped right before I did.

Her attendants quickly silence her with an injection. She slumps forward, knocked unconscious in a matter of seconds. She looks even more frail and breakable than before. Like me, nine other detainees stand bolstered in numerous restraints. Of the nine other faces, I only recognize two.

I'm shaking and can't stop myself. The room is cold, and the metal pushing against my skin to hold me upright is uncomfortably chilly. My bones feel fragile beneath my skin, as if I could fall apart from a single wrong movement. Even if I wanted to revolt, I physically can't. I'm not sure who all has noticed that I'm conscious, so I try to keep my movements subtle.

THE REVELATION

The white fluorescent lights around us intensify. I want to close my eyes and disappear, but I'm more afraid of what I will miss if I don't stay alert. The arching walls of the semicircular room rise to meet a high glass wall in front of me. From the way we are positioned, the glass seems to serve as a large observation window, shielding us from whoever is watching on the other side. Whatever the case, I have a good vantage point to observe the room and the additional people behind me.

As I stare at my reflection in the glass, I feel like I'm watching an animal subdued in a trap. Is that what we are to them? Tears pool in the corner of my eyes at the humiliating thought. The ten of us barely have any covering over our bodies.

I hear a few one-way conversations around me, so the attendants must be receiving orders from earpieces.

"We're ready for the observation team to enter," a female voice calls from out of sight.

Within a few seconds, a door in the wall's reflection releases a hydraulic sigh. Several people dressed in gray bodysuits casually make their way to tiered observation seats sectioned off behind us. Like the attendants, these people are wearing face masks with a reflective strip running across their hidden eyes. The rest of their faces are exposed behind clear masks. They must feel safe behind the clear bolted covering concealing them in the observation area. Their entry door hisses as it closes shut again.

I look back to Rhysk. Her eyes are locked ahead of her as if she is trying to burn a hole in the glass. I wish she would look my way. I want her to know she's not alone, assuming she recognized me. Surely she did? She's the only source of comfort I have in this room. A surge of ice-cold liquid pinches into the veins in my neck and forearms. My nine counterparts grimace too, so I know I'm not alone in my pain.

I listen to pieces of the light conversations passing back and forth between the onlookers in the observation deck to see if I can make sense of why any of us are here.

"I didn't see anything worth bidding on last time, so I'm hoping this bunch will be worth the trip," a strangely accented voice grumbles behind me.

"They haven't provided us with sufficient eugenic statistics on half this group," another man complains. "You can't expect someone to invest without being informed."

"You know that's how they get you here," a throaty voice scoffs. "You can drown yourself in eugenic reports, but there's nothing like seeing it live."

"Look at that one. He's adorable," a female voice comments, pointing at me dotingly as if I were an animal on display in a pet shop window.

"Preparing phase two of revelation," a woman announces through the surrounding speakers, and all the curious voices in the designated viewing area go silent. The room holds its breath. The silence breaks a moment later as brassy, automated hums coming from the other side of the wall vibrate the floor.

"Revelation fifty percent complete," the announcer narrates.

Fifty percent of what? I'm positioned on the far right of the room with only one young man to my right. The clean thrumming sounds move from the far side of the room in tandem with a violet light source scanning smoothly from my left toward me.

"Revelation eighty percent complete."

THE REVELATION

I look back at Rhysk, and she's staring at me. She mouths something I can't understand. But she sees me, so we're not alone. I focus harder, even though my eyes are weak. She tries again, but I can't read her lips.

A faint scream breaks my focus, but it's not coming from this side of the wall. The attendants' hands simultaneously cover their ears, as if the noise is amplified within their earpieces. A violent pounding sounds from behind the glass directly in front of me. It strikes again and again until a long crack splits my reflection in half. Behind me, the observers' screams fill the room. In the fragmented reflections of glass, I watch them stumbling over their seats toward the door.

"They're trying to break through! Get them out. Now!" the narrating attendant yells while the observers panic.

"What's happening?" I ask the attendant assisting me, but she ignores me.

"Are the evac receptors charged?" she yells to the lead attendant, who is still cupping her hands over her earphones. "We need to know now!"

The lead attendant removes her left hand from her ear and holds one finger up high, signaling for everyone to wait. Even though the deep poundings cracking the viewing wall have subsided, our attendants scramble to our sides, unbuckling us and injecting us again with yet another needle.

A moment later, she screams "Now!" and my personal attendant begins tapping a quick sequence on the panel attached to my seat restraints, and her counterparts do the same for the other nine captives. This initiates a transformation sequence of the ten restraining devices, which shape-shift in sync to envelop all ten of us into pod-like structures.

Rhysk's capsule swallows her, and I can only see her

face through a thin, clear strip on the shell's casing. The lady assigned to Rhysk's device slaps another pad, which recreates the same engulfing black smoke I witnessed when Hara was first teleported away. A moment later, the dark swirl dissolves again within the capsule, leaving only an empty harness inside.

My own pod envelops me, and the seal pops shut. Overcome by the anticipation of teleporting once again, I begin hyperventilating. The soft hum of oxygen pumping into my shell attempts to stabilize me. I am powerless to escape the tortuous sensation I know is coming, so I whisper "Help me" over and over again, even though I know no one is coming.

I think of my parents and Jaykin, and then of my bed at home. Every thought I'm pulling to bring me comfort suddenly gives way to nauseating hypersensitivity followed by tormenting numbness. The feeling takes me like a storm, pushing me into the in-between as I let go of consciousness.

A sharp, stabbing pain sinks deep into the back of my neck. My entire body tingles as if tiny pins are lightly poking into my skin. My eyes open to soft light, and my focus strains to pull my surroundings together. Merrin is standing by my side again.

"Whoa, whoa. Lay back," he says.

Knowing he's here instantly helps me to relax as much as I can into my stiff bed. The medical room looks familiar, even though my mind is too hazy to recall from where.

"Take it easy. You need to rest," Merrin suggests.

My mouth is dry, so when I try to ask where I am, only a few syllables come out.

"You're back with me," a different voice says from behind

THE REVELATION

my head. Jerrico, my attendant from when I first awoke in the Revelation Territory, comes around the side of my bed to wave before continuing to adjust one of the intravenous cords slithering behind my shoulder like a cold snake.

"No!" I scream, jerking away from him while swinging to keep his hands away from me. My stomach spasms, and a cold shudder washes over my body as I remember the aching prickle from the last shots I was given before I was transported to the observation lab.

"Stop! It's okay. You're okay. He's here to help you," Merrin says, forcing me to lie back again. "We got you."

I cover my face with my hands and close my eyes, still seeing the fresh images of Rhysk, Hara, and the seven other people strapped down like animals. Where is Rhysk? As soon as the thought hits my mind, I realize Merrin doesn't know she's here.

"Here," Merrin says, bringing some water to my mouth. I take the cup from him and gratefully down every drop. I lie back and catch my breath again. My head feels like a cloud of thick fog.

"You with me?" Merrin asks, and I realize I've zoned out. I can barely contain telling him about seeing Rhysk, but at this point, I don't know if anything I say could interfere with me finding Ruma.

"Yes," I finally respond, still struggling. My disjointed thoughts seem to make my head tighten with pressure.

"Okay, good. Just relax. Jerrico is going to get you back to normal. You just have to let him help you," he reassures me as Jerrico carefully administers a fresh batch of an unidentified medication into my veins while monitoring my readings.

My fingers repeatedly squeeze into my palms, and my toes

press firmly against the metal bar fixed at the end of my bed, just so I can feel some sense of being grounded.

"Where did you go? Before I could get up off the ground, you had already disappeared, and your clothes and your T13 unit were just laying where you stood."

"I don't know how to explain it," I tell him hazily, which is mostly true, but considering my mental exhaustion and not knowing whether I can trust Jerrico, I decide it's better not to explain what I saw.

"Tell me something you remember," he suggests, trying to pull more information from me before he's interrupted by an unfamiliar raspy voice that draws my attention to the doorway.

"Don't worry about him. I'll take care of your friend," an elderly man weakly says while locking eyes with me. His skin shines so pale under the white light that he almost looks as if he's glowing. A gray suit covers his narrow figure with several sharp edges, which almost appear like starched feathers.

"Dr. Voorst," Jerrico says, addressing the unexpected guest with a respectful head bow.

Even though his strained smile gives way to very few wrinkles, there's a certain quality that makes him seem much older. Maybe it's his bald head or his frail posture.

"Well, everything you've been doing looks as if it's working," he says, acknowledging Jerrico's efforts with a simple open palm that folds back over his right hand.

"Thank you. I'm doing what I can," he says with a short-lived smirk.

Dr. Voorst addresses me again. "Your friend Wyatt has done a good job of watching over you, but I'll be taking over from here."

THE REVELATION

"Who?" I ask, and then I catch Merrin's wide eyes.

"Wyatt. Your friend," Jerrico says, noticing the flicker of confusion in my eyes before I can conceal it.

Dr. Voorst makes no effort to hide his suspicion of my answer, so I try and recover.

"Sorry. My head feels really foggy," I say, which is still true.

He pauses, narrowing his eyes while letting a stretch of silence weigh over the room.

"Tell me your name," he demands, slightly tilting his gaunt face.

I can't remember my fake name, and my mind completely freezes over.

"Eden needs rest," Merrin says, covering for me.

Dr. Voorst ignores Merrin's request. His thin, dry lips part as he stares at me, frozen, as if struck by a sudden epiphany.

"You're not who you say you are, are you?" he asks, his eyes bright and wild. "That's why she tried to get to you."

Who was trying to get me? He quickly raises his forearm to his lips and whispers, "Send Reaper assistance to my location."

My eyes catch movement at the door behind us. Rose hastily rushes into the room with a duffle bag thrown over her shoulder. Armed with a small gun, she aims and fires at the old man.

A thin projectile flies from the barrel and strikes just above his pointed collar. His crisp gray eyes widen as he tries to claw the protruding object out of his skin, but his body falls limp to the ground as if he's been deflated.

"What are you doing?" Jerrico asks, horrified.

Rose points the weapon directly at him. "It's a tranquilizer. Shut your mouth, or you're next."

Keeping her aim, Rose moves hastily to lock the door.

"They're onto us," she says, addressing Merrin directly. "You'll both be staying with me."

"Wait, what? What do you know?" I ask Merrin, completely lost.

"They made me promise not to tell you anything for your safety," Merrin tells me, struggling to stay calm.

"There's a reason someone tried to break through that wall," Rose explains. "They don't know why, but it's enough to make them suspicious of everyone who was on your side of the wall."

"Who was trying to get me?" I ask.

"For your protection, I can't tell you anything more. Just follow my instructions."

Rose bends over the old man's contorted body and snatches something from his pocket.

"Rhysk is here," I blurt out to Merrin. "They've got her. They had us locked up in these machines and people were bidding on us," I say, struggling to control my anger.

Merrin stands in shock, his mouth open.

"You've got to reel him back in," Rose says to Merrin, shaking her head as she begins dragging the old man's limp body across the floor toward the back corner of the room. She struggles to pull him as she walks backward.

"You going to help me?" she asks Jerrico, who hasn't moved since Rose tranquilized the old man. "I can always blame this on you."

Jerrico reluctantly assists her.

"Merrin. Who is coming for me?" I ask, my voice shaking.

"I'm so sorry. I promised I wouldn't put you in danger—"

"Answer me!" I scream.

THE REVELATION

"It's Ruma!" Merrin yells back, gritting his teeth as he firmly grabs my arm. His voice fades to a whisper. "She's here, and now she knows you're here. But you've got to calm down or you'll mess everything up."

Rose drops the man's limp arms back to the floor and stares silently between the two of us. "Hide him in the cabinets," she orders Jerrico.

"I'll be blamed for this for sure," Jerrico mutters, seemingly on the verge of tears.

"After tonight, you're the least of their worries, right before Dr. Voorst. Now shut him up in there," Rose fiercely commands Jerrico. She then steps toward me. "Ruma recognized you through the glass. She almost fucked everything up, and you're about to do the same if you don't shut your damn mouth. That's all you have to do. Can you do that?"

"How did she—"

"I am asking you. Yes or no?"

"Yes," I say, feeling sweat dripping down my forehead.

"Good. Now, you can sit there, or you can help us hide this son of a bitch so we don't get caught."

"Who is he?" Merrin asks, helping Jerrico fold the old man's bony legs into the cabinet.

"My boss," she says plainly.

Jerrico holds open one of the storage closet doors, and Merrin and Rose quickly work to finish shoving her boss's sedated body inside.

"Here. Take this," she says, walking over to meet me, her hand extended. I try to examine what she's holding first, but she impatiently slaps it into my hands before I get a good look. "Take it!"

"What is it?" I ask, examining the thick card.

"Security authorization. We'll need it."

I stare at the card in my hand, unsure of where to put it.

"Look at me," she says, gently turning my face with her hand. "Pull it together."

She is only a few inches away from my face and is staring directly into my eyes. Something about her reminds me of Anger. She doesn't bother waiting for my response. Rose seems like an entirely different person.

She moves toward the door, where she digs through the white duffel bag she brought into the room upon her arrival. I place the card inside my left pants pocket while she pulls out two pairs of bright silver boots. She gives one pair to each of us, along with two solid tan jumpsuits.

"Let's do one thing at a time. Jerrico, help them dress," she manages to say gently. "Oh, and here are their weights." She passes him two encumbered straps.

"What are those for?" Merrin asks.

"Just strap them around your waist," Jerrico says firmly, and we do so.

We throw on the bodysuits first and then step into our new boots. They're surprisingly light and fit well as I secure the straps above my ankle. Rose's boss apparently busted his nose when his face hit the floor, so Rose hastily cleans up the smeared trail of blood while we dress.

"Listen to me," Rose whispers. "You're not supposed to leave this room, but only a few people know that." She briefly tosses her head toward the cabinets where they stored the body of her unconscious boss. "Your shoes have tracking devices in the soles. The floors are constantly scanning, so there are certain rooms you cannot enter without triggering security. Although I gave you shoes from someone who has access, you

THE REVELATION

have to match the approximate weight of whoever's shoes you are wearing at the access doors."

Merrin taps his waist where the weighted straps rest. "Got it."

"We've been given a small window of time to move you out of here with suspended security surveillance. We'll need to move quickly, but *don't* bring attention to yourself. If we're caught, it's over. Understand?"

"No," Merrin says bluntly, "but we're used to that." He nods at me. "Let's do this."

"Okay," I respond, trying to assure myself as much as them.

"Ready?" she asks Jerrico as she heads for the door. Jerrico, still pallid and distraught, follows close behind her. I look at Merrin for affirmation. Of course he doesn't have any better idea of what we should do. He makes the first move toward the door as Rose disappears beyond the exit.

"Wait," I whisper to Merrin. "Why do you trust her?"

"I don't trust *her*. I trust what I think's motivating her," Merrin says, nodding for me to follow him.

"What's that?" I ask, feeling very aware of his growth in maturity.

"Revenge," he says before leaving me to follow him out of the room.

Trying to embrace the small amount of faith I have amidst overwhelming uncertainty, I follow after Rose, Jerrico, and Merrin, hoping that somehow I'll find Ruma along the way.

Once in the hallway, we try to move inconspicuously while catching up to Rose. The reflective metal walls and rich copper floors look very similar to the hallways where I first met Rose. At every doorway, she scans her eyes and fingers over a holographic screen. She stops occasionally to study an illuminated three-dimensional map on a slender device running across the length of her forearm, similar to our T13 units.

"We're almost there," she whispers into her device as we move.

She stops abruptly and places her hand against an empty metallic-gray wall. A keypad becomes visible around her hand, and within seconds, the outline of a doorway appears as if from nothing.

"And some places," she continues, "you have absolutely no business going."

The door slides into the ceiling, the perfectly white walls of the hallway look more like a passageway into the afterlife.

"Keep quiet," Rose says to Jerrico as sweat drips from his forehead. "If they find out, I'll make sure your name is mentioned with mine." Without making eye contact, he hastily nods before stepping through the doorway. The sliding wall retreats back toward the ceiling and the doorway's seal vanishes once again as if it never existed.

"This way," Rose says, retracing a portion of our steps until we turn down yet another hallway and pass through an automated doorway into a small elevator. The clear revolving door closes behind us.

We stand behind Rose as she presses the necessary buttons to keep us moving. From behind, I notice a long scar on the side of Rose's neck. Even though she seemed much more cordial and professional when I first met her, she's slowly starting to remind me of Anger.

"We're in the lower access areas now, so more people will be around. Stay close. We don't need to stand out. Stay calm

THE REVELATION

and follow me," Rose lightly commands, changing her voice back to her familiar cheery inflection.

The elevator doors split open, and just as Rose warned, several new faces pass by. Numerous people are wearing red-and-white uniforms identical to my own. I keep my eyes to myself. Rose looks ahead, unbothered, only speaking when prompted by someone else's passing greeting.

"Please tell me what we're doing," I whisper, dipping my head down toward Merrin's shoulder as we walk.

"I really don't know," he confesses, shaking his head. "I'm just sticking to my part of the mission."

"What's your part?"

"Taking care of you," he says. "Deep breaths. Okay?"

I keep my eyes wide, peering into every passing window lining the new stretch of hallway. From a few quick passing glances, I notice masked scientists shrouded in full white body suits, busily engaging with a plethora of scientific equipment. I'm sure the odds are against me, but I can't help but hope to catch a glimpse of Rhysk to make sure she's okay. I wonder what Merrin thinks, knowing she's here, but there's no telling if we'll be able to have a moment alone to talk. We continue passing through a high archway and into an expansive circular atrium hosting numerous floors above us and significantly more people.

Some wear the familiar red and white-accented uniform, but now several other outfits mix among the crowd. I've determined everyone's attire distinguishes their rank or purpose in the Revelation Territory's social hierarchy. The mostly solid-colored jumpsuits, with varying numbers of arm and leg stripes, seem to make up one tier. A few rare people model the same sharp-edged design Rose and her boss wear.

Another tier dresses in black form-fitting armor, and they stand guard in pairs all throughout the atrium. I dodge the eyes of these Legionnaires, who stand alert as we cross to the opposite side of the commons area.

I'm not certain, but from the look of the exorbitant use of rich white marble and gold trim within the structural formations of the massive atrium, I assume we're just beyond the other side of the lavishly decorated edifice Merrin and I were marveling at before Hara and I were teleported away. Almost hidden amongst the bustling crowd is a small herd of men and women formally dressed in business attire, huddling together as a tour guide provides a live narration describing the functioning significance of each tiered level. The guide points toward the direction where we just came, and I pick up her sentence.

"...is our Biochemical Research wing, and to the right, beneath the beautiful silver installation of our Revelation Territory symbol, poised between the outstretched angel wings, you'll notice the entrance to our Intake and Rescue Rehabilitation branch, where we give a second chance at life to many people who otherwise wouldn't be alive without our help."

The small crowd seems to easily swallow her lie with nods and approving comments. I would be curious to see how the tour group would've reacted if they'd seen Rhysk and I pinned half naked beneath the painful medical restraints back in the observation lab. The guide herds her cluster of followers into one of the many elevators symmetrically positioned throughout the atrium. The elevator columns function as the supporting pillars of the atrium's infrastructure.

A group of eight armed Legionnaires files out of one of

THE REVELATION

the elevators and rushes directly at us. I freeze for a moment and bend down to fasten my shoe, attempting to hide my face. I'm afraid any second they'll tackle me to the floor. I stay low to the ground as they brush between the other Revelation Territory inhabitants and eventually weave past me. My forehead instantly feels hot, and my palms begin feeling sticky with sweat as I rise to catch up with Merrin and Rose.

"Where do you think they're going?" someone asks. Without stopping, we move along, knowing exactly where they are headed. I wonder how long it will take them to find Rose's boss stuffed inside the cabinets.

We approach one of the exits leading outdoors and pass a small line of people who, with the help of armed guards, are filing through a security checkpoint.

"Eden, you and Wyatt can use the security cards I gave you to get through this checkpoint. Ride the platform lift all the way up to the observatory. Wait for me there," Rose instructs us before whispering, "Where's your card?"

I'm glad she's remembering to use our fake names because that's the last thing on my mind. I reach for my pockets and immediately remember I put the security card in my pants right before I changed into my current uniform.

"I don't have it," I say, weighted with disappointment. "We changed clothes."

Rose hesitates for a moment, so we stop. She makes a decision quickly, and we continue toward a black-armored Legionnaire who appears to be in control of a smaller, exclusive line. A nearby sign reads DESIGNATED CLEARANCE FOR INTERDEPARTMENTAL PERSONNEL.

Rose tries to walk straight through but is stopped by a large woman who's a few inches taller than Merrin.

"Wait! Wait. Where are you going?" she asks, timidly holding out her hands in protest.

"I'm taking these transfers to their new housing pass. I called it in over an hour ago," Rose responds sternly.

"What's your name?" the woman asks Rose while barely acknowledging us.

Rose bears the full weight of her eyes over the young woman before curtly saying, "Dean McLoud."

The woman's expression shifts distinctly, as if she's been hit in the face by a bucket of cold water.

"I'm... I'm sorry. I didn't recognize—" she stammers before another, older woman, someone I'm assuming is her superior, steps in.

"Excuse me," she says to her subordinate. "What's the issue here? Has she been given authorization?"

"Yes. Well, she says she has. This is Dean McLoud, ma'am," she says with conviction.

"I know who she is. That's not what I asked. Do they have their entry cards?"

"I... I don't know, ma'am. I haven't asked yet. Do you have your entry card, ma'am?" she asks Rose.

Before Rose can answer, the tall woman's commander says, "There's no way we can let anyone through without their entry card."

"Look," Rose says, holding her ground. "Now's not the time for games. My father has demanded to meet with me before his provincial order address. I told a friend I'd do her a favor and take these new intakes to their housing pass, and yes, one of them already lost his ID, but if you'd like to explain to my father why you've detained an interdepartmental dean for the

THE REVELATION

simple matter of a new recruit misplacing his *temporary* ID, I'll gladly call him now."

The subordinate's lips purse together tightly. Her boss begins to speak before changing her mind, but her mouth is open as if she still wants to say something. She robotically extends a handheld device toward Rose, who kindly offers up her T13 unit for scanning.

Once she is cleared, Rose instructs Merrin to offer up his card, and after a few reassuring beeps signal that all is well, we're cleared to enter. Whatever power stands behind Rose's name, it certainly seems have been enough to intimidate our way through. After the visibly miffed boss walks away, her subordinate offers a hasty apology. Rose nods and flashes a forced but gracious smile before leading us onward.

Not far ahead, we queue up in a line leading down a darker passageway that ends before a carousel of short platforms. Small groups of about eight people at a time board the platforms before being taken up a tunnel at a steep incline.

Rose pulls us on with a group of five, and we shuttle upward through the softly glowing tunnel. After three brief stops, we're the only three remaining on our platform. One more short trip releases us at the foot of a spiraling stairwell.

We head up the winding stone-carved staircase until we step into a large glass observatory. I can see the night sky clearly, and I can't tell if the protective shield over the Revelation Territory is transparent from the inside or if the simulated sky is just indistinguishably realistic.

Some Revelation Territory inhabitants linger at the half dozen stargazing outposts, but we take no additional time to admire the night sky. Instead we follow Rose's hasty steps out onto a balcony, nearly circumnavigating the exterior of the observatory.

"This way," she orders without checking to see if we're still following her. "The cameras up here are barely monitored, so they were the easiest to hack."

We pass a few quiet conversations in the dark and make our way to an uninhabited corner of the balcony. Rose reaches underneath a nearby bench and retrieves a black bag before emptying its contents in front of us.

"So here is the part where I have to trust you both have had training," she whispers as she begins securing a rappelling rope to a camming device. "We're going to move through a restricted sector of woods, but first we need to grapple down quickly before anyone sees us. Now's as good a time as ever. I'll go first, and I trust you'll follow."

"*Please*, Rose, can you tell us where we're going?" I ask as patiently as I can.

Rose climbs onto the stone ledge. "I had all incoming and outgoing signals blocked from your T13 units. Otherwise you would have received a secondary update about today's mandatory meeting, the provincial order address—that's where we're going."

"But they'll be looking for us," I say, wondering if anyone has discovered that we're missing from wherever we're supposed to be.

"I don't make messes I can't clean up," she says. "Now let's go. You don't want to miss this."

After a short moment of contemplation, I look at her and nod. She clamps the rappelling bracers on the ledge and then passes us our connecting hooks.

"Watch me," she says while quietly instructing us on how to prepare ourselves before the jump.

THE REVELATION

"And the rest is up to you," she says before rappelling over the edge and disappearing below.

"Do you think she'll be there?" I ask Merrin while he attaches his harness.

"Ruma? Or Rhysk?" he asks, hoisting himself over the wall.

"Both."

"I don't know, but there's one way to find out."

Without hesitation, he disappears into the night. Merrin has already committed to whatever mission Rose threw at us by flinging himself after her, so I choose to trust him.

I reach out to connect my waist to the harness. All the while, I'm second-guessing myself. My hands brace tightly onto the ledge as my legs fling over the side.

In this moment of darkness, there is nothing else left for me to do but let go and hope when my feet hit the ground, I can find the courage to not let fear, uncertainty, and the agenda of strangers distract me from my own purpose. I'm here to find Ruma.

CHAPTER 21

As soon as my feet hit the ground, I unclip from my rappelling rope and leave the towering wall of the observatory behind. Moving quickly through the thick bramble of trees is difficult to do, especially considering Rose also has ordered us to step quietly. I've mostly given up on stealth and simply try to keep the volume of my twig and leaf crunching to a minimum. Rose occasionally stops to shush us. Through the cracks between branches and clusters of green leaves, I see small dots of lights and a collection of various buildings.

My stomach rumbles. I haven't eaten anything since Rose stole us away earlier today. At this point, I don't think she's planning on stopping for a meal anytime soon. We tread onward.

"Look straight ahead," Rose tells us. "You see those white orbs? That's where we are going."

Gauging distance through the dense woods is difficult, but around one hundred yards away, a few white orbs dimly glow like fallen stars.

THE REVELATION

I hear something swooping through the air just above my head, and I hit the ground. When I look up, the dark shadow of a large owl is flying away through the treetops. It hoots in the night, expressing its displeasure with us trespassers. Merrin helps me up. I brush off the wet leaves sticking to my hands and knees. The glowing orbs aren't far.

Murmurs of a gathering crowd become louder the closer we get to the opposing edge of the woods. When we come upon a semi clearing, I look up and see the moon, nearly full, spilling its light down onto the Revelation Territory. I feel a little hollow knowing it can't see me through the expansive shield stretching over the sky above.

"Okay. Here. This is good enough. We'll need to wait here," Rose says quietly between breaths while scanning over the twisted bushes and crooked trees as if looking for someone.

"Wait for what?" Merrin asks, squatting down on his heels.

As if in answer, a violent rumbling from the branches above makes us all scatter for cover. The sound of impact against the ground is much too heavy to be an owl. A different shadow kneels before us before standing up straight. We wait for Rose to make the first move to determine if we should surrender, run, or fight.

Rose spits out a few curses. "Jael! You scared the shit out of me."

"You can't be on time for anything," a woman's voice says from beneath her black mask.

"I'm here, and I've delivered on my end," Rose says. "You could try saying *thank you*."

"If it'll make you feel better," the muffled voice says teasingly.

"Is that Anger?" Merrin quietly asks me in disbelief.

"She just called her Jael," I say, even though in my mind her voice now sounds all too familiar.

"Now you care about my feelings?" Rose asks, approaching the woman. "You must really miss me."

"I wouldn't say that," Jael says, removing her helmet.

It *is* Anger. She and Rose embrace one another tightly.

Just the sight of Anger's face triggers a spark of rage and disgust inside me. I'm so furious that I can't even speak.

"Who is Jael?" Merrin asks, edging away from Anger to stand by my side.

"You're looking at her," Rose says, stepping back to look at Anger, who blithely stands with her arms crossed.

"She never told us her real name," Merrin says, buttering every word with annoyance.

"She's always been Jael to me," Rose says.

"How do you know one another?" Merrin asks.

"We're sisters. Obviously not biological, but we might as well be," Rose says.

"I don't know about that," Anger playfully objects.

"Why did you let them capture us?" I ask Anger as my face flushes with heat. Her avoidance of acknowledging how she left us to be beaten and thrown around by the Legionnaires fuels my revulsion.

"I set a trap and they took the bait," she says nonchalantly.

"They weren't bait," Rose corrects.

"I can't exactly walk right in to the Revelation Territory anymore," Anger explains. "I have to find more creative ways to get us in."

"We needed a way to get you into the Revelation Territory on our terms," Rose adds.

"Why?" I ask brashly, balling up my fists tightly.

THE REVELATION

"Can't say," Anger asserts.

"Not right now," Rose clarifies before asking Anger, "So you feel like we can make it back out through the caves?"

Their dismissively vague answers grate against my nerves.

"With them guiding us, yes," Anger says.

"How did you settle them trying to break through the wall?" Anger asks Rose.

"Dr. Wade helped downplay the whole thing and blamed it on one of the attendants miscalculating Ruma and Drove's dremaline dosage. Of course, since their genetic reversals weren't appropriately suppressed, Dr. Voorst was all over it. He was already complaining because the shots you gave them made it almost impossible to pull a clear reading of their DNA, so they were only expecting to run the RNA diagnostics for Darvin."

"Good. That's why I gave it to them," Anger says.

"I know. I'm just saying he was the only one I know of who suspected anything, but I took care of him," Rose clarifies.

"How do you know?"

"I know," Rose assures her.

"Where is Ruma?" I ask.

"You'll know more later," Rose says, trying to placate me.

"That's not good enough!" I'm not interested in staying quiet anymore.

"Lower your voice," Anger commands quietly. "I told you. Giving you answers now would just make you more of a liability."

I take a deep breath in and feel my chest swell. I have patience for Rose, but I'm quickly reminded I have none left for Anger.

"I'm not going anywhere unless you tell me where Ruma is."

Anger steps up, inches in front of my face and spits her words at me. "My world doesn't revolve around you or Ruma, and neither does theirs," she says, pointing to Rose and Merrin without looking away. "I've done nothing but keep you alive, so the last thing I owe you is an explanation for my actions. If this mission goes to shit, when they're torturing you, you'll be thanking God that I didn't tell you a damn thing."

"Who are *they*?" I yell loudly.

Anger shoves her hands against my chest, causing me to fly at least ten feet backward through the air and then down into the dirt and leaves. After my initial shock of hitting the ground, I notice a bright swell of color directed from a nearby orb. At first I thought the impact of the hit affected my vision, but in the new light, I can see everyone else facing the orb as well.

"Stop!" Rose yells before adjusting her tone. "Stop it. Now they've sensed you. They'll send Reapers. We can't risk this getting messy."

Rose pins Anger's arm by her side. Anger quickly snatches it free while Merrin rushes to help me up.

"This is already messy. That's all we've got. Even Falyn is suggesting our best chance is to execute the twins' backup escape," Anger says, struggling to keep her composure.

"What are Reapers?" Merrin asks Rose as he pulls me to my feet.

"They're Revelation Territory agents, specifically armed and trained to suppress any unauthorized use of genetic-reversal abilities. They have no respect for personal space, I can assure you of that."

THE REVELATION

"So in other words, Anger just screwed up," I say, trying to get under her skin.

Rose surprisingly nods in agreement.

"I'm sure as hell not going to let him scream every word he says," Anger asserts bitingly.

"Oh, so throwing him within reception of the Reaper orbs was the best solution to that problem? That last thing we need is a swarm of drones on our ass," Rose snaps, and the two sisters begin arguing.

I feel trapped in my own skin. I'm tired of walking blind in the obscurity of Anger's secrets, and for better or worse, I follow my sudden impulse to run. I can't beat Anger, but I know my strengths. I quickly turn in a full sprint, hurtling through the overgrowth toward the lights. I figure the closer I get to the orbs, the more likely Anger will refrain from using her abilities in fear of giving away our location.

A quick thumping of feet hits the ground behind me. I hope it's Merrin, but I don't turn around to confirm. Once through the clearing, I see we've been at the edge of one of the four housing passes. The units are small but look unexpectedly cozy. I would've expected high-rising, close-quarter bunks with no privacy. When I finally risk looking back over my shoulder, I'm relieved to see Merrin close on my heels.

"What are you doing?" he says, stretching his voice just far enough for me to hear.

I honestly don't know, so I can't answer him. Ahead, I see two men in uniforms with their backs to me. I quickly realize I have no idea what they'll do if they see me. A small part of me regrets running, so I decide I've got to get out of sight again—just not anywhere in the company of Anger. With the mandatory provincial order address, I'm hoping everyone will be away from their homes.

Ahead, I see a small orange house with unkempt shrubbery and no sign of interior lights. I make a break for the front door. There's no handle, only an electronic keypad, which I assume reads handprints.

I curse to myself as Merrin reaches me.

"Have you lost it? You can't just break into someone's house and disappear."

My shoulder involuntarily slams into the door as Anger crashes into me. The door gives way, and I fall to the floor inside the home.

All the air leaves my lungs. My vision goes dark, and I feel myself about to pass out. My shoulder throbs as I lay face first on an unfamiliar carpeted floor. As I finally regain my breath, my eyes pull back into focus. The familiar bright light of the Reaper orb illuminates a square portion of the home's interior through the open frame of the front door.

"Get inside," Rose says. "I'll make up an excuse. You just keep them quiet."

Anger quickly pulls the door back in place, bringing almost total darkness back into the room. Even in the blackness, Anger shifts her way across the room with ease until a thin slit of light appears from where she peeks through the window curtains.

"Are you okay?" Merrin whispers to me.

"Quiet. I need to hear," Anger spits back at him.

I hear a faint clicking sound behind me, and when I turn, there's a small head of a flame. The flame brightens in a moment, revealing an elderly woman shrouded in the red-orange light of a candle.

THE REVELATION

"If you move, I'll stick you with electricity," the old woman says, accenting every word.

I'm partially mesmerized in terror. We all freeze, including Anger, who looks straight down at the floor without turning around. Holding the candle out ahead of her, the old woman steps cautiously toward Anger.

"Who are you?" she asks curiously, nodding in Anger's direction. The candle flutters quietly, trembling in the woman's hand.

Squinting in disbelief, Anger slowly shifts her feet around to face the old woman before saying, "I thought you would've been dead by now."

No sooner do the words leave her mouth than she is hit by a streak of electricity streaming from the old woman's outstretched fingertips. Anger's body locks tight as she hits the floor. The white light from the outside orbs shine through the small slit between the curtains. Even after the bright stream of electricity ceases, Anger continues to convulse in the candlelight.

"Stay back," the old woman commands us.

We back into the wall, and a hanging picture shatters at our feet. Merrin quickly apologizes. The woman seems uninterested in his apology as she moves over to Anger's body. Even while feeling terrified, seeing Anger shocked unconscious for the second time in the past few days is satisfying.

The elderly woman stoops down and picks up Anger's hand, examining it closely in the candlelight. Anger no longer moves. The old woman sighs and carefully places the candle on the floor beside Anger's body. I can't tell if Anger is breathing.

"I knew it. That bitch stole my ring," she grumbles while removing Anger's ring from her limp hand.

Merrin and I exchange a quick glance.

"Why did she come here?" the old woman demands of us.

"We don't know, but we don't like her either," Merrin spits out.

"I'm... we're... we're trying to get away from her," I respond more specifically.

She glances back and forth between the both of us before walking over to the living room window, poised beside her neatly organized bookshelf. Her hair is well kept, still holding a dirty-blonde color, resting just above her shoulders. Her wrinkled skin appears only a few shades darker than her off-white cardigan.

She pinches back her beige drapes just enough to peek one eye outside.

"Then hide yourselves in my bedroom. Both of you. Now," she commands, shooing us toward the nearest door. "I'll take care of her for you."

We hastily follow her instructions and shut ourselves in darkness. I walk my hands like a pantomime across the wall, touching frames and wall hangings, bumping into occasional furniture before I feel the soft, thick drapery covering the window. A thin strip of warm light squeezes through the bottom of the old woman's bedroom door as she turns on her lights.

"Help me, please! Help!" we hear the old woman yelling more feebly than she previously sounded as she steps outside. She continues her plea as I whisper for Merrin to join me at the window.

I look out from behind the small break between curtains. My limited view allows me to see Rose watching as two Reapers hastily leave their conversation with her to move toward the house we're in. After checking the T13 unit on her arm, Rose stealthily moves in the opposite direction, away from us, disappearing from view behind the neighboring houses.

"We should hide in case someone peeks into the room," Merrin suggests.

I can hear the Reapers at the old woman's front door, but the conversation through the wall is muffled.

"She tried to attack me. I-I don't know who she is," the old woman shakily tells the two Reapers. They exchange a quick narration of details, and suddenly the old woman is thanking the Reapers for saving her life. I return to the window to see the men carrying Anger between their arms.

The door to the bedroom creaks open again as the honey-gold living room lights backlight the old woman's small frame.

"It's safe to come out," she tells us reassuringly.

Curious to hear what happened to Anger, Merrin and I follow her into the light. She directs us where to sit in her living room by tapping the air with her finger toward two separate chairs turned inward between an intricately crafted side table. We sit for a moment in silence.

"Where is she?" Merrin asks softly.

"Gone. I called in a few Reapers to drag her out. They're always looking for something to do, so no worries there."

The elderly woman's thin frame wouldn't intimidate anyone at first glance. Her sharp, pale face could even be considered friendly if she weren't currently wearing a scowl. Her hazel-blue eyes sparkle in the lamplight. I can't decide if she's charming or insane, but I'll give anyone a chance who stands up to Anger.

"I'm Maybeth," she tells us.

"Nice to meet you," Merrin says, standing up to extend his

hand, but he suddenly pulls it back as he thinks better of it. I'm assuming he's remembering the strange sensation we felt from shaking hands with Edwin and Brooks.

"I won't shock you. I promise," she says, chuckling lightly. "Unless you cross me—then all bets are off." She extends her hand.

Merrin timidly obliges, and I do the same after I see no harm is done. Unlike Edwin and Brooks, her hand doesn't leave mine feeling tingly.

"You boys are handsome. What're your names?"

"I'm Wyatt," Merrin says, looking at me to see if I'm going to answer truthfully.

"Darvin Flint," I say. "And his name is Merrin."

Merrin shakes his head, and Maybeth squints her eyes at us.

"They told us to not tell anyone our names here, but they didn't tell us why, and I'm sick of their games, so I don't care anymore," I explain, releasing a tight breath. It's as if a rope has been untied from around my lungs.

"Why'd they tell you that?" she asks, finally settling down in a dark wooden rocking chair.

I look to Merrin, still wondering what he knows. He releases his breath and closes his eyes for a moment before reopening them to speak.

"Rose said our real names could potentially be tied to Anger through K-Balt, depending on if she talks under pressure. The Legionnaires caught her in Anger's black suit when she left Widow's, and when they interrogated Widow, she lied, confirming their assumptions that K-Balt was the one they call the Death Angel, who they blame for originally attacking the Legionnaires that tried to intercept us. Rose knew you wouldn't care about protecting Anger's identity, so she asked me to promise to keep our names secret so it wouldn't compromise our chances of getting out safely."

Clearly bemused, Maybeth takes a moment to look Merrin over.

"I'm sorry," he adds. "I wanted to tell you earlier, but I was afraid if I did, I would put us both at risk."

"Why am I pretending to be Eden?" I ask, still dumbfounded as to why they would hide me behind my cousin's name.

"You were right about the bites. Anger injected us with something that scrambled our blood result when they tested us. They apparently already have your DNA in their database, so they were prepared to say you were Ruma's cousin if any genetic similarities showed up on the readings."

Maybeth raises her eyebrows. "I don't know what you've gotten into, but I'll tell you this. You can't play with spiders without getting caught in their webs."

"Yes, ma'am," Merrin says. "I think for us, it's more like we stumbled into the web, and now we're trying to get out."

"I know the feeling," she says. "I've lived half my life feeling like that."

"I'm sorry to hear that," Merrin offers. He extends his hand toward Maybeth once more. "My real name is Merrin Palice."

Maybeth accepts his hand. "I appreciate your honesty. Nice to meet you, Merrin."

As they release hands, she returns Anger's ring to her right index finger.

"So that's your ring," I say, pointing to it as she spins it over her knuckle.

"I wouldn't have taken it back if it wasn't," she says. "It

used to be hers, but she traded it for my black-gold Revelation charm."

"What do the letters stand for?" I ask, eyeing the ring while sitting up in my chair.

"On the inside? Her grandfather's initials. Edwin Clayton McLoud. I'm sure you recognize the name."

Merrin and I both hesitate to nod, unwilling to admit we don't know the name. We both know Edwin, the twin we met a few days ago, but she's clearly referring to another Edwin. "Edwin's great grandfather, Shalland McLoud, was the founder of RedCloud Industry. Of course, now they call it an empire."

"*Her* family owns RedCloud?" Merrin asks. "There's no way."

"Sure there is. She was adopted," she says, pushing herself up to her feet. "You boys want something to eat or drink? I've got peanut butter crackers."

"No, ma'am," I say, still dumbfounded by this info about Anger, but Merrin accepts some. I change my mind and correct my response when I remember how hungry I am.

"They called Rose Dean McLoud," I whisper to Merrin in disbelief. "If Anger is her adopted sister, she had to have grown up as a McLoud at some point."

"So RedCloud is named after their family," he says softly, just now making the connection. "What happened to her?"

A dish clangs loudly in the sink, and Maybeth apologizes for the noise and for what she considers a mess. Her small round kitchen table is set for four, as if she could be expecting to serve dinner at any moment. Overall, her home is small and much cleaner than I would expect it to be from the outside. She keeps several indoor plants, which seem to stretch out

THE REVELATION

happily in their colorful pots. Numerous pictures of birds and feathers hang neatly on the walls.

Merrin quietly mouths something at me I can't understand, so he whispers a little louder. "What do we do?"

I shrug. I don't particularly care what we do as long as I can try to find Ruma without anyone dragging us around in the dark or injecting me with mysterious medicine. Maybeth returns, carefully balancing two drinks in separate glasses along with six peanut butter crackers and diced apples for us to share.

"I got her good, didn't I?" Maybeth says, smiling as she recounts shocking Anger. "Normally they have me shot full of meds that suppress my genetic reversal, but they've been slacking since I always give them a hard time." She passes along our snacks. "I didn't think I'd ever see her again. I promise you, she deserved it. What I did to her, I mean." She rests back in her chair.

"We know she did," I agree, thinking about all the times I wished I could've done the same but couldn't.

Maybeth smiles approvingly. I decide I like her.

My first bite makes the stiff muscles in my jaws sting. We both quickly inhale the crackers and apple slices.

"A little carbonation and a snack always makes me feel better," she says happily. "You know, Jael can see in the dark, so I'm surprised she didn't beat me to the punch. What's wrong with her face? She looks different."

"What do you mean?" I ask, puzzled.

"Her face. She doesn't look like I remember her. Her hair, the scars. I couldn't have picked her out of a crowd just looking at her, but I felt her energy before she even came inside. Of course, her voice is the same."

"She's always looked that way to us," I say, wondering what Anger could've been though for her appearance to change.

"She can see in the dark?" Merrin asks, and I suddenly remember Anger leading us through the pitch-black tunnels of Beggar's Grave with ease.

"It's not that impressive compared to her biggest downside, which is her personality," Maybeth says, her face sour.

I haven't seen my grandmother on my mom's side in two years because of travel restrictions, but Maybeth's spunk reminds me of her.

"When I first got here," Maybeth continues, "this place looked like a vacation spot, but really it's like the devil's timeshare."

"Did you ever meet twins named Edwin and Brooks?" Merrin asks. I never would've thought to ask her, but now I'm curious. His question strikes a chord with her, as she hesitates to respond.

"How do you know them?" Maybeth asks, bemused.

"We met them in the mountains just outside of here a few days ago. You just reminded me of them with how you can use energy," Merrin hastily explains.

"So they're still alive," she says, smiling brightly. "You know, they used my DNA to create them."

"What do you mean *create* them? Who created them?" I ask, almost afraid to hear her answer.

"Those self-righteous fools trying to play God. That's what they do here. Some religions say we were all made from dust, so if that's true, when dust plays God, it just makes a big mess for him to clean up."

Merrin and I sit quietly, neither of us knowing how to respond. My mind flashes with memories from the lab, where

THE REVELATION

the attendants strung up Rhysk, Hara, me, and the other captives for the bidders. I remember one of them mentioning the word *eugenics*. I quickly string that thought together with my hazy recollection of a room full of vertical liquid tanks that held developing babies, one of which was thrown away as if it were trash. Was that what they were trying to do with me?

"How long have you two been here?" Maybeth asks, quickly changing the subject.

"We've only been here a couple days," Merrin tells her.

She pauses a moment and stares him down. "You don't have to lie. I'm not interested in stories that aren't real."

I can't help but be confused.

"I'm not lying. Anger turned us over to the Revelation Territory agents two days ago—"

"Who is Anger?" she asks.

"Jael. We call her Anger," Merrin clarifies.

"Oh. I would've come up with something a bit nastier myself," she says, smugly raising her eyebrows. "But keep going."

"But ever since we got here," I continue, "we've been swept away to wherever they want us. Anger's sister, Rose, seemed like she was trying to help us escape—"

"Escape? It's a rare act of God to escape from here."

"Or maybe we don't know why we're really here. All I know is they said my sister is here, and I want to find her," I say.

"What did you say your last name was?" Maybeth asks me. Her eyebrows have dropped down, shadowing her eyes.

"It's Flint," I say.

Her head lifts slightly, and her eyes become more visible. She opens her mouth as if to say something, and then pauses again. Maybeth pushes herself up from her flowery red cushion and makes her way toward me. I watch her carefully, and I flinch when she carefully puts her fingers under my chin. She gently turns my head toward the lamp light.

"Ruma. Ruma Flint," she says, lightly gasping as her fingers raise in front of her lips. "You're her brother. Your energy feels so much like hers."

"How do you know her?" Merrin asks as I sit stunned in silence.

"We were assigned to the same mandated task group several times. Does she know you're here?"

"She does now," Merrin says, catching my eyes.

"How did you meet Ruma?" I ask, repeating Merrin's question as adrenaline nearly takes over my entire body. For all I know, Maybeth might have spent more time with my own sister than I have.

"I met her several years ago. I used to mainly work in horticulture before I retired. She wasn't there long before they took her away. We had many good conversations, and when they took her, I knew she must've been special to them."

"What do you mean, *special*?" Merrin questions, sitting forward in his chair.

"Now, I want you both to listen to me carefully," Maybeth says. "I've lived nearly half of my life as a prisoner of this terrible place. They'll confuse you with all the nice empty things they have to offer, and then the masks come off when they offer you up for sacrifice on a scientific altar. That's what they did to me. They told me I was special right before they violated my body for every ounce of genetic information they could find. Then they gave me food and a roof over my head like they were doing me a favor. I've been here forty-three years, and I don't see the beauty in the flowers or pause when

I feel a fake breeze. Not anymore. It's all tainted." She stops, having to catch her breath. She's shaking with fresh emotion.

"How'd you get here?" I ask, giving her a moment to breathe.

"I assume the same way you did, more or less. I was exposed to perducorium a long time ago when my husband and I took our kids camping. We knew it was risky, but we were sick of living in fear. Fear isn't always a bad thing, if you haven't learned that yet."

Maybeth walks over to an antique chest sitting beside the hearth of her barren fireplace. She carefully opens the lid, and after a moment of digging, she pulls out a weathered photograph. She walks back across the living room and hands me the picture.

"That's my family there," she tells us while I carefully hold the photo so both Merrin and I can see. In the picture, Maybeth's eyes sparkle just as brightly as they do now on a younger version of her beautiful face. One arm is wrapped around her uniformed husband, and the other is draped over the youngest of her two sons.

"If they found this, they would destroy it," she tells us.

"Why?" I ask, feeling a fresh longing to reach into my pockets to grab my lost pictures and fire starter.

Maybeth gently takes back the photo with a wrinkled hand. She stares at the picture in silence, quietly losing herself in memories.

"If they can erase your past, it's easier to control your future," she mumbles, as if the same words have fluttered across her mind so many times that they've become dull. Her smile fades, giving way to the resting wrinkles of her cheeks.

"What happened to them?" Merrin asks cautiously.

She returns to her red-cushioned chair and carefully places the picture on her side table before sitting down.

"One of them came out of nowhere. A Stone jumped on my youngest, so I attacked. It was instinct. They left us all for dead, and when RedCloud found us, I was somehow still alive."

We watch curiously as she pulls up the bottom of her pants leg.

"I know it doesn't look like it, but my leg here is fake," she says, giving it a good tapping with her finger. "It's the only gift I ever found useful from RedCloud. Once I healed up, they shipped me here. And that was it."

"So you haven't seen your family since then?" Merrin asks. I'm sure it's hard for him to reconcile hearing about unprovoked Stone attacks while knowing in his parents' case, they were wrongfully targeted.

She softly shakes her head and says, "I don't even know if they're alive."

"I'm so sorry," I offer as sincerely as I can.

"They still have my love. That'll never change."

She stares at the floor for a moment, squeezing her interlaced fingers perched on her lap. I decide not to push her with any more personal questions. Merrin seems to have fallen quiet. I'm sure the parallels between his and Maybeth's shared experience of losing family members has triggered him. I try to shift the conversation away to distract them both.

"Have you ever tried to escape?"

"Yes. Yes, I did," Maybeth says, lifting her eyes. "Once. And that was the last time I saw Jael. She had a plan, and I helped her. She's a bitch, but a brilliant bitch at that. When we got to the end, things didn't go as planned, and she left me

THE REVELATION

behind as bait. And I'll never forgive her..." Her words trail off as her narrow face hardens.

"So that's why you attacked her," Merrin says, sighing sympathetically.

"That, yes, but you both seem like you've spent enough time with her to know I had a few *other* reasons."

I laugh for the first time since being in the Revelation Territory. Maybeth's spirit has warmed me up, and for a moment, I forget where I am.

"We've been confused from the beginning," Merrin tells her. "Anger intercepted us after an Ops mission went wrong, and ever since, she's been dragging us around, feeding us bits and pieces of hope to keep us curious."

Maybeth smacks her lips. "She's not giving you real hope. I know people like Jael. If they can keep people mistaking manipulation for divination, they have you right in their pocket. The Revelation Territory is a dog, and RedCloud is its master. The master trains and keeps the dog alive in exchange for loyalty and protection. The dog feeds off of people like you and me, so who's really to blame? The dog or the master?"

"I'd say both," Merrin answers, even though I assumed her question was rhetorical.

"Maybe," she says, nodding her head.

We all turn toward the front door when we hear a thudding knock. Merrin and I stiffen in our chairs, afraid to move, awaiting Maybeth's orders.

"Go hide back where you were. Quietly," she whispers while grabbing the picture of her family, which she buries deep inside her trunk.

"It's Rose," I hear before we make it past the guest bedroom doorway. "Please let me in. I'm not armed. I just want to talk."

Again, Merrin and I freeze, confounded by the potential consequences of me running away and Anger getting taken away by the Reapers. Maybeth makes her way to the door, where she presses a panel initiating a live video feed on the backside of the door, as if the door itself were transparent. Rose isn't alone.

Maybeth turns to us. "Do you trust these two?"

Merrin and I fixedly stare at the screen as my heart squeezes beneath my chest.

"Yes," I say, struggling to speak. "Yes. The girl is our friend."

I haven't figured out whether I trust Rose or not, but somehow she has returned with Rhysk by her side, so I'll have to take my chances.

CHAPTER 22

"Fair warning," Maybeth says plainly to us before opening the door. "If anything doesn't feel quite right, I'm going to shock them."

We both nod.

There appears to be no locking device on the door, and I'm thankful because earlier when Anger threw me into the door it would've been a lot more painful. Maybeth pulls on the handle of her front door. Rose and Rhysk stand before us with glistening sweat running down their faces.

"May we please come in?" Rose pleads with Maybeth.

"That's what I intended when I opened the door," she says, waving them in.

The hum of the nearby crowd has grown since the last time I heard it outside, and the walls of the house muffle the announcements sounding in the air from the loudspeakers. Rose and Rhysk step inside timidly. Under the present circumstances, I don't know how to greet Rhysk, so I keep my distance. Her wavy brown hair appears slightly more disheveled than usual. The weight of her exhaustion hangs on her shoulders and downtrodden face. When our eyes connect, I nod but say nothing, still feeling residual shame from last seeing one another in the dehumanizing conditions of the lab.

Maybeth shuts the door and invites her new guests to sit down. Rose refuses the offer.

"We can't stay long," she says. "More Reapers will be here shortly. I don't have time to navigate a conversation. Is surveillance enabled in your home?" she asks Maybeth directly.

It was until I fried the circuits. They gave up on installing new systems for me a long time ago."

Rose lowers her voice to a whisper. "We've organized an escape. Tonight. There are about forty evacuees preparing to leave as we speak, so listen carefully. Darvin, Merrin, both of you have been assigned under my wing."

I feel relief hearing her use our real names, but the word *escape* makes the back of my neck pickle. I don't plan on leaving here without Ruma, but before I can protest, Maybeth says, "I recognize you." She steps closer to Rose. "You're a McLoud, aren't you?"

"Yes," Rose answers firmly, keeping a strong posture, as if bracing for impact.

"Then I don't trust a damn word you're saying," Maybeth says, cocking her eyebrows down while extending her hand toward Rose. A small storm of energy twitches across her fingers.

"Don't!" Rhysk yells, stepping in front of Rose. "She's helping us!"

"What did she do to Jael?" Rose asks Merrin and me.

"I knocked her ass out, is what I did," Maybeth answers. "Jael used me as bait in her last escape plan twenty years ago. The hell if I'm gonna let you do the same to these boys."

"She was only eighteen!" Rose argues, standing her ground.

"And I haven't seen my family in forty-three years," Maybeth throws back. "I've spent well over half my life away from everyone I love. There's no forgiveness for people like her."

Rose's face turns solemn. "I'm so sorry she did that to you, and I don't blame you for hurting her. Maybe she deserved it, but without her help, a lot of people will be stuck here forever. They don't deserve that either, including these three," Rose pleads, gesturing toward Rhysk, Merrin, and me.

"Jael can rot in here for all I care," Maybeth says without hesitation.

"No. No one deserves that. My father adopted Jael just so he could infect her for a RedCloud marketing campaign for perducorium treatments."

"That's a load of shit," Maybeth says dismissively.

"No, it's not," Rose asserts, stepping toward Maybeth with both hands submissively poised in front of her. "He wanted to appear empathetic with his consumers. It all backfired on him when her body genetically reversed the disease, so he threw her away here to cover everything up. And I sure as hell know she wouldn't tell you that."

Maybeth's hazel-blue eyes sparkle with the reflection of electricity popping between her fingers.

"Please. Help us," Rhysk says in not much more than a whisper.

"Your heritage is sour," she says, pursing her lips as she

THE REVELATION

addresses Rose. "Even if you're telling the truth, your father's sins don't justify Jael's disgusting selfishness. But I won't let my bitterness interfere with these boys' chance to escape." Maybeth lowers her hands, and the electric buzzing subsides. She steps toward Rose until she's only an arm's length away. "And if you're lying, I will come after you. Now, what do you need?"

"I need to take Darvin and Merrin to go to the provincial order address," Rose tells us. "You know everyone's mandated to go, and I'll certainly be expected to be there. We don't want to raise any unnecessary red flags."

"Won't they be looking for us?" I ask.

"Yes and no," Rose says. "We've covered most of our tracks."

"Sounds like a trap to me," Maybeth spouts back.

"No. Not this time. Our diversion will happen there. We need to be as inconspicuous as possible. They'll know the diversion when they see it, and most likely there will be widespread panic. This will be our chance to escape through the designated exit point. I'm assuming you both can swim," Rose says, waiting for our response.

We both assure her we can, even though I'm uneasy imagining why she asked us if we could.

"And what if things don't go as planned?" Maybeth inquires.

"We've run into a lot of that, and more now, thanks to you. Our success depends on Anger's ability to execute her end of the mission, so I've already got people on her."

"Do you plan on sticking around here as a traitor to your father's legacy?" Maybeth asks Rose.

"I'll worry about myself," Rose insists, letting a moment

of silence hang as she glares at Maybeth. "If everything goes well, you and I should be able to keep our secrets and stay here."

Maybeth barks out a laugh. "I have no intention of staying here if the party is leaving. Jael owes me a ticket out of here. Give me that, and I'll keep your secrets."

An aggressive pounding thuds on the front door, pulling us all out of the conversation.

"Prepare for entry," a Reaper yells assertively. "Your safety will be determined by your cooperation."

"Shit," Rose whispers through her teeth, moving her back away from the door.

"Here we go again," Maybeth says, exasperated, rolling up her sleeves.

Within seconds, four Reapers covered in black-and-red bodysuits storm Maybeth's house. Each of them points their firearm at us, but not at Maybeth.

"Don't mess with my guests! And get your damn boots off my carpet."

"We're taking them in," one of the masked Reapers says, "and we'll be coming back for you. The provincial order address is mandatory."

"Oh, hell. I've missed those things for the past two years, and all of a sudden you're interested in what I do with my time? Mrs. McLoud here beat you to the punch anyway. She brought these kids to convince me to go to that crazy propaganda meeting."

"Yes. I apologize, but we were just about to leave before you came," Rose offers.

"I have to ask you to step aside, Dean McLoud," another

THE REVELATION

Reaper says while the others quickly bind the rest of us with our arms behind our backs.

"Don't be dramatic," Maybeth says, trying to wiggle free. "She said we were about to leave. They just spent the last fifteen minutes convincing me, and I finally decided to go, but hell, if you want to take me away for truancy, that will be one more meeting I can miss without having to waste my life away."

Two of the Reapers look at each other. One shakes his head as the other frowns at Rose.

"You expect us to believe that load of shit? You've been defiant at best since the first time I met you," the lead Reaper says to Maybeth.

"Maybe you never tried kindness. I can smell fake from a mile away," Maybeth says, scoffing.

"So you're saying after all the shit you've given us for the past two years when you've been subpoenaed, these people here just pop by, and all of a sudden convince you to go?"

"Like I said, you'd be surprised how far a little kindness can go," Maybeth asserts. "Not one of you thanked me for not shocking you this time. I'd hate to change my mind."

"You know she won't go," the Reaper behind me says, slighty releasing his vise grip on my arms.

"Try me," Maybeth says defiantly.

After a short moment of silence, the lead Reaper says, "Hell. All right. If you go, we'll release your new friends here and escort you all there. If not, you're all going down by force."

"Then let us go. You've already made us late," Maybeth scolds. "I'm not going looking like this. Let me just put on some lipstick."

The lead Reaper subtly nods at his men, and they

immediately begin loosening the bonds from our arms.

"Thank you," Rose says curtly. Her McLoud family position seems to award her little favoritism with the Reapers. I'm surprised she hasn't used her position as a threat.

"I sure hope they've spiced up these dull meetings in the last two years," Maybeth says with freshly dressed red lips, giving one last jab at the Reapers as they file us out the door.

The Reapers walk closely behind us. We follow the softly glowing pathway as we maneuver our way past a sign that reads BEASLEY PASS.

Even though Maybeth claimed to be worried about us being late, she clearly is uninterested in punctuality, as she takes her time walking. I see Merrin whisper a question to Maybeth, and she doesn't bother to hide her answer.

"I guess they figure it's just easier to wait for me to die than to deal with me. I always give 'em a good zap," she tells him, laughing to herself.

As we move toward the growing collection of voices and broken chants, my back tingles with cold shivers. The night sky is dark and shiny, like a fresh coat of black paint. Hot acid leaps up my throat as my stomach churns the peanut butter crackers we ate earlier. I walk just behind Rhysk, keeping a short distance while trying to figure out what I could say to her. She slows her steps and falls in stride beside me. She touches my shoulder, and I unintentionally flinch.

"You okay?" she asks timidly, folding her arms tightly underneath her chest.

I nod. "Yeah."

We walk in silence for a few uncomfortable seconds.

"What do you think they were doing to us?" she asks, quietly staring ahead of us.

THE REVELATION

"I don't know," I say uselessly, too afraid to admit they most likely were advertising our DNA for use in eugenics. Does she know her genetic-reversal abilities? I'm still unsure of mine. Rose mentioned that I was genetically resilient to perducorium, but I'm not sure if that was real or a part of the whole Eden Evans charade.

"They told us you were dead. Both of you," she whispers. We walk beneath the silvery glow of lamp lights periodically placed between the symmetrical rows of trees bordering the walkway.

"Who? What do you mean?"

"Our Special Ops commanders," she says. "I thought you were dead. That was what I was trying to tell you back when I saw you in that insane lab. I bet they said the same about me back in New Province Guard after they took me."

As we approach the end stretch of homes in Beasley Pass, several winding walkways funnel into one long road periodically marked by massive stone archways. We're heading straight for a high-rising coliseum shaped like a giant geometrical flower blooming into the night sky. The whole structure glows like moonlight.

"How did you get here?" I ask her.

"I'm guessing the same way you two did. We were set to go out on a mission, and I got called back for an inspection before we left. I don't remember what they did, but the next thing I knew, I woke up here."

I shake my head. "That's not what happened to us. We carried out our mission, and people died. Merrin saw his parents. They were fully turned Stones. I don't think they expected that, and then it was just chaos. They left us behind, but I think that was an accident." I let my voice trail off because suddenly I'm doubting my own interpretation of what happened.

"I don't know how to say this without it sounding bad…" Rhysk says, her eyes darting aimlessly over the walkway. She looks at me. "But I'm glad you're here."

I don't know how to respond, but I get the feeling she understands. Merrin looks over his shoulder to check in and turns around once I dip my head to signal I'm good. Merrin offers Maybeth his arm for stability, but I think she accepts more to enjoy the temporary comfort of his company.

Other than the Reapers silently following us, there are no other faces in sight. As we approach the entrance to the coliseum, the crowd's murmuring subsides as a female's voice narrates the opening statements of the provincial order address. We reach the main entryway of the coliseum, and the Reapers escort us through the security checkpoint. I didn't notice Rose reengaging our T13 units, but the security workers scan us in, and we enter without issue.

The crisp white banners streaming down from the ceiling hang the Revelation Territory's emblem above our heads. The dark glass walkways wind gracefully against sharp supporting walls that overlap and fold over one another like flower petals.

"No one should bother you while you're here," Rose says. "You'll need to keep your units on for now."

Our glass pathway winds its way up alongside the exterior walls of the coliseum. We periodically pass live holographic projections of the woman currently addressing the crowd inside. Each step takes us higher above the surrounding housing passes that stand against the base of the stadium.

On the larger empty faces of the walls, additional two-dimensional projections depict the narrating woman as she

THE REVELATION

stands amongst the burning remnants of a small town. She's reporting on location somewhere as smoke rises from small pockets of flames surrounding her. The visual perspective pans away from the woman to piles of lifeless bodies strewn across the ashen ground. Human limbs bend and tuck over one another like tangled branches. The images twist my stomach and make my neck spasm. I want to look away. How can this be real?

"This is just one example of the deadly footprints left behind every day from the thousands of Stone hordes terrorizing the unguarded settlements throughout New Province," the woman narrates with conviction.

Merrin's narrow eyes and clenched jaw are sharply locked while he watches the surrounding screens. As I follow closely behind him, I wonder if the vilifying portrayals of the Stones feels like a personal attack on his parents.

Rose passes under a tunneling archway guarded by two armed Reapers, which leads into the coliseum's interior, where several thousand inhabitants of the Revelation Territory encircle the stage. We pass rows of unfamiliar faces, all reflecting the various hues of light cast from the numerous projections as we find our way to our seats.

"You're going to have to sit me down. My legs are giving out," Maybeth says without bothering to whisper.

Rose helps her into an empty seat at the end of a nearby aisle, but every other seat around us is filled.

"Are you going to be okay here by yourself?" I whisper to her, and Rose pulls at my arm.

"I'll just be taking a nap," Maybeth says, smiling up at me as she squeezes my hand. "And don't leave me here, or I might just have to make a scene," she calls out after Rose, drawing the uncomfortable attention of several quiet faces around her.

I return a soft smile and nod silently to assure her I won't. We continue walking around a peripheral tier between two levels of seats for almost a minute before we turn down a set of steps to find four empty seats, which Rose has been tracking down for us with her T13 unit. My eyes run over the tiers of seats, once again wondering if I might find Ruma, even though it's been so long that it's possible I wouldn't even recognize her if I saw her.

I enter the aisle after Rhysk, Merrin is behind me, and Rose sits beside him on the end of our row. Everyone around us stares with unbroken focus up at the 360-degree video screen poised like a halo in the center of the stadium. The screens fade to black, and a widespread holographic scene projects like a live-action performance at the heart of the coliseum's central stage.

A young, dirt-weathered woman holding a baby in one arm and the hand of her young daughter with her other hand pleads from every screen, saying, "Any hope for peace depends entirely on the support of the Revelation Territory. Your cooperation and sacrifice are our only hope for survival."

I adjust myself in my seat, and my right knee lightly touches Rhysk's leg. She doesn't bother to move. I've been starved of connection for a while now, so even this small amount of contact brings me comfort.

"What is she talking about?" Merrin says, leaning over to whisper.

I shake my head and shrug.

Simulated gray smoke swirls over the central projection as the scene fades away to the deep-red Revelation Territory emblem. A man rises from a small group of individuals seated

THE REVELATION

around the center stage. He walks through the remnants of smoke until he's poised directly below the seal. His elaborate white suit, accentuated with golden trim and buttons, neatly contrasts with a pointed scarlet collar rising just above his ears.

A closeup of his face takes my breath. I fixedly stare in denial until Rhysk's hand suddenly grips the side of my leg, and I know she must recognize his face as well. The bold contrast of his cold blue eyes and ebony skin makes him instantly recognizable.

"That's High Commander Nebbuck," Merrin whispers, squeezing my arm. I just barely nod in acknowledgment.

"Why is he here?" Rhysk asks quietly.

I have no response because I have no idea. The last time I saw him he was helping me out of a net Rhysk had trapped me in back during our Stone encounter simulation at Special Ops training. *What did he say to me?*

"Please stand for the supplication of Bishop Isaac Kane," High Commander Nebbuck says, placing his right hand over his heart. His left arm rests by his side with his palm facing up, as if he's preparing to receive something. Every person in the coliseum stands and emulates the gesture. Following Rose's lead, we do the same.

"May we hold close the Great Maker's heart," he recites, "the pieces he's shared among his people, as we are but scattered seeds cast on borrowed earth. Let our hands bear the light of our offering."

In near-perfect harmony, a bone-shaking roar of voices joins him, chanting together, "Sacrifice, serve, and preserve." It's so loud it triggers a cold shiver down my arms and back. Everyone sits, and we wait in silent anticipation as High

Commander Nebbuck introduces Emperor Ruvis McLoud before returning to his seat amongst the five throne-like chairs positioned just behind the main podium.

"That's him. He's the leader of RedCloud Empire," Rhysk shakily whispers in my ear.

"Rose's father," I say, looking to Rose, who stares ahead.

An elderly man previously standing in front of the center throne passes Nebbuck and takes his place behind the podium. My eyes shift from the center stage up to the video screen, where I can see up close. His long silver hair shines like polished wax as it lightly touches his thin shoulders. The entirety of his white suit emanates like moonlight, with the exception of his high crimson collar. All of his fingers bear golden rings that match the Revelation Territory emblem hanging around his neck. He leans into the silence, and his green eyes pan across the crowd before him. The entire audience seems transfixed by the presence of Emperor McLoud as we watch him closely on the massive screens.

"Redemption," he says, letting the word echo around us before continuing.

"What has been lost and stolen from us will be returned. The generations before us bore the weight of devastation as their homes were swallowed by black fire with their families inside. Every word spoken in love, every treasure earned though sweat and blood, all of it reduced to ash and disease just two hundred odd years ago."

The entire audience hangs on the edge of his words in complete silence.

"Resilience. Pulling life from the hands of that which is dead. Our foreign enemies in Naroke anointed death as the unwelcome author of our history. For the last two centuries,

THE REVELATION

we as a people have rewritten the dark pages of our past. This stirring beneath the ashes began with the resilient ones like my great-great-grandfather, Shalland McLoud, who refused to be defeated by those carrying an intemperate lust for destruction without a just cause. Holding true to the visionary revelations he received during his years at the Patmos Monastery, he and his son, Redderick McLoud, my great-grandfather, founded the Revelation Territory we have long called home. It is my desire and great privilege to honor my heritage and yours by continuing the work that was started long ago to reclaim what was stolen from our people."

Merrin leans over and whispers, "I'm so confused."

I turn my head to respond and lock eyes with a patrolling Reaper a few rows back. Rose redirects our attention toward Emperor McLoud. After a moment of listening, I look again to my left to see the Reaper's face studying the screen on his forearm. I watch him briefly before he catches my eyes once more. I look away but keep his movements within my peripheral vision.

"What are you looking at?" Rhysk asks from my right.

"There's a Reaper back there who's watching us."

"There's two of them now," Rhysk mutters, shifting her hair to cover the side of her face.

I don't dare look to confirm.

"They're coming our way," she says, facing forward again.

I try to continue listening to the words of Emperor McLoud's speech, but his words wash out like water poured over my ears. A shudder starts in my stomach and sinks down into my legs, causing my knees to tremble. If we're taken away by the Reapers, we could miss the only opportunity we might ever have to escape. What if Ruma escapes without me?

Even now, Rose's eyes don't move away from Emperor McLoud. Rather than watching the screens, she's looking down to where he stands on the stage. Her jaws seem tight, but her eyes glisten with tears. Her lips move subtly. I can't read what she says, but Merrin passes along the message.

"Do as they ask. Stay together."

I say the same to Rhysk. A moment later, the first Reaper reaches us, grabbing Rose forcibly by the arm.

"The four of you, come with us. Now."

"Watch your grip," Rose says through her teeth.

A few people watch us curiously while others remain captivated by Emperor McLoud's speech. Rose turns to us and calmly nods, so we file out of the aisle in order. My mind begins producing an excessive number of hypothetical conclusions as to what the Reapers know and what they will do to us once we leave the coliseum.

I've completely forgotten Maybeth until we approach her seat. She stands, drawing the attention of the guards, who know her well. Her blue eyes sparkle wildly under the white lights. I know she's planning something terrible.

I'm startled by a deep boom that suddenly sends a shudder throughout the coliseum and its inhabitants. The crowd collectively murmurs as the Reaper directly in front of me touches his ear and immediately turns toward the center stage, where Emperor McLoud is suddenly being escorted away by a squad of Reapers, along with Nebbuck and the three others previously sitting on the five thrones. Even through the stirring turmoil of the crowd, my ears follow a distinct whistle from above.

THE REVELATION

My attention turns toward the top of the coliseum. Within seconds, the top of the domed roof shrieks as it rips open with searing red flames.

CHAPTER 23

I instinctively drop to the floor, and invasive heat envelops my entire body. A chorus of screams erupts, and I hear the deep, metallic cracking of the coliseum's ceiling structure as giant beams rain down onto the center stage where Emperor McLoud was speaking only moments before. I'm yanked up from the floor as I struggle to stand in the chaos. My mind clicks into autopilot. Although my heart feels stuck in my throat, we quickly shove past panicking bodies funneling out of the exit.

"Where is Maybeth?" I scream to Rose, who leads us through the shifting maze of bodies as we retrace the steps from only minutes earlier.

I'm not sure when this happened, but I'm holding Rhysk's hand. My fingers tightly entwine around hers as we rush forward. I look back over my shoulder and find Merrin. He's only a couple of steps behind us, protecting Maybeth as they navigate through the turmoil together. Fresh blood stains

THE REVELATION

both of them. I don't know which one of them is bleeding. Rose leads the way in front of a panicking crowd stampeding behind us.

Ahead, another mob of people spills out of an exit like angry hornets leaving their broken hive. Several distressed faces turn our way, choosing the same exit path ahead. A young dark-haired girl falls to the ground and disappears underneath the feet of others desperately trying to escape. I want to save her, but pushing back against the streams of panicking people is impossible. There's nothing I can do.

A numbing flood of adrenaline makes everything around me seem surreal. I clutch Rhysk's hand in mine, holding on to the only thing that feels real. I look again to find Merrin still close behind. He's always been bigger and stronger than I am, but I'm amazed he and Maybeth have been able to keep up with us.

We pass several projections still live-streaming a feed of where Emperor McLoud once stood. Now there is nothing to see but billowing fire and smoke, which only heightens the sense of chaos.

When we finally face the main exit where we first entered, I can see another swell of flames whipping the darkness off in the distance. The structural ceiling panels shielding the Revelation Territory from the outside world flicker sporadically like strobing lights. Black smoke rises and spills into the night sky through the one gaping hole above the coliseum. Rose leads us to the left side of the exit behind a buttressing pillar carved in the shape of an anemone flower, like the ones my grandmother used to grow. We stop momentarily to regroup amongst the storming hysteria surrounding us.

"Is she okay?" Rose asks Merrin, trying to decipher where the blood came from.

"I think so," he yells over the uproar, panting for air as he drops to his hands and knees.

Maybeth's eyes are closed. She's struggling to catch her breath. I step closer and rest my hand on her arm. She tries to say something, which gets lost in the turmoil.

"What did you say?" I ask, leaning in closer.

"I said I finally went to a meeting worth going to," Maybeth says, smiling even though I can tell she's in pain.

"We've got to move toward our extraction point," Rose commands. "There's no time."

"I'll carry you," Merrin says to Maybeth between heavy breaths.

"No, you won't," she says sternly.

"I can do it," I say, reaching for her, but she pushes against me and hits my hand away.

"No. Stop. Don't worry about me. I'm slow, but I'm not crippled. This is your time. Now get," she yells, slapping Merrin on the back. He hesitates for a moment, but Rose doesn't. Merrin and I both kiss Maybeth on the cheek and hastily chase after Rose with Rhysk by our sides. I throw a few glances over my shoulder until Maybeth disappears behind the streams of people as we dodge our way through the chaos. My insides feel weighted from the guilt of leaving her behind.

"What are they doing?" Merrin asks, turning our attention to a group of individuals wearing Falcon-like gear. They're swiftly guiding some of the Revelation Territory inhabitants into small upright vessels no bigger than a ground convoy.

"They're escaping," Rhysk says, without stopping. Within seconds of loading, the escape pod fires into the air, bursting

THE REVELATION

through one of the ceiling panels before disappearing into the night. Heavy rain begins falling, too quickly to be real, dousing the monstrous flames engulfing the coliseum.

Swarms of drones appear without warning over our heads. The numerous hordes fly in assorted groups separated by color schemes. My eyes follow the streams of several different groups, which seem to be performing different tasks based on the color of their swarm. The small white drones busily dress the wounds of the coliseum's exterior dome while a larger horde of black drones aggressively pours out through the newly created exit.

As we maneuver our way through the paths of Beasley Pass while trailing behind Rose, I notice the Reaper orbs have transformed into protective shells for those needing to take refuge from danger.

Our surroundings become vaguely familiar, and I turn to my right and locate Maybeth's house, less than a hundred feet away. I wonder if that's where she will be returning if she makes it that far.

"This way!" Rose yells back at us. Rhysk and I run side by side, and Merrin follows close behind. Rose charges toward the tree line, where we reunited with Anger not long ago.

A small group of gunmen wearing camouflage Falcon-like gear seems to be flagging us down. To my left, another group of six or seven Revelation Territory inhabitants merge with our group. At first I prepare to attack, but they don't make any hostile moves toward us. Another small group joins them shortly after. There must be around twenty or more of us together now, running for cover amongst the trees.

Without time to be careful, our feet strike the ground hard. We take turns falling and helping each other up. As the gunmen receive our groups, another woman leading her group yells, "Drones!"

The armed guards form a firing line behind us. These drones rip through the overhead foliage like fierce red birds. The gunmen's bullets drop several of them with precision, but two make it past their defense and descend into our group.

One snatches someone up from the back and carries her off into the night while she screams. Rhysk screams my name just in time for me to turn around to see a second drone wrapping its robotic claws around her arm and lifting her into the air. She's only a few feet away, so I jump up and grab one of the drone's mechanical talons as tightly as I can. The drone pulls both of us into the sky.

One of the gunmen fires a risky shot that luckily strikes the drone instead of us, and we briefly drop low enough for someone else to grab a hold of my feet. The same gunman sprints to meet us, and we all work together to hold the drone down while the gunman fires several shots directly on top of the drone until it's destroyed.

Merrin and two others meet us, so now the seven of us have to catch up with the pack ahead. I don't know who my new friends are, but Rhysk and I probably owe them our lives.

We catch up to the others just as the tree line breaks open into a small clearing at the base of the Revelation Mountains. Rose stays back to meet us as the rest of the group huddles by the edge of a natural spring spilling into the mouth of a large cave.

"Are there any others behind you?" she asks us, out of breath.

"Not that we know of. We wouldn't have left them behind if they were," one of the males who helped save us says.

THE REVELATION

"We need to get her some help," one of the women who stayed behind with Merrin tells Rose. While she inspects Rhysk's bloody arm, I feel guilty for not noticing she was hurt. Rose drops one of her packs to the ground and quickly tends to Rhysk's wounds.

"Why are we waiting?" Merrin asks, resting his hands on his knees to catch his breath.

"We're not the only ones escaping. There should be close to thirty of us. Anger is leading her group here as we speak."

"But she was captured," I say.

"I know. She was planning on that anyway, so we can thank your friend Maybeth for unwillingly assisting us," Rose says while applying a final protective layer of wrapping. At the mention of her name, I choose to believe Maybeth made it safely back home.

"We had to cut all communication signals, so we'll have to trust she'll find us shortly. I'm sure the Reaper's drone swarms will be trying to herd them too. If they miss the checkpoint, we cut our losses," she says sternly. Her countenance has changed so drastically since the first time I met her I'm not sure I would recognize her now if I hadn't been with her the entire way.

"How are we getting out of here?" Rhysk asks, eyeing the shadowed brush we came from.

"We'll leave soon enough. They're passing out submersion masks and oxygen tanks by the cave over there. You'll need one."

As I inspect the serene pool of water flowing out from the cave's mouth like a dark bib, I realize this is why Rose asked us if we could swim.

"I'll get ours," I say to Merrin and Rhysk as I walk over to the spring's edge.

"I'm coming with you," Rhysk says, gently touching the bandage wrapped over her arm as she joins me.

One of the group leaders passes out the masks and small oxygen tanks, which connect to each other easily.

"I can't believe this," she says to me as we stop just beyond earshot of the small line ahead of us.

"What do you mean?"

"All of this. How did we grow up not knowing about this place? Or genetic reversal? Or any of it?"

I look around at the many unfamiliar faces, faces that seem just as frightened as I am. A young girl around Jaykin's age sits crying alone on the ground about thirty feet away. Another older boy closer to my age walks over and sits by her side. My bottom eyelids fill with tears.

"I don't know," I say as my exhausted mind fights uncertainty.

Rhysk continues. "They have videos of a war going on somewhere close by that we didn't even know existed, and we're a part of it, but we don't even know how. Our Guard cities aren't just keeping the Stones out—they're keeping us disconnected from the rest of the world. We've been living in the dark."

Her words resound deep within me. I wish I could be at home to talk with my parents and ask them questions about their experiences in purge camp and the outside world beyond Southern Guard. I don't know if my parents have been sheltering me from the outside unrest or if the walls surrounding our city have blinded them too. Rhysk is waiting for me to respond, so I push past my thoughts.

THE REVELATION

"We don't know what's true here. It seems like people will tell you anything to make you do what they want."

She seems ready to say something, but in the end, she says nothing. Even though we've been talking for less than a minute, it feels much longer.

"They're here. Everyone get ready," Rose commands, drawing our attention behind us.

I freeze in anticipation of the next group. Ahead, through the branches of the trees where we came, I see several people running our way. Rose doesn't seem alarmed, so I try to remain calm.

One man emerges, and another shortly after. A third figure appears wearing all black, and from her gait and posture, I recognize Anger. I immediately step in her direction. As the fourth and fifth come into view, they look behind them, watching as the last two members of their group break into the moonlight. An intimidatingly large man is carrying a small woman in his arms. In the night, his dark skin shines with fresh sweat. As I move closer, I see the man gently setting Maybeth down. *Thank God.*

Anger greets Rose, and they exchange a few words.

"Are you good?" Rose asks Anger.

"Yeah. We got the Revelation siblings. The others left with Falyn in the pods. It just worked better that way."

"Where's Dr. Wade?" Rose asks, concerned.

"He's out. He made it out with Falyn's Saints too. Now it's up to us."

"Okay. Okay," Rose repeats between taking in a few deep breaths.

"Darvin," Anger calls. "Come here."

I can hear my own heartbeat thumping through the veins in my inner ears.

"I have someone for you to meet. Or meet again," she says, motioning for me to follow her.

"No need to reintroduce us," Maybeth says wryly.

Anger ignores her and nods toward a young woman who arrived with their group right before Maybeth. Her long dark hair is mostly pulled behind her head, but a few locks have fallen over her eyes and cover some of her face.

When she steps from the hanging shadows of the trees, she pulls her hair behind her ears, and the light of the moon catches in her eyes. Anticipation draws me forward a few steps before I stop in disbelief. When she reaches me, her hand comes up slowly from her side as she timidly touches my face, as if she's unsure if I am real.

"Darvin," she whispers.

Hearing her say my name stuns me. Her thumb wipes one of the tears falling down my face, and then she's crying too. I see so much of Mom and Jaykin in her face that I feel like I'm seeing all three of them at once, and I embrace her. My arms tremble around her back as her arms squeeze tightly around my ribs.

I'm afraid this somehow isn't real, that she'll suddenly disappear from my grasp. As she lays her head across my shoulder, I listen to the quick puffs of air blowing against my arm as she cries. I feel her hair beneath my jaw and her fingers clenching my shirt.

She's real. For the first time in thirteen years, I let myself fully believe Ruma is alive.

CHAPTER 24

Finally within my arms, Ruma doesn't feel like the sister I've held in my mind for the past thirteen years. I feel an unexpected reverence for her, as if she's a legend who somehow magically emerged from the pages of a childhood fairytale. My imagination had oversimplified Ruma before this moment. I physically and emotionally preserved her in the state I last remembered her in, which wasn't much more than the shell of a memory formed in the mind of a five-year-old. Now that Ruma is within my grasp, I'm aware of how far time and distance have removed me from who she has become.

The night goes quiet. I notice several unfamiliar faces seem to have stopped to watch us meet. Our hug is short-lived, as Anger breaks us up, dousing the sentiment from our reunion. "This can wait. Time to move."

Ruma and I both seem to be suspended in the same state of shock, and I'm not sure I would've been able to speak to her even if Anger gave us a chance. Anger pushes Ruma away

THE REVELATION

from me and rushes her over to where they've laid out the remainder of the submersion masks. As she walks, Ruma looks back at me over her shoulder, and we exchange a subtle nod.

"Brooks, get ready to lead the first group," Anger calls out. "Edwin, stay behind to take the second. Keep an eye out in case anyone in Brooks's group gets left behind."

I didn't catch it before, but the two men who arrived with Ruma's group are the twins.

"Good to see you again," Brooks says, grabbing my shoulder from behind. He smiles and waves before helping Ruma secure her mask.

"I told you we could deliver," Edwin says, playfully punching my arm as he passes by to assist Brooks.

"You have the guide suits, right?" Brooks asks Anger. She throws two wet suits in his direction.

"Let's hope they're charged," Edwin says, stripping down to his underwear.

"Everyone make sure you grab a mask and oxygen tank," Anger says. "Brooks and Edwin, get your groups prepped and briefed. Now."

Merrin walks Maybeth toward the water's edge, so I join them. I don't know how to be around Ruma. A real stranger has taken the place of the familiar memories and ideas I held of who my sister was.

The wind sounds through the jittery branches of trees like muffled static. Most of our group stands huddled at the stone edge of the natural pool. We hook around the far left of the group just as Brooks and Edwin break the surface of the water. As they submerge themselves, their black wet suits turn bluish-white, like starlight. Rhysk joins us as Merrin,

Maybeth, and I fasten our masks to our faces and connect them with the oxygen tanks.

"We'll need to move quickly and stay together," Anger says. "Navigating the underwater caverns is very tricky. There will be a few tight squeezes, but the first order of business is to keep calm. It's essential to keep a hold of the guide rope, but if worse comes to worst, you should be able to follow the headlights attached to everyone's masks ahead of you."

"I can't swim," one of the girls in our group says in a panic.

"Hang on to the guide rope or stay here. Those are your options. Time to move out." Anger starts shoving the more timid members of the group into the water.

Brooks resurfaces to initiate the distribution of the guide rope, which is attached to an underwater propelling device. He grabs the handles of the mechanism and quickly submerges again, glistening like a sinking treasure below the water's surface. My nerves begin bubbling up inside of me as Merrin, Rhysk, and I position ourselves at the rear of the line. The members of the first group take turns disappearing beneath the water.

"Drove," Anger calls to the large man who came with Maybeth.

"You're taking care of Maybeth. Pull her with you. Ruma, you follow behind for support."

Ruma nods, and I can't help but wonder what her prior encounters with Anger have been like.

As Anger commands the remaining people in our group to submerge, a hollow blast ruptures through the trees and interrupts her instructions. The surge of energy knocks everyone down except for Drove. Most of us tumble hard over the ground, and a few others fly through the air and crash

THE REVELATION

down into the water. Several nearby trees crack, splintering open as they tumble over one another like slain giants.

My ears ring as I dazedly lift my head up off the grass. I see Merrin on the ground a short run away. He isn't moving. Pushing myself back up, I turn around to find Rhysk emerging from the water. She was blown back at least twenty feet. A few masked heads disappear, submerging in the water behind me while I scramble toward Merrin. Another explosion throws me into the dirt again. I crawl the last few feet to reach Merrin and pull myself over his body. He's unconscious and barely breathing. I helplessly try shaking him awake before I begin dragging him backward toward the water.

Not far from where I'm struggling to pull Merrin, Drove scoops up Maybeth in his arms. Sporadic lights zip by us from within the dark forest and explode against the face of the mountain cave. Drove's body locks tight, and he drops to the ground. Maybeth falls from his arms, and her fingertips are glowing white. I can't make out what she's screaming, but she's pointing toward Merrin and me. Drove quickly pushes himself back up and bolts to my side.

"I got him! Go!" he yells as he throws Merrin over his shoulder with incredible ease.

"Maybeth!" Ruma screams from behind me.

I stand in awe as Maybeth walks carefully toward the illuminated trees. Her arms glow in unison with brilliant streaks of lightning pulsing from her hands like a violent lightning storm. Each powerful blast shakes the ground.

Ruma clutches my arm from behind and drags me back toward the mouth of the cave.

"Stay with me," she says as we both run toward the water's edge. Rhysk meets us, and I grab her hand as the three of us sprint for the water. I turn back one last time and see Anger side by side with Maybeth, wildly expelling her own forces of energy into the night.

Dozens of Reapers spill from behind the tree line around fifty yards away as drone swarms weave through the branches above their heads. One of the bright lights from the tree line strikes Maybeth, and she drops to the ground.

"No!" I scream, only able to stop a moment before Ruma pulls me forward again.

I don't look back, so I can at least pretend there's a possibility Maybeth will get back up. Maybe Anger will save her. As I run, I cough until I gag, as if my body is trying to throw up the emotions I can't swallow. My heart wants to sink, but my inner grit kicks me into survival mode. We all secure our submersion gear once again before stepping over the water's edge.

Once we're nearly waist deep in the frigid water, I help Drove fasten Merrin's mask and oxygen tank. He's still unconscious but breathing. We all plunge into the depths of the spring, furiously swimming down to escape the chaos behind us. The water temporarily shocks my nerves as my skin tightens from the cold.

As I'm submerged, I hear persistent thumps sounding around me before streaking lines of red lasers pierce the water. The searing streams boil the surface water above us before being weakly refracted by the water. The full-bodied moonlight provides just enough light to see, so we don't have to turn on our headlights for now, which could make us easy targets. The cavernous rock structures look like the inner organs of the mountain, hungry to swallow us alive.

The guide rope must be somewhere ahead, out of reach,

THE REVELATION

so we're left without a clear path. For a moment, we all seem to be swimming on top of one another, and I begin to panic.

A gentle glow from my left catches my attention as an illuminated body glides past me to the front of our group. From the body size and appearance, I figure Anger has successfully escaped and is now leading the way with her glowing wet suit. I push the thought of Maybeth sacrificing herself out of my mind. I let the comforting glow swimming ahead calm me as I focus on the simple task of following the light. The depths of the underwater cave make the world above the surface feel much farther away.

Eventually, Drove turns on his headlight, and the rest of us do the same. He seems to be maintaining a steady hold of Merrin, and I can't tell if he's still unconscious or not. Rhysk and I have spent a lot of hours in aquatics training, but Ruma easily outmaneuvers us both and stays close behind Anger.

The underwater expanse within the caves astounds me with its immensity. Thankfully, the walls have enough breadth to allow us to swim comfortably. The pressure of the water pushes against my head. I swim steadily and relax my breathing to stay calm. I have no clue how long the oxygen in my tank will last. As I follow Ruma, she stops as if caught off guard. We haven't been told if there is animal life in the water, so I stay alert.

Instead, Ruma swims upward and off track of where Anger is taking us. A single faint light shines through the dark water where Ruma is heading. She swims off in its direction. I try to signal to the others behind me, but they seem to be confused as to what's going on.

Ruma disappears into the darkness behind her headlight. I watch the faintly glowing light until it meets with the other distant light and then quickly begins growing brighter as it approaches us. A few moments later, Ruma returns with a previously lost member of the first group tucked under her arm.

Thankfully, Anger must have noticed we were no longer behind her because she's back, waving her glowing arms to direct us through the jagged underwater tunnels. Our path seems to level out. Groups of small fish move in unison on the peripheral of our headlights. Their scales cast a cold, dim glow back toward us, like distant stars in a fading sky. Larger, solitary fish float by as unwanted shadows.

Ahead, I see a particularly narrow cut in the rock formation, which Anger is approaching. Around fifteen feet below, my headlight reflects off the shiny metal of the underwater propelling devices that the twins were using, which have now been discarded because of their size. She stops for a moment, as if to reassure us to follow her through the tunnel. With a bit of a struggle and careful maneuvering, she forces her way through the cramped opening to the other side. The pass only seems to be about ten feet long, but it's narrow enough to raise my heart rate for fear of getting stuck.

Ruma goes second, coercing whomever she rescued to follow her. The squeeze is tight but manageable for both of them. Assuming Edwin and Brooks made it through, Merrin would be able to make it through the gap if he were conscious, but pulling him to the other side will prove to be much more difficult. I'm the closest to the crevice, but I hesitate to swim through. Rhysk grabs my arm for a moment before quickly shooting through, only bumping the rocks a few times. She's the smallest in the group.

A light shines through the hole now. I know it must

THE REVELATION

be Rhysk looking back. Her light is about the only thing encouraging me to move forward. I've always hated cramped spaces, but potentially getting wedged in a dark underwater crevice heightens my anxiety to a completely different level.

Drove nudges me from behind. When I turn and face him, he taps his and Merrin's oxygen meters. Every passing second, our supplies are dwindling. When I face the rock opening again, the light hasn't moved. My eyes focus on it, and I swim forward.

The space between the rocks isn't wide enough for me to sufficiently bring my elbows beside me, so I enter in a streamlined position with my arms stretched out in front of me. My knees and elbows occasionally strike against the rock walls, but this only drives me forward with more ferocity.

My feet thrash around, searching for a foothold, and once I find one, I thrust myself forward. I'm sure I've bruised or bloodied the skin on my shoulders, but this is a small price to pay as I swim free past the opposite end of the tunnel.

Rhysk meets me and quickly directs my attention toward the rest of our group, which continues to swim upward without Merrin and Drove. The cave walls around me form a rough cylinder around twenty feet wide that rises like a tower toward the water's surface.

I look back from where I came and see Drove's light shining through from the other side of the tunnel. Rhysk tugs my arm, encouraging me to keep going, but I shake my head to let her know I won't continue without Merrin. A dark shadow quickly darts toward us. Rhysk and I both panic, screaming into our masks. As the figure nears, I realize it's Anger. I'm assuming her suit and headlight have lost their charge. Shielding her eyes with one hand, she signals for us to keep swimming as she dives farther down to assist Drove and Merrin. Maybeth told us Anger could see in the dark, but I had no idea her night vision was powerful enough to navigate black water.

Accepting that Anger is the most qualified to get Merrin through the cramped tunnel, Rhysk and I reorient ourselves and continue toward the lights. I follow her up as we chase the collection of headlights flickering a lengthy distance above us.

Even though I've grown more accustomed to the cold, my body temperature has dropped. My motor skills feel less responsive. My best defense is remembering my training to focus on steadying my breath to lower my heart rate.

A collection of headlights smears over the ripples in the water's surface just a short swim away. A deep, resounding hum charges the black water around Rhysk and me, causing our bodies to vibrate. The harrowing bellow encapsulates us in such a way that it's as if the mountain itself is groaning in pain.

The vibrations only last a few seconds, but a series of additional booms resonate through the water. As we look down, our headlights reflect off a rising cloud of murky water where we last saw Anger, Merrin, and Drove.

The turbid swell swallows both of us as we swim up. Panic rises from within my stomach. My vision is completely obstructed, so all I can do is swim blind, hoping that eventually I'll find the surface.

Through the thick, opaque water, a soft orange glow refracts into the water above me. The surface is near. Although the water provided us security and relief from the Reaper and drone ambush, I'm exhausted from navigating the frigid obscurity. My feet are numb as I struggle through the last few strokes to the surface.

THE REVELATION

When we break into the air, one of the twins pulls Rhysk and me from the water. The low-hanging rock domes overhead look like a thick collection of decaying bones. My body trembles uncontrollably. I throw off my mask and oxygen gear as I'm pulled onto a smooth stone ledge surrounding the mouth of the spring.

I put the rest of my strength into crawling toward a nearby fire, my teeth chattering. My fingers quiver over the slippery rock faces, and my knees sting from occasional brushes against jagged rocks.

The others from the group before us huddle together, trying to soak in the heat emanating from the inner ring of firelight. I fumble over strangers as if they're inanimate objects and try to position myself closer to the fire. With some resistance, I'm finally able to get close enough to the fresh heat throbbing against my skin. My body continues trembling and feels as if it's powering down, but I force myself to roll over to face the water's edge. I watch the water, waiting for Merrin to surface. My effort to clench my jaws fails to keep my teeth from chattering.

As if from a dream, I hear a gentle choir of voices singing in my ears. Am I close enough to freezing to hear angels? My eyelids are heavy, and as I lie on my side, the once frigid water soaking my skin lifts off in thin, steamy clouds.

The distant, unintelligible melodies beg my eyes to close, but I hold them open. Drove and Anger emerge from below the water's surface, dragging Merrin to the stone shore. He made it. My eyes give way to the unbearable weight of exhaustion, and the distant voices lull me into stillness.

CHAPTER 25

Hear my voice, I'll lead you on
Find my face among the stars,
Embrace the warmth that comes with dawn,
Like morning light, I'm never far.

I hear my mother's faint voice singing from her bedroom. I remember the tune as the words settle clearly in my mind. I jump from my bed, running across my house and into her bedroom. I find the room empty except for a single abandoned birdcage covered in cobwebs, resting in the back corner by her window. My mother isn't there, but the soft words of her song continue to ebb and flow in the rushing wind that beats through the broken window.

Feel the winds of hope blow strong,
Rise like birds above your seas,
The sky is where your heart belongs
In all these things, that's where I'll be.

THE REVELATION

I whisper the words with her as my eyes open to dim, flickering shadows chasing the light between crevices in the cave's ceiling. A thin wool blanket lies over my body, and it wasn't there when I first fell asleep. Gentle singing draws my attention. I roll over to find Ruma sitting upright a few feet away. She looks as if she's trying to quietly sing her mind to sleep.

"Did Mom teach you that song?" I ask, my voice low. Her eyes open, and it takes her a second to realize where the question came from.

"Yeah," Ruma says, her gaze falling to the dancing flames.

"You sound like her," I say.

Ruma says nothing as she studies my face, as if she's still unsure if I am real.

"I was just dreaming about that song. I guess I heard you while I was sleeping."

Suddenly, I remember Merrin. After watching him be knocked unconscious by the Reapers' blast and dragged by Drove through the underwater caves, I'm worried about how much physical damage he endured. I throw off my blanket and sit up to scan the sleeping bodies sprawled around me.

"He's fine," Ruma whispers, pointing over to her left about fifteen feet away. "He came to after you fell asleep."

My legs feel unsteady as I stand. I have to catch myself with my hands as I fall over someone's leg. I carefully hop over the members of our group and sit down by his side.

"They kept him awake for as long as they could," she explains. "He was confused but still asking about you."

A bundle of blankets covers him. I place my hand on the blankets to make sure he's breathing.

"Don't wake him. He needs rest."

I look around once more, scanning the cave for Rhysk.

"She's behind you," Ruma tells me. "By the second fire."

The tightness in my chest releases like steam leaving a kettle as I breathe out.

"Thank you," I say, momentarily taken aback by how perceptive Ruma is.

Once I find Rhysk, I settle back down to sit by Merrin, but I stay facing Ruma. We sit in silence for a short while. I try to count the shadows of people on the ground, but some blend into others, so I give up.

Ruma stands up and moves closer to the fire to warm her hands.

"Where are we?" I whisper, looking around at the staggering umber walls of the hollow caverns.

"Somewhere beneath the Revelation Mountains," she responds, shrugging her shoulders and rubbing the fire's heat between her palms.

Seeming satisfied with the warmth she's collected from the flames, Ruma stands and whispers, "I want to show you something. Come with me."

"Now?"

"Yeah. I think you'd like to see it."

Ruma and I seem to be the only ones unable to sleep, so I nod, following her as she steps between the gaps among the ones sleeping around us. The cave walls narrow ahead into the opening of a dark tunnel. As we move away from the fires behind us, I rely on the faint reflections of light caught in the water trickling down the cave walls to guide me.

"We're not far," Ruma assures me.

She steps into the mouth of the tunnel, and we both brace our hands against the damp walls so our fingers can help us

THE REVELATION

walk along with our feet. A cold breath of wind sweeps through the hollow just as we turn a bend. The night sky peeks through the eye of an opening ahead.

Ruma guides me to the tunnel's end, where an eight-foot circular window overlooks rows and rows of mountains, like stormy waves crashing amongst the sea of stars. She sits down on a smooth stone ledge and lets her legs hang off the edge. I sit beside her and do the same.

"It's beautiful," I say, and she nods in agreement.

I stare at the moon and try to imagine its light washing over my face. I've spent so many nights sharing the company of the stars, wondering where Ruma was, but tonight we get to sit together.

"The moon feels different," Ruma says, breaking the silence while gazing off into the night sky.

"What do you mean?" I ask.

"It just feels real, like it can see me again without the glass ceiling in the way," she says, breathing in the night as her light-green eyes softly catch the moonlight.

"Yeah," I say in agreement, and we return to silence. For all the unanswered questions I've accumulated in my head over the years, I can't seem to think of anything worth interrupting the beauty of this moment.

"What's it like out there now?" she asks, looking over the distant mountains.

"I don't know," I tell her. "I only know Southern Guard. We haven't been to Northern Guard in a couple years either."

"Are Nona and Papa still alive?" she asks.

"Yeah. They're still good as far as I know," I say, smiling, reminded of how much she's missed over the past thirteen years.

"They told me you all died from perducorium," she says, staring out into the darkness.

"*What?* No," I say, confused.

She nods once, and her face remains unchanged. All this time, I was so busy thinking of the questions I would ask her that I never imagined what questions she might have for me.

"We're all still alive," I say, looking straight into her eyes. "And we never gave up hope that you were alive."

"I'm not alive. Not anymore," she says, pulling her knees in close to her chest. Still no emotion registers on her face.

"What do you mean?" I ask.

She shakes her head as her legs begin to bounce within her arms. "I'm not her anymore. They ruined her."

"Yes, you are. You're still my sister," I tell her, reaching out to touch her arm, but she flinches away.

"I don't have a family anymore," she says, obstinately getting to her feet.

"Yes, you do."

"No!" she yells, looking me in the eyes for the first time since we've stepped out into the night. "You don't understand."

"We never forgot you," I say, desperate to reassure her.

"You have no idea what I am," she says, gritting her teeth. Suddenly, her eyes turn bright yellow, nearly glowing in the dark. As I look at her, her complexion changes before my eyes, and I flinch away. Within a few seconds, her skin seems to be shriveling and thickening at the same time. I jolt backward, scrambling a few feet back into the tunnel.

The silhouette of Ruma's thick frame looks frighteningly unfamiliar as the moonlight splits over the cracks of her ashen skin. She doesn't look away from me. Her eyes burn bright,

THE REVELATION

like gold flames. In a matter of seconds, she's transformed herself into a Stone.

"You don't know me anymore," she says, her voice now much rougher than before.

As quickly as her mutation took over her, the transformative effects of perducorium recede out of view as if they never existed. This process normally takes several weeks to complete for a Stone, but as Ruma sits back down, breathing heavily, she looks no different than she did when she first sat down on the mountain ledge. With my back pressed up to the cave wall, I'm afraid to move.

I know Ruma saw the fear and even disgust across my face as I looked at her. She knows it. I saw it in her eyes too. It's what I've been trained to feel. From as early as I can remember, I've been taught about the life-threatening dangers of perducorium.

My adrenaline still burns hot inside of me, but I move against my fears and step toward Ruma. My hands shake slightly, so I tuck them between my crossed arms. Ruma is my sister, and I'm her brother, but we don't know one another anymore.

"I think we've both changed," I say. "I've only been gone a few weeks, but I'm not the same person I was when I left home. We may not know each other anymore, but maybe that's something we can figure out together."

Ruma looks back over her shoulder, and I extend my trembling hand toward her.

"I'm still your brother," I say, keeping my hand extended, waiting for her to respond.

"You don't have to do this," she says, as if trying to dismiss me from an obligation to be kind.

I lean a little farther toward her, reaching my hand a little closer to hers. "I'm Darvin. Your brother."

Ruma hesitates. Her lips push together and scrunch up toward her nose. She casually untucks her hands to shake mine. Ruma feels more real to me this time, even more so than when we first hugged before escaping. Tears slip down my face, and I let them.

When she lets go, my hands are no longer trembling. I sit down beside her, giving her a few feet of space. "You have another brother," I tell her. "*We* have another brother. His name is Jaykin."

"What?" she asks, halfway pushing herself up from the ground.

"Jaykin. He's ten now. He looks more like Dad than we do."

When she looks at me, the corners of her mouth rise just enough for me to know she cares.

"He really wants to meet you," I tell her. "We never gave up on believing you were alive. Never."

She nods subtly. From the way she's squinting, I can tell she's sorting through her thoughts. Ruma breathes in a sudden breath of cool air that quickly quivers back out as she exhales, like she's letting go of something.

"How did you find me?" she asks.

"It just kind of happened. Everything seemed to be falling apart, and then somehow we ended up with Anger, and that eventually led us to you," I tell her, wishing I had a more meaningful answer.

"So you trust her?" she asks, trying to rub the night's chill from her skin.

"God, no. But I didn't really have a choice."

THE REVELATION

"Maybeth told me about her," Ruma says. "She hated her, but she still talked about her like she was a legend."

"So you were close to Maybeth?" I ask, knowing the ache I felt from knowing her less than a day would certainly be much worse for Ruma.

She doesn't respond for a moment, and then she nods.

I stop to take a moment to breathe. My body feels stiff and exhausted. I don't have enough mental space to process everything that's happening. I don't know what Ruma has been through, but I'm sure she needs to feel safe and understood by someone.

The sound of a glass bottle breaking catches our attention. Both of our heads turn toward the tunnel. The bright orange glow of a torch fills the cave before dimming, leaving only the edges of light behind. Ruma gets up first and signals for me to follow her. Together, we pursue the flickering tail of light lingering a short distance away within the hollow.

We find an arching stone entrance to another tunnel, previously covered by darkness, splitting off from the passageway where we first entered. The echoes of another bottle shattering momentarily stop us in our tracks. Still unsure of who could be following us after escaping beneath the underwater caves leading out of the Revelation Territory, Ruma and I move cautiously.

We warily chase the distant flickers of firelight as they paint the edges of the carefully inlaid bricks lining the narrow tunnel. The damp air smells bittersweet, like mildew and aged wood.

After we sneak a few paces past the archway, the light disappears entirely, and we're left to carefully shuffle our way toward the distant echoes of voices in the dark. I gasp as a rat scampers at my feet. Ruma reaches back and grabs my arm tightly. A wooden door gently creaks from its hinges as Ruma pushes her way into another stretch of the winding tunnel. Flickering lights hang somewhere ahead, gradually providing more light as we cautiously approach the growing sounds. I quickly realize the distorted voices belong to Anger and Rose.

The narrow hallway ends suddenly, opening into a small vaulted cavern filled with wine barrels and shelves stocked with bottles. The only visible light comes from lanterns mounted on the cave walls. We stop to listen out of sight at the edge of the passageway.

"You think you're in control, but you're not. Your hate for him is driving every decision you make," Rose says.

"Speak for yourself, because I don't give a fuck about him," Anger says.

"Oh. So you don't care? He sacrificed you, his own daughter, to promote his industry, and you just let that go," Rose says, dousing her words with sarcasm.

"I'm not his goddamned daughter, Rose. You are."

"They raised you in our home knowing he would infect you all along—"

"My God," Anger says.

"Let me finish. And when he dumped you off at the Revelation Territory to cover up your genetic reversal—"

"I know what happened to me."

"I don't think you do," Rose asserts. "Either you're in denial, or I don't think you get it."

"*I* don't get it?" Anger repeats, laughing. "Then I'm glad as fuck you're here to explain how I should feel. Thank you, Rose. But if you really want to help, you can toss me that dark bottle by your head."

THE REVELATION

"I think you've had enough," Rose says. Another bottle crashes against the cave walls. "Would you stop?" Rose hisses.

We wait for Anger's response. I realize I've been mostly holding my breath this whole time.

"If he didn't die tonight, I'm going to kill him," Anger says, breaking the silence. "It will be him, or whoever is at the top of RedCloud when I get there. I'm telling you, so when it happens, you'll know it was me." Another bottle shatters against the stone wall.

I step forward until I can see parts of their figures between stacked barrels and holes in the sparsely filled wine racks where bottles used to be. Anger walks over to where Rose is sitting and grabs another bottle of wine. Rose tries to take it from her sister's hand, but Anger snatches it away. After she sits on top of a wine barrel, she knocks the glass bottle head off against the wall closest to her. A splatter of dark-red wine drips thickly down the wall like fresh blood.

Anger raises the bottle in the air toward Rose. "To our father."

Rose says nothing. She stands, pushes her chair in at the small wooden table where she was sitting, and leaves as Anger pours the wine from the bottle's shattered neck onto the floor.

"Let's go," Ruma whispers, already on the move.

We hastily make our way back through the dark tunnels as we return to the mountain caverns, where our companions are still sleeping. I rush to resituate my blanket beside Merrin, and Ruma settles herself where I found her upon waking up.

I close my eyes, and Anger and Rose's conversation begins rolling over in my head. My mind takes inventory of every word I can remember, even though I'd much rather be sleeping. *She was intentionally infected? Does she really want to murder the emperor of RedCloud?* After a few restless minutes of mulling over questions with no answers, I decide to distract myself by singing the same song I dreamed my mother was singing to me.

    I quietly mumble the words of the first verse to myself. Once I whisper the line, *Like morning light, I'm never far*, I repeat the phrase to myself a few times as a quiet mantra, and then silently inside my own head, until the words become the anthem that carries me back into the darkness of sleep.

CHAPTER 26

"Darvin, it's time to move."
I wake up to Rhysk gently shaking my shoulder. Most everyone is already up and moving around. Merrin is awake but still lying on his back.

I reach over to check on him.

"You okay?" I ask.

He doesn't answer but nods his head slightly. His disquieting response leaves me feeling uneasy, but considering what he's been through in the past several hours, I'm thankful he's alive and responding. I see some people passing out bottles of water and food. I'm not sure what time of day or night it is, but I decide to grab breakfast for Merrin and me.

I get up slowly. My joints and muscles complain from sleeping on the stone floor with little padding. The blanket helped, but not nearly enough. My blood feels extra thick in my body, as if it's trying to pull me back down so I'll stay asleep. One of the girls handing out breakfast comes in my direction. I meet her to get some food, and we exchange smiles.

THE REVELATION

"Can I have another for my friend?" I ask. She hands me an additional bottle of water and two pieces of some type of bread baked with dried fruit. I'm not sure where it came from, but I'm grateful.

She has her blonde hair pulled back behind her head except for one strand, which hangs across her face. A small patch of dried blood has settled above her left eye. I can tell she's had a rough night like the rest of us.

I thank her, and she smiles kindly in return and makes her way over to Merrin, kneeling beside him with his breakfast. Drove walks over to Merrin and forces him to his feet. It's good to see him standing again. I keep the extra rations in case I find someone else who hasn't eaten yet.

I'd guess there are around twenty-five of us. Three men and two women are holding firearms. I don't know who most of these people are or what role they had in the Revelation Territory, but whatever the case, we're on the same team now. One of them saved Rhysk's life last night by downing the drone.

That reminds me that I haven't thanked the two guys who stayed behind to help us last night. In the darkness and chaos, I didn't get a good look at their faces. I look around the room to see if I can recognize them and quickly spot a familiar face. He begins walking toward me. After a moment, my mind pulls his name back into memory: Endon.

"I don't know how I haven't seen you this whole time," Endon says to me. "You're Eden, right?"

"Darvin, actually," I say, and he gives me a confused look. "I'm sorry. When we met the first time, they told me to tell people my name was Eden. My real name is Darvin."

"Darvin," he says. "That's okay. You weren't the first to lie to me when I got to the Revelation Territory, so it's not a big deal."

"You want some breakfast? I have two," I tell him, and he gratefully accepts.

A gray-haired woman bumps into me and distractedly apologizes, busying herself by lighting the wicks of several lanterns. She passes them around to whomever will take one, including Rhysk.

"Where's your sister? Is she here with us?" I ask Endon. For a moment I panic, wondering if she was the one who was snatched away by one of the drones.

"No, but as far as I know, she escaped with Falyn's crew."

"How do you know Falyn?" I ask.

"Everyone knows him," Endon says. "But I've never actually met him."

"Me either. I was just with Anger in the Black Valley when she met with him—"

"Did you get to see him?" Endon asks in disbelief.

"No. They met late at night, and I was asleep by then."

"I can't believe you went to sleep and missed meeting Falyn Dire."

"I don't really know anything about him," I say, wondering what I missed.

"He's the leader of the Saints. They're all anti-RedCloud dominance, and they want to make sure the four Guard cities, and any Guards to come, can self-govern. So they're demanding a balance of power between industry and government. He organized this whole infiltration of the Revelation Territory. I mean, not all of this. I heard Anger planned the second branch of the escape with our group, but he organized the attack

THE REVELATION

during the provincial order address. They're saying it's the first successful breach of the Revelation Territory ever."

"I guess we're still not in the clear yet," I tell him, wondering if there are Reapers and Legionnaires circling every inch of the Revelation Mountains, waiting to pounce on us.

"Apparently they already staged a fake escape with transport aerocrafts several hours ago to throw them off our trail," Endon explains, taking a big bite out of his bread.

"I didn't even know this place existed until a week ago," I say.

"You weren't the only one. I can promise you that."

Two of the armed men in our group work together to throw buckets of water on the last coals still glowing in the fires. The embers release a long, smoky sigh as their last breaths join together to form swirling gray clouds of smoke that flow against the low rock ceilings. The lantern lights dye the smoky haze bright orange.

Anger emerges from the same hallway where Ruma and I found her last night when she was drunkenly arguing with Rose in the wine cellar. She seems to have sobered up. Either that or she's just hiding it well.

"We have to move now. Quietly," she announces before turning around and going back the way she came. "We'll take a short passageway up to the lower levels of the monastery, and then we'll move to our extraction point."

"Let's go," Rose reiterates and follows her out.

Rhysk joins me, and we join Merrin.

"Are you going to be okay?" I ask him.

"Yeah. I think I got it. Just keep an eye out for me."

"We've got you," Rhysk says. I know she doesn't know

Merrin very well, or me, for that matter, but I can sense her loyalty is strong.

After deciding Merrin is okay to move without his assistance, Drove moves forward, connecting with Ruma, and they lead the way through the tunnel ahead of us. Drove's head is only a few inches away from the ceiling, and his shoulders nearly span the width of the tunnel.

Rhysk, Merrin, and I follow them through the passageway and past the wine cellar. The fragrance of freshly spilled wine from last night hits my nose like a fermented ghost. We reach a winding stone staircase that leads us upward. Remnants of old spiderwebs drag over my head. I swipe them away as best I can. The cut stones and mortar framing the stairs look like they've grown tired as they sink into one another.

"Drove," Anger calls down from above. "We need you."

We continue around the last bend of the staircase to find a wrought-iron door barring our escape.

"Where is he?" Anger asks, sounding annoyed.

"I'm here," Drove answers, pushing his way up front.

"Take care of this," she commands, pointing to the iron gate. "Keep it on the hinges."

"He was supposed to unlock it," Edwin says, clearly frustrated.

Drove instructs the people up front to move back, so we shuffle a few steps back down. He places his hands firmly between the thick decorative swirls of iron and takes a deep breath. Once he begins to pull, I hear a series of harsh pops as the metal lock snaps apart like a dry twig. Drove gently swings the iron door, its hinges still intact, back against the rock wall for easy passage.

Other than the few initial gasps, Merrin, Rhysk, and I seem

THE REVELATION

to be the only ones the least bit impressed by Drove. I wonder how many of them have unique abilities of their own that I've yet to see. I'm still unsure why Rhysk and I would've been a part of the apparent Revelation eugenics screening in the lab if we both didn't have some type of genetic resilience. Whatever the case, the three of us move forward with the group in silent awe, following the others into yet another stretch of tunnels.

Thankfully, this length of winding stone hallway stands a few feet higher, so I don't feel as cramped. The walls bear several identical nooks, burrowed into the stone where small delicately carved angels stand watching us along the way. The white necks of the burning candles, which stand melting beside the angelic marble figures, let me know someone has recently walked this hall who didn't come with us.

We slowly travel through the labyrinth of passageways until Rose signals for us all to stop. Merrin bumps into the back of me and nearly makes me fall. Our group rests in a pocket of darkness between the glowing halos of candlelight. The front of the line freezes at the foot of a steep flight of stone stairs.

At the top of the steps, a single candle flickers into view, spilling ebbing waves of light down the stairs. As prisoners of the shadows, we all watch a gray-cloaked figure descending toward us with a candle in hand. We wait for Anger's move, hoping she'll do whatever it takes to keep us from being recaptured.

The figure stops just as the edge of his small flame touches our group. The features of his face are lost among his pale wrinkles and his long, crawling beard.

"You could've waited for the other key," the old man says as his raspy voice tumbles through the silence.

"You were late," Brooks says dryly as he and Edwin begin ascending the stairs.

"I don't keep time. It keeps me," he says, extending his hand toward Brooks. When the twins reach him, they exchange a quick embrace before Brooks nods his head to signal us to continue onward.

"Keep moving," Anger commands.

"Who is that?" Merrin whispers, as if I'll have an answer.

Edwin and Brooks carefully guide the old man back up the stairs as Anger stealthily follows behind with the rest of us.

Rhysk whispers from beside me. "Did they ever make you do that virtual inauguration experience about the history of the Revelation Territory?"

"Yeah. We both did," I whisper close to her ear, nodding back at Merrin. "Rose took us through it herself."

"I think we're underneath the Patmos Monastery," she says. "We've got to be."

We come to another abrupt stop as we reach a straight stretch of an arched stone corridor. Anger, Edwin, and Brooks split up between our group to make sure everyone hears our instructions.

Edwin comes to the back where we are. "Listen carefully. Just beyond that door ahead, there's a chamber where about two dozen of the Patmos monks are sleeping. It's about four in the morning, so we're hoping to pass through unnoticed. If we're detected, they could notify the Revelation Territory, and within minutes, the tail of our escape could get chopped off. You understand?"

We nod before he continues. "We'll pass down the center between the two rows of beds and go up a short flight of steps. Once we make it through the next door, we'll take an

THE REVELATION

immediate right down a straight passageway leading to an exterior balcony, where we'll be extracted. Got it?"

"What happens if we wake them?" Rhysk whispers.

"Our old friend should've taken care of that. They should be out for a few hours. Your only goal is to exit as quickly and as quietly as possible. We'll take care of the rest. Don't make a sound, and we'll have no problems."

Our schedule must be extremely tight because Anger is already moving her crew toward the double wooden doors. We step just behind the heels of those in front of us. I make eye contact with Ruma, who nods reassuringly before turning forward again.

Once we're all in line, the stillness is almost unbearable. Anger signals for all of the lantern lights to be extinguished as the old man pulls a thick iron key from within his cloak. We wait for our next move in the dark.

For a few seconds, I hear nothing but the slight whistle of someone breathing through their nose. My ears pick up the soft crunch of the key turning within the door's lock. A thin, vertical strip of light appears and slowly widens as the old man carefully pushes open the chamber door. The painful creaking of the iron hinges interrupts the silence. The rusted pins squeal while rotating in their sockets. My neck tightens, and I hold my breath.

Shadows ahead of me slip quickly though the cracked doorway, one after the other. The old man holds the door as we all pass, treading lightly as if entering the den of a beast. My fingers shake out in front of me as I feel my way forward, trying not to run into Rhysk.

As I push through the doorway, I see low-burning candles hanging on to their last breaths beside each bed. On the right wall, high, slim transom windows allow a definitive amount of moonlight into the chamber. One square falls directly on the pale oval face of one of the monks, his features surrounded by gray hair and a thick beard. His mouth is agape in a way that makes him look as much dead as he does asleep.

Several identical banners hang symmetrically above our heads, decorating the thick wooden I-beams supporting the steeply vaulted ceilings. Above the double doors ahead, a life-sized statue of a robed man is poised inside a recess in the brick wall.

Anger has already reached the doors at the top of a half flight of stairs. We all have to pause in place while she unlatches the locked bars keeping us inside. Again, the clicks of the lock attempt to warn the monks of our passing, but as far as I can tell from scoping the room, we remain unnoticed. Anger's figure slides out of view, and she's the first of us to make it safely to the other side.

The statue seems to be the only one aware of our presence. As I move closer toward the figure, I can more clearly see three coins resting in his outturned hand. His other hand holds a double-headed wooden staff. I begin ascending the steps below the shrine just as Merrin loses his footing behind me. He catches himself on the stairs and nearly makes me fall after grabbing my leg. Merrin and the three others behind him momentarily stiffen. I do the same. My eyes are the only part of me scanning the room for any response to Merrin's untimely clumsiness. One of the monks rolls over in his bed and pulls his thin blanket up to his chin.

I prepare to run, but fear keeps me in place. After a moment, I realize that by some miracle, we haven't been detected, and I slip through the door without further hesitation.

THE REVELATION

To my right, the stretch of hallway leading to the exterior terrace is not much more than thirty feet away. The rest of our group has already made it outside the ajar terrace doors. The cool freshness of the outside air washes over my skin like liquid moonlight. With Merrin and the others behind me, I quickly step to meet Anger, who holds the door with one hand, waving us forward with the other.

She startles, peering over our shoulder and screaming, "Get down!" A bolt of panic surges through my body. Covering my head, I fling myself to the floor and feel Merrin drop over my legs. From behind us, a burst of sound and light flashes, illuminating the entire hallway as if lightning has struck.

I wince as something splatters over my back from behind. My body tingles with energy, but I don't feel pain. While lying on the ground, I feel someone's blood dripping over my arms. I look up at Anger rising from the floor just in front of me. The blast ripped away the interior framing of the balcony doors where she had been standing a moment ago. My ears ring and my eyes struggle to shake out the blurry haze obstructing my vision.

Once back on her feet, Anger immediately stretches her hand toward whoever attacked us from behind, and I hear a complex crunching sound. Not until I roll over and turn around do I realize the sound came from the crumbling bones snapping within the body of an armed monk patrolling the halls. My heart roars in my chest, and I can barely breathe. The cloaked monk drops to the floor as a disfigured corpse beside the glowing barrel of his oversized laser. In the torchlight, his blood pours out from his body and flows between the cracks in the stone floors.

Rhysk and I move to help Merrin and the blonde girl who

handed me my breakfast get up off the floor. The weapon used to attack us dismembered the last two escaping members of our group. Fragments of their bodies litter the floor around us.

Merrin begins panicking, frantically wiping pieces of wet flesh off his body. Still in shock, the blonde girl can barely move. My hand slips off the blood running down her arm as I pull her to her feet. I can't tell whether it's her blood or the blood of the ones who were killed behind her. Thankfully, Merrin seems to have no physical injuries. Even in his state of near hysteria, he helps me lead the dazed girl toward the exterior balcony.

"Run!" Anger yells to us.

We hastily follow Anger's orders. Feeling a fearful deference to her power, I don't even feel comfortable looking at her. Once we pass through the doorway and into the open air, we see the others have already boarded three separate aerocrafts, all of which reflect the night sky as a form of camouflage.

A steep, retractable walkway extends down to the terrace floor. The last of us load into the same aerocraft as Rhysk, Ruma, and Drove.

Once we fling ourselves into an open seat and strap over our safety harnesses, Anger commands the pilot to leave. In seconds, we're flying over the Revelation Mountains in the silence surrounding the electric trills of the engines.

I can barely hear the gentle murmuring of the engines as all three of the aerocrafts accelerate into the air. The night is quiet as I sit covered in someone else's blood while we leave the mountains behind. I imagine Maybeth's body lying alone not far from the cave pool where we escaped. It's not fair that I'm flying away from the Revelation Territory after being held

THE REVELATION

captive for just a few days when she's the one who spent over half her life there as a prisoner. Will her children ever know her story? I'm unaware of time, and nothing feels real except for the breaths I draw in and let out.

I sit blankly in a state of shock, keeping my eyes shut to block out everything around me as much as I can. After a few minutes of refusing to open my eyes, I feel a soft, damp cloth sliding over my arm. When I open my eyes and look down, Rhysk is sitting beside me, wiping the dried blood from my skin.

Once she sees I'm awake, she says, "Hold this. You got it?" She leaves the freshly stained towel in my hand. I rub it between my fingers to finish cleaning the remaining blood off.

"You finished?" Rhysk asks, extending her hand to take my towel.

"Yeah. Thank you," I say, quietly handing it back to her, wishing I could relieve her golden eyes of their sadness.

She tosses the towel underneath her seat and pulls something from inside of her pocket.

"Hold out your hand," she tells me.

"Why?" I ask curiously as I open my palm toward her.

Rhysk's soft fingers briefly slide across my palm as she lays the flint fire starter and the picture of my mother I thought I had lost in my hand.

"Where did this come from?" I ask, stricken with disbelief and gratefulness for the small piece of home she's returned to me.

"Anger told me to give it to you. She said you dropped it."

When I look at Anger, she's squatting behind the pilot, scanning the instrumental readings. I hold both items in my hand and rub them with my thumbs. I hold the picture of my mom close and wonder what she would say if she were here right now, riding over the distant lands of New Province with the daughter she hasn't seen in over thirteen years.

My shirt is still wet with blood, so I carefully take it off. My undershirt is thankfully much cleaner.

Rhysk helps me wash my arms and neck with damp wipes she pulls from a pack resting beside her seat.

"Is that your mom?" Rhysk asks, taking a hold of my forearm.

A lump rises in my throat, and all I can do is nod.

"She looks like both of you," she says, gently sliding the cold wipe across the side of my neck.

I breathe deeply for a few seconds until my throat releases its tension. "These are the only pieces of home I have," I say.

"What's that?"

"It's a flint fire starter," I tell her. "My dad gave it to me. You open it here and split it apart. These two ends strike together, and it makes a spark."

"Can I try it?" she asks, intrigued.

"Yeah." I hand it over. She strikes the two pieces of flint together, and several bright sparks fly out before quickly disappearing into the floor between our feet. The volume of sparks startles her, and she drops one of the flint ends on the ground. The metal casing holding the flint breaks off at the bottom, and as I pick it up, I realize there's a detachable chamber I never noticed before.

"I'm so sorry. I didn't mean to—"

"No. It's okay," I say. "I think you can just put this back on." I pick up the separate pieces to inspect them. A tiny persistent light is flashing inside the bottom of the capsule piece previously connected to the fire starter.

THE REVELATION

"What is that?" I mumble to myself.

Rhysk assumes I'm asking her and takes the piece from my hand.

"It looks like a tracking device. My dad sells these at his shop. Did you know this was in here?" She inspects it more closely.

"No. Are you sure that's what this is?" I ask uneasily.

She nods. "My parents made me carry one every time I left Southern Guard. Maybe your dad was trying to do the same thing."

"I wouldn't think he would be like that, but if they've been tracking me, they would've known my location was away from New Province Guard. I don't even know if they know I'm alive. Do you think someone has contacted our families?"

"I don't know. I don't even know where we're going now," she says, as if she's just now fully realizing this.

"We're going home," I say reflexively, but as I say the words, I feel a sudden stab of uncertainty.

"Darvin," Rhysk whispers, leaning in close by my ear. "Look who we're with. They told us back at Ops that you and Merrin died. They could've easily said the same about me after I was captured. I don't think they would just let us go home. I think it's much bigger than that."

The blonde girl sitting a seat over to my right interrupts our conversation.

"There were two parts to our escape. Our groups were only half of it as far as I know." Her voice sounds dry and somewhat spacy, almost as if her mind is elsewhere rather than trying to have a conversation. "We'll probably meet up with Falyn Dire and his Saints. They have the other group with them," she finishes. I didn't realize until now that she has a touch of a foreign accent.

"What's your name?" I ask.

"Talliph. And yours?" she asks, combing her fingers through her matted hair without looking at us. We both answer, and she repeats, "Rhysk and Darvin. Nice to meet you."

"What do you know about Falyn Dire?" Rhysk asks.

"Not much," she says as she begins licking the tips of her fingers and wiping the bloodstains off her forearms.

"Here. Let me help you," Rhysk says, handing her another cloth. Talliph takes the fabric and holds it in her shaky hands, staring at her fingers as they pinch the edges of the cloth.

"Are you okay?" Rhysk asks her.

Talliph pauses for a moment and looks at Rhysk as if she doesn't understand the question. After a moment of quiet, Talliph leans over to me and whispers, "Can I ask you something?"

I nod. "Yes."

"What happened back there?" she says, slowly beginning to use the wet cloth to rub the red smudges from her skin.

I look down at the partially dried stains on both of our clothes and the wadded-up shirt at my feet. I settle back into my seat, and I can't bring myself to say anything.

"The girl. She was nice to me. That's all," Talliph says before sitting back as well to stare at the ceiling.

The cabin falls into silence. I close my eyes as I'm pulled toward an inner urge to pray. I don't pray a lot, but when I think to, I feel peace. My lips move, but I don't let any words come out loud enough to be heard. I pray for my family, my friends, safety, peace, comfort, and lastly for purpose. *God, help me make my own choices.*

"Everyone get up!" the copilot screams over his shoulder, startling us. "Get up! Now! We have to eject. They're about to fire on us. Grab the chutes underneath your seats!"

Everyone is alert and responding, and most of us snatch up our chutes in a matter of seconds. Merrin can't seem to unlatch his, so I help him get his free. The copilot quickly shows us how to attach them around our bodies as well as which cord to pull. Unnerving beeps wail from within the cockpit.

The pilot engages the exit doors at the back of the aerocraft, which open to darkness and growling winds. The freezing cold air whips around us. The copilot inspects Drove's chute and gives him the signal to exit. Without hesitation, he jumps, and not five seconds later, Ruma disappears into the night behind him. Talliph shakes her head after she is cleared to go.

Her face is completely drained of color, pale like the shade of moonlight. She's hyperventilating.

"Go!" the copilot screams, but she's not moving. Rhysk moves around him and grabs Talliph's hands, locking eyes with her.

"I've got you. Be brave," Rhysk yells over the whirling air while leading her toward the exit ramp. Talliph follows reluctantly. Once they are close enough to the edge, Rhysk nods at her and flings them both into the night.

"She's on autopilot. Get the fuck out!" the pilot yells as he rushes from the cockpit. The rest of us jump together.

I've practiced air evacuations dozens of times, but this is only my second real experience. Adrenaline swells hot inside me. Above us, the moon hides behind a veil of clouds, which allows minimal light to illuminate the ground far below. I have no point of reference for when I should pull my chute, and I'm afraid to pull too early in case the others are still dropping above me.

A fiery cloud interrupts the night. An explosion roars above the surging air. The bright glow of what's left of our aerocraft falls out of the sky, fading like a dying ember thrown off by a current of smoke.

I try stabilizing myself on my stomach as best I can with the wind forcefully pushing against me. The expanded canopy of a chute below reflects just enough moonlight to warn me it's time for me to do the same. I roll out of the way, nearly crashing into someone. I release my own chute and begin my final descent. My harness snatches me upward as the belly of my chute fills with air.

Most of my energy reserve feels depleted as I quietly drift toward the ground. This moment of falling from the sky is one of the few times I've been alone in weeks. A part of me wishes I could land by myself and hide in the background of someone else's world. I close my eyes and let the wind wash over my skin as I glide toward the ground.

When I open my eyes, I can see the high grass of an open prairie shining softly a few hundred feet below. My feet steady for impact. After a short trot, I throw off my chute, fall to the ground, and roll onto my back. I hadn't noticed the stars when I was closer to them, but now, from below, they comfort me.

Jaykin and I used to sneak out and climb the Outer Wall after my parents went to bed. We would lie on our backs for hours, counting to see who saw the most shooting stars. Some nights we'd see none, and others we'd see almost twenty.

Voices around me are calling, but I don't bother to answer.

THE REVELATION

None of us are going anywhere, and they'll find me soon enough. I squeeze my fire starter and the picture of my mother in my pocket, wishing they'd somehow transport me back home. My eyes trace the host of stars above, winking with soft whispers of light. They know all the secrets of the dark, and yet every night, they wash over the sky like tiny sparks of hope.

"I'm bringing Ruma back," I whisper to the endless sky, imagining my words will find their way home.

CHAPTER 27

What little heat the sun poured over the earth during the day has drained from the grasslands. My skin tightens from the cold night air. I'd rather be alone, but my need to find warmth is more pressing. As I reconvene with the group, they're wrapping themselves in their parachute canopies, which are also designed to serve as thermal blankets.

Merrin, Rhysk, Ruma, Drove, Talliph, and I sit huddled together while Anger and the pilots organize a secondary rescue for our group. I still don't trust Anger, but for all the times I've disliked and even hated her, I feel a flicker of admiration and appreciation for her involvement in helping rescue Ruma.

We've more or less settled down now after exhaling the adrenaline from our bodies. Using their communication devices, the pilots occasionally converse with their distant counterparts flying far away. The incoming voices sound muffled, and the radios only catch broken pieces of the wrinkled sound waves spilling out.

THE REVELATION

I hear one of the pilots say, "They'll be dispatching Legionnaires."

"We're sending coordinates now."

That's all they care to offer us before continuing the rest of their hushed conversations in private.

Under the stars, I sit quietly, listening to our small group exchanging stories and pieces of information they haven't been able to share for lack of time and safety.

"How did you end up in the Revelation Territory?" Merrin asks Rhysk, who is sitting in the tall grass between Merrin and me.

"I have no idea," she says. "I woke up there almost two weeks ago. All I remember before that is that I got called back for a secondary inspection after they canceled our ops mission, and at some point they must have drugged me, and then I woke up there."

"What about you?" Merrin asks, looking at Talliph.

"I was there since about a year ago," Talliph says. "I left my home country to visit New Province after Nebbuck contacted my family to recruit me. I convinced my parents to let me go, but I never made it to New Province Guard. It was just like tonight. There were ten of us, and our plane engine died before my group arrived. Two of the parachutes didn't work on the way down. Eight of us made it, but one of my good friends and another girl, they both—" Talliph stops talking, but she's said enough.

"I'm sorry to hear that," Rhysk offers.

"Where are you from?" Drove asks Talliph. His voice is deep and smooth, like the low tones of a cello.

"Dalivia," she says. "I haven't met anyone here who's been there. And you?" She asks, returning the question to Drove.

"The island of Barottosse, not far from Solyn." His strange accent is much thicker than Talliph's. Again, we all seem at a loss for geography. Ruma isn't responsive. She's lying on her back with her hands tucked behind her head as she nibbles on a dried stem of grass.

"How long were you there?" Merrin asks Drove.

"I was taken from my country when I was twelve years old, so fourteen. Fourteen years."

"So you haven't seen your family in fourteen years?" I question.

He shakes his head. "No. Only in my dreams."

"Did you ever try to escape?" Rhysk asks.

"They had videos of my city burning. My family was killed in a rebellion, so I had nothing to run to."

"Drove, they showed me videos too," says Ruma, sitting up, finally joining the conversation. "But they couldn't have been real. My family is still alive. Maybe yours is too."

"What videos?" I ask her.

"They weren't real, so it doesn't matter now," she says unconvincingly, lying back again as if to retreat from the conversation.

"They showed you videos of your family dying that weren't real?" Rhysk asks in disbelief.

"Apparently, but that was years ago," she says, covering her mouth as she yawns.

Drove suddenly becomes quiet as he sits staring at the ground.

"What about the war?" Talliph asks.

"Which war?" Rhysk asks.

"The war in your capitol and in the Guards. That's where you are from, right?" she asks.

THE REVELATION

"We're from Southern Guard," I say, "but there's no war going on, unless something big has happened since we've been gone these past couple weeks."

Talliph squints her eyes and tilts her head. Her lips move as if she's debating whether she should speak before she asks, "You were at the provincial order address, yes?"

We nod, and Rhysk confirms, "Yeah. I didn't understand what all of that was about."

"Me either. What war were they talking about?" Merrin asks her.

Talliph looks at Merrin, Rhysk, and I, reading our faces with hard suspicion in her eyes.

"We've seen it. Ever since I've been here; it's almost every week," she tells us.

"There have been loads of warfront videos," Ruma confirms, sitting upright.

"What have you seen?" Rhysk asks.

"Everything. The Stones destroying cities, RedCloud pushing them back, New Province Operatives resisting RedCloud Legionnaires. We've seen a lot," Ruma says, stopping after reading the clear confusion on our faces. "So that's a load of shit too?" She runs her hands over her long hair as she whispers, "No fucking way."

"I don't understand," Talliph says as her eyebrows push down heavily.

"We know the Stones are out there," I try to clarify, "but there's no war in New Province. So I don't know what that was all about."

I can sense uncovering the inconsistencies in what they've been told is making everyone uncomfortable. We share a moment of silence as our minds try to reconcile our conflicting stories.

"They were breaking us," Ruma finally says. "And they did." She pauses and exhales a thin cloud of air before continuing. "I've never told anybody this before because I didn't think it mattered, but when I was helping Salom sneak through the insides of the Outer Wall after he was attacked by that Stone, he told me the Stone spoke to him. The Stone told him he didn't want to hurt him, but he had to. He *told* Salom that. I don't know if someone made him do it, but he could've killed Salom. Nothing was stopping him, but he didn't. That doesn't sound like a monster to me."

Thirty yards away, under cover of one of the few trees visible beneath the moonlight, the pilot's communication device sounds with a muffled string of words. We all turn our heads and listen intently. He has a quick exchange with his copilot before they both run through the thick grass to where we're sitting.

"We've arranged for a nearby shuttle drone to intercept us at this location. Prepare to leave."

"Shuttle drone?" Merrin says. "They only go between the Guards and New Province Guard."

"Are we going home?" I ask.

"Uh, yes," the pilot distractedly responds as his eyes search for distant lights out in the darkness.

"Really?" Merrin asks, apparently to make sure what he heard was right.

I imagine seeing my mom and dad's faces when I step through the front door of my home. Hugging my parents, and Jaykin jumping onto my back. As I imagine Ruma walking in,

THE REVELATION

I realize I have no idea if or how she'd be allowed to enter Southern Guard, even with her genetic reversal.

"How will Ruma even get inside?" I ask, wondering why no one else has mentioned it before now.

"We'll take care of all of that," Anger says, her eyes lingering on me, as if trying to read my reaction.

"Why are we going to Southern Guard?" Rhysk asks. Why is she questioning them about taking us home?

"Staying overnight in the Greylands could kill us," the pilot responds. "We don't know what's out here."

I turn to look at Ruma, but she's not where I last saw her. For a few seconds, I can't find her anywhere, but I catch a shadow moving out around forty feet away.

"Ruma!" I yell, immediately regretting bringing everyone's attention to her. I sprint after her, and she begins to run too.

The grass around me isn't very high, but there are a few low-lurking plants I have to dodge in pursuit. She's a fast runner, but I can tell I'm closing the gap between us.

"Darvin!" Merrin yells. He must be following me.

"Stay back! I got her," I yell, unsure if he can hear me. After a few seconds of running, I look back and see he's stopped pursuing us.

I'm heaving in breaths now, but I'm closing in on her. She's slowed down, but she's not giving up. I reach out to grab her, and she swings her arm behind her and strikes the side of my face, sending me to the ground. She throws herself off balance and falls a short distance ahead of me.

My jawbone and upper neck burn from the fresh blow. My forearm also stings from scraping across the ground. I feel fresh blood dripping down my elbow as I dazedly try standing back up.

"What are you doing?" I scream. I can't make sense of why she hit me. She brushes herself off without seeming to care about the damage she inflicted on me. She continues walking away in the direction she was running. I follow as anger runs hot within me, propelling me after her.

"Where the hell are you going?" I ask.

She's mumbling to herself, but I can't make out what she's saying.

"Are you crazy?" I yell, following her now inconsistent path. "I risked my life looking for you, and you're going to run off right before we get home?"

She stops and stands still. When I reach her again, she turns around, and her appearance freezes me. Her face is like that of a Stone. The deep, gray lines of hardened skin split across her complexion like parched land. Even in the darkness, the glow of her yellow-gold eyes flares like wind-blown coals. My eyes flick away.

"Look at me!" she screams.

I don't want to look at her, but I feel compelled by her intensity.

"I can't be this. I can't. They'll take me back. I can't go back," she says, shaking her head.

"No, they won't. I won't let that happen," I say, trying to reassure her while I feel myself shaking.

"You can't save me," she yells, heaving in a few deep breaths. "Look what I am," she says, struggling to control herself. "When they told me my family died, I grieved for all of you, but there was a part of me that was relieved no one would ever have to know me like this."

"But you can control it. They don't have to know," I insist.

"But *I* know," she says. "Those walls were made to keep

THE REVELATION

people like me out. I can't hide from who I am. I can't do it."

We both stand partially bent over, trying to catch our breath. I don't know what to say, but I feel compelled to try.

"Who you are isn't gone. We remember you."

"You were *five*, Darvin. You never knew who I was. I don't know what you want from me, but I can't fix whatever it is you feel like you lost. I can't even do that for myself."

"That's not what we want. Maybe I don't know who you were, but I always knew you were my only sister. We don't even have pictures of you, but I dreamed about you all the time. Even Jaykin asks Mom to tell him stories about you at night before he goes to bed. I wasn't holding on to some ideal image of who you could be. None of us were. We held on to our love for you. We don't need you to fix anything. We just want you home again."

Ruma's dark Stone complexion begins returning to her natural appearance. Tears slide down her cheeks. Her eyes release their harsh, tawny coloring and regain a more pleasant shimmer under the silent stars.

"I can't go back," she says quietly.

"Yes, you can. You're not a monster. You're not. That's the word for the people who took you from us. We've got to get away from them. Right now, all we have is home."

"They'll come after us. They need me," she says.

"Who? For what?"

She shakes her head.

"For what?" I ask again.

Silence.

"I'm trying to understand, but I can't if you won't talk to me," I say, struggling to hide my frustration. "I'm sick of feeling like I'm the only one who doesn't know anything."

We stand in silence. I don't know what else to do. Feeling I have nothing left to say that could convince her to return home, I begin walking back to the group.

I don't make it far before she says, "They're not taking us home."

I stop for a moment to see if she'll continue.

"Did they tell you it was me and Drove who tried to break through the observation wall to get to you?" she asks. "They knew all along if I didn't see you myself, I wouldn't believe you were alive even if they told me. They knew I'd need a reason to care about escaping. And they were right."

I take a moment to absorb what she's saying before turning around to face her again.

"How did you recognize me?" I ask gently, not wanting to deter her from saying more.

"You look the same," she says, shrugging. "Just older."

My mind begins filling with questions.

"Why do you think they aren't taking us home?" I ask.

"This was never about a charity rescue. They wouldn't risk that much to help us without expecting something from us in return. Anger wants us for something. We are her currency, and she'll use us to get whatever it is she wants. I don't plan on being used by anyone else if I can help it. At least not on their terms."

I cover my face with my hand, feeling a wave of shame for being so ignorant to think that Anger, at least on some level, might have cared enough about doing what was right to help me find Ruma again.

"They told us to hide our identities when we got there, and Merrin said it was to protect Anger from being tied to us," I say, offering Ruma what little information I know.

THE REVELATION

Ruma shakes her head, and her eyes shift around as she forms her thoughts. "That's not the only reason they hid your names," she says softly. "The whole revelation process is all about genome mapping and genetic engineering. If the Revelation Territory could have full access to your DNA, then they'd have the paternal chromosomes they're missing from me. They hid you because they knew you'd be too valuable to the Revelation Territory. Both of us are."

Neither of us seems to know where to go from here. Time isn't on our side with the shuttle drone approaching, and I know the rest of our group is wondering why we've run off.

"I can't leave my friends. I don't know what we should do, but I can't leave them," I tell her, still unsure of what to do next.

"We'll figure it out—no shuttle drones, no escorts, and on our own time. With our friends," Ruma says, pausing a moment before brushing past me and heading back to the group. She doesn't have to say anything else. I know she's with me. We slowly step through the grass toward Merrin, who is still patiently waiting where he first stopped chasing after us.

"So... Rhysk. She's a friend?" Ruma asks, and I hesitate to answer because I can't tell if she's asking if I trust her or if there's something more between us.

"I trust her," I say.

"That's good." We take a few more steps. "Looks like she *trusts* you too."

I look at her with a straight face, waiting for her to say something else about Rhysk and me, but she continues looking ahead.

"I'm sorry I hit you," she adds.

"I guess that's what brothers and sisters are supposed to do," I say, and a thin smirk draws over her face.

"So how are we going to do this?" I ask her.

Before she answers, we both hear raised voices arguing from where we left the others. Merrin, not far ahead of us, turns around and darts back toward the group. We both sprint after him.

"Stay back!" I hear the head pilot yell into the night. It's not until we've reunited with the group that I see he's holding Talliph hostage with a blade at her neck. The copilot stands back, holding a gun, alternating his aim from one person to the next, excluding Anger and his pilot.

"What the fuck's happening?" I ask.

"I said I was leaving," Rhysk explains, "and they said they'd cut her throat if I tried. Seems like I might be important to them."

"No one's leaving," the pilot growls.

Anger looks furious. "We really could've done this without a knife."

"Maybe I'm the only one taking our orders seriously," he shouts back at her. "I plan on delivering my end of the deal."

"Let her go," Ruma demands. "You're hurting her."

Talliph shakes in the pilot's grasp. She's clenching her teeth as she struggles to breathe. The pilot has her right arm pinned up behind her head with his arm, and he steadies the knife against her neck with the other.

"You have your own tricks," the pilot says, staring wide-eyed at Ruma. "This is mine."

As he speaks, faint lights rise and fall across his face—the shuttle drone is approaching. The lights brighten, casting long shadows across the tawny grass. I wait for Anger to intervene, but she's just waiting.

"They need to shut off the lights," the copilot says, but the pilot doesn't respond. The familiar croon of a shuttle drone grows in my ear, increasing in tandem with the luminosity of the spotlights.

I look at Ruma. Even though the copilot is aiming at her chest, her eyes are locked on me. Neither one of us intends to get on the shuttle drone. Ruma's eyes move away from me toward Drove. The dark outline of his body accentuates his size against the approaching light.

Ruma speaks a few words in a language I don't understand. Drove nods his head, then leaps like a beast with incredible agility toward the copilot, who fires on him. The blasts ring deep within my ears.

Rhysk screams when the pilot slits Talliph's throat. She drops to the ground, clutching her neck with both hands. Ruma rushes the pilot, who accepts her challenge, posturing himself in a defensive stance. Drove takes several direct hits before reaching the copilot. My jaw drops as he rips both arms off the copilot, who screams inhumanly while still standing upright. After tossing the severed arms aside, Drove silences the copilot, smashing his head with both fists.

Just before Ruma collides with the pilot, she slides into his legs and intercepts his wrist as he attempts to stab her. His legs buckle, and he drops hard to the ground. Rhysk rushes to where Talliph lies shaking in the grass. Merrin and I sprint toward the pilot as Ruma regains her footing.

"Don't!" I yell, stopping a short distance away from the pilot. He has his previously concealed firearm drawn and pointed at Ruma. We're all partially blinded by the nearing shuttle drone's lights and the whirling dust that's kicking up from beneath its hovering turbines.

Within seconds, the vehicle stops only a few yards from where I stand. The shock-absorbing anchors touch down in high grass as the thrumming engines power down. The side of their transport bears the New Province symbol of a singular eye of providence poised within a triangle above the head and between the outstretched wings of a phoenix. As soon as the armored doors fling open, a dozen operatives rush out and quickly surround our group. While barking voices shout commands for us to drop to the ground, my eyes cut to Anger, who still hasn't moved.

"No!" Ruma screams.

Drove abruptly ends his charge toward the pilot, who fires a singular shot in his direction. The bullet ricochets off Drove's chest and disappears into the night. A part from a short-lived wince of pain, Drove seems unharmed. The New Province operatives split their aims between everyone except the pilot and Anger. Anger remains little more than a bystander, watching the situation unfold as if she were powerless.

"Nobody move," one of the operatives orders us from behind.

We remain frozen while the pilot cautiously steps away to stand by Anger's side. The operatives slowly close the distance between us. The beaming headlights of the shuttle drone outline them from behind.

"Commander Elite. Captain Zell," the commanding officer says, greeting Anger and the pilot while he walks toward them.

"We encountered some unexpected retaliation that altered our exit plans," Anger finally says. "Our group is accounted for

THE REVELATION

with the exception of Hara Coven. She should be arriving by a different transport tonight."

"What happened to her?" the captain asks, looking at Talliph lying motionless by Rhysk's side.

"That one tried to kill us," the pilot says, blatantly lying. "We should still take her body."

"Anger, what's happening?" I ask, but she won't look at me. My eyes follow the pilot, who steps toward Rhysk as she cradles Talliph's body in her arms.

"Get up," the pilot commands Rhysk, but she doesn't move.

"Do as he says," the commanding officer tells Rhysk as he directs his firearm at her. "Stand up and put your hands behind your head. Captain Zell, cuff her."

"Yes, sir," the pilot responds, pulling his cuffs from his back pocket.

"There will be no need for that," Anger says, overriding the commanding officer.

Rhysk refuses to cooperate. Her fierce eyes hold fast to Captain Zell as he approaches, as if she's preparing to fight him.

"Step away! Now!" the commanding officer yells again.

After a few seconds of silence, Rhysk gently settles Talliph's head against the ground. She stands up and slowly begins stepping backward. Her fingers dig against the palms of her hands as she joins Merrin and me. The pilot stands over Talliph's motionless body and nudges her with his boot.

A horse whinnies from somewhere in the night, just beyond the circle of light provided by the shuttle drone. The familiar sound of horse hooves pounds toward me. Anticipating the unexpected rider, everyone silently stares over Anger's shoulders. My ears lead my eyes as I spot a dark horse and its cloaked riders as they draw the aim of the operatives.

The horse halts only a few yards away from Anger and snorts as its front legs punch into the ground. The lights pouring from the shuttle drone allow me to see that both riders are covered by dark matte full-body protective armor with clear shields over their faces. The bright glares reflected by their masks make it hard to distinguish their features.

Without an introduction, the lead rider asks, "Who will speak for this group?" An amplifier attached to her black helmet magnifies her voice.

"I will," Anger says, stepping toward the rider. "Who the hell are you?"

"My name doesn't matter, just my business," the rider says as her passenger dismounts from the horse.

"Stay back," Captain Zell warns, but neither of the two seems afraid.

"I'd be careful with those weapons," the rider says smoothly. "We're not alone."

Anger's eyes scan over darkness. I know she may be seeing something the rest of us can't, but her face hides it well.

"What do you want?" Anger demands impatiently.

"I would like to speak with Darvin Flint."

Hearing my name makes my skin stiffen like she's thrown a bucket of ice-cold water over my head. I'm not sure how to respond. I can't make any words come out.

"I know it's one of you, unless you've stolen something that doesn't belong to you," she says.

This statement only furthers my confusion. No one on my side offers any help. She looks down at the object in her hand, and a small white light blinks as she makes her way to my side.

"I'm Darvin," I'm finally able to say.

"That would have been my guess," she says, clearing her throat. "You still have it on you after all this time. To be honest, I figured someone must have found you dead and stolen it off of you."

I want to ask her what she's talking about, but as my hand moves toward my pocket, I realize she's tracked me down using the flint fire starter my dad gave me the day I left Southern Guard.

"Go ahead. Let me see it," she says, waving the receiving end of the tracking signal. "For the past few weeks, it's just been a dot on a screen for me."

I pull the tracking device out to confirm I'm the one she's looking for.

"You know him. Can you confirm that's him?" the rider asks her passenger.

As the young girl approaches me, the center beam of the captain's flashlight strikes her body. She shields her eyes from the light, so I can't see her face. Her pale skin and bright-red hair glow within the condensed circle of light. A dark suit blackens the rest of her body to blend with the darkness. As the light shifts away from her eyes, the girl's hand drops down to her side so I can clearly see her face.

"Don't come any closer," the commanding officer demands as she stops in place about ten feet away.

"Silver?" I ask, unable to make sense of why she's standing in front of me so far from Southern Guard.

"Yes, it's him," Silver tells the rider. "And that's Merrin, too. Hello, Darvin," she says, offering a hint of a smile.

Rhysk whispers, "Who is she?"

When I don't immediately answer, Merrin says, "They grew up together."

"What are you doing here?" I ask Silver.

"We've been tracking you for weeks," she says calmly.

"We don't have time for this," Anger cuts in. "We're leaving."

"Darvin and Merrin will be coming with us. The rest of you are free to leave," the rider responds firmly.

"Stand down," Zell orders the rider as he walks toward her. "We have orders from the New Province Guard to escort these citizens to the capital."

"I'm sure you do, but it will be in everyone's best interest, including yours, if Darvin comes with us," she says, coldly confident.

"That's not happening," Anger says, as she too walks toward the rider.

"It's time for you to leave," the commanding officer asserts.

A guttural scream of pain turns my attention back to Captain Zell. Talliph clings to the same knife used to slit her throat, which is now wedged deep in Zell's back. I'm confounded that she's even alive. She drags the knife down his spine until he drops to the ground. She slumps beside his body as dark blood spills across the dry yellow grass. Still on her knees, Talliph pulls the knife out of his back while holding her throat with her right hand. I hadn't noticed until now that she doesn't appear to be bleeding. This must be an effect of her genetic reversal. The operatives turn their weapons toward Talliph as Anger screams, "Hold your fire! Don't shoot!"

The dark horse whinnies as the rider retreats into the darkness, leaving Silver behind. I exchange glances with

THE REVELATION

Rhysk, Merrin, and Ruma all in a moment. None of us know what to do.

"Darvin," Silver says, getting my attention. "Don't be afraid."

I stare back at her feeling more perplexed than when I first recognized her face only moments ago. Why would she tell me not to be afraid when she's just been abandoned?

"I'm not leaving them," I tell her, nodding towards Ruma, Rhysk, and Merrin.

"Gas them. Now!" Anger commands, and three of the operatives spray clouds of yellow fog from their tanks as the familiar gas stings my nose. Drove tries to charge the operatives but quickly falls to his knees. We all cover our faces and cough against the fumes while scrambling away.

In the distance, the sound of feet pounding the ground stampedes toward us. Merrin passes out, falling to the ground beside me. Ruma and Drove succumb to the fumes only a few yards away from him. Rhysk and I pull one another onward as we stumble away from the stinging vapor. Emerging from the gas with her protective helmet, Silver rushes to our sides to help us escape the putrid gas. Once out of reach of the fumes, I turn to see the operatives huddling together with their weapons directed toward the near thunderous charge of dark shadows rushing toward them.

Rhysk breathes heavily as I hold her in my arms. Silver sits down by my side as the bellowing roars close in. I freeze again, petrified as a horde of Stones materializes from within the darkness to meet the radiant, red beams streaming from the operatives' singeing lasers.

CHAPTER 28

There's something about risk and fear coming together that exposes what matters in my heart. When I know what I'm afraid of losing, I know why I'm living. In this moment, I choose to embrace the face of fear and death while protecting the ones around me.

"Hold her for me!" I tell Silver, who takes Rhysk. As heavy shadows bound over me and recklessly smash into the hastily disbanding group of operatives, I help drag Ruma and Merrin back toward where Rhysk and Silver are sitting until we're all together.

The avalanche of Stones moves so fast through the lingering gas and fresh clouds of smoke that I can't be sure if there are a dozen or a hundred of them.

The two operatives that managed to avoid being instantly crushed by the Stones desperately spray their red laser streams wherever they can. I recognize the surge of firepower from their wasp-links as they strike the attacking Stones like

THE REVELATION

serpents, taking several of them down. The chaotic screams of pain pinch my ears.

For a moment, the firing stops, and the Stones scramble back into the darkness just beyond the smoke and streaks of wildfire left behind by the lasers. Only two operatives remain standing, and Anger is nowhere in sight. Guns still poised and ready to fire, they both carefully maneuver over the bodies of the Stones and their fallen companions.

"Stay back," one of them shouts. Together, they rush toward the belly of the shuttle drone. As they run, one of the gassing guns used against us moments before raises off the ground from beside the lifeless body of a fallen operative. The gun floats by itself through the air until it reaches the two operatives nearly at the shuttle drone. Suddenly, their masks fling off their faces, and the stinging yellow clouds engulf them. They quickly fall to the ground. I don't need to see Anger to know she's responsible, but as soon as they hit the ground, she emerges back into plain sight.

Small patches of fire left behind by the lasers wash through the dry grass like a wave spreading over the shore. Anger treads across the flames, approaching where our small group rests huddled together. From behind us, trotting hooves signal the rider is coming back to us. After coming to a halt, the rider carefully removes her helmet. Her hair flows over her pale face. She's breathing heavily, looking back and forth among all of us. Following her lead, the Stones cautiously emerge from the rolling smoke.

"Keep your distance," the rider commands Anger. The Stones stand only ten feet away from our sides. Their thick, broken skin looks like cracked marble. I begin shaking and hold Ruma tightly while I stare at the Stones around us.

Whether I'm resilient to perducorium or not, the instincts ingrained in me from being constantly warned of the disease's life-threatening affects still make me terrified of them.

Observing Anger's face, I know she's choosing her words carefully. Depending on whom this woman works for, our group's genetic resilience could either make us enemies or very valuable captives.

"Who do you work for?" Anger asks the rider, unafraid of the growing group of Stones surrounding her.

"The domina of the Breakers Guild," the rider answers, and she asks the same question of Anger.

"Myself," Anger responds. "What do you want with them?" She tilts her head toward us.

The rider clears her throat. "I'm a deliverer, not an informer."

Anger stills without breaking eye contact with the rider. In the momentary silence, somewhere off in the night, I hear a lone wolf howl, as faint as the light of the stars.

"What do you want with me?" I ask, hoping to understand why Silver, the rider, and a group of displaced Stones would travel this far to find me.

Silver turns to face the rider, who nods, giving her approval to speak.

"We've been tracking you for weeks. The day you left Southern Guard, I was told to place a screen mirror on your brace-comm and follow you to New Province Guard."

As she speaks, I remember my awkward encounter with Silver the morning Dad walked Merrin and me to East Gate.

"The Breakers Guild got me on the shuttle drone, but somehow someone in New Province got word of what we were doing, so they gassed us all when we got off the train, and

THE REVELATION

when I woke up, I was locked away. We have guild members in New Province who arranged for my release, and by that time, you were already scheduled for your first ops mission, where they planned for you to be reported as missing in action. That was going to be their cover so they could indefinitely use you for hematology studies that might help to advance the development of New Province's perducorium research programs."

I look to Anger, who seems just as perplexed as I do, but she says nothing as Silver continues.

"We stole your Falcon gear, hoping to delay your participation in the mission so we would have more time to plan a way to intercept you, but we didn't have enough time. We lost you until one of our members picked up a signal from you in the Black Valley. I don't know if you noticed, but he found you and tried to plant a photo of your family that your dad gave us in your pocket. Anger was too close to—"

"Wait, wait. My dad? My dad was helping you track me?" I ask.

"We went to him after they reported you missing so they would know you weren't dead," Silver explains. "Both of you." She looks to Merrin, who is still unconscious on the ground beside me.

I feel a small burden release from inside. My family is aware that Merrin and I are alive. Do they know about Ruma? I push the thought aside for the moment. "But why were y'all going through that much trouble to find me?"

The rider answers for Silver. "The Breakers Guild works to aid and reunite families affected by the PRA's systematic abuse of perducorium-related tactics of oppression."

"Bullshit," Anger says. "They weren't looking for *you*.

They were looking for someone with your DNA. That's what everyone wants, isn't it?" She takes a step closer to the rider, whose sharp face pulls even tighter as she dismounts her horse to close the distance between her and Anger.

"I don't know who you people are except for Darvin," the rider responds, pointing her tracking device at me. "I've been given orders to deliver him through the walls of Southern Guard—those are orders I fully plan on following."

"I understand. But there are some things you can't plan for," Anger says.

The rider takes a sudden step backward. Her face strains as if she's in pain. A high-pitched whistle fills my ears as the rider suddenly rises nearly fifteen feet into the air. The Stones collectively gasp as the rider struggles to breathe with her arms pinned at her side.

Silver screams, standing helpless and terrified as the dark-haired woman remains suspended under Anger's control. She steps back from Rhysk.

"Put her down!" I yell at Anger, realizing now why she gassed the remaining two operatives. With no New Province witnesses, her word and authority will easily stand against ours, even if we tried to convince others of her hidden identity and abilities.

"What's happening?" Silver yells, reaching for me with a trembling hand.

From within the horde of Stones, a long spear launches through the air and narrowly misses Anger. She flinches, and the rider drops to the ground hard. I hear a crack, and the rider screams in pain; she's broken at least one of her legs. The Stones charge Anger in a furious rush, and she swiftly unleashes her power against them. My body remembers

THE REVELATION

the high-pitched ringing and skin-shaking force Anger used against the Legionnaires as energy waves explode from her, flinging the Stones through the air as easily as the wind throws leaves.

Silver covers her ears. High in the night sky, a resonating thrum of firing aerocraft engines replaces the piercing sounds of Anger's attacks as a RedCloud Legionnaire ship materializes from within the darkness.

In the chaos, the remaining Stones scatter wildly in every direction. Anger screams, "Darvin!" and when I look at her, she yells, "Load them in the shuttle drone!"

I stare at her, wondering why she helped me to begin with. I remember Widow telling me before we left her house in the Black Valley. *Follow her. She knows what she's doing.* Whatever secrets Anger has kept from me haven't kept me from finding my sister. I've never trusted her because I don't understand her, but for everything I don't know about Anger, I do know I'd rather be with her than intercepted by a RedCloud Legionnaire ship.

"Come with us," I yell to Silver, whose eyes are strung with panic and confusion. "Help me, please!" I beg, grabbing her hand. "We need to get them to the shuttle drone."

Without looking me in the eyes, she shakes her head as if she's unsure of what she's doing, but after we work together to help Rhysk to her feet, Silver hastily stumbles toward the shuttle drone while Rhysk leans against her shoulder for support. I grab Ruma and follow right behind Silver as we load them into our only hope of escape.

Silver and I return for Merrin, and my adrenaline pumps as we pick him up off the ground. Silver stops what she's doing and stares wide-eyed behind me. With Merrin weighing heavy in my arms, I turn to see Anger with her hands quivering violently by her sides. Faint, pulsing white waves of light fire from her outturned palms and strike the Legionnaire ship. It struggles to maintain control, barreling from side to side less than a hundred feet above us.

I try not to fall as we make our way to the shuttle drone. The ship's engines bellow loudly, fighting against Anger's hold while trying to regain control. After loading Merrin through the open hatch doors, I watch the massive Legionnaire ship sink like a fallen giant, exploding against the ground in a blinding swirl of fire. The rush of hot air burns my eyes, and I drop to the ground.

When I lift my head, the once-dark night sky glows bright orange from the swelling firelight. Struggling to regain her footing, Anger pushes herself upright. Drove and the rider lift off the ground, floating in our direction as Anger guides them along with her to the shuttle drone. Silver's hair reflects the radiance of the surrounding flames. I have to call her name to break her attention away from burning wreckage. With Anger close by me, Silver keeps her distance as we all head for the shuttle drone.

In this moment, there are no words left to exchange between Anger and me. Once we situate everyone inside the doors, Anger sits in the driver's seat and begins following the navigation system back toward the main roads leading to the capital in New Province Guard.

As soon as we begin moving, Ruma stirs, coughing and rubbing her face. I crawl out of my seat to get to her, asking if she's okay. She doesn't respond. Still covering her face, she shifts her body sideways in her chair, leaning against her headrest.

THE REVELATION

"Give her some time," Rhysk mumbles from her seat.

For a moment, I gently rest my hand on Ruma's arm and watch her breathing.

"She'll be all right. You should rest too," Rhysk says.

I'm too exhausted to disagree, so I return to my seat beside Rhysk.

"It could be worse," she whispers, her eyes lingering on mine before she lays her head back to rest.

Silver tries to comfort the rider, whose name I still don't know. The woman trembles in pain, her hands and seat smeared with her own blood. Silver's eyes almost look empty. I feel like I've betrayed her by unintentionally leading her into Anger's mysterious crusade for control that no one seems to fully understand.

"Give her two of these," Anger suggests, tossing back a medicine bottle she dug out from within one of the front compartments of the shuttle drone.

Silver catches the small container and immediately looks to me. I nod approvingly. Even though I'm unsure of what pills Silver is holding, I'm almost certain the rider will have no better options for alleviating her pain.

"Here," Rhysk says, handing Silver a partially full bottle of water she scrounged from beneath her seat to go with the medicine. Silver thanks her and places the pills in the woman's mouth before tipping the water bottle to her lips. With nothing left to do, the two of them try to rest, hoping time will eventually help ease her pain.

I close my eyes, leaning back in my stiff seat between Rhysk and Merrin. As we hover over the dark grasslands, I imagine having to explain to Merrin what happened while he was unconscious and then seeing the disappointment on his face when he finds out we still aren't heading home. I'm not sure what Anger wants with me, but I don't want it to interfere with the well-being of anyone here.

After riding for a few minutes in silence, Ruma's weak voice calling my name draws my eyes open.

"Yeah?" I say, feeling slightly disoriented.

"Do you have the picture?" she asks, still sitting beside Drove, who has yet to wake up.

As I look at Ruma, I'm suddenly taken by a rush of many emotions at once. For thirteen years, she lived in our hearts as the relentless and mysterious ache that touched our dreams, family dinners, birthdays, and Christmas mornings. I easily could have never seen Ruma again, just like Maybeth's two sons, now grown if they're still alive, who will live the rest of their lives with the impossible hope of one day seeing their mother again. But now, by some unexplainable miracle, Ruma is sitting in front of me.

My eyes water as I reach in my pocket for the picture of our family. I carefully step over Rhysk to keep from waking her and place the photo in Ruma's outstretched hand. After her first glance, she looks away for a moment before letting her eyes return to our family. Her eyebrows drop down, pushing out the tears that begin to fall down her cheeks. As I watch her cry and breathe in and out slowly, a subtle and unexpected smile moves over her lips.

"He does look more like Dad than we do," she says, still staring at our family.

The thought of seeing Jaykin triggers a strange blend of comfort and a longing ache.

"You'll see them again," Ruma tells me, wiping her face dry with her fingers, "But this time we'll be together." She

THE REVELATION

holds the picture close to her chest and lays her head back to close her eyes.

While the rest of the shuttle drone sleeps, I sit worrying about my parents and Jaykin. Since leaving home, the only thought that kept me from feeling guilty for leaving my family has been the thought of finding Ruma, and I've done that.

Now, having no idea where Anger could be taking us as she quietly drives through the nearly barren Greylands, I wonder if the sacrifices I've made to find Ruma could cause me to lose the very ones who drove me to find her.

–THE END until the next BEGINNING–

ACKNOWLEDGMENTS

I have an immeasurable amount of appreciation for everyone involved in helping me create my first novel. I can think of few things that have brought me greater joy than having the people I love actively support, value, and invest in my dream of writing a book.

Thank you to Mrs. Ann Smith, my high school ELA teacher, for both capturing and sharing the magic of literature and language with me for four years. Experiencing your classroom was the closest I've ever felt to attending Hogwarts.

Thank you to the ones who cared enough to read the roughest versions of *The Revelation*. I genuinely couldn't have completed this process without your insightful corrections, visionary suggestions, and motivating encouragement. Jackson Sharpe, Carrie Beth Davis, Collin Kimmons, John Sharpe III, Courtney Sharpe, Caroline Sharpe, John Sharpe Jr., Mabeth Beasley, Frances Sharpe, and Gwen Banks—you all taking the time to read and value my story was one of the greatest acts of love I have ever received.

Thank you to my cousin and lifelong friend, Kyla Legaspi, for paying for the cover design. Your kindness inspires me to look for ways I can invest in other people's dreams.

Thank you to my close friends and extended family members for holding me accountable, keeping me writing by persistently asking when my book was coming out. I very much appreciate every question, conversation, and shared social media post. The collective support I have received from each of you has sustained and encouraged me to believe that my story and my voice have a meaningful place in the world.

Thank you to Crystal Watanabe and her incredible team at Pikko's House for providing legendary editing services. I've learned so much from working with you that I feel like I'm walking away from this process with an additional degree in story crafting and revisions. Thank you for being so incredibly gracious and giving of your time and expertise.

Finally, thank you to every person who takes the time to read about Darvin Flint and his journey through New Province to reunite his family. I hope you can enjoy seeing pieces of yourself reflected back to you through the characters as you partake in their stories.

Made in the USA
Coppell, TX
18 February 2021